An Ensuing Evil

and Others

✧

By Peter Tremayne

*forthcoming

— AN —
ENSUING EVIL
AND OTHERS

Fourteen Historical Mystery Stories

PETER TREMAYNE

St. Martin's Minotaur
New York

www.minotaurbooks.com

Design by Jonathan Bennett

Library of Congress Cataloging-in-Publication Data

Tremayne, Peter.
   An ensuing evil and others : fourteen historical mystery stories / by Peter Tremayne.
—1st St. Martin's Minotaur ed.
      p. cm.
   ISBN 0-312-34228-4
   EAN 978-0-312-34228-9
   1. Detective and mystery stories, English.   2. Historical fiction, English.   I. Title.

PR6070.R366E575   2006
823'.914—dc22

                                                        2005049772

10 9 8 7 6 5 4 3 2

ACKNOWLEDGMENTS

"Night's Black Angels," originally published in *Royal Whodunnits*, edited by Mike Ashley (UK: Robinson, 1999; US: Carroll & Graf, 1999).

"An Ensuing Evil," originally published in *Shakespeare Whodunnits*, edited by Mike Ashley (UK: Robinson, 1997; US: Carroll & Graf, 1997).

"Methought You Saw a Serpent," originally published in *Shakespearian Detectives*, edited by Mike Ashley (UK: Robinson, 1998; US: Carroll & Graf, 1998).

"The Game's Afoot," originally published as "Let the Game Begin!" in *Much Ado about Murder*, edited by Anne Perry (US: Berkley Books, 2002).

"The Revenge of the Gunner's Daughter," originally published in *The Mammoth Book of Hearts of Oak*, edited by Mike Ashley (UK: Robinson, 2001).

"The Passing Shadow," originally published in *Death by Dickens*, edited by Anne Perry and Martin H. Greenberg (US: Berkley, 2004).

"The Affair at the Kildare Street Club," originally published in *New Sherlock Holmes Adventures*, edited by Mike Ashley (UK: Robinson, 1997; US: Carroll & Graf, 1997).

"The Specter of Tullyfane Abbey," originally published in *Villains Victorious*, edited by Martin H. Greenberg and John Helfers (US: DAW Books, 2001).

ACKNOWLEDGMENTS

"The Siren of Sennen Cove," originally published in *Murder in Baker Street*, edited by Martin H. Greenberg, Jon L.Lellenberg, and Daniel Stashower (US: Caroll & Graf 2001).

"The Kidnapping of Mycroft Holmes," originally published in *The Strand Magazine* (US: Issue #X, May–September 2003).

"A Study in Orange," originally published in *My Sherlock Holmes*, edited by Michael Kurland (US: St. Martin's Minotaur, 2003).

"The Eye of Shiva," originally published in *The Mammoth Book of Historical Detectives*, edited by Mike Ashley (UK: Robinson, 1995; US: Carroll & Graf, 1995).

"Murder in the Air," originally published in *The Mammoth Book of Locked Room Mysteries and Impossible Crimes*, edited by Mike Ashley (UK: Robinson, 2000; US: Carroll & Graf, 2000).

"The Spiteful Shadow," originally published in *The Mammoth Book of New Historical Whodunnits*, edited by Mike Ashley (UK: Robinson, 2005; US: Carroll & Graf, 2005).

For a good friend,
Maurice McCann,
who appreciates the
short mystery tale

CONTENTS

— PREFACE —

My name now appears to be irrevocably identified as the creator of Sister Fidelma, my seventh-century Irish sleuth. From time to time, readers write to me expressing surprise at having discovered that I have written mysteries set in other historical periods and cultures.

It reminds me of when I was a young aspiring writer. I was attending a launch party for a new Nicholas Blake thriller. Nicholas Blake was the pseudonym of the United Kingdom's poet laureate of the time, Cecil Day Lewis (1904–1972). I had the temerity to ask the great man why he wrote detective stories under a pseudonym. He took my question in good humor. "Because, young man," he said graciously, "a poet can't write detective stories." He was then drawn away into the wine-guzzling throng, leaving me to ponder on his enigmatic response.

It was some time before I understood what he meant. When a writer is known for producing a certain "product," it is thought that the public won't allow him to produce anything different. Poor Arthur Conan Doyle; he was driven to killing off his creation, Sherlock Holmes, in his desire to get recognition for his historical novels. It didn't work. He had to resurrect Sherlock Holmes, and never fulfilled his ambition to be acclaimed as a great historical novelist.

I am not so extreme as to want to kill off Sister Fidelma to make my point. But the fact is that I have written other tales. As well as my own character creations, sleuths created by other writers in the genre have always fascinated me. I suppose my very first crime mystery novel was a genuflection to Ernest William Hornung

(1866–1921) and his creation, Raffles, the "gentleman burglar" whose first stories appeared as *The Amateur Cracksman* in 1899. Only three books of the adventures of Raffles and his fumbling, unwilling accomplice, Bunny Manders, were published, but they achieved a special place in literary criminology. So I decided to continue the Raffles saga with a novel, *The Return of Raffles*.

The current collection of short stories is put together to demonstrate my fascination with historical settings for crime, ranging from eleventh-century Scotland to the twenty-first century—set somewhere thirty-two thousand feet above the earth!

The title of the first story, "Night's Black Agents," might well be taken from the quote from Shakespeare's *Macbeth* and does feature that Scottish monarch, but this is a story of the real historical High King of Scotland, who ruled from 1040 to 1057. There is no real Shakespearean connection. This tale takes place in 1033, seven years before MacBeth (a better way of Anglicizing his real name of MacBheatha mac Findlaech) was elected High King, but just one year after he became *mórmaer*, or "provincial ruler," of the province of Moray. The murder of Malcolm Mac Bodhe, the brother of MacBeth's wife, Gruoch, is recorded in the ancient annals. Who was responsible? In this tale, it is MacBeth who investigates.

Like most writers, however, I am an enthusiastic admirer of William Shakespeare and a frequent attendee at the Globe Theatre in London. I cannot thank the shade of the late Sam Wanamaker (1919–1993), the actor and director who was the driving force in the project to build an authentic replica of Shakespeare's Globe Theatre in its original location on London's south bank, called Bankside. It was while having a coffee at The Globe after a performance that I conceived the idea of a Shakespearean detective. Master Hardy Drew was the Constable of the Bankside Watch. The crimes he has to solve all occur in and around the Globe. "An Ensuing Evil" was written first and relates directly to events arising from the first performance of *All Is True*, later printed as *Henry the Eighth* on June 24, 1613. This was followed by "Methought You Saw a Serpent," inspired by *All's Well that Ends Well,* over which there is some disagreement when it was written. I have opted for 1601 and linked it to the execution of Queen Elizabeth I's one-time favorite, the Earl of Essex. Finally, there is "The Game's Afoot," inspired by a line from *The Life of King Henry the Fifth.*

Some readers may note that the name of Master Hardy Drew is my genuflection to a couple of mystery series that I enjoyed in my youth. The Stratemeyer Syndicate in the United States had conjured into being two series featuring teenage detectives—The Hardy Boys in 1927, written by Franklin W. Dixon, and Nancy Drew in 1929, written by Carolyn Keene. Both were in-house pen names. Seventy years later, the books are still being produced and broadcast on radio and television.

From Shakespeare's London, we move on to the early nineteenth century, during the Napoleonic wars. The action of "The Revenge of the Gunner's Daughter" takes place during the siege of Copenhagen in September 1807. The Royal Navy bombarded Copenhagen for four days, even though Britain and Denmark were not at war. The attack was to persuade the Danish Regent to surrender his fleet to Britain so that it would not be captured and used by the French. Since I was twelve years old, I have been a devotee of C. S. Forester, devouring all the Hornblower novels. I was intrigued with the idea of how a murder on board a Royal Navy ship o' war in Napoleonic times might turn out.

We move on to the mid-nineteenth century and the immortal Charles Dickens. "The Passing Shadow" not only features that redoubtable writer as the detective, but also his "sidekick" son-in-law, Charles Collins, a writer, as well, and the brother of Wilkie Collins, who is credited with writing the first modern detective novel: *The Moonstone* (1868). Although Dickens and his in-laws intrigued me, it was the location that drew me to write the story. It is set in the ancient fifteenth-century tavern, The Grapes, in London's Narrow Street, standing by the River Thames, near Wapping Steps. It was a favorite location for Dickens, and in addition, his godfather used to be a ship's chandler nearby. Dickens's father had stood the young boy on a table in that little tavern and made him sing to the assembly. Dickens describes the inn in *Dombey and Son* (1848) and used it as a major setting in *Our Mutual Friend* (1864). It still stands, and I have often been there, imagining Dickens in the little crowded bar. I once hired the tiny restaurant room upstairs, overlooking the brooding Thames waters, for a birthday celebration for my wife, Dorothy. How could a writer not use such a location to set a Victorian London detective tale?

I doubt whether any writer of mysteries in the world has not been tempted to write a Sherlock Holmes tale, even if they have not actually done so. There are five of my own Sherlock Holmes tales here. The link among all five tales is that I have depicted Sherlock Holmes's background as an Anglo-Irish one. His creator, Arthur Conan Doyle, was the grandson of John Doyle (1797–1868), an impoverished Irish Catholic who left Dublin in his mid-twenties because the Penal Laws discriminating against Catholics prevented him from earning a living as a portrait painter. He became a famous cartoonist in London. One of his sons moved to Scotland, married an Irish girl, Mary Foley, and Arthur Conan Doyle was born in Edinburgh. The Sherlock Holmes tales are replete with Irish names. One thinks of the names of Holmes's chief enemies, Moriarty and Moran, for a start. Conan Doyle was all too well aware of his Irish ancestry and background. I have opted for Holmes paralleling the educational career of his fellow Irishman, the poet and playwright, Oscar Wilde. Holmes first studies at Trinity College, Dublin, and then obtains a scholarship to Oxford. "The Affray at the Kildare Street Club," set in Dublin, is, according to my chronology, his first case. The stories are often inspired by throwaway references in Conan Doyle's own stories. For example, "The Specter of Tullyfane Abbey" derives from the line in "Thor Bridge," where reference is made to an unrecorded case concerning James Phillimore, "who stepped back into his house to get his umbrella and was never seen again." And in "The Siren of Sennen Cove," we learn what Holmes was doing when, according to "The Devil's Foot," he wrote his monograph on *Chaldean Roots in the Ancient Cornish Language*. These stories, then, are my "hat doffing" to one of the greatest detective writers of all time.

The period of the British Raj in India always intrigued me as a boy. I was fascinated not so much by Rudyard Kipling's tales but by those of Talbot Mundy (1879–1940), one of the bestselling adventure thriller writers of the early twentieth century. Mundy had an adventurous life himself; son of a well-known British military family, expelled from the famous Rugby School, he went to the colonies, adventuring in India and Africa, where he misbehaved and served jail sentences before arriving in New York in 1909 under his assumed name of Mundy. In 1911 he began to write for magazines. He became a U.S. citizen in 1917. Several of his books were made into films, notably his *King of the Khyber Rifles* (1916), filmed once by John Ford with Victor McLaglen as the hero in 1929, and then by Henry King in 1954 with Tyrone Power as the star.

Back in the 1970s, a good friend, the American publisher Donald M. Grant, asked me if I knew anything about Mundy's early life. At that time it remained a mystery, because Mundy was not his original name. Don asked me whether, if I could crack the Mundy mystery, I would write a biography for him. I was optimistic. However, from 1976, when Don first suggested the book, it took several years of painstaking research, and it was not until 1984 that Don was able to publish my biography *The Last Adventurer: The Life of Talbot Mundy*.

"The Eye of Shiva" is just the sort of setting in British India that Mundy worked in as a young man and which he later portrayed so vividly in his many novels and stories. I decided to publish this under an old pseudonym of mine, Peter MacAlan. I wrote eight novels under that name, but Mr. Tremayne outgrew Mr. MacAlan.

Finally, I come to the late twentieth or even early twenty-first century.

When anthology editor Mike Ashley asked me if I could write a "locked room" mystery but one with a difference, I thought I would try to come up with the ultimate locked-room tale. How could a man be murdered in a toilet on an aircraft at thirty-two thousand feet, being shot while the door remained locked from the inside and without anyone noticing anything untoward? As Mike observed when he first published the story, "How much more impossible can you get!"

To conclude this volume, it would be impossible to avoid an encounter with the lady my readers see as their favorite sleuth—Sister Fidelma, the seventh-century Irish religieuse who is a *dálaigh* or "advocate" of the ancient Irish law courts. In this new tale, "The Spiteful Shadow," which has not appeared in either of the Sister Fidelma short story collections *(Hemlock at Vespers* or *Whispers of the Dead)*, Fidelma is at the ancient abbey of Durrow in another encounter with her old friend and mentor Abbot Laisran. Laisran has a mystery on his hands: Is one of his religious possessed by a malevolent and vengeful spirit?

So these are my mystery short story offerings. Most are slightly different from my usual fare of Sister Fidelma but, hopefully, for the reader, they will all prove equally as enjoyable.

—Peter Tremayne

An Ensuing Evil

and Others

❧

— Night's Black Agents —

Good things of day begin to droop and drowse;
While night's black agents to their preys do rouse.
                                        —*Macbeth*, Act III, Scene ii

I t is plainly murder, my lord," the elderly steward announced unnecessarily.

What else could a stab wound in the back mean but murder? It
would hardly be self-inflicted. The fact that Malcolm, the son of
Bodhe, prince of the House of Moray, lay stretched on the floor of
his bedchamber with the blood still seeping across his white linen
nightshirt did not need a fertile imagination to conjure an explanation of what had befallen the young man.

The corpse lay facedown on the wooden floorboards, clad in
nothing else but the shirt, which meant that he had just left his bed
to greet his killer. A bloodstained knife had fallen nearby, apparently
dropped by the assassin in his haste to be gone.

MacBeth, son of Findlay, the *Mòr-mhaor* or petty king of
Moray, which was one of the seven great provincial kingdoms of
Alba, answering to no man except the High King, whose capital was
south in Sgàin, stared down with a grim face. Indeed, this was his castle, and the dead man was his wife's brother. He stood with a cloak
wrapped around his shoulders to protect him from the night chill. It
had been but only a few minutes ago when he had been roused from
his sleep by his anxious steward and requested to come quickly to
the bedchamber of Malcolm.

It certainly needed no servant or seer or prophet to tell Mac-Beth that someone had entered this chamber and brutally struck down the young prince and then discarded the weapon.

"Is the castle gate still secured?" he demanded, his voice raised as if in irritation and glancing into the corridor, where a warrior of his personal bodyguard stood impassively.

"Aye, noble lord," replied his steward, an elderly man named Garban. "As custom decrees, the gate was secured at nightfall and will not be opened before dawn. Your warriors still stand sentinel at the gate and walk the ramparts."

"So the culprit may yet be within these walls?"

"Unless he has wings to fly or be a mole that can burrow under the walls," agreed the old servant.

MacBeth nodded in grim satisfaction. "Let it continue to be so, for we many yet snare this evildoer. Now where is Prince Malcolm's servant? Why is he not here?"

"He was injured, noble lord. He now is being attended to, for in truth, he received a blow to the head, which caused it to bleed. He it was who discovered the body of his master."

"Then send for him straightaway, Garban. And send for my brehon to oversee these matters, according to the law. There is little time to delay in our pursuit of this assassin."

While a king or even a chief could be a judge and arbitrator in the law courts, it was, by law, known that a professional and qualified lawyer, a brehon, had to sit with the king to ensure the letter of the law was obeyed and a fair judgment delivered.

The old steward was turning toward the door when there was a cry at the portal, and MacBeth turned to see his newly wed wife, the Lady Gruoch, standing there, a hand to her mouth. Garban, the steward, jerked his head to her in nervous obeisance before he hurried forward to carry out MacBeth's instructions.

MacBeth turned to his wife. He had thought her still sleeping when he had left the bedchamber to follow Garban. "Madam, I am afraid your brother is dead," he greeted her quietly, not knowing what else to say but the blunt truth.

Lady Gruoch had seen much violence in her five and twenty years. It had been only one year ago that her first husband, Gille-comgàin, the previous petty king of Moray, had been slaughtered in his castle near Inverness with fifty of his warriors. The castle, with its occupants, had been razed to the ground with fire. No one was caught, but whisper had it that the man who ordered the deed was none other than the man whose bed she now shared and who had been acclaimed with the mantle of *Mòr-mhaor* to replace her dead husband. Yet the Lady Gruoch had long been persuaded to discount such a notion, and she had come to love the young red-haired monarch who offered her and her baby, the young Prince Lulach, his protection.

Gruoch had not been in the castle of Gillecomgàin at the time of the attack but away visiting with her newly born son. The people of Moray, bereft of their ruler, turned to MacBeth, whose father Findlay had been king before Gillecomgàin. For kingship, like chieftainship, descended by the rule of the ancient laws of the bre-hons and not by the inheritance of the firstborn male. A king, or chief, had to be of the blood, but they were elected to their office by their *derbhfine*, four male generations from a common great-grandfather. The law of succession had always been thus so that the most worthy and able should succeed.

No one questioned that MacBeth was worthy or that he was able. Indeed, he was also of the blood royal, for he was grandson of the High King, Malcolm, the second of his name to sit on the throne at Sgàin. Thus the red-haired young noble had been duly installed as the petty king of the province.

Within the year, MacBeth had convinced the Lady Gruoch that he had not been responsible for her husband's death and had won her love. Scarcely a month had passed since their marriage, at which he had even adopted her son, the baby Lulach, as his own. Yet the evil whispers still remained, and some said that he was ambitious and was only reinforcing his claims to the High Kingship because Gruoch, too, had been the grandchild of a High King, Kenneth III, who had died some thirty years ago. Only in these lands, which comprised the former ancient kingdoms of the Cruithne, was a succession through the female allowed by Brehon Law, but the Pictish custom, as it was called, had not been claimed since Drust Mac Ferat ruled over two hundred years before. So the gossip did not hold water.

More logical tongues pointed out that the Lady Gruoch's brother, Malcolm Mac Bodhe, as grandson to Kenneth III, had a more popular claim to the throne as next High King. Even if he had not, it was well known that Malcolm II, who had sired only daughters, did not favor his grandson MacBeth, or, indeed, any member of the Moray House. The old king favored his grandson, Duncan Mac Crinan, the son of the Abbot of Dunkeld, and son of his eldest daughter.

The old king and his grandson, Duncan, were of the House of Atholl, and they maintained they had a superior right to the High Kingship at Sgàin than the House of Moray, even though his second daughter, the Lady Doada, had married Findlay of Moray and was MacBeth's mother. The death of Gillecomgàin in the previous year was attributed by many of the House of Moray as being a deed carried out at the whispered order of Malcolm II to ensure that Duncan was placed on the throne. Gillecomgàin alive had been a threat to Atholl's claims. Gillecomgàin had been slaughtered. But Malcolm Mac Bodhe, grandson of Kenneth III, had become the next challenger to the continued Atholl dominance at Sgàin. Some were already acclaiming him as successor to Malcolm II.

But now Malcolm Mac Bodhe, too, was dead; lying on the floor of his bedchamber in MacBeth's castle. Murdered.

The young king appeared troubled as he stood regarding his tearful wife, who stood, leaning against the doorjamb, her breast heaving, a hand across her trembling mouth.

"There will be many who will blame me for this death, my lady," MacBeth addressed the grief-stricken young woman quietly. He held out a hand to comfort her.

She took it and gave a single heartrending sob, trying, at the same time, to gain control over her feelings. The years of threatening danger had taught her to suppress her emotions until she could indulge in them without distraction.

"How so, my lord?" she asked, succeeding in the effort.

"They will say that I have killed, or had killed, your brother, in order to secure my place nearer the throne at Sgàin."

The woman's eyes widened, and she shook her head vehemently. "I will swear that you never left my side since we parted from my brother after the meal last night."

"Can you so swear?"

"Aye, I can, for I have not closed my eyes these last hours. You know well that I am still beset by nightmares and have visions of our being burnt while we slept, as happened to my . . . as happened to Gillecomgàin, your cousin. I heard Garban come into our chamber and ask you to follow him here—that is why I came after you to see what was amiss."

"They will say that your witness for me is what might be expected of a wife or that you had good cause to see your brother dead so that your husband could claim the throne that you might sit by his side as queen at Sgàin. Indeed, some might even say that, while I slept, you did the deed yourself for ambition's sake."

The Lady Gruoch paled as she stared at him. "What fiendlike creature will people have me be?" she whispered in shock. "To kill my own brother? Even to think such a thought is to pronounce speculations hateful to the ears of any justice."

"It may be said just the same," pointed out MacBeth impassively. "Many things are said and done in the court of my grandfather at Sgàin. I do not doubt that the vaulting ambition of my cousin Duncan, the son of my mother's own sister, will do more than make hateful speculations to secure the throne. His father, the unnatural abbot of Dunkeld, even tries to poison the entire Church against anyone who stands as rival to the resolution of his son to secure the throne."

"I fear that it is so," sighed Gruoch. "I have long labored, as you know, in the belief that the destruction of Gillecomgàin was brought about by your grandfather, who encouraged the rumors which laid the deed at your door."

MacBeth lowered his head. It was true that rumors still circulated accusing him of Gillecomgàin's death. "There will be more whispers yet," he agreed heavily, "unless we speedily resolve this unnatural death of your brother."

A tall elderly man stood at the door. It was clear that he had just come from a deep sleep. His hair was a little disheveled, and his clothes had not been put on with care.

"Garban has informed me of these tragic events, noble lord," the man muttered, his eyes moving swiftly from MacBeth to Gruoch and to the body on the floor. They glinted coldly in the candlelight and seemed to miss nothing.

"I am glad that you have come, Cothromanach. It needs your skilled touch here, for I was saying to the Lady Gruoch, there are many who will wish to taint me with this killing. Your word is needed that this matter has been properly conducted and resolved so that none may level any accusation against me."

Cothromanach, the brehon, set his face stonily. "The truth is the truth. I am here to serve that truth, my lord."

MacBeth nodded. "Indeed, let us proceed with logic. Garban has told you that we have a witness to this deed in the prince Malcolm's servant?"

Cothromanach nodded. "I am told that he has been sent for."

"He has. The Lady Gruoch and I were in our bedchamber until Garban summoned me. The Lady Gruoch says that she is prepared to state that I did not rouse from our bed all night. I have told her that her testimony might be dismissed on grounds of her relationship to me."

The brehon pursed his lips wryly. "Madam, is there any other witness that will say that you and your husband did not stir until Garban summoned your husband here?"

Gruoch thought a moment and then nodded in affirmation. "Little more than an hour ago, I asked my maid Margreg to bring me mulled wine to help me sleep. She entered our chamber with the wine while my husband slept on obliviously."

MacBeth raised his eyebrows in surprise. "I did not hear her."

"You were tired, my lord, after yesterday's hunt and last night's feasting."

"This is true. So Margreg brought wine and saw me sound asleep beside you? This, you say, was but an hour ago?"

"It was so."

MacBeth turned to the brehon. "And I was roused to come here but a quarter of the hour past, and if the deed were committed not long before, it would mean that we have the best witness yet in the maid."

"What makes you think the deed was done but an hour ago?" queried the brehon.

"Easy to tell. We have a witness to the deed." He turned to his wife to explain. "I have sent for your brother's servant, who, it appears, was attacked by the assassin. He has already indicated the time to my steward, Garban."

The Lady Gruoch stared at him in surprise. "This servant was attacked by the assassin? Then we have no need fear our innocence of the deed."

MacBeth sighed: "Perhaps," he said softly. "Truth does not still malicious tongues."

"You sound defensive, lord," observed the brehon. "As if you already stand accused and found guilty."

"It is why I want you to examine this matter closely, Cothromanach. I fear it may be so unless I demonstrate that I had no hand in this. Now, here comes Garban and Malcolm's servant. Do return to our chamber, my lady, and dress yourself, for it is near dawn and this may be a long day." He paused and turned to Cothromanach. "That is, unless you wish the lady to stay?"

The elderly brehon shook his head. "I have no objections to the Lady Gruoch withdrawing."

As Gruoch left the chamber with a single glance back to where her brother's body lay, old Garban came forward. Behind him followed a younger man, tall and well built. There was a gash over his eye that still seeped blood. His face was pale, and he walked with an unsteady gait. He stood hesitating before MacBeth, looking from him to the brehon.

Old Garban gave him a gentle nudge forward.

"Tell my noble lord your name, boy."

The young man took a pace forward. "I am called Segan, noble lord," he muttered, his eyes downcast.

"How long have you been in the service of the prince Malcolm?"

"I have served him ever since I can remember, and my father before me was a steward in the house of his father, the prince Bodhe."

"Then this will not take long, Segan. Tell us the circumstances in which you received this blow to your head and how you discovered the prince?"

"Little to tell, indeed, noble lord. Prince Malcolm had retired after the feasting last evening and went straightaway to his bed. He told me that he would not want me until the morning. So I, too, went to my bed—"

"Which is where?" Cothromanach, the brehon, suddenly interrupted.

"In that small chamber opposite," the young man indicated through the open door.

Garban, the steward, intervened with a clearing of his throat. "I placed the servant there so that he might be near his master in case of need," he explained to the brehon.

"What then?" MacBeth did not wait for the brehon to acknowledge the explanation.

"I fell asleep. I do not know what time I was awakened nor what had awakened me. Perhaps it was the sound of something falling to the ground. I roused myself and listened. All was quiet. I went to my door and opened it. I thought that I heard a sound from Prince Malcolm's room.

"Wondering if anything was amiss, I went to his door and called softly. There was no answer. I was just about to turn back into my chamber when I heard a distinct sound from this room. I called Prince Malcolm's name and asked if he needed anything.

"There was no response, and so I tried the chamber door. It was secured."

"Secured?" interposed Cothromanach quickly.

"It was Prince Malcolm's custom to secure the door to his bed-chamber from the inside." The young servant hesitated and dropped his gaze. "These are troubled and dangerous times, lord. There are many who would not weep over Prince Malcolm's death."

"Go on," the brehon instructed.

"I called again. Then I heard the bolt being withdrawn. I tried the handle and this time the chamber door swung open. I took a step inside and saw the prince even as you see him now, lying on the floor there. The blood on his shirt and the knife at his side."

MacBeth glanced toward the brehon and saw his puzzled gaze. He preempted the question. "You saw Malcolm lying there and saw all this clearly? How so?"

"How so?" repeated the young man in a puzzled tone, not understanding what he meant.

"Was the room not in darkness?"

"Ah." Segan shook his head. "No, there was a candle alight by the bedside, even as it is now."

MacBeth turned to examine the candle and saw that scarcely a half-inch of tallow was left flickering in its holder. Satisfied, Mac-Beth turned back in time to see the young man wince and stagger a little.

"Are you hurt?" intervened the brehon anxiously.

"I am a little dizzy still. Yet I rebuke my own stupidity," lamented the young man. "I cannot believe that I could be such a dimwit. Seeing the body, I took two steps toward it, and then something hit me from behind. Now I realize, whoever had drawn the bolt still stood behind the door, and who would it be but the assassin? I came in, like a lamb to the slaughter, and thus he could strike me down from behind."

Old Garban nodded in support. "It could happen to anyone, seeing their lord dead. It was a natural error. No blame to the young man."

MacBeth nodded absently, but Cothromanach was examining the young man with his sharp eyes. "Yes. It was an action not governed by thought. So you say that you were struck from behind? What then?"

The young man frowned at the elderly man. "Then?"

"Yes, what happened then?" pressed Cothromanach.

"I must have fallen unconscious to the floor, for the next thing I knew, I came to with blood on my head and a throbbing which was more agonizing than anything I can remember. I was lying just there." He pointed downward. "Then I remembered the prince and raised myself. It was obvious that he was dead. I turned, the door was closed and no one else in the room. I left the chamber and went in search of Garban. I roused him and he came here. He then sent me to his wife to clean my wound while he went to tell you of this news."

Garban now intervened once more in support. "This is true. The young man roused me, and I put on my clothes and hurried here while my wife tended to his wound, which was bleeding more profusely than it is now. Having ascertained what Segan had said was true, I felt I should come to rouse Lord MacBeth. The rest is as he knows."

MacBeth turned to Cothromanach. "Indeed. I immediately followed Garban here. My wife followed moments later. That was when I sent Garban to you and asked him to bring Segan back here."

The brehon stood, head bowed in thought for a moment. "How long, Garban, do you estimate the time between you being roused by Segan and you rousing the lord MacBeth?"

The old man held his head to one side and thought. "Scarce five to ten minutes, Cothromanach."

"And you, Segan, is there any way you can estimate the time you lay unconscious?"

"Not long, I think. It may have been a matter of minutes."

"What makes you say so?"

"The candle. I said it was burning when I entered. It had not burnt down too much when I regained consciousness. And, even now, you can see it still flickering there."

MacBeth went toward the table to examine the candle, noting the spilled grease on the table and the floor. He bent down and picked up a stub of tallow and frowned in annoyance at Garban. "These chambers should be better cleaned," he snapped, throwing the tallow at his steward, who caught it and began to apologize.

Cothromanach hid his impatience. "It is not the time to discuss the dilatory habits of the servants, noble lord."

MacBeth looked guilty and turned back to Segan. "So the chamber was well lit? Did you get any impression of your assailant?"

Segan looked puzzled. "Impression. I did not see him at all."

"Yet you are certain that it was a male?"

Segan was now entirely bewildered.

"If you did not see who struck the blow," explained MacBeth patiently, "how can you tell it was a man?"

In spite of himself, Segan raised a laugh. "I cannot imagine a woman delivering the blow that would have laid me low, noble lord."

"Perhaps not," agreed MacBeth. He turned to the brehon and saw the man still examining Segan's features thoughtfully. MacBeth turned back to Segan and suddenly realized what puzzled the brehon. "But there is a question that intrigues me. You say that you were struck from behind?"

"Yes, noble lord. Had it been from the front, I would have seen my assailant," he added patiently.

"Quite so. Then how is it that your wound is on your forehead and not on the back of the head?"

Segan's eyes widened, and he raised his hand automatically to his forehead as if to touch the gash that was there. "I was struck from behind, noble lord," he insisted. "I feel the hurt there even now. So *that* I know as a fact. Perhaps, as I fell, I also struck my forehead."

"There is no other explanation," agreed the brehon quietly. "There is too much of Malcolm's blood on the floor to see where you might have fallen. Well, there is little more we can discover from this young man, I think."

"I have no further questions, Segan. I suggest Garban take you back to his wife to have your wound examined further. It looks a bad gash, and a bruise surrounds it."

"I would rather lie down a few moments, lord," said Segan, but Garban took his arm with a firm grasp and smiled.

"Plenty of time after my wife has made a poultice for that cut and bruise."

Alone in the room, MacBeth turned to the brehon. "What do you think?"

Cothromanach shrugged. "Little to think about, noble lord. There are few facts at our disposal to make any clear deductions."

"The facts seem that the killer gained entrance to this chamber and stabbed Prince Malcolm. The body falling to the floor must have alerted his servant, Segan, who came to the door. The killer had secured the door but, hearing Segan call out, realized that if he remained locked without, he would raise the alarm and the assassin would not be able to escape. So he slid the bolt and waited behind the door."

Cothromanach smiled. "I cannot fault your logic, noble lord."

MacBeth continued, warming to the theme. "Standing behind the door, the assassin waited as the young man opened the door. The killer relied on the fact that the young man would react at the sight of Malcolm lying in his bloodstained shirt on the floor; he knew that the servant would take an involuntary step forward into the room. That was when the blow was struck. Then the killer left the room."

"Again, the logic is without a fault."

MacBeth smiled thinly. "If nothing else, I answer to logic," he replied complacently.

"Very well, my lord. Let us turn logic to the following matters. Firstly, let us regard the body of the prince."

MacBeth looked down, his face wrinkled in distaste. "What can we learn from it except that the killer stabbed the prince in the back?"

"That he did so presents us with an important question that needs a resolution."

"How so?"

"We have heard that the prince was in fear of his life for the reasons well known to you, noble lord. He slept at night with his door bolted from the interior. How, then, when his assassin came to his chamber, did he gain entrance?"

MacBeth raised his eyebrows and turned to examine the door. The bolt was in place, and there was no sign of any undue violence being used against the lock. He did not have to go to the small window in the chamber, for he knew that it was a long drop into a rocky ravine through which a river meandered. There was no way anyone would climb in through that window. He would take an oath on it.

"If—" He paused and framed his words slowly. "—if the door was bolted, then Malcolm himself must have let his killer into the chamber."

Cothromanach made a gesture of approval. "In order to do that, the prince Malcolm must have known his assassin. He must have known him well enough to have trusted him, to have let him into his bedchamber while not yet dressed and—"

MacBeth interrupted, for now he saw what the elderly brehon

was getting at. "He must have trusted him to be able to have turned his back on him, for the two stab wounds are in the back. The killer, as Malcolm turned away from him, stabbed him twice."

"Then dropped the knife and was turning to go—"

"When he was interrupted by Segan?"

"Perhaps," the brehon said. "Yet what would be the motive for such a deed?"

"Surely the motive is obvious? Malcolm was a popular candidate for the High Kingship. The likely motive was to eliminate him."

"So we are saying that whoever did this deed was a servant of Duncan who aspires to the throne?"

MacBeth nodded and then grimaced. "You are forgetting my claim, for with the prince Malcolm gone, I am now the head of the House of Moray and challenger to the kingship at Sgàin."

Cothromanach smiled briefly. "I have not forgotten. Nor have I forgotten that you are not the only one who stands to gain."

MacBeth frowned. "Who?"

"The Lady Gruoch would benefit by your elevation to the kingship."

For a moment MacBeth stood in anger, but then he shrugged as if in acceptance. "You mean more than she would have done had her brother gained the throne?"

"Of course. Much more. However, this is hardly a woman's work."

"With that, I agree." MacBeth was emphatic.

The door opened, and Garban the steward reentered. "Segan is having his wound redressed. Can I render more assistance?"

"Find the maid Margreg and bring her here," instructed Mac-Beth.

The brehon held up a hand to stay him. "You knew the prince Malcolm well, didn't you?"

Garban blinked in surprise and shrugged. "That is common knowledge. I was employed in the house of Bodhe before I took service with my lord MacBeth. I taught young Malcolm to ride his first horse. His death grieves me sorely."

14

"Indeed," sighed the brehon, and dismissed him with a wave.

When Garban had gone, MacBeth turned to Cothromanach. "Let us hear from the maid's own lips that we were in our beds at the time the deed was done," he told the brehon. "Then you may be able to quench any malicious rumors which may be spread about us."

"You are sensitive on this matter," observed the brehon.

"I know my grandfather, the High King, and my cousin, Duncan Mac Crinan," MacBeth said grimly.

"So be it," Cothromanach sighed.

Margreg was young and youthful, scarcely seventeen. She was dark haired, fair skinned, and attractive, and what is more, she knew it. There was a boldness about her that might have been interpreted by some as a speculative lasciviousness.

She entered the chamber, dropped a half-curtsy to MacBeth, and was about to acknowledge the venerable brehon when her eyes caught sight of the body on the floor. Her features wrinkled distastefully, but she did not avert her gaze.

"The brehon wishes to ask you a few questions," MacBeth said, stepping to one side and motioning the brehon to proceed.

"You are maidservant to the Lady Gruoch?"

"You know so," retorted the girl with confidence. "You are as familiar with this castle as I am."

Cothromanach suppressed a sigh of irritation. "This is an official inquiry, girl. Just answer my questions and leave your impudence for those who appreciate it."

The girl pouted in annoyance. "Yes. I am maid to the Lady Gruoch."

"How long have you held that position?"

"Full one year since she came to this castle with her baby in search of sanctuary."

"Did you attend your mistress at bedtime."

"I did. Her dressing room is next door to the bedchamber, and that is where the baby, Lulach, sleeps, and that is where I sleep, as well. I helped her undress and prepare for bed. That was just after the feasting."

"So you sleep in the next chamber. Were you disturbed in the night?"

"Yes. I awoke and heard the baby coughing. He is a good little soul but inclined to a night cough. So I arose and tended the child. I had quietened him and was about to go back to bed when I heard a door open and footsteps in the corridor. Curiosity made me go to the door, and I looked out."

MacBeth had turned with a frown. "What time was this?"

The girl shrugged. "I have no means of knowing, my lord. It was dark and cold, and the embers in the fire I had built in the chamber were gray." She turned to Cothromanach. "I try to keep a fire going through the night for the good of the baby. Warm air eases his poor little chest."

"You said that you went to the door and looked out," MacBeth observed heavily. "What did you see?"

"The Lady Gruoch, walking down the corridor. She was carrying something in her hand."

"How could you see that it was her? Did you or she have a candle?" asked the brehon quickly.

The girl shook her head. "No. There are torches kept alight in the corridor there."

"So the Lady Gruoch left the bedchamber during the night?" pressed MacBeth unnecessarily.

"What time did she return?" demanded the brehon.

"I do not know. Having seen that it was my lady, I simply returned to my bed, for it was chill, as I have said, and I was asleep in no time."

"Were you disturbed again?"

"Yes. I thought me barely asleep when I awoke and found my lady bending over me. She said she could not sleep and asked me to prepare her a goblet of mulled wine. I did so."

"And you had no idea when that was either, I suppose?" sighed MacBeth.

"Oh yes. It was not long before Garban came and knocked at your chamber door. I prepared the wine and went in, finding the lady Grouch sitting up in bed. You were there also, my noble lord, fast asleep by her side. I don't think that you had been disturbed at all during the night, for you were deep in sleep and . . . and snoring with a sound fit to wake the dead." She grinned provocatively at him.

"How long was it before Garban came to our chamber?" he snapped.

"I went back to bed but could not sleep. Perhaps he came within the hour. I cannot be sure, only that it was not very long."

The brehon looked troubled. "The Lady Gruoch told you that she could confirm you were by her side all night. Yet now we find that she left the bed, and who is to provide her with an alibi? We must send for her again."

Lady Gruoch stood before them shortly afterward. She looked guilty but not alarmed. "Yes. I left the chamber. I have already told you that I do not sleep well. That was the reason why I asked the maid Margreg to fetch me mulled wine."

"But you were seen going down the corridor," pointed out the brehon. "Where did you go, lady?"

The Lady Gruoch raised her chin defiantly. "If you must know, I came to see my brother."

MacBeth looked unhappy. He glanced at Cothromanach, who was gazing thoughtfully at her. "This is a sensitive matter, lady. You know of what you might be accused? You know why I need to clarify the matter?"

"I know it well enough, my lord. But I came here for a purpose that I would keep between myself and his soul. All you need to know is that my brother was well and alive when I came here. Furthermore, when I left him, he was still alive and well."

"That is not all I need to know, madam!" MacBeth almost shouted.

"Softly, noble lord," intervened the brehon. Then he turned to Lady Gruoch. "But in truth, the noble lord is right, madam. We need to know the reason that you came here like a thief in the night. What intercourse could you have with your brother that needed such secrecy as to be conducted in the blackness of the night, that needed to be kept secret from your own husband?"

The Lady Gruoch was flushed and unhappy. She gazed at Mac-Beth for several moments and turned back to the brehon. "Very well. You will already have the evidence, so I will confess to you."

MacBeth groaned helplessly. "Evidence? What are you saying, lady?"

"It is common knowledge that my brother, Malcolm, was going to claim the High Kingship when my husband's grandfather dies or abdicates the throne at Sgàin. It is well known that MacBeth's cousin, Duncan, is favored to succeed. Yet he is not the choice of the people, even in Atholl. My brother planned to raise the clans of Moray against Sgàin. For that he needed money. I was given many jewels by my husband as wedding gifts when I married him. Much that I owned perished in Gillecomgàin's castle. So I decided that my brother could make better use of the gifts from MacBeth."

"You say that you brought these jewels to your brother in the middle of the night?" asked MacBeth doubtfully.

"It was just after midnight, an appointment that I had arranged with my brother last evening so that no one would know of the gift."

"Was his door secured?"

"Yes. It was bolted, but he opened when he heard my voice call to him."

"You say that you left him alive?"

"I did so. He secured the door after me."

"And you went straightaway back to your bedchamber?"

"I did. And that was, as I say, just after midnight."

"The trouble is that you have no witness that he was alive when you left here," the brehon sighed.

"I did not think I needed a witness. I understood from Margreg that the servant Segan disturbed the killer and was knocked unconscious by him some hours after I left my brother. That shows that I am innocent of the deed."

As she had been speaking, the elderly brehon had been examining the room very carefully.

"What is it?" demanded MacBeth curiously. "What do you seek?"

Cothromanach looked at him and smiled thinly. "Why, a bag of jewels, what else?"

Lady Gruoch stared at him in disbelief. "You found no jewels? But that was the evidence that I thought you had and would trace them to my ownership. Why . . ."

MacBeth, ignoring her, was also searching the room carefully. Finally he stood before her.

"There are no jewels here, madam," he observed heavily.

"I do not understand it. He would not have given them to anyone else for safekeeping unless . . ." Her eyes widened as she stared at her husband.

MacBeth turned to the brehon. "Do we not have another motive before us, Cothromanach? The assassin was not solely a murderer but a thief."

"It would appear so. Yet, let me remind you, noble lord, that the killer, thief or no, was still known to the prince. Why else would the killer be let into the chamber, why else would the prince have turned his back on the hand that then struck him down?"

MacBeth bowed his head in thought. Then he smiled grimly. "I have an idea. Garban!"

The servant came forward.

"Are the gates still secured and my sentinels in place?"

"Not even a mouse could have left this castle without them being aware of it, noble lord."

"Good. Then we shall search for Lady Gruoch's jewels. I doubt whether our assassin has had time to dispose of them."

"Very well, noble lord. Where shall I start?"

MacBeth looked through the opened door into the corridor. "We will start with Segan's chamber, it being nearest. Proceed, Garban. You, madam, will return to your chamber until I send for you."

MacBeth and Cothromanach followed the elderly steward into the servant's bedchamber. As Garban entered, he seemed to stumble and reached out a hand to steady himself on the wall. He cut short an exclamation and brought his hand away. His fingertips were stained with blood.

MacBeth asked Garban to bring a candle, which he did. There was a small patch of blood on the wall, at shoulder level.

Garban began to make a diligent search, and it was not long before, examining beneath the bed, he emerged with a cry of triumph. He held out a small leather sack. They watched with fascination as he opened it and poured its contents on the bed. The muddle of jewels glittered and sparkled in the candlelight.

"Are they the jewels that you gave to the Lady Gruoch?" demanded the brehon.

"They are, indeed," replied MacBeth with satisfaction. "Garban, fetch the servant Segan back here, but do not mention this discovery to him."

"I understand, noble lord," Garban said with a grim smile.

Cothromanach the brehon looked thoughtfully at MacBeth. "Did you expect to find the jewels here?"

"As soon as I heard my wife's explanation—yes. I began to understand how and why this foul deed was done."

"Explain your deduction, my lord."

"Not hard. This is what I believe happened: Maybe the prince Malcolm told his servant that he would be receiving the jewels from his sister. Maybe Segan saw the Lady Gruoch come to his master's chamber and observed her entering with the sack. It was not politics that motivated Segan but greed. He waited until the castle was quiet and then he went to rouse his master by tapping at the door. Malcolm let him into the chamber, half-asleep. Seeing only Segan, a servant he trusted, he turned his back on him. That was when Segan struck. Two swift but fatal stabs in the back. He found the sack of jewels and took them back to his own bedchamber and hid them where we have now discovered them."

"How then did Segan receive his own injuries?"

"Easy to tell. He had his story ready, that the murderer had stood behind the door and had given him a blow on the head which rendered him unconscious so that he could not recognize who it was. But this was the difficult part. Have you ever tried to give yourself a blow on the back of the head? Nevertheless, he needed some visual sign to show that he had been attacked. In fact, I might not have spotted the flaw in his story had not you realized it."

"That the injury was in the front?"

"Exactly. He went to the wall and banged his head against it, causing the abrasion. Then he pretended that he had just come round and went to rouse Garban with the news of his attack."

MacBeth suddenly smiled and pointed to a small bloodstain on the wall. It was shoulder high, where a man might have banged his head to make the abrasion. "I presume we do not have to explain that mark away?"

The brehon sighed. "It is a stupid man who leaves such a trail of clues."

Just then Segan entered the chamber with Garban close behind him.

He stared from MacBeth to the brehon with a slight flicker of puzzlement in his eyes. Then his glance fell on the bed and the pile of jewelry.

"My lord, this . . . ," he began, taking a step forward.

Then he froze, his eyes round in surprise. He half twisted and attempted to reach for something at his side. Garban withdrew the six-inch blade from the young man.

He watched dispassionately as the servant fell to the floor.

There was no need to examine the body. Segan was dead long before he hit the floor.

"He was reaching for his knife," Garban explained. "He meant to harm you, noble lord."

"A pity," muttered Cothromanach. "Better to have him live awhile and receive his punishment as a warning to all thieves and murderers."

"Indeed," MacBeth acknowledged grimly. "Have the body removed, Garban, and have those jewels gathered up and returned to the Lady Gruoch. I will walk a way with you, Cothromanach."

The brehon glanced at him. "You are still anxious, noble lord?"

"There are still willing tongues to spread rumors. Many will be quick to lay the blame for this at my door."

"Have no fear. I shall write my account to my fellow brehons throughout the land. They shall know what has transpired here."

MacBeth smiled in thanks and, hauling his cloak more tightly around his shoulders, turned and made his way back to his bedchamber. Dawn now filled the castle with a gray, cold light.

After the morning meal, while the light was still gray and cold, MacBeth found old Garban on the ramparts of the castle.

He was standing in a quiet corner away from the scrutiny of the guards, leaning with his back to the ramparts. "A close call, noble lord," observed the old man as he turned and peered over the ramparts, looking down into the rocky ravine below. "I had to kill him."

"Indeed you did," agreed MacBeth, pleasantly enough. "Yet the plan was nearly ruined by not clearing away the extra candle stub."

"It is easy to make a mistake. But all ended well. After Lady Gruoch left her brother, I knocked on the door, and the prince opened it, knowing it was I. The problem was that his falling body was heard by Segan, who came and knocked on the door. Had I not opened, he would have roused the entire castle. So I let him in and gave him a blow on the back of the head. While he lay unconscious, I struck him on the temple, for I knew that this might arouse suspicion.

Then I hid the jewels in his bedchamber, in case we needed evidence, and also spread his wall with his blood to make it look as though he had faked his wound by dashing his forehead there. Then, to confuse him over the time the deed was committed, I exchanged the burning candle with a new one, which would put his timing out by an hour or two."

"That was the mistake you made, in dropping the stub of the first candle on the floor and not taking it with you," observed Mac-Beth. "It could have made the brehon suspicious."

"None of us are perfect, noble lord," sniffed the old servant.

"True enough."

"And now you stand one step closer to the throne at Sgàin, noble lord. Prince Malcolm is no longer your rival, and the Lady Gruoch is there to support you."

"True again."

"You have much to thank me for, noble lord." Garban smiled. "I trust I will be properly rewarded."

"That I have and that you shall," agreed MacBeth, and turning swiftly, he gave the old man a violent push, sending him flying over the rampart. There was scarcely time for Garban to scream as he plummeted downward into the rocky chasm below.

MacBeth turned and, seeing that he was unobserved, allowed a smile of satisfaction to spread over his features.

━ An Ensuing Evil ━

Yet I can give you inkling
Of an ensuing evil . . .

—Henry VIII, Act II, Scene i

I t's a body, Master Constable."
Master Hardy Drew, Constable of the Bankside Watch, stared in distaste at the wherryman. "I have eyes to see with," he replied sourly. "Just tell me how you came by it."

The stocky boatman put a hand to the back of his head and scratched as if this action were necessary to the process of summoning up his memories. "It were just as we turned midriver to the quay here," the wherryman began. "We'd brought coal up from Greenwich. I was guiding the barge in when we spotted the body in the river, and so we fished it out."

Master Drew glanced down to the body sprawled in a sodden mess on the dirty deck of the coal barge.

The finding of bodies floating in the Thames was not an unusual occurrence. London was a cesspool of suffering humanity, especially along these banks between London Bridge and Bankside. Master Drew had not been Constable of the Watch for three years without becoming accustomed to bodies being trawled out of this stretch of water whose southern bank came under his policing jurisdiction. Cutthroats, footpads, and all manner of the criminal scum of the city found the river a convenient place to rid themselves of their victims. And it was not just those who had died violent deaths who were disposed of in the river, but also corpses of the poor, sick and diseased, whose relatives couldn't afford a church burial. The pollution of the water had become so bad that this very year a water reservoir, claimed to be the first of its kind in all Europe, had been opened at Clerkenwell to supply fresh water for the city.

However, what marked this body out for the attention of the constable, among the half-dozen or so that had been fished from the river this particular Saturday morning, was the fact that it was the body of a well-dressed young man. Despite the effects of his immersion, he bore the stamp of a gentleman. In addition, he had not died of drowning, for his throat had been expertly cut—and no more than twelve hours previously, by the condition of the body.

The constable bent down and examined the features dispassionately. In life, the young man had been handsome, was well kempt. He had ginger hair, a splattering of freckles across the nose, and a scar, which might have been the result of a knife or sword, across the forehead over the right eye. His age was no more than twenty-one or twenty-two years. Master Drew considered that he might be the son of a squire or someone in the professions—a parson's son, perhaps. The constable's expert scrutiny had ruled out his being of higher quality, for the clothes, while fashionable, were only of moderately good tailoring. Therefore, the young man had not been someone of flamboyant wealth.

The wherryman was peering over the constable's shoulders and sniffed. "Victim of a footpad, most like?"

Master Drew did not answer, but keeping his leather gloves on, he took the hand of the young man and examined a large and ostentatious ring that was on it. "Since when did a footpad leave jewelry on his victim?" he asked. He removed the ring carefully and held it up. "Ah!" he commented.

"What, Master Constable?" demanded the wherryman.

Drew had noticed that the ring, ostentatious though it was, was not really as valuable as first glance might suggest. It boasted no precious metals or stones, thus fitting the constable's image of someone who wanted to convey a sense of style without the wealth to back it. He put it into his pocket.

There was a small leather purse on the man's belt. Its mouth was not well tied. He opened it without expecting to find anything, so was surprised when a few coins and a key fell out. They were as dry as the interior of the purse.

"A sixpenny piece and three strange copper coins," observed Master Drew. He held up one of the copper coins. "Marry! The new copper farthings. I have not seen any before this day."

"What's that?" replied the wherryman.

"These coins have just been issued to replace the silver farthings. Well, whatever the reason for his killing, robbery it was not."

Master Drew was about to stand up when he noticed a piece of paper tucked into the man's doublet. He drew it forth and tried to unfold it, sodden as it was.

"A theater bill. For the Blackfriars Theatre. A performance of *The Maid's Tragedy*," he remarked.

He rose and waved to two men of the watch, who were waiting on the quay with a cart. They came down onto the barge and, in answer to Master Drew's gesture, manhandled the corpse up the stone steps to their cart.

"What now then, Constable?" demanded the old wherryman.

"Back to your work, man," replied Master Drew. "And I to mine. I have to discover who this young coxcomb is . . . *was,* and the reason for his being in the river with his throat slit."

"Will there be a reward for finding him?" the wherryman asked slyly. "I have lost time in landing my cargo of coal."

Master Drew regarded the man without humor. "When you examined the purse of the corpse, Master Wherryman, you neglected to retie it properly. If he had gone into the river with the purse open as it was, then the interior would not have been dry, and neither would the coins."

The wherryman winced at the constable's cold tone.

"I do not begrudge you a reward, which you have taken already, but out of interest, how much was left in the purse when you found it?"

"By the faith, Master Constable . . . ," the wherryman protested.

"The truth now!" snapped Master Drew, his gray eyes glinting like wet slate.

"I took only a silver shilling, that is all. On my mother's honor."

"I will take charge of that money," replied the constable, holding out his hand. "And I will forget what I have heard, for theft is theft and the reward for a thief is a hemp rope. Remember that, and I'll leave you to your honest toil."

One of the watchmen was waiting eagerly for the constable as he climbed up onto the quay. "Master Drew, I do reckon I've seen this 'ere cove somewhere afore," he said, raising his knuckles to his forehead in salute.

Master Drew regarded the man dourly. "Well, then? Where do you think you have seen him before?"

"I do be trying 'ard to think on't." His companion was staring at the face of the corpse with a frown. "'E be right. I do say 'e be one o' them actor fellows. Can't think where I see'd 'im."

Master Drew glanced sharply at him. "An actor?"

He stared down at the theater bill he still held in his gloved hand and pursed his lips thoughtfully. "Take him up to the mortuary. I have business at the Blackfriars Theatre."

The constable turned along the quay and found a solitary boatman soliciting for custom. The man looked awkward as the constable approached.

"I need your services," Master Drew said shortly, putting the man a little at ease, for it was rare that the appearance of the constable on the waterfront meant anything other than trouble. "Blackfriars Steps."

"Sculls then, Master Constable?" queried the man.

"Sculls it is," Master Drew agreed, climbing into the small

dinghy. The boatman sat at his oars and sent the dinghy dancing across the river to the north bank, across the choppy waters, which were raised by an easterly wind.

As they crossed, Drew was not interested in the spectacle up to London Bridge, with its narrow arches where the tide ran fast because of the constriction of the crossing. Beyond it, he knew, was the great port, where ships from all parts of the world tied up, unloading cargoes under the shadow of the grim, gray Tower. The north bank, where the city proper was sited, was not Constable Drew's jurisdiction. He was constable on the south bank of the river but he was not perturbed about crossing out of his territory. He knew the City Watch well enough.

The boat rasped against the bottom of Blackfriars Steps. He flipped the man a halfpenny and walked with a measured tread up the street toward the tower of St. Paul's rising above the city, which was shrouded with the acrid stench of coal fires rising from a hundred thousand chimneys. It was not far to the Blackfriars Theatre.

He walked in and was at once hailed by a tall man who fluttered his hands nervously. "I say, fellow! Away! Begone! The theater is not open for another three hours yet."

Master Drew regarded the man humorlessly. "I come not to see the play but to seek information." He reached behind his jerkin and drew forth his seal of office.

"A constable?" The man assumed a comical woebegone expression. "What do you seek here, good Constable? We have our papers in order, the license from the Lord Chamberlain. What is there that is wrong?"

"To whom do I speak?" demanded Master Drew.

"Why, to Master Page Williams, the assistant manager of our company—Children of the Revel." The man stuck out his chin proudly.

"And are any of your reveling children astray this afternoon?"

"Astray, good master? What do you mean?"

"I speak plainly. Are all your company of players accounted for today?"

"Indeed, they be. We are rehearsing our next performance, which requires all our actors."

"Is there no one missing?"

"All are present. Why do you ask?"

Master Drew described the body of the young man that had been fished from the river. Master Page Williams looked unhappy.

"It seems that I know the youth. An impetuous youth, he was, who came to this theater last night and claimed to be a playwright whose work had been stolen."

"Did he have a name?"

"Alas, I have forgotten it, if I were even told it. This youth, if it be one and the same, strutted in before the evening performance of our play and demanded to speak with the manager. I spoke with him."

"And what did he want?" pressed Master Drew.

"This youth accused our company of pirating a play that he claimed to be author of."

Constable Drew raised an eyebrow. "Tell me, was there reason behind this encounter?"

"Good Master Constable, we are rehearsing a play whose author is one Bardolph Zenobia. He has written a great tragedy titled *The Vow Breaker Delivered.* It is a magnificent drama. . . ." He paused at the constable's frown and then hastened on. "This youth, whom you describe, came to the theater and claimed that this play was stolen from him and that he was the true author. As if a mere youth could have penned such a work. He claimed that he had assistance in the writing of it from the hand of some companion of his—"

"And you set no store by his claim, that this play was stolen from him?"

"None whatsoever. Master Zenobia is a true gentleman of the theater. A serious gentleman. He has the air of quality about him. . . ."

"So you know him well?"

"Not well," confessed Master Williams. "He has been to the theater on diverse occasions following our acceptance of his work. I believe that he has rooms at the Groaning Cardinal Tavern in Clink Street—"

"Clink Street?"

It was across the river, in his own Bankside jurisdiction.

"What age would you place this Master Zenobia at?"

"Fully forty years, with graying hair about the temples and a serene expression that would grace an archbishop."

Master Drew sniffed dourly. Theater people were always given to flowery descriptions. "So did the youth depart from the theater?"

"Depart he did, but not until I threatened to call the watch. When I refused to countenance his demands, he shouted and threatened me. He said that if he did not recover the stolen play or get compensation, his life would be in danger."

"His life?" mused Master Drew. "Marry! But that is an odd thing to say. Are you sure he said it was *his* life in danger, not the life of Master Zenobia? He did not mean this in the manner of a threat?"

"I have an ear for dialogue, good master," rebuked the man. "The youth soon betook himself off. It happened that Master Zenobia was on stage, approving the costumes for his drama, and so I warned him to beware of the young man and his outrageous claims."

"What did he say?"

"He just replied that he would have a care and soon after departed."

"Is he here today?"

"No. He told me he would be unable to see the first performance of the play this afternoon but would come straightway to the theater after the matinee."

"A curious attitude for an aspiring playwright," observed Master Drew. "Most of them would want to be witnesses to the first performance of their work."

"Indeed, they would. It seems odd that Master Zenobia only calls at our poor theater outside the hours of our performances."

Constable Drew thanked the man and turned out of the theater to walk back to the river. Instead of spending another halfpenny to cross, he decided to walk the short distance to the spanning wooden piles of London Bridge and walk across the busy thoroughfare with its sprawling lopsided constructions balanced precariously upon it. Master Drew knew the watch on the bridge and spent a pleasant half an hour with the man, for it was midday, and a pint of ale and pork pie at one of the grog shops crowded on the bridge was a needed diversion from the toil of the day. He bade farewell to the watch and came off the bridge at the south bank turning west toward Clink Street.

The Groaning Cardinal Tavern was not an auspicious-looking inn. Its sign depicted a popish cardinal being burnt at the stake. It reminded Constable Drew, with a shudder, that only the previous year some heretics had been burnt at the stake in England. Fears of Catholic plots still abounded. Henry, the late Prince of Wales, had refused to marry a Catholic princess only weeks before his death, and it was rumored abroad by papists that this had been God's punishment on him. Protestants spoke of witchcraft.

Master Drew entered the tavern.

The innkeeper was a giant of a man—tall, broad shouldered, well muscled, and without a shirt but a short, leather, sleeveless jerkin over his hairy torso. He was sweating, and it became evident that he was stacking ale barrels.

"Bardolph Zenobia, Master Constable?" He threw back his head and laughed. "Someone be telling you lies. Ain't no Master Zenobia here. He do sound like a foreigner."

Constable Drew had come to the realization that the name was probably a theatrical one, for he knew that many in the theater adopted such preposterous designations.

He repeated the description that Master Page Williams had

given him and saw a glint of anxiety creep into the innkeeper's eyes.

"What be he done, Master Constable? 'E ain't wanted for debt?"

Master Drew shook his head. "The man may yet settle his score with you. But I need information from this man, whoever he is."

The innkeeper sighed deeply. "First floor, front right."

"And what name does this thespian reside under?"

"Master Tom Hawkins."

"That sounds more reasonable than Master Zenobia," observed the constable.

"Them players are all the same, with high-sounding titles and names," agreed the innkeeper. "Few of them can match their name to a farthing. But Master Hawkins is different. He has been a steady guest here these last five years."

"He has his own recognizances?"

The man stared at him bewildered.

"I mean, does he have financial means other than the theater?"

"He do pay his bills, that's all I do say, master," the innkeeper replied.

"But he is a player?"

"One of the King's Men."

Master Drew was surprised. "At the Globe Theatre?"

"He is one of Master Burbage's players," confirmed the innkeeper.

Constable Drew mounted the stairs and knocked at the first floor, front right door. There was no answer. He did not hesitate but entered. The room was deserted. It was also untidy. Clothes and papers were strewn here and there. Master Drew peered through them. There were some play parts and a page or two on which the name *Bardolph Zenobia* was scrawled.

He took himself downstairs and saw the big innkeeper again.

"Maybe he has gone to the theater?" suggested the man when he told him the room was deserted.

"It is still a while before the time of the matinee performance."

"They sometimes hold rehearsals before the performance," the innkeeper pointed out.

Master Drew was about to turn away when he realized it would not come amiss to ask if the innkeeper knew aught of the youth whose body had been discovered. He gave the man a description without informing him of his death. But his inquiry was received with a vehement shake of the head.

"I have not seen such a young man here nor do I know him."

Constable Drew walked to where the Globe Theatre dominated its surroundings in Bankside. Master Hardy Drew had been a boy when the Burbage brothers, Cuthbert and Richard, had built the theater there fourteen years before. Since then the Globe had become an institution south of the river. It had first become the home of the Lord Chamberlain's Men, who, on the succession of James VI of Scotland to the English throne ten years ago, had been given gracious permission to call themselves the King's Men. Master Drew knew Cuthbert Burbage slightly, for their paths had crossed several times. Cuthbert Burbage ran the business side of the theater while his brother, Richard Burbage, was the principal actor and director of the plays that were performed there.

Master Drew entered the doors of the Globe Theatre. An elderly doorman came forward, recognized the constable, and halted nervously.

"Give you a good day, Master Jasper," Master Drew greeted him.

"Is aught amiss, good master?" grumbled the old man.

"Should there be?" The constable smiled thinly.

"That I would not know, for I keep myself to myself and do my job without offending God nor the King nor, I do pray, my fellow man."

Master Drew looked at him sourly before glancing around. "Are the players gathered?"

"Not yet."

"Who is abroad in the theater?"

Master Jasper looked suspicious. "Master Richard Burbage is on stage."

The constable walked through into the circular auditorium, leaving the old man staring anxiously after him, and climbed the wooden steps onto the stage.

A middle-aged man was kneeling on the stage, appearing to be measuring something.

Master Drew coughed to announce his presence.

Richard Burbage was still a handsome man in spite of the obvious ravages of the pox. He glanced up with a frown. "And who might you be, you rogue?" he grunted, still bending to his task.

Drew pursed his lips sourly and then suddenly smiled. "No rogue, that's for sure. I might be the shade of Constable Dogberry come to demand amends for defamation of his character."

Burbage paused and turned to examine him closely. "Are you a player, good master?"

"Not I," replied Drew, "and God be thanked for it."

"How make you freely with the name of Dogberry, then?"

"I have witnessed your plays, sir. I took offense to the pompous and comical portrayal of the constable in Master Shakespeare's jotting. *Much Ado about Nothing* was its title and, indeed, Master Burbage, *Much Ado about Nothing* was a title never more truly given to such a work. 'Twas certainly *Much Ado about Nothing*."

Richard Burbage stood up and brushed himself down, frowning as he did so. "Are you, then, a critic of the theater, sir?"

"Not I. But I am a critic of the portrayal of a hardworking constable and the watch of this fair town of ours."

"How so, good master?"

"I judge because I am a constable myself. Constable of Bankside in which this theater is placed."

"Ar't come to imprison me for defaming the watch then, sir?" asked Burbage stiffly.

Master Drew chuckled with good humor. "Marry, sir, there be

not enough prisons in the entire kingdom wherein to imprison everyone who makes jest of the constable and his watch."

"Then what—?"

"I am seeking one Tom Hawkins."

Burbage groaned aloud. "What has he done? He is due on stage in an hour or so, and I fear we have no competent understudy. Do not tell me that you mean to arrest him? On what grounds?"

"I come not to arrest anyone . . . yet. Where is Master Hawkins?"

"Not here as yet."

Master Drew looked round. There were a few people in corners of the theater, apparently rehearsing lines. "What play are you rehearsing?" he asked with interest.

"Will Shakespeare's *Famous History of the Life of King Henry VIII.*"

"Ah, that is a play that I have not seen."

"Then you would be most welcome to stay. . . ."

"Does Master Hawkins take part in this play?"

"He does, for he is Cardinal Campeius," came Burbage's immediate response. "It is a part of medium tolerance, a few lines here and yonder."

"The elderly harassed-looking doorman approached Burbage. "I declare, Master Richard, that the fools have not sent us gunpowder. What shall I do?"

Burbage took an oath by God and his angels that all except himself were incompetent fools and idlers. "Go directly to Master Glyn's gunsmithy across the street and take a bucket. Return it filled with gunpowder, and tell Master Glyn that I will pay him after this evening's performance."

The old man went scurrying off.

"Gunpowder?" Master Drew frowned. "What part has gunpowder to do in your play?"

Burbage pointed to the back of the theater. "We have mounted a small cannon in one of the boxes on the second floor. The box will not be hired out during any performance."

"And what will this cannon do, except blow the players to king-dom come?" demanded the constable wryly.

"Not so, not so. In act two, scene four, we have a grand scene with everyone on stage and the king and his entourage enters, with princes, dukes, and cardinals. It is a grand entrance, and Will Shakespeare calls for a sennet with divers trumpets and cornets. I thought to add to the spectacle by having a royal salute fired from a cannon. It will just be the ignition of the gunpowder, of course, but the combustion shall be explosive and startle our dreaming audi-ence into concentration upon the action!"

Master Drew sniffed. "I doubt it will do more than cause them to have deafness and perhaps start a riot out of panic for fear that the papists have attacked the theater." He was about to settle down to wait for Tom Hawkins when he had a further thought. "In truth, turning to concentration reminds me that I would have you set your mind upon a youth whose description I shall presently give." He quickly sketched the description of the youth whose body they had fished out of the river.

Richard Burbage's reaction was immediate. "God damn my eyes, Master Constable, I have been searching for that miscreant since this morning. He failed to turn up at the rehearsal, and I have had to give his part to his friend. Where is the execrable young rogue?"

"Dead these past twelve hours, I fear."

Richard Burbage was shocked. He clapped his hand to his head. But the main reason for his perturbation was soon apparent. "A player short! If ever the gods were frowning on me this day . . ."

"I would know more about this boy . . . ," insisted the constable. Richard Burbage had turned to wave to a man who had just entered the theater.

Master Drew recognized Richard Burbage's brother, Cuthbert, immediately.

"A good day to you, Master Constable. What is your business here this fine Saturday?" Cuthbert Burbage greeted him as he came forward.

His brother raised his hands in a helpless gesture. "Fine Saturday, indeed, brother! Tell him, Master Constable, while I am about my business. It lacks only an hour before the play begins." He turned and scurried away.

Quickly, Master Drew told Cuthbert Burbage of what had passed.

"So, young Oliver is drowned, eh?"

"Oliver?"

"That was the lad's name, Oliver Rowe. Did he fall drunk into the river to drown?"

Master Drew shook his head. "I said we hauled him from the river, not that he drowned. Young Oliver Rowe had his throat slit before he went into his watery grave. It was not for robbery either, for he still had money in his purse and"—he pulled out the ring from his pocket—"this ring on his finger."

Cuthbert let out an angry hiss. "That, sir, is theater property. No more than a simple actor's paste. A cheap imitation. I had wondered where it had gone. Damn Oliver—"

"He is damned already, Master Cuthbert," interrupted Master Drew.

Cuthbert hung his head contritely. "Forgive me, I quite forgot. I was thinking of his making off with theater property."

"Had this Oliver Rowe been long with you?"

"A year, no more."

"A good actor?"

"Hardly that, sir. He lacked experience and dedication. Though, I grant, he made up for his lack with a rare enthusiasm."

"Would anyone wish him ill?"

"You seek a reason for his murder?"

"I do."

"Then I have none to give you. He had no enemies but many friends, particularly of the fairer sex."

"And male friends?"

"Several within the company."

"Was Master Hawkins a particular friend of his?"

"Hardly. Tom Hawkins is twice his age and an actor of experience, though with too many airs and graces of late. He is a competent performer, yet now he demands roles which are beyond his measure. We have told him several times to measure his cloth on his own body."

"Where did this Oliver Rowe reside?"

"But a step or two from here, Master Constable. He had rooms at Mrs. Robat's house in the Skin Market."

A youth came hurriedly up, flush-faced, his words tumbling over themselves.

Cuthbert Burbage held up a hand to silence him. "Now, young Toby, tell me slowly what ails you?"

"Master Burbage, I have just discovered that there is no gunpowder for the cannon that I am supposed to fire. What is to be done?"

Master Drew pulled a face. "If I may intervene, Master Burbage? Your brother has sent old Jasper across to the gunsmithy to purchase this same gunpowder."

The youth gave Drew a suspicious glance and then left with equal hastiness. "I will ascertain if this be so," he called across his shoulder.

Cuthbert Burbage sighed. "Ah, Master Constable, the play's the thing! The player is dead—long live the play. Life goes on in the theater. Let us know what the result of your investigation is, good master. We poor players tend to band together in adversity. I know young Rowe was impecunious and a stranger to London, so it will be down to us thespians to ensure him a decent burial."

"I will remember, Master Cuthbert," the constable agreed before he exited the theater.

It took hardly any time to get to the Skin Market, with its busy and noisome trade in animal furs and skins. A stall holder pointed to Mrs. Robat's house in a corner of the market square.

Mrs. Robat was a large, rotund woman with fair skin and dark hair. She opened the door and smiled at him. *"Shw mae. Mae hi'n braf, wir!"*

Constable Drew glowered at her ingenuous features. "I speak not your Welsh tongue, woman, and you have surely been long enough in London to speak in good, honest English?"

The woman continued to smile blandly at him, not understanding. *"Yr wyf yn deal ychydig, ond ni allaf ei siarad."*

A thin-faced man tugged the woman from the door and jerked his head in greeting to the constable. "I am sorry, sir, my wife, Megan, has no English."

Master Drew showed him his seal of office. "I am the Constable of the Watch. I want to see the room of Master Oliver Rowe."

Master Robat raised his furtive eyebrows in surprise. "Is anything amiss?"

"He is dead."

The man spoke rapidly to his wife in Welsh. She turned pale. Then he motioned Master Drew into the house, adding to his wife: *"Arhoswch yma!"*

The constable followed the man up the stairs for five flights to a small attic room.

"Was there an accident, sir?" prompted the man nervously.

"Master Rowe was murdered."

"Diw! Diw!"

"I have no understanding of your Welshry," muttered the constable.

"Ah, the loss is yours, sir. Didn't Master Shakespeare give these words to Mortimer in his tale of *Henry the Fourth?* . . ." The man struck a ridiculous pose. "I will never be a truant, love, till I have learn'd thy language; for thy tongue makes Welsh as sweet as ditties highly penn'd—"

Master Drew decided to put an end to the man's theatrical eloquence. "I come not to discuss the merits of a scribbling word-seller nor his thoughts on your skimble-skamble tongue," snapped the constable, turning to survey the room.

There were three beds in the room. Two of them untidy, and there were many clothes heaped upon the third. There were similarities to the mess he had observed in Hawkins's room. A similar pile of untidy papers. He picked them up. Play scripts again. He began to go through the cupboards and found another sheaf of papers there. One of them, he observed, was a draft of a play—*Falsehood Liberated*. The name on the title page was *Teazle Rowe*.

"What was Master Rowe's first name?" he asked the Welshman. He had thought the Burbages had called Rowe by the first name of Oliver.

"Why, sir," confirmed the man, "it was Oliver."

"Did he have another name?"

"No, sir."

"Can you read, man?"

The Welshman drew himself up. "I can read in both Welsh and English."

"Then who is *Teazle* Rowe?"

"Oh, you mean Master Teazle, sir. He is the other young gentleman who shares this room with Master Rowe."

Constable Drew groaned inwardly.

He had suddenly remembered what Page Williams, at the Blackfriars Theatre, had said. What was it? Rowe had complained that Bardolph Zenobia had stolen a play written by Rowe with the help of his friend.

"And where is this Master Teazle now?"

"He is out, sir. I don't suppose he will return until late tonight."

"You have no idea where I will find him?"

"Why, of course. He is doubtless at the theater, sir."

"The theater? Which one, in the name of—!"

"The Globe, sir. He is one of Master Burbage's company. Both Master Rowe and Master Teazle are King's Men."

Master Drew let out an exasperated sigh.

So both Rowe and his friend Teazle were members of the same company as Hawkins, alias Bardolph Zenobia?

Rowe had accused Hawkins of stealing a play that both he and Teazle had written and of selling it to the Blackfriars Theatre. A pattern was finally emerging.

"When did you last see Master Rowe?"

"Last night, sir," the reply came back without hesitation.

"Last night? At what hour?"

"Indeed, after the bell had sounded the midnight hour. I was forced to come up here and tell the young gentlemen to be quiet, as they were disturbing the rest of our guests."

"Disturbing them? In what way?"

"They were having a most terrible argument, sir. The young gentlemen were quite savage with each other. *Thief* and *traitor* were the more repeatable titles that passed between them."

"And after you told them to be quiet?"

"They took themselves to quietness and all was well, thanks be to God. Sometimes Master Teazle has a rare temper, and I swear I would not like to go against him."

"But, after this, you saw Master Rowe no more?"

The man's eyes went wide. "I did not. And you do tell me that Master Rowe is dead? Are you saying that—?"

"I am saying nothing, Master Robat. But you shall hear from me again."

The play had already started by the time the constable reached the Globe again.

He marched in past the sullen old doorman and examined the auditorium. The theater was not crowded. It being a bright summer Saturday afternoon, many Londoners were about other tasks than spending time in a playhouse. But there was a fair number of people filling several of the boxes and a small crowd clustering around the area directly in front of the stage. He noticed, in disapproval, the harlots plying their wares from box to box, mixing with fruit-sellers and other traders, from bakers' boys and those selling all kinds of beverages.

Master Drew saw a worried-looking Cuthbert Burbage coming toward him.

"Where is Master Hawkins?" he demanded.

"Preparing for the second act," replied the man in apprehension. "Master Constable, swear to me that you will not interrupt the play by arresting him, if he be in trouble?"

"I am no prophet, Master Burbage," returned the constable, moving toward the area where the actors were preparing themselves to take their part upon the stage. He looked at them. What was the part that Hawkins was said to be playing—a cardinal? He picked out a man dressed in scarlet robes.

"Are you Master Hawkins?"

The actor raised a solemnly face and grimaced with contempt. "I am not, sir. I play Cardinal Wolsey. You will find Cardinal Campeius at the far end."

This time there was no mistake. "Master Thomas Hawkins?"

The distinguished-looking cleric bowed his head. "I am yours to command, good sir."

"And are you also Master Bardolph Zenobia?"

The actor's face colored slightly. He shifted uneasily. "I admit to being the same man, sir."

Master Drew introduced himself. "Did you know that Master Oliver Rowe has been discovered murdered?"

There was just a slight flicker in the eyes. "It is already whispered around the theater from your earlier visit, Master Constable."

"When did you first learn of it?"

"Less than half an hour ago, when I came to the theater."

"When did you last see Master Rowe?"

"Last evening."

"Here, at this theater?"

"I was not in last night's performance. I went to stay with . . . with a lady in Eastcheap. I have only just returned from that assignation."

"And, of course," sneered the constable, "you would have no difficulty in supplying me the lady's name?"

"None, good master. The lady and I mean to be married."

"And she will be able to tell me that you were with her all night?"

"If that is what you require. But not just the lady but her father and mother, for she lives with them. They own the Boar's Head in Eastcheap and are well respected."

Master Drew swallowed hard. The alibi of a lady on her own was one thing, but the alibi of an entire respectable family could hardly be faulted.

"When last did you see Master Rowe?"

"It was after yesterday afternoon's performance. Rowe asked me to go with him to a waterside tavern after the matinee performance. I had an appointment across the river before I went on to Eastcheap and could not long delay. But Rowe was insistent. We wound up by having an argument, and I left him."

"What was the argument about?"

Hawkins's color deepened. "A private matter."

"A matter concerning Master Bardolph Zenobia's literary endeavors?"

Hawkins shrugged. "I will tell you the truth. Rowe and a friend of his had written a pretty story. Rowe wanted help in finding a theater to stage it."

"Why did he not take it to Burbage?"

"Sir, we are the King's Men here. We have a program of plays of surpassing quality for the next several years from many renowned masters of their art, Master Shakespeare, Jonson, Beaumont, Fletcher, and the like. Master Burbage would not look at anything by a nameless newcomer. Rowe knew I had contacts with other theaters and gave me the script to read. The basic tale was commendable, but so much work needed to be done to revise it into something presentable. I spent much time on it. In the end, the work was mine, not Rowe's nor that of his friend."

"I suppose by 'his friend,' you mean Teazle?"

"Yes, Teazle."

"So you felt that the play was your own to do with as you liked?"

"It *was* mine. I wrote it. I will show you the original and my alterations. At first, I asked only to be made a full partner in the endeavor. When Rowe refused, saying the work was his and his friend's alone, I put the name of Zenobia on it and took it to Blackfriars. I told Rowe after I had sold it and offered to give him a guinea for the plot. I did not wish to be ungenerous. He refused. Rowe found out which theater I had sold it to and even went to the theater after I had left him last night, claiming that I had stolen the work.

"But from what was said yesterday afternoon, I had the impression that Rowe might have accepted the money if Teazle had not refused his share of the guinea. Rowe told me that Teazle thought him to be in some plot with me to cheat him and share more money after the play was produced. I told Rowe that it was up to him to make his peace with Teazle. I think a guinea was a fair sum to pay for the idea which I had to turn into literature."

"I doubt whether a magistrate would agree with your liberal interpretation of the law," Master Drew replied dryly. "Has Master Teazle spoken to you of this business? Where is he now?"

Hawkins gestured disdainfully. "Somewhere about the theater. I avoid him. He has a childish temper and believes himself to be some great artist against whom the whole world is plotting. Anyway, I can prove that I am not concerned in the death of young Rowe. I have robbed no one."

"That remains to be seen."

Master Drew left him and went to the side of the stage. The third scene of the second act was closing. The characters of Anne Bullen and an Old Lady were on stage. Anne was saying,

> —*Would I had no being,*
> *If this salute my blood a jot; it faints me,*

to think what follows.
The queen is comfortless, and we forgetful
In our long absence: pray, do not deliver
What here you've heard to her.

The old lady replied indignantly: "What do you think me?" And both made their exit.

All was now being prepared for the next scene.

Master Drew glanced around, wondering which of the players was Teazle.

Something drew his eye across the auditorium to the box on the second story in front of the stage. Someone was standing, bending over the small cannon that had been pointed out to the constable earlier. Master Richard Burbage had explained that the cannon would herald the scene with a royal salute, followed by trumpets and cornets, and then the King and his cardinals would lead a procession onto the stage.

The muzzle of the cannon appeared to be pointing rather low.

The constable turned to find Master Cuthbert Burbage at his shoulder.

"That is going to stir things a little." The business manager of the theater, who had observed Master Drew's examination, grinned.

"Your brother has already explained it to me," the constable replied. "The cannon will be fired to herald the entrance of the procession in the next act, but isn't the muzzle pointing directly at the stage?"

"No harm. It is only a charge of gunpowder which creates the explosion. There is no ball to do damage. Take no alarm; young Toby Teazle has done this oftimes before."

Master Drew started uneasily. "That is Master Teazle up there with the cannon?"

A cold feeling of apprehension began to grip him as he stared at the muzzle of the cannon. Then he began to move hurriedly toward the stairs on the far side of the auditorium, pushing protesting spectators out of his way in his haste. He was aware of Cuthbert Burbage shouting something to him.

By the time he reached the second floor, he was aware of the actors moving onto the stage in the grand procession. He heard a voice he recognized as the actor playing Wolsey. "Whilst our commission from Rome is read, let silence be commanded." Then Richard Burbage's voice cried: "What's the need? It hath already publicly been read, and on all sides the authority allow'd; you may then spare that time." Wolsey replied: "Be't so. Proceed."

The cacophony of the trumpet and cornets sounded.

Drew burst into the small box and saw the young man bending with the lighted taper to the touch hole. On stage he was aware that the figures of Burbage's King, and the actors playing Cardinal Wolsey and Cardinal Campeius, the urbane figure of Hawkins, had come to the front of the stage and were staring up at the cannoneer, waiting. The constable did not pause to think but leapt across the floor, kicking at the muzzle of the small cannon. It jerked upward just as it exploded. The recoil showed that it had been loaded with ball; its muzzle had been pointed directly at the figure of Cardinal Campeius. The hot metal crashed across the interior of the theater and fell into the thatch above the stage area.

There were cries of shocked surprise and some applause, but then the noise of the crackle of flames where the hot metal landed on the dry thatch became apparent. Cries of "Fire!" rose on all sides.

Master Drew swung round only to find the fist of the young man, Toby Teazle, impacting on his nose. He went staggering backward and almost fell over the wooden balustrade into the crowds below as they streamed for the exits of the theater.

By the time the constable had recovered, the young man was away, leaping down the stairs and was soon lost in the scuffling fray.

Master Drew, recovering his poise, hastened down the steps as best he could. The actors, with Cuthbert Burbage, were pushing people to the exits. The dry thatch and tinder of the Globe were like

47

straw before the angry flames. The theater was becoming a blazing inferno.

Master Drew groaned in anguish as he realized that the young man was lost among the crowds now and there was never a hope of catching him.

It was more than nine months later, in the spring of the following year, 1614, that the new Globe Theatre eventually rose from the ashes. This time it was erected as an octagonal building with a tiled roof replacing the thatch. Fortunately no one had been injured in the fire, and all the costumes and properties had been saved thanks to the quick wit of the actors, and all the manuscripts of the plays had been stored elsewhere, so the loss was negligible.

Apart from Master Oliver Rowe, two other players were not present to see the magnificent new Globe Theatre. Master Tom Hawkins was languishing in Newgate Gaol. However, he was not imprisoned for the fraudulent misuse of another playwright's work. In fact, *The Vow Breaker Delivered* had been taken off on the third night and had made a loss for the Blackfriars Theatre. No, Master Hawkins was imprisoned for breach of promise to the young lady who lived at the Boar's Head Tavern in Eastcheap. As Constable Hardy Drew remarked, *The Vow Breaker Delivered* had been an inspired prophetic title, as apt a title as could have been chosen by Master Bardolph Zenobia.

The other missing player was Master Toby Teazle.

It was the very day after the new Globe Theatre had opened that Constable Drew was able to conclude the case of the murder of Master Oliver Rowe, sometime one of the King's Men. Master Cuthbert Burbage asked Constable Drew to accompany him to the Hospital of St. Mary of Bethlehem.

Drew was mildly surprised at the request. "That is the hospital for the insane," he pointed out. Most Londoners knew of Bedlam, for as such the name had been contracted.

"Indeed it is, but I think you will want to see this. I have been asked to identify someone."

An attendant took them into the gray-walled building, which was more of a prison than a hospital. The stench of human excrement and the noise arising from the afflicted sufferers was unbelievable. The attendant took them to a small cell door and opened it.

A young man crouched inside in the darkness was bent industriously over a rough wooden table. There was nothing on it, yet he appeared to be in the act of writing in the blackness. His right hand held an invisible pen, moving it across unseen sheets of paper.

The attendant grinned. "There he is, good sirs. He says he's a famous actor and playwright. Says he is a King's player from the Globe Theatre. That's why you were asked here, good Master Burbage, just in case there might be truth in it."

The young man heard his voice and raised his matted head, the eyes blazing, the mouth grinning vacuously. He paused in his act of writing.

It was Toby Teazle.

"Ah, sirs," he said quietly, calmly regarding them. "You come not a moment too soon. I have penn'd a wondrous entertainment, a magnificent play. I call it *The Friend's Betrayal*. I will allow you to perform it but only if my name should go upon the handbill. My name and no other." He stared at them, each in turn, and then began to recite.

> 'Tis ten to one this play can never please
> All that are here; some come to take their ease
> And sleep an act or two; but those, we fear,
> We have frightened with our cannon; so, 'tis clear,
> They'll say, 'tis naught . . . naught . . .

He hesitated and frowned. "Is this all it is? Naught?" He stared suddenly at the empty table before him and started to chuckle hysterically.

As Constable Drew and Master Cuthbert Burbage were walking back toward Bankside, Drew asked: "Were those his own lines which he was quoting with such emotion?"

Master Burbage shook his head sadly. "No, that was the epilogue from *Henry VIII*. At least, most of it was. The poor fellow is but a poor lunatic."

Master Drew smiled wryly. "Didn't Will Shakespeare once say that the lunatic, the lover, and the poet are of imagination all compact?"

METHOUGHT
━ YOU SAW A SERPENT ━

Methought you saw a serpent.
            —*All's Well That Ends Well*, Act I, Scene iii

M aster Hardy Drew, the newly appointed deputy to the Constable of the Bankside Watch, gazed from the first floor latticed window onto the street, watching in unconcealed distaste as a group of drunken carousers lurched across the cobbles below. The sounds of their song came plainly to his ears.

> *Sweet England's pride is gone!*
> *Welladay! Welladay!*
> *Brave honor graced him still*
> *Gallantly! Gallantly!*

The young man turned abruptly from the window back into the room with an expression of annoyance.

On the far side, seated at a table, the elderly Constable of the Bankside Watch, Master Edwin Topcliff, had glanced up from his papers and was regarding the young man with a cynical smile. "You have no liking for the popular sympathy then, Master Drew?" the old man observed dryly.

Hardy Drew flushed and thrust out his chin. "Sir, I am a loyal servant of Her Majesty, may she live a long life."

"Bravely said," replied the constable gravely. "But, God's will be done, it may be that your wish will be a futile one. 'Tis said that the

Queen's Majesty is ailing and that she has not stirred from her room since my lord Essex met his nemesis at the executioner's hands."

It had been scarcely two weeks since the flamboyant young Robert Devereux, Earl of Essex, had met his fate in the courtyard of the Tower of London, having been charged and found guilty of high treason. Rumor and disturbances still pervaded the capital, and many of the citizens of London persisted in singing ditties in his praise, for Essex had been a hero to most Londoners, and they might even have followed him in overturning the sour, aging Queen, who now sat in solitary paranoia on the throne in Greenwich Palace.

It was rumored that the auspices were evident for Elizabeth's overthrow, and even the usually conservative Master William Shakespeare and his theatrical company had been persuaded to stage a play on the deposing and killing of King Richard II but a couple of weeks before Essex's treason was uncovered. It was claimed that many of Essex's supporters had, after dining together, crossed the Thames to the Globe to witness this portentous performance.

In the middle of such alarums and excursions, young Master Hardy Drew had arrived to take up his apprenticeship in maintaining the Queen's Peace with the aging constable. Drew was an ambitious young man who wanted to create a good impression with his superior. The son of a clerk, he had entered the Inns of Court under the patronage of a kindly barrister, but the man had died, and Hardy Drew had been dismissed because of his lowly birth and lack of social and financial support. So it was, he found himself turning from one aspect of law to another.

Old Master Topcliff rubbed his nose speculatively as he examined his new assistant. The young man's features were flushed with passionate indignation. "I would not take offense at the songs you hear nor the people's sympathies, young man. Times are in a flux. It is a time of ebb and flow in affairs. I know this from reading the Almanacs. What is regarded as seditious today may not be so tomorrow."

Master Drew sniffed disparagingly. He was about to make a rejoinder when there came a banging at the door, and before he or

Master Topcliff could respond, it burst open and a young man, with flushed features, his chest heaving from the exertion of running, burst into the room.

"How now? What rude disturbance is this?" demanded Master Topcliff, sitting back in his chair and examining the newcomer with annoyance.

The youth was an angular young man of foppish appearance, the clothes bright but without taste. Topcliff had the impression of one of modest origins trying to imitate the dignity of a gentleman without success.

"I am from the Globe Theatre, masters," gasped the young man, straining to recover his breath. "I am sent to fetch you thither."

"By whose authority and for what purpose?"

The young man paused a moment or two for further breaths before continuing. He was genuinely agitated. "I am sent by Richard Burbage, the master of our group of players. The count has been found murdered, sirs. Master Burbage implores you, through me, to come thither to the crime."

Topcliff rose to his feet at once. "A count, you say?"

"The Count of Rousillon, master."

Topcliff exchanged an anxious glance with his deputy. "A foreign nobleman murdered at a London theater," he sighed. "This does not augur well in the present travails. There is anxiety enough in this city without involving the enmity of the embassy of France."

He reached for his hat and cloak and signaled Master Drew to follow, saying to the youth: "Lead on, boy. Show us where this Count of Rousillon's body lies."

The Globe Theatre was a half a mile from the rooms of the Constable of the Bankside Watch, and they made the journey in quick time. There were several people in small groups around the door of the theater. People attracted by the news of disaster like flies to a honey pot.

A middle-aged man stood at the door, awaiting them. His face bore a distracted, anxious gaze, and he was wringing his hands in a helpless, almost theatrical gesture. Hardy Drew tried to hide a smile, for the action was so preposterous that the humor caught him. It was as if the man were playing at the expression of agitated despair.

"Give you good day, sir," Master Topcliff greeted breezily.

"Lackaday, sir," replied the other. "For I do fear that any good in the day has long vanished. My name is Burbage, and I am the director of this company of players."

"I hear from your boy that a foreign nobleman lies dead in your theater. This is serious."

Burbage's eyes widened in surprise. "A foreign nobleman?" He sounded bewildered.

"Indeed, sir, what name was it? The Count of Rousillon. Have I been informed incorrectly?"

A grimace crossed Master Burbage's woebegone face. "He was no foreign nobleman, sir."

"How now?" demanded Master Topcliff in annoyance. "Is the constable to be made the butt of some mischievous prank? Is there no murder then?"

"Oh, yes. Murder, there is, good Constable. But the body is that of our finest player, Bertrando Emillio. He plays the role of the Count of Rousillon in our current production."

Master Topcliff snorted with indignation.

"An actor?" Master Topcliff made it sound as though it was beneath his dignity to be called out to the murder of an actor. He gave a sniff. "Well, since we are here, let us view the body."

Burbage led them to the back of the stage, where several people stood or sat in groups quietly talking amongst themselves. One woman was sitting sobbing, comforted by another. Their whispers ceased as they saw the constable and his deputy. From their appearance, so Drew thought, they were all members of the company of actors. He glanced across their expressions, for they ranged from curiosity to distress to bewilderment, while others seemed to have a tinge of anxiety on their faces.

Burbage led them to what was apparently a small dressing room, in a darkened corridor behind the stage, which was full of hanging clothes and baskets and all manner of clutter. On one basket was a pile of neat clothes, well folded, with leather belt and purse on top.

In the middle of this room lay the body of a young man, who in life and been of saturnine appearance. He was stretched on his back, one arm flung out above his head. The eyes were open, and the face was masked in a curious expression as if of surprise. He wore nothing more than a long linen shirt that probably had once been white. Now it was stained crimson with his blood. It needed no physician to tell them that the young man had died from several stab wounds to his chest and stomach. Indeed, by the body, a long bone-handled knife, of the sort used for carving meat, lay discarded and bloody.

Master Topcliff glanced down dispassionately. Death was no stranger to the environs of London, either north or south of the river. In particular, violent death was a constant companion among the lanes and streets around the river.

"His name is Bertrando Emillio, you say? That sounds foreign to me. Was he Italian?"

Master Burbage shook his head. "He was as English as you or I, sir. No, Bertrando Emillio was but the name he used for our company of players."

Master Topcliffe was clearly irritated. "God's wounds! I like not confusion. First I am told that he is the Count of Rousillon. Then I am told he is an actor, one Bertrando Emillio. Who now do you claim him to be?"

"Faith, sir, he is Herbert Eldred of Cheapside," replied Burbage unhappily. "But while he treads the boards, he is known to the public by his stage name—Bertrando Emillio. It is a common practice among us players to assume such names."

Master Topcliff grunted unappeased by the explanation. "Who found him thus?" he asked curtly.

As he was asking the question, Master Drew had fallen to his knees to inspect the body more closely. There were five stab wounds to the chest and stomach. They had been inflicted as if in a frenzy, for he saw the ripping of the flesh caused by the hurried tearing of the knife, and he realized that any one of the wounds could have been mortal. He was about to rise when he saw some paper protruding under the body. Master Drew rolled the body forward toward its side to extract the papers. In doing so, he noticed that there was a single stab wound in Bertrando's back, between the shoulder blades. He picked up the papers, let the body roll into its former position on its back, and stood up.

"Who found him thus?" Master Topcliff repeated.

"I did," confessed Master Burbage. "We were rehearsing for our new play, in which he plays the Count de Rousillon. It was to be our first performance this very Saturday afternoon, and this was to be our last rehearsal in the costumes we shall wear. Truly, the stars were in bad aspect when Master Shakespeare chose this day to put forward his new work."

"You are presenting a new play by Master Shakespeare?" queried Hardy Drew, speaking for the first time. He had ascertained that the papers under the body were a script of sorts, and presumably the part was meant for Bertrando.

"Indeed, a most joyous comedy called *All's Well That Ends Well*," affirmed Burbage, albeit a mite unhappily.

"Let us hope that it pleases the loyal subjects of the Queen's Majesty better than your previous production," muttered Master Drew.

Master Topcliff shot his deputy a glance of annoyance before turning back to Burbage. "This is a comedy that has turned to tragedy for your player, Master Director. All has not ended well here."

Burbage groaned theatrically. "You do not have to tell me, sir. We must cancel our performance." His eyes widened suddenly in realization. "Z'life! Master Shakespeare is already on his way from Stratford to attend. How can I tell him the play is canceled?"

"Isn't it the custom to have an understudy for the part?" asked Hardy Drew.

"Usually," agreed Burbage, "but in this case, Bertrando was so jealous of his role that he refused to allow his understudy to attend rehearsals for him to perfect the part. Now the understudy has no time to learn his part before our first performance is due."

"What is known about this killing?" interrupted Master Topcliff, bored with the problems of the play-master.

Burbage frowned. "I do not follow."

"Is it known who did this deed or who might have done it?"

"Why, no. I came on the body a half an hour since. Most of us were on stage reading our parts. When Bertrando did not come to join us, I came here in search of him and found him as you see."

"So you suspect no one?"

"No one would wish to harm Bertrando, for he is one of . . . *was* one of our most popular players with our audiences."

Hardy Drew raised an eyebrow. "Surely that would not endear him to his fellow actors? What of this understudy that he has excluded from rehearsals? Where is he?"

Burbage looked shocked. "You suspect one of our players of such a deed?" he asked incredulously.

"Whom should we suspect, then?" demanded Master Topcliff.

"Why, some cutthroat from the street who must have entered the playhouse in pursuit of a theft. Bertrando surprised the man and was stabbed for his pains. It seems very clear to me, sir."

Hardy Drew smiled thinly. "But not to Master Topcliff nor myself," he replied quietly.

Master Topcliff looked at his young deputy in surprise and then swiftly gathered his wits. "My deputy is correct," he added, addressing Burbage.

"Why so, sir?"

Master Topcliff gave a shrug. "You tell him, Master Drew."

"Easy enough. Your Bertrando, master-player, did not enter this room to surprise a thief. Bertrando was already in this room.

Someone then entered while he was presumably dressing to join you on stage. The purpose of that person was to kill him."

Burbage looked at him incredulously. "Do you have the second sight? By what sorcery would you know this?"

"No sorcery at all, sir, but by using my common sense and the evidence of my eyes."

Master Topcliff was regarding his deputy anxiously. He did not like the word *sorcery* being leveled at his office. Such a charge could lead to unpleasant consequences. "Explain yourself further to the good Master Burbage," he suggested uneasily.

"I will and gladly. There was a single stab mark in Bertrando's back. I would say that the culprit entered the dressing room while Bertrando was donning his clothes with his back to the door. He had only his shirt on. The murderer raised the knife and stabbed Bertrando between the shoulder blades. It was a serious wound, but Bertrando was able to turn—with shock and surprise he recognized his assailant. The assailant in a surge of emotion, raised the knife and struck not once, not twice, but in a frenzy of blows, born out of that emotion, delivering five more stabs to Bertrando's chest, each a mortal wound. That is an indication of the rage that the murderer felt towards him. Bertrando sank to the floor. Either he was already dead or dying within seconds."

Master Topcliff looked on approvingly. "So you think this was done by someone who knew Bertrando or whatever his name is?"

"Sir, I am sure of it. No cutthroat would commit a murder in such a fashion. Nor is there sign of any theft."

"How can you be so sure?" demanded Burbage.

Master Drew turned to the neat pile of clothes on top of the basket. "I presume that these are Bertrando's clothes of which he divested himself, stacking them neatly there as he changed for the stage?"

Burbage glanced at the pile as if seeing the clothes for the first time. "Yes," he admitted. "Yes, I recognize his jacket. He was a vain man and given to gaudy colors in jacket and hose."

Master Drew pointed. "Then I suppose that the leather belt and purse is Bertrando's also?"

Burbage's eyes widened. "That they are," he agreed, seeing where the logic was leading.

Master Drew leaned forward, picked up the purse, and emptied the contents into his hand. There fell into his palm a collection of coins. "Would a thief, one who had been prepared to murder so violently to secure his theft, retreat leaving this rich prize behind? No, sir, I think we must seek other reasons as to this slaughter."

Burbage bowed his head. His nose wrinkled at the smell of blood, and he sought permission to cover the body with a sheet.

"Now," Drew said, turning to Burbage, "you say that most of you were on stage when you noticed that Bertrando was missing from your company?"

"That is so."

"Can you recall anyone who was not on stage?"

Burbage thought carefully. "There were only a few that were latecomers, for I needed everyone on stage to rehearse the final scene; that is the scene set in the Count of Rousillon's palace, where the King and all the lords, attendants, and main characters gather."

Master Hardy Drew hid his impatience. "Who was not with you then?"

"Why, Parolles, Helena, Violenta . . . oh and young Will Painter."

"You will explain who these people are."

"Well, they are all characters in our play. Well, all except Will Painter. He was the understudy for Bertrando, who was excluded from the task. The only thing I could give him to do was to be a voiceless attendant upon our King."

Master Drew scratched his chin. "And he was one with a motive, for, with Bertrando dead, he could step into this main role and win his reputation among the luminaries of your theater. Fetch this Will Painter to us."

Will Painter was scarcely as old as Hardy Drew. A fresh-faced youth, well dressed and with manners and mode of speech that displayed an education that many theatrical players did not possess.

"Will Painter? That is a familiar name to me." Master Drew greeted, having once more sought the permission of his superior to conduct the inquiry.

"It is my father's name also, and he was admired as a writer of plays," replied the youth, nonchalant in manner.

"Ah, indeed. And one who provided well for his family. It is strange that his son would seek such lowly footings in the theater."

"Not so." The youth flushed. "To rise to be a master-player, one must know and experience all manner of theatrical work."

"Yet, methinks that you would have preferred to play the role of the Count de Rousillon in this new comedy?"

"Who would not cast an envious eye at the leading role?"

"Just so. Did you cast such an envious gaze in Bertrando's direction?"

The youth flushed in annoyance. "I do not deny it."

"And were you irritated beyond endurance by the fact that Bertrando was so jealous of his part that he refused that you understudy him in rehearsal?"

"Irritated by his popinjay manners, yes. Irritated, yes, but not beyond endurance. One must bear the ills with the joys of our profession. I admit that I liked him not. But dislike was not enough to slit his throat."

"Slit his throat? Why do you use that expression?"

Will Painter frowned. "I do not understand."

"What makes you think that his throat was slit?"

"Why, Master Burbage waxing lyrical about a cutthroat having entered the theater in search of plunder and killing Bertrando. What other method would such an assassin use?"

Master Drew uncovered Bertrando's body.

Will Painter saw the stab wounds and turned his face away in disgust. "I liked him not, but 'tis oppressive to see a man so reduced as this."

"And you cannot hazard a guess to the identity of anyone who would wish him so reduced?"

The young actor shrugged. "In truth, if I were to name one, I would name many."

"How so? Master Burbage says he was well disposed to the entire company?"

The youth was cynical. "Well disposed, but more to the feminine gender of our company than aught else."

"Women?" asked Master Topcliff, aghast. "Do you mean that you have women as players?"

"Aye. Master Burbage experiments in using women to play the female roles, as is common in Europe. Bertrando cast his net like a fisherman and trawled in as he could. However, he lives . . . *lived* with Hester at the Mermaid Tavern in Mermaid Court."

"Hester? And who is she?"

"The maid that plays Helena in our comedy. I saw Bertrando and Hester arrive at the theater together. She was already dressed for her part, and so Bertrando went towards the dressing room, presumably to change. I saw Bertrando no more."

"Did you go near the dressing room?"

"Not I. I went off to seek a flagon of ale in the Globe Tavern opposite, and there I remained until I heard the sound of disturbance. Master Fulke will tell you that I departed as he arrived, for he brushed past me as I quit the theater, although he didn't greet me."

"Master Fulke? And who is Master Fulke?"

"You have not heard of Raif Fulke, who plays the part of Parolles in our play?"

"Parolles?" mused Master Drew. "Let me stick with Master Fulke and not be confused by such a choice of names. You say that Master Fulke brushed past you?"

"I did."

"Did he go to speak with Bertrando or Hester?"

"I did not stay to see, but I think not. He is at enmity with them, for Hester once lived with Master Fulke and he bears no fondness for Bertrando. It is well known that Fulke is jealous of Bertrando and his success both on stage and with women."

"Well, Master Painter, do you go to call this Hester here, but do not go beyond the confines of the theater until we tell you."

The girl Hester came almost immediately.

Old Master Topcliff and his assistant, aware of the niceties and refinements, had stopped her from entering the dressing room with the dead body and proceeded to question her outside. She was an attractive woman whose silk gown may have seen better days but which still enhanced the contours of her figure, leaving little to the imagination. That she had taken the news of the death of her lover badly was written on her tearstained features. Her skin was pale and her eyes red with sobbing.

"I hear you were Bertrando's lover?" began Master Drew without preamble.

The girl sobbed and raised a square of muslin to the corner of her eye and dabbed it. "Lover? I am Mistress Herbert Eldred," she announced, raising her chin slightly. "So have I been these past two years. I have a paper to prove it."

Master Drew blinked, but it was the only expression that he gave of surprise.

Master Topcliff sighed as if totally puzzled. "Faith! Who is Herbert Eldred?" he demanded in bewilderment.

Master Drew glanced swiftly at him. "The actor, sir, Bertrando Emillio. Herbert Eldred is his real name."

"Ah, I had forgotten. Why these people cannot stick to one name, I have no understanding." He looked hard at the girl. "I am of the impression that no one in this company of players knows that you were married?"

"Herbert—Bertrando as was—felt it better that we keep our marriage a secret lest it impede his career. If you want proof of our marriage, then I have—"

Master Topcliff made a dismissive gesture with his hand. "No need for proof at this stage. So, if you are the dead man's wife, you, therefore, had no cause to kill him?"

The girl stared at him in indignation. "Of course I had no cause to kill him! But there be others. . . ." She hesitated as if regretting what she had said.

Hardy Drew was swift to follow her words. "Others?"

Her eyes were now narrowed in suspicion. "But why speak of that when I understood that a thief had attacked him and killed him?"

"Who told you that?"

"It is common talk among the players."

"Were you in this part of the theater while the others were gathering on stage for the rehearsal?" pressed Drew without answering her previous question.

"For a moment, no more."

"When did you last see Bertrando?"

"I came with him from our lodgings to the theater. I left him to change for the rehearsal while I did the same, and then I went to the stage, but Bertrando was not there. When he did not come, Master Burbage went to fetch him."

"You left him well?"

The girl pursed her lips in a grimace. "Bertrando was always well. I left him entering that room behind you. Is that—?"

Master Drew nodded in answer to the unfinished question. "Please wait for us in the theater and send us who plays the part of Violenta."

A tall fair-haired young girl appeared shortly after Hester Eldred had left them. From a distance, she looked the picture of maidenly virtue and innocence. Only when she grew near did Hardy Drew see the hard lines around the mouth, the coldness of the blue eyes, and the smoldering resentment in her features. Her body was too fleshy and would grow to fat in middle age, and the pouting mouth would turn to an ugly form.

"I am Nelly Porter," she announced, her voice betraying signs of the West Country. "What is your need of me?"

"I understand that you play the part of Violenta in this new drama?"

"A joyous 'comedy,'" she sneered. "And what of it? I have played many parts in the French theater."

"How well did you know Bertrando?"

She gave a raucous laugh. "As well as any maid who trod the boards of this theater, aye, and who came within the grasp of the pig!"

"There is hatred in your voice, mistress," intervened Master Topcliff mildly.

"Hatred enough," affirmed the girl, indifferent to his censure.

"Hatred enough to kill him?" demanded Hardy Drew.

"Aye, I'll not deny it. I could have killed the pig who ravished girls and left them to bear his children and fend for themselves."

"He did that to you?"

"So he did. Two years ago. But my child died."

"And did you kill him for vengeance' sake?"

"No, that's God's truth. But I do not grieve nor do I condemn his killer. If that is a crime, I am ready to be punished."

"You are honest enough with your dislikes. Where were you just before the rehearsal?"

"I was late getting to the theater from my lodgings, that's all."

"Did anyone see you arrive at the theater?"

"None that I know of. I went straight to the stage on my arrival, so only the people there saw me."

"I see. Wait for us now on stage and send us the actor who plays Parolles. I believe his name is Master Fulke."

She walked away without another word, and they watched her go before exchanging glances.

"She is not exactly grieving over her former lover's death," Master Topcliff observed, stating the obvious.

Master Fulke was poised, could pass as a gentleman, but was not exactly handsome. He was too round of the face, and too smooth of skin and too ready with an ingratiating smile.

"Well, Master Fulke . . ."

"You want to know where I was before I joined the gathering on the stage?" Fulke greeted a little breathlessly.

"You seem to know my mind," replied Drew gravely.

The genial actor shrugged. "It is hard to keep a secret among so small a company. I was delayed, if you wish to know. I arrived late at the theater—"

"Late from where?"

"From my lodgings in Potters Fields. I have a room in the Bell Tavern overlooking the river."

"That is but ten minutes' walk from here."

"Indeed so."

"Why were you delayed?"

The man rolled his eyes expressively. "A rendezvous." He smiled complacently.

"And this, this *rendezvous,* it made you late arriving? Did anyone see you arrive?"

"I brushed by that young upstart, Will Painter."

"But you did not see Bertrando?"

Master Fulke sneered. "Bertrando! Yes, I saw *Master Herbert Eldred.* He, too, had a rendezvous. . . . I saw him go to his dressing room. Then I saw someone enter after him. It was not my concern. So I went on my way to join those on stage for the rehearsal." He sniffed. "We were fifteen minutes into the rehearsal when Master Burbage began to worry that Eldred had not appeared. I told Burbage where he might be found."

Master Topcliff tried to suppress his excitement. "God's wounds, man! Do you tell me that you actually saw his murderer?"

"No, I do not, sir. I said I saw someone enter his dressing room after Eldred had gone in. I have no way of saying this was the murderer. I did not stay longer, as I said, but passed on to the rehearsal."

"Describe the person," Topcliff ordered sharply. "Who else would it be but the murderer?"

"A man, short of stature, of wiry appearance, I would say. He wore his hair long and dark, underneath a feathered hat. There was a short cloak. He wore boots. The colors were dark and tailored in the latest fashion. I could see no more in the gloom of the passage. In truth, though, there was something familiar about him, though I cannot quite place it. It may come to me later."

Master Topcliff was pleased. He dismissed Master Fulke and turned to Hardy Drew with grim satisfaction on his face. "Well, at least we know our killer was a man, and that he was no common cut-throat but someone who could afford to dress well."

Drew looked at his mentor blankly. "Yet this does not lead us any closer to apprehending the man."

"There are too many of this description on the streets of this city for us to single one out and charge him," agreed the old constable.

"Do you plan to leave it so?"

"For the time being. Come, Master Drew. I will have a word with this Burbage and his players before they are dismissed."

The company was standing or sitting on stage in gloomy groups. A tall balding man, well dressed, was engaged in earnest conversation with Burbage.

"Ah." Burbage turned. "This is the constable, Will. Master Topcliff, this is Master Shakespeare."

The balding man inclined his head to the constable. "What news? Can you say who engineered the death of our player, sir?"

"Master Fulke saw the murderer enter your actor's dressing room and has given a full description—"

There was a gasp from several members of the group, and all eyes turned to Master Fulke, who momentarily stood with flushed surprise. He had not expected the constable to reveal his attestation.

"So you mean to arrest the culprit?" queried the playwright.

"Not immediately, Master Shakespeare. We will consider our

move for a while. Master Fulke here has given a good description, but he has not, so far, recalled where he has seen the person before, though he is sure he recognized him. We will wait to see if his memory improves."

Fulke made a move forward as if to deny the constable's interpretation, but Master Topcliff turned and glared at the man, so that Fulke lowered his head and hurried off.

The old constable turned to the assembly and bowed low, flourishing his hat.

As he left the theater, Master Drew came trotting in his wake. "I do not understand," he ventured as he hurried to keep up with the long strides of the constable.

Master Topcliff paused in the street and turned to him. "Are you city bred or country bred, young man?"

"City bred, Master Constable."

"I thought so. I am country bred and raised in the fields of Kent. When the quarry goes to ground, what does the huntsman do? You know not? Of course, you know not. What is done is that you prepare a lure."

Hardy Drew frowned. "Then you have prepared Fulke as a bait in a trap?"

"If our murderer is one of the gentlemen of Master Burbage's company, he will come this night to make sure that Master Fulke's memory does not return."

"A harsh judgment on Fulke if we are not there when the murderer visits him."

"Indeed, but be there we will. We will go to the lodgings of Master Fulke and prepare our snare with Fulke as the unknowing decoy."

Master Drew looked at the old constable with a new respect. "And I thought . . ."

Master Topcliff smiled. "You must learn the ways of the gamekeeper, young man, and learn that it is always best to tell the poacher where you have set your traps for him."

They took themselves to the Bell Tavern in Potters Field. A few coins pressed in willing hands were able to secure a booth with curtains from which they could view the front entrance of the tavern. This station fell to Master Topcliff, while Hardy Drew, being the younger and hardier, took up his position at the rear entrance of the tavern, so that either entrance to Fulke's rooms might be observed.

A little the worse for drink, Raif Fulke entered the tavern toward ten o'clock and made his way immediately up to his room.

It was well after midnight that there was a scream, and the innkeeper's wife came running to Master Topcliff, her eyes wide and frightened. "'E's dead. Master Fulke is killed!"

Master Topcliff called to a young man hefting barrels to run around the back of the inn and inform Master Drew. Master Topcliff tried to make for the stairs but found the innkeeper's wife clinging to his sleeve and expanding in detail on her fright.

No one had entered from the back door; of that Hardy Drew was certain. He hurried into the inn and up the back stairs to the bedchambers. He saw one of the doors open at the end of a corridor and ran in.

Master Raif Fulke lay on the floor. A candle burned nearby, but it scarcely needed the light to see that there was dark blood oozing from several wounds on the man's chest. Miraculously, Fulke's chest still rose and fell. He was not yet dead.

Drew knelt by him and raised his head. "Who did it, Fulke, who did it?"

The actor opened his eyes. Even in his condition, he smiled, though grimly. "I would not have known him . . . ," he wheezed painfully. "Like Rousillon, I knew him not. . . . Why? Why, young sir? Jealousy is a fierce foe. That was the reason."

He coughed suddenly, and blood spurted from his mouth.

"Take it easy, Fulke. Name the man."

"Name? Ah . . . for, indeed, he was mad for her, and talked of Satan, and of Limbo, and of Furies, and I know not what. . . ."

He coughed again and then smiled, as if apologetically.

"The web of our life is of a mingled yarn, good and ill together; our virtues would be proud if our faults whispered this not; and our crimes would despair, if they were not cherished by our virtues."

"The name, man, quick, give me the name."

Fulke's breathing was hard and fast. "I am a'feared the life of Helena . . . was foully snatched . . ."

"Helena?" demanded Drew. "Do you say that Helena, Hester Eldred, that is, is now in danger from this man?"

Fulke forced a smile.

"Helena? Methought you saw a serpent . . ." he began.

Drew compressed his lips in irritation.

"Concentrate, Fulke, name your assailant."

Fulke coughed again. He was growing weaker and had not long. "The play . . . the play's the thing . . ."

Then his eyes dilated and for the first time he realized that he was going to die. The moment of truth came for Master Fulke in one horrible mute second before he fell back and was dead. Master Topcliff hurried in, having shaken off the terrified innkeeper's wife.

"Did he say aught?" he asked breathlessly.

Drew shook his head.

"He was rambling. His last words were something about the play being the thing . . . what thing?"

Master Topcliff smiled grimly.

"I fear it was only a line from Master Shakespeare's tragedy of the Prince of Denmark. I recognize it well, for it is a play of murder and intrigue that held much meaning for me. 'The play's the thing wherein I'll capture the conscience of the king.' No use to us. This is my fault. I was too confident. I let this murderer out of my grasp."

"How did he get in? I can swear that he did not pass me at the back door."

"Nor from the front," vowed Master Topcliff.

He peered round. The window was still open, the curtain flapping. There was a small balcony outside, built out above the waters of the Thames. The river, smelly and dirty, was lapping just below.

The window and balcony were on the side of the building, for it was built sideways onto the river, and was blind to the scrutiny of anyone watching the front and back.

They stared out onto the darkened waters. The assailant must have come by rowing boat and pulled up against the wall of the inn, under the balcony. It was high water, and easy to pull oneself up toward this balcony and then climb through Fulke's window.

"Our man will be long gone by now. Now, truly, all we can do is return to our lodgings and secure a good night's repose. Tomorrow morning, I think we will have another word with Master Will Painter. Logic shows him as our likely suspect."

Hardy Drew sighed with exasperation as he stared down at the actor's body. "Faith, he rambled on so much. Had he known he was dying, I doubt whether he would have quoted so much from his part in this play."

He suddenly spied a sheaf of papers on the bed. Bending, he picked them up and perused them.

"*All's Well That End's Well,*" he quoted the title. "A bad ending for some."

He was about to replace it on the bed when he spotted a line on the pages to which the play script had fallen open. "Methought you saw a serpent," he whispered. He turned to the old constable. "Are you sure those words 'the play's the thing' comes from this other tragedy you mentioned? Are they not used in this new play?"

"I have seen the tragedy of the Prince of Denmark, but I have not seen this new comedy, nor has anyone else, remember? They were just rehearsing it for its first performance."

"True enough," Drew replied thoughtfully. After a moment or so, with a frown gathered on his forehead, he tucked the play script under his arm and followed the old constable down the stairs, where Master Topcliff gave instructions about the body. There was nothing further to do but to return to their lodgings.

It was morning when Master Topcliff, sitting over his breakfast, observed a pale and bleary-eyed young Hardy Drew coming into the room.

"You have not slept well," he observed dryly. "Does death affect you so?"

"Not death. I have been up all night reading Master Shakespeare's new play."

Master Topcliff chuckled. "I hope that you have found good education there?"

Drew sat down and reached for a mug of ale, taking a mouthful. He gave an almost urchinlike grin. "That I did. I found the answer to many mysteries there."

Master Topcliff gave him a hard look. "Indeed?"

"Indeed. I learnt the identity of our murderer. As poor Raif Fulke was trying to tell me—the play's the thing, the thing which reveals the secret. He was quoting from the play so that I might find the identity of his assailant there. But you are right—that line does not occur in this play, but the other lines he quoted do."

An hour later they stood on the stage of the Globe with the players gathered in somber attitude about them. Burbage had recovered his shock of the previous day and was now more annoyed at the loss of revenue to his theater by the delays. "How now, Master Constable, what now? Two of our good actors are done to death and you have named no culprit."

Master Topcliff smiled and gestured to his deputy. "My deputy will name the assailant."

Drew stepped forward. "Your comedy says it all," Drew began with a smile, holding up the play script. "Herein, the Count of Rousillon rejects a woman. She is passionate to have him. She pursues him, first disguised as a man."

There was a muttering.

"The story of the play is no secret," pointed out Burbage.

"None at all. However, we have Bertrando, who actually plays Rousillon, in the same situation. He is a man of several affairs, our

Bertrando. Worse, he has rejected a most passionate woman, like Helena in the story. Bertrando is married and likes to keep his marriage a secret, is that not so, Mistress Eldred?"

Hester Eldred conceded it among the expressions of surprise from the company.

"So one of his lovers," continued Hardy Drew, "that passionate woman, likes him not for his philandering life. Having been rejected, like Helena in the play, she pursues him. However, unlike the play, she does not seek merely to win him back, but her intention is to punish him. She stabs him and ends his life."

"Are you telling us that a woman killed Bertrando?" gasped Burbage. "But Fulke saw a man enter the dressing room."

"Fulke described a man of short stature. He was positive it was a man. Unfortunately, we"—he glanced at his superior—"decided to allow Fulke to act as bait by pretending he knew more than he did. Thus lured out, the assailant murdered Fulke before we had time to protect him. Luckily Fulke was not dead. He survived long enough to identify his assailant. . . ."

He turned to Hester Eldred. She read her fate in his eyes, leaped up with a curse, and ran from the stage.

Master Topcliff raised a hand in signal, and a burly member of the guard appeared at the door and seized her.

A babble broke out from the company.

Burbage raised his voice, crying for quiet.

Nelly Porter moved forward. "I thought you were going to accuse me. I was Bertrando's lover, and thanks to him, my child died. I had more reason to hate and kill him than she did."

Hardy Drew smiled softly. "I did give you a passing thought," he admitted.

"Then why—?"

"Did I discount you? When we arrived, Hester was on stage in a dress. Now her part, as I read the play, calls for her, as Helena, to appear in men's clothes. Yet she clearly told us that she had arrived at the theater with her lover, left him to change while she went to change herself. Presumably from her own clothes she would change into that of her part as a man. But Will Painter said that he saw her arrive with Bertrand, in men's clothes ready for her scene. She told me that she had left Bertrando and went to change into the clothes for her scene. When we came to the theater, she was in a dress and had been so from the time of the rehearsal. She had, therefore, killed her husband while in the male clothing, changed into a dress, and joined you all on stage."

"But her motive? If she was passionately in love with Bertrando, why would she kill him?"

"The motive is as old as the Earth. Love to hatred turned. For Bertrando was just as much a ladies' man during his marriage as ever he had been. Hester as his wife could not abide his philandering. Few women could. She did not want to share him with others. I could feel sympathy for her had she killed in hot blood. But she planned the scene and brought her victim to the theater to stage it. She also killed Fulke when she thought that he had recognized her—"

"Who knows," intervened Master Topcliff, "maybe he had recognized her. Didn't Will Painter say they had lived together before she took up with Bertrando? Painter implied that Fulke still loved her. Even when dying, perhaps for love, he could not name her outright but, for conscience' sake, gave you the coded clue instead?"

"One thing this deed has also killed," interrupted Master Burbage. "We shall no more experiment with women as players. They bring too many dangers with them."

Master Hardy Drew turned and smiled wanly at Master Topcliff. "By your leave, good Master, I'll get me to my bed. It has been a tiring exercise in drama." He paused, smiled, and added with mocking tone. "The king's a beggar now, the play is done."

The Game's Afoot!

The game's afoot!

—*Henry V*, Act III, Scene i

W hen the shrill voice of a boy, accompanied by an incessant thudding against his door, awoke Master Hardy Drew that morning, the Constable of the Bankside Watch was not in the best of moods.

He had retired to his room, which he rented above the Pilgrim's Wink Tavern, in Pepper Street, in the early hours that morning. Most of the night he had been engaged in dispersing the rioters outside the Cathedral of Southwark. It had been a well-organized protest at the publication of the Great Bible, which had been authorized by King James. The Great Bible had been the production of fifty scholars from the leading universities, resulting in a work that the King had ordained to be the standard Bible used throughout his realms.

While it had been obvious to Master Drew that the Catholics would seize the opportunity to express their outrage at its publication, he had not expected the riots organized by the Puritan Party.

Not only were there rumors and reports of popish plots and conspiracies this year, but the activities from the extreme Protestant sects were far more violent. King James's moderate Episcopalian governance angered the Puritans also. Only last month the Scottish Presbyterian reformer, Andrew Melville, had been released from the Tower of London in an attempt to appease the growing anger. The King had admitted that his attempt to break the power of the

Presbyterian General Assembly in Scotland had not met with success. Rather than placate the Presbyterians, Melville's release had increased the riots, and he had fled into exile in France where, rumor had it, he was plotting his revenge. James had fared little better with imposing his will on the English Puritans.

The kingdoms of England and Scotland echoed and reechoed with treasonable conspiracies. Indeed, a few months previously, another attempt to install James's cousin Arabella Stuart on the throne had resulted in the unfortunate lady being confined to the Tower. Times were dangerous; Master Hardy Drew had been reflecting on this while quelling the outburst of anger of Puritan divines. Even his position of constable was fraught with political danger. There were many who might falsely inform on him for his religious affiliations or, indeed, for his lack of them, in order to secure the position of constable for themselves together with the small patronage that went with it.

The knocking increased in volume, and Master Drew rolled out of his bed with a groan. "Ods bodikins!" he swore. "Must you torture a poor soul so? Enter and have a good reason for this clamor!"

The door opened a fraction, and a dirty young face peered round.

Master Drew glared menacingly at the child. "You had better have a good reason for disturbing my sleep, little britches," he growled.

"God save you, good master," cried the young boy, not entering the room. "I've been sent to tell you that a gen'lemen be lying near done to death."

Master Drew blinked and shook his head in a vain attempt to clear it. "A gentleman is—? Who sent you, child?" he groaned.

"The master what owns the inn in Clink Street. The Red Boar, Master . . . Master Pen . . . Pen . . . some foreign name. I can't remember."

"And precisely what did this Master Pen ask you to tell me?" Master Drew inquired patiently.

"To come quick, as the gen'lemen be stabbed and near death."

Master Drew sighed and waved the child away. "Tell him that I'll be there shortly," he said.

Had the news been other than that of a gentleman stabbed in an inn, he would have immediately returned to his interrupted slumber. London was full of people being stabbed in taverns, alleys, or along its grubby waterfront. They were usually members of the lower orders of society, whom few people of quality would miss, much less shed a tear over. But a gentleman . . . now that was a matter serious enough to bring a Constable of the Watch from his warm bed.

Master Drew splashed his face with cold water from a china basin and hurriedly drew on his clothes. Below, in the tavern, he spent a half-pence on a pot of beer to cut the slack from his dry throat and, outside, chose an apple from a passing seller to munch for the balance of his breakfast.

Clink Street was not far away, a small road down by the banks of the Thames, along the very Bankside that was Master Drew's main area of responsibility. He knew of the Red Boar Inn but had little occasion to frequent it. Perhaps *inn* was too grand a title, for it was hardly more than a waterfront tavern full of the usual riffraff of the Thames waterfront.

There was a small crowd loitering outside when he reached there. A small boy was holding forth to the group, waving his arms and pointing up to a window. Doubtless, this was the same urchin who had brought the message to him. The boy pointed to the constable as he approached and cried, "This is 'im naw!" The small crowd moved back respectfully as Master Drew halted before the dark door of the inn and pushed it open.

Although the morning was bright outside, inside candles were alight, but even so, the taproom was still gloomy, filled with a mixture of candle and pipe smoke, mingling with odors of stale alcohol and body sweat.

A thin, middle-aged man came hurrying forward, wiping his

hands on a leather apron. He had raven-black hair but his features were pale, which caused his shaven cheeks to have a bluish hue to them.

"We do be closed, good sir," he began, but Master Drew stopped him with a cutting motion of his hand.

"I am Constable of the Bankside Watch. Are you the host of this tavern?"

The man nodded rapidly. "That I do be, master."

"And your name?"

"Pentecost Penhallow."

Master Drew sniffed in disapproval. "A Cornishman by your name and accent?"

"A Cornishman I do be, if please you, good sir."

Master Drew groaned inwardly. This day was not starting well. He did not like the Cornish. His grandfather had been killed in the last Cornish uprising against England. Not that he was even born then, but there were many Cornish who had come to London during the reign of the Tudors and stayed. He regarded them as a people not to be trusted.

The last uprising had been caused by the introduction of the English language into church services in Cornwall. The Cornish rebels had marched into Devon, even captured the suburbs of Exeter after a siege before defeating the Earl of Bedford's army at nearby Honiton. That was where Master Drew's grandfather had been killed. The eventual defeat of the Cornish rebels by Lord Grey, and the systematic suppression of the people by fire and sword, the execution of their leaders, had not brought peace to Cornwall. If anything, the people had become more restless.

Master Drew knew that the English Court feared a Catholic-inspired insurrection in Cornwall, as well as other of the subject nations on the isles. Cornwall was continuing to send her priests to Spain to be trained at St. Alban's College of Valladolid.

Master Drew took an interest in such things and had read John Norden's recent work surveying Cornwall, in which it was reported that, in the western part of the country, the Cornish tongue was most in use among its inhabitants. Master Drew felt it best to keep himself informed about potential enemies of the kingdom, for these days they all seemed to congregate in the human cesspool that London had become.

He realized that the innkeeper was waiting impatiently.

"Well, Master Pentecost Penhallow," he asked gruffly, "why am I summoned hither?"

"If you would be so good as to go above the stair, good master, you may find the cause. One of my guests who do rent the room above do be mortally afflicted."

Master Drew raised an inquisitive eyebrow. "Mortally afflicted? The boy said he was stabbed? What was the cause? A fight?"

"No, no, good Master Constable. He be a gentleman and quite respectable. A temperate, indeed he be. This morning, as is my usual practice, I took him a noggin of mead. He do never be bestirring of a morn without his noggin. That 'twas when I discovered he be still abed with blood all over the sheets. Stabbed he be."

"He was still alive?" demanded Master Drew, surprised.

"And still be but barely, sir. Oh, barely!"

"Godamercy!" exclaimed Master Drew in annoyance. "Still alive and yet you sent for me and not a physician?"

Pentecost Penhallow shook his head rapidly. "Oh, sir, sir, a physician was sent for, truly so. He do be above the stair now. It be he who do be sending for thee, Master Constable."

The constable exhaled angrily. "What name does your gentleman guest go by, and which is his room?"

The innkeeper pointed to the head of the stair. "Master Keeling, do be his name. Master Will Keeling. The second door on the right above the stair."

Master Drew went hurrying up the stairs. On the landing he almost collided with a young girl carrying a pile of linen. He caught himself, but the collision knocked some sheets from her hand onto the floor. The constable swiftly bent down and retrieved them. The young girl was an exceptionally pretty dark-haired lass of perhaps no more than seventeen years. She bobbed a curtsy.

"Murasta, mester," she muttered, and then added in a gently accented English, "Thank'ee, master."

The constable gave a quick nod of acknowledgment and entered the door that the tavern owner had indicated.

A thin-faced man with a shock of white hair, clad in a suit of black broadcloth, making him appear like some Puritan divine, was sitting on the edge of a bed. On it a pale-faced young man lay against the pillows. Blood stained the sheets and pillows. Some bloodstained clothes were pressed against the man's chest.

The thin-faced man glanced up. "Ah, at last. You have not come a moment too soon to this place, Master Constable. He has barely a moment more of life."

"God send you a good morrow, Doctor Tate," replied Constable Drew in black humor. He knew the elderly physician and acknowledged the man before he moved to the bedside.

The young man was, indeed, barely conscious and obviously feverish. There was a bluish pallor that lay over his skin, which showed the swift approach of death.

"Master Keeling," he said loudly, bending to the dying man's face. "Who did this thing? Who stabbed you?"

The young man's eyes were open, but they were wandering about the room. He seemed to be muttering something. The constable leaned closer. He could just hear the words, and their diction indicated a person of some education.

"What's that you say, good fellow? Speak clearly if you can."

The lips trembled. "Oh for . . . for a Muse of fire . . . that would ascend the . . . the brightest heaven of invention . . ."

Master Drew frowned. "Come, good fellow, try to understand me. Answer you my simple question. . . . What manner of knave has done this to you?"

The young man's eyes brightened, and Master Drew suddenly found a hand gripping his coat with a power that one would have not thought possible in a dying man. The lips moved; the voice was stronger. "Once more unto . . . unto . . ." He began to cough blood. Then suddenly he cried loudly, "Let the game begin!"

The voice choked in the man's throat. The pale blue eyes wavered, trying to focus on the constable's face, and then the pupils dilated as, for a split second, the young man realized the horror of the imminent fact of death.

The constable gave a sigh and removed the still-clutching hand from his jacket and laid it by the side of the body. He whispered softly: "Now entertain conjecture of a time, when creeping murmur and the pouring dark fills the wide vessel of the universe. . . ."

"What's that?" demanded the physician grumpily.

"No matter," Master Drew replied as he moved aside and gestured to the body. "I think he has run his course."

It did not need the physician's quick examination to pronounce that the man was dead.

"What was the cause of death?" asked Master Drew.

"A thin blade knife, Master Constable. You will see it on the table where I placed it. It was left in the wound. One swift incision was made in the chest, which I deduced caused a slow internal bleeding, thus allowing him to linger between life and death for the last several hours."

"Presumably not self-inflicted?"

"Most certainly not. And you will notice that the window is opened and a nimble soul might encounter little difficulty in climbing up with the intention of larceny."

"You have an observant eye, Master Physician." The constable smiled thinly. "Can it be that you are interested in taking on the burdens of constable?"

"Not I!" laughed the physician. "I need the prospect of a good livelihood."

Master Drew was turning the knife over in his hands. It told him nothing. "Cheap," he remarked. "The sort that any young coxcomb along the waterfront might carry at his waist. It tells me little."

Doctor Tate was covering the body with the bloodstained sheet. "Poor fellow. I didn't understand what he was saying at the end. Ranting in his fever, no doubt?"

"Perhaps," replied the constable. "But articulate ranting nonetheless."

Doctor Tate frowned. "I don't understand."

"Perhaps you don't frequent the Globe?" The constable smiled. "He was reciting some lines out of Master Shakespeare's play *The Life of King Henry the Fifth*."

"I didn't take you for one who frequents the playhouses."

"A privilege of my position," Master Drew affirmed solemnly. "I am allowed free access as constable. I find it a stimulation to the mind."

"There is too much reality to contend with than living life in make-believe," dismissed Doctor Tate.

"Tell me, good Doctor, did the young man say aught else before I came?"

"He said nothing but raved about battles and the like. Something about St. Crispin's Day but that is not until next October, so I do not know what he meant by it."

The physician had turned from the body and was packing his small black bag.

"I can do no more here. The matter rests with you. But I would extract my fee before I depart."

"Take your fee and welcome," sighed the constable, glancing round the room. It was untidy. It appeared as if someone had been searching it, and he asked the physician if the room had been disturbed since he had arrived.

The physician was indignant. "Think you that I would search for a fee first before I treated a gentleman?" he demanded.

"Well, someone has been searching for something."

"And not carefully. Look! Some jewels have been left on the table there. I'll take one of those pearls in lieu of a coin of this realm."

Master Drew pulled a cynical face. "A good profit in that, Doctor Tate. However, I'll not gainsay your right."

The physician swooped up the pearl and held it up to the light. The smile on his face suddenly deepened into a frown, and he placed the pearl between his teeth and bit sharply. There was a crack, and the physician let out a howl of rage. "Paste, by my troth!"

Master Drew walked over and examined the other pieces of jewelry scattered nearby. There were some crushed paste jewels on the floor. A small leather purse also lay there with a few coins in it. He took out the coins.

"Well, paste jewels or no, he was not entirely destitute. There is over a shilling here, which will pay for a funeral if we cannot find his relatives. And here, good physician, three new pennies for your fee." He grinned sourly. "I wager that the three pennies are closer to the value of your service than ever that pearl, had it been real, would have been."

"Ah, how is a poor physician to make a decent living among the impoverished derelicts along this riverbank, Master Constable? Answer me that, damme! Answer me that!" The physician, clutching his coins, left the room.

Master Drew gazed down at the shrouded body of the young man and shook his head sadly.

An educated young man who could recite lines from popular theatrical entertainment but who used cheap paste jewelry. Surely this was a curious matter? He turned and began to search the room methodically. The clothes were many and varied, and while giving an appearance of rich apparel, on closer inspection were actually quite cheap in quality and often hastily sewn.

He noticed that there were some papers strewn around the room, and bending to pick them up, he saw a larger pile on the floor under the bed. He drew these out and examined them. It was a text of the play *The Life of Henry V* by Will Shakespeare. The lines of Henry V had been underlined here and there.

"Well, well, Master Keeling," the constable murmured thoughtfully. "This sheds a little light in the darkness, does it not?"

He gathered up the script and turned out of the room, closing the door. There was nothing more he could do there.

The innkeeper was awaiting him at the bottom of the stair. He appeared anxious. "The physician says the gentleman do be dead now, Master Constable. Did he identify his assailant?"

"Indeed he is, Master Penhallow. Some words with you about your gentleman guest." Master Drew frowned suddenly, and an idle thought occurred to him. "Pentecost, is that your first name, you say?"

"That it be," agreed the man, somewhat defensively.

"Your parents being no doubt pious souls?"

"Not more so than anyone else." He was defiant, but then he realized what was in the constable's mind. "Pentecost be a good Cornish name; the name of my mother's family. *Pen ty cos* means 'dwellers in the chief house in the wood.'"

Master Drew found the explanation amusing. "Well now, Master Pentecost Penhallow, how long has Master Keeling been residing here?"

"One, nay two months."

"Do you know what profession he followed?"

"Profession? He be a gentleman. What else should he do? You've seen his clothes and jewels?"

"Is that what he told you? That he was a gentleman?"

The innkeeper's eyes narrowed suspiciously.

Suddenly a dark-haired woman appeared from a shadowy corner of the tavern. Twenty years ago, she must have looked much like the young girl whom he had encountered on the landing, thought Master Drew. She began to speak rapidly to him in a language that Master Drew did not understand. It sounded a little like Welsh, but he guessed that it was Cornish.

"Wait a moment, good woman," protested Master Drew. "What is it you say?"

84

"Meea navidna cowza Sawsneck," replied the woman in resignation.

"Taw sy!" snapped her husband, turning with an apologetic smile to the constable. "Forgive my wife, sir. She be from Kerrier, and while she has some understanding at her of English, she does not be speaking it."

"So, what does Mistress Penhallow say?"

"She complains about the late hours Master Keeling did keep, that's all."

"Was he late abroad last night?"

"He was."

"When did you last see him alive?"

"At midday, but my wife saw him when he came in last night."

He turned and shot a rapid series of questions at his wife in Cornish.

"She says that he came in with his friend, another gentleman, about midnight. They were a little the worst for drink."

The woman interrupted and repeated a word that sounded like *tervans.*

"What is she saying?" demanded Master Drew.

"That they were arguing, strongly."

"Who was this man, this friend?"

There was another exchange in Cornish, and then Master Penhallow said, "My wife says that he was a young man that often used to drink with Master Keeling. Another gentleman by name of Cavendish."

A satisfied smile spread over Master Drew's face. "Master Hal Cavendish? Was that his name?"

"That do be the name, Master Constable. A fine gentleman, I am sure. Have you heard tell of him?"

"That I have. You say that the two came here last night, drunk and arguing? Is it known when Master Cavendish left Master Keeling's room?"

"It was not by the time that my wife and I retired."

"Where were you when Master Keeling came in that you did not see him?"

"I was out . . . on business."

"On business?"

The man hesitated, with a swift glance at his wife, as if to ensure that she didn't understand; then he drew the constable to one side. "You know how it be, good master." He lowered his voice ingratiatingly. "A few shillings can be made from cock fights—"

"*Kessynsy!*" sneered his wife.

"You were gambling, is that it?" Master Drew guessed the meaning of her accusation.

"I was, master. I confess I was."

"So you did not return until late? Was all quiet then? . . . I mean, you heard nothing of this argument overheard by your goodwife?"

"All was quiet. The place was in darkness."

"And when was this?"

"About the middle watch. I heard the night crier up on the bridge."

London Bridge stood but a few yards away. Master Drew computed that was between three and four o'clock. He rubbed his chin thoughtfully. "And did your daughter notice anything before she went to bed?"

Master Penhallow's brows drew together. "My daughter?"

"The girl that I met on the landing; I presume that she is your daughter? After all, she addressed me in your Cornish jargon."

A look of irritation crossed the man's face. "I do be apologizing for that, master. I know 'tis thought offensive to address one such as yourself in our poor gibberish. I will speak harshly to Tamsyn."

Master Drew stared disapprovingly at Pentecost Penhallow, for he heard no genuine regret in his voice.

What was it Norden had written? *And as they are among themselves litigious so seem they yet to retain a kind of concealed envy against the English who they affect with a desire of revenge for their fathers' sakes by whom their fathers received their repulse.* He

86

would have to beware of Penhallow's feigned obsequiousness. The man resented him for all his deferential speech, and Master Drew put it down to this national antipathy.

"Is that her name? Tamsyn?" he asked.

"Tamsyn Penhallow, if it please you, good master."

"Did she notice anything unusual last night."

"Nay, that she did not."

"How do you know?"

"Why, wouldn't she be telling me so?"

"Perhaps we should ask her?"

"Truly, good Master Constable, we cannot oblige you in this, for she had only just left to go to the market by the cathedral."

Master Drew sighed. "I will be back soon. In the meantime, no one must enter into the room of Master Keeling. Understand?"

Pentecost Penhallow nodded glumly. "But when may we clear the room, master? It is not pleasing to have a corpse lying abed there for when the vapors do be emanating—"

"I will be back before midday," the constable cut him short, and left the Red Boar Inn, still clutching the script he had gathered from the floor of Keeling's room.

Although it was still early in the day, he made his way directly to the circular Globe playhouse, which was only a ten-minute walk away. He was greeted by the elderly gatekeeper, Master Jasper.

"A good day, Master Constable. You are abroad early." The old man touched his cap in respectful greeting.

"Indeed, I am, and surprised to see you here at this hour."

"Ah, they are rehearsing inside this morning." The old man jerked his thumb over his shoulder.

"I had hoped as much. I'll lay a wager with you, good Jasper." The constable smiled in good humor. "I'll wager you what new play is in rehearsal."

The old doorkeeper laughed. "I know well enough not to lay wagers with the Constable of the Watch. But for curiosity's sake, do make your guess."

"The Life of King Henry the Fifth."

"The very same," chuckled Master Jasper in appreciation.

"Is Master Hal Cavendish playing in it?"

"You have a good memory for the names of our players," observed the old man. "But young Hal Cavendish be an unhappy man because Hal cannot play Hal in this production."

"Explain?" asked Master Drew, allowing the old gatekeeper a few moments to chuckle at his own obscure joke.

"Young Hal Cavendish fancied himself as playing the leading part of King Hal but now must make do with the part of the Dauphin. He is bitter. He is understudying the part of King Hal, but if he could arrange an accident to he who plays the noble Harry Fifth, young Cavendish would lief as not be more than content."

Master Drew stroked the side of his nose with a lean forefinger. "Is that the truth of it?"

"Aye, truth and more. Hal Cavendish is a vain young man when it comes to an assessment of his talents, and that is no lie. Mind you, good Constable, all those who tread the boards beyond are of a muchness in that vanity."

"Do you also have a player called Will Keeling in the band of King's Players?"

To Master Drew's surprise, Master Jasper shook his head.

"Then tell me, out of interest, who plays the part of Henry the Fifth, whose role Hal Cavendish so desires?"

"Ah, a young Hibernian. Whelton Keehan. He has newly joined the company."

Master Drew raised a cynical eyebrow. "Whelton Keehan, eh. What manner of young man is he? Can you describe him?"

Master Jasper was good at descriptions, and at the end of his speech, the constable pursed his lips thoughtfully. "I would have a word with Master Cavendish, good Jasper," he said.

The old man saw the grim look in his eyes. "Is something amiss, Constable?"

"Something is amiss."

Master Jasper conducted the constable through the door and led the way into the circular auditorium of the theater.

An elderly lean-faced man was standing on stage with a sheaf of papers in his hand. There were a few other people about, but the central figure was a young man who stood striking a pose. One hand held a realistic-looking sword, while the other hand was on his waist and he was staring up into one of the galleries.

"Crispian Crispian shall never . . . ," he intoned, and was interrupted by an angry stamp of the foot of the lean man, who shook his wad of paper at him.

"God's wounds! But you try my patience, Master Cavendish! *Crispin* Crispian shall ne'er go by—! Do you aspire to rewrite the words of Master Shakespeare or can it be that you have grown indolent as the result of your previous success as Macduff? Let me tell you, good Master Cavendish, an actor is only as good as his last performance. Our production of *Macbeth* ended last night. You are now engaged to play the Dauphin in this play of *Henry the Fifth*, so why I am wasting time in coaching you to understudy the part of King Hal is beyond me."

The young fair-haired man waited until the torrent had ended, and then he began again.

> *Crispin Crispian shall ne'er go by*
> *From this day to the ending of the world*
> *But we in it shall be remembered.*
> *We few, we happy few, we band . . .*

His voice trailed off as he suddenly noticed Master Hardy Drew standing nearby with folded arms.

The lean-faced man swung round. "And who might you be, who puts my players out of rhythm with their parts? Can you not see that we are in rehearsal?"

Master Drew smiled easily. "I would have a word with Master Cavendish."

"Zoots!" bellowed the man, and seemed about to launch into a tirade when Master Jasper drew him to one side and whispered something.

"Very well, then," sighed the man in irritation.

"Ten minutes is all we can spare. Have your word, master, and then depart in peace! We have a play to put on this night."

The young man was frowning in annoyance as Master Drew approached him. "Do I know you, fellow?" he demanded haughtily.

"You will, fellow," the constable replied in a jaunty tone. "I am Constable of the Bankside Watch."

The announcement registered little change of expression on the player's features. "What do you want of me?"

"I gather that you are a friend of Master Whelton Keehan."

Hal Cavendish's features formed a grimace of displeasure. "A friend? Not I! An unwilling colleague on these boards, this will I admit to. But he is no more than an acquaintance. If he is in trouble and needs money to bail him, then pray go to Master Cuthbert Burbage, who manages our company. Perhaps he will feel charitable. You will not extract a penny from me to help him."

"I am afraid that he is beyond financial assistance." Master Drew smiled grimly. Then without explaining further, he continued: "I understand that you accompanied him back to his lodgings last night?"

Hal Cavendish sniffed dismissively. "If you know that, then why ask?"

"Let me make it plain why I ask." Master Drew's voice rose in sudden anger at the young man's conceit. "You stand in danger unless you answer me truthfully. Why was he known at his lodgings as Will Keeling?"

"It's no crime," Cavendish replied indifferently. "He was but a few months arrived in this city from Dublin and thought to better his prospects by passing himself off as a English gentleman at his lodgings. Poor fool—he had not two farthings to jingle in his pocket. I'll grant you, he was a good actor, though. He borrowed props from here, costumes and paste jewelry to maintain his image at his lodgings and thus extend his credit with that sly old innkeeper. Ah . . . tell me, has his ruse been discovered? Are you carting him off to debtors' prison?" Hal Cavendish began to laugh in good humor.

Master Drew waited patiently for him to pause in his mirth. "Why should that give you cause for merriment, Master Cavendish?"

"Because I now can play the part of King Hal in this production. Keehan was never right for the part. In truth, he was not. A Hibernian playing King Hal! Heaven forfend! That is why we argued last night."

"Tell me, Master Cavendish, how did you leave Master Keehan? What was his condition?"

"Truth to tell, I left him this morning," the young man admitted. "He was not in the best of tempers. We had been drinking after the last performance of *Macbeth* and visited one or two houses of . . . well, let us say, of ill repute. Then we fell to discussing tonight's play."

"You were arguing with him."

"I do not deny it."

"About this play?"

"About his inability to play his role. He had the wrong approach to the part, which rightfully should be mine. He had the audacity to criticize my part as the Dauphin, and thus we fell to argument. A pox on the man! May he linger a long time in the debtors' jail. He deserves it for leading the innkeeper's daughter on a merry dance with his assumed airs and graces. She, being a simple, country girl, was beguiled by him. There is no fun in debauching the innocent."

Master Drew raised an eyebrow. "Debauching? In what way did he lead Master Penhallow's daughter on?"

"Why, in his pretense to be an English gentleman with money and fortune. He gave the poor Penhallow girl some of his worthless jewels and spoke of marriage to her. The man is but a jack-in-the-pulpit, a pretender."

The constable considered this thoughtfully. "You say that Keehan promised to marry the Penhallow girl?"

"Aye, and make her a rich and great lady," agreed Cavendish.

"He gave her paste jewels?"

"Poor girl, she would not know the like from real. I think she had set her heart on being the mistress of some great estate which only existed in Keehan's imagination. He gambles the pittance that Master Burbage pays us and visits so many whorehouses that I doubt if he has not picked up the pox, which will cook his goose the sooner. I have never known a man who had such an excess of love for his own self. I rebuked him for it. By the rood! He had the audacity to recourse to a line from this very play of ours, *Henry V* . . ."

The young man struck a pose.

" 'Self love, my liege, is not so vile a sin as self-neglecting.' One thing may be said of Master Keehan, he never neglected himself."

"This Master Whelton Keehan does not sound the most attractive of company," agreed the constable.

"I doubt not that this view is shared by the father of the Penhallow girl. I never saw a man so lost for words when he espied Master Keehan treading the boards last night and realized that Keehan was none other than his gentleman lodger."

"What?" Master Drew could not stay his surprise. "Do you mean to tell me that Master Pentecost Penhallow knew that his lodger was a player and residing at the Red Boar under a false name?"

"He knew that from last night. He was there in the ring having paid his penny entrance to stand in the crowd before the stage. Keehan did not see him, but I did. In fact, as I was coming offstage, Master Penhallow accosted me to confirm whether his eyes had played him false or not. I had to confess that they had been true. He went away in high dudgeon. He was in no better spirits when I saw him later at the Red Boar."

"You saw Master Penhallow at the Red Boar? At what time was this?"

Master Cavendish considered for a moment. "I confess to having indulged in an excess of cheap wine. I scarcely recall. It was late, or rather, it was early this morning. He was coming in as I was going out."

The elderly white-haired man came forward, clicking his tongue in agitation. "Sirrah! Can you desist with your questioning? We have a play to rehearse and—"

Master Drew held up his hand to silence him. "Cease your concern, good master. I shall leave you to your best efforts. One thing I have to tell you. You must find a new player for the part of King Hal this evening. Master Keehan is permanently indisposed."

"Confound him!" cried the elderly man. "What stupidity has he indulged in now?"

Master Drew smiled grimly. "The final stupidity. He has gotten himself murdered, sir."

Arriving back at the Red Boar Inn, he found Master Pentecost Penhallow moodily cleaning pewter pots. He started as he saw the dour look on the constable's face.

"You lied to me, Master Penhallow," Master Drew began without preamble. "You knew well that Will Keeling was no gentleman, nor had private mean. You knew that he was a penniless player named Keehan."

Pentecost Penhallow froze for a moment, and then his shoulders slumped in resignation. "I knew," he admitted. "But I only knew from last night."

"Are you a frequent playgoer then, Master Penhallow?"

The innkeeper shook his head. "I never go to playhouses."

"Yet you paid a penny and went to the Globe last night. Pray, what took you there?"

"To see if I could identify this man Keeling . . . or whatever his name was."

"Who told you that he was a player there?"

"Two days ago, one of my customers espied him entering the inn and said, 'That's one of the King's Players at the Globe.' When I said, nay, he be a gentleman, the man laid a wager of two pence with me. So I went, and there I saw Master Keeling in cavorting pretense upon the stage. God rot his soul!"

"So you realized that he was in debt to you and little wherewithal to honor that debt?"

"Indeed, I did."

"So when you returned home in the early hours of this morning, you went to his room and had it out with him?"

When Penhallow hesitated, Master Drew went remorsefully on.

"You took a knife and stabbed him in rage at how he had led you and your family on. I gather he gave faked jewels to your daughter and promised marriage. Your rage did wipe all sense from your mind. It was you who killed the man you knew as Will Keeling."

"I did . . . ," began Master Penhallow.

"*Na! Na, tasyk!*" cried a female voice. It was the young woman the constable had seen on the landing that morning. Penhallow's daughter, Tamsyn.

"*Cosel, cosel, caradow,*" Penhallow murmured. He turned to Master Drew with a sigh. "This Keeling was an evil man, Constable. You must appreciate that. He used people as if they meant nothing to him. Yet every cock is proud on his own dung heap. He crowed at his vice when I challenged him. He boasted of it. His debt to me is but nothing to the debt that he owed my daughter, seducing her with his glib tongue and winning ways. All was but his fantasy, and he ruined her. No man's death was so richly deserved."

The young girl came forward and took her father's arm. "*Gafeugh dhym, tasyk,*" she whispered.

Penhallow patted her hand as if pacifying her. "*Taw dhym, taw dhym, caradow,*" he murmured.

Master Drew shook his head sadly as he gazed from father to daughter and back to father. Then he said, "You are a good man, Master Penhallow. I doubted it for a while, being imbued with my prejudice against your race."

Penhallow eyed him nervously. "Good Master Constable, I understand not—"

"Alas, the hand that plunged the dagger into Master Keehan was not your own. Speak English a little to me, Tamsyn, and tell me when you learnt the truth about your false lover?"

The dark-haired girl raised her eyes defiantly to him.

"*Gorteugh un pols!*" cried Penhallow to his daughter, but she shook her head.

She spoke slowly and with her soft accent. "I overheard what was said to my father the other night; that Will . . . that Will was but a penniless player. I took the jewels which he had given to me and went to the Dutchman by the Blackpriars House."

Master Drew knew of the Dutchman. He was a jeweler who often bought and sold stolen goods but had, so far, avoided conviction for his offenses.

"He laughed when I asked their worth," went on the girl, "and said they were even bad as faked jewels and not worth a brass farthing."

"You waited until Will Keehan came in this morning. But he came in with Hal Cavendish."

"He was in an excess of alcohol. He was arguing with his friend. Then Master Cavendish departed, and I went into his room and told him what I knew." Her voice was quiet, unemotional. But her face was pale, and it was clear to Master Drew that she had difficulty controlling her emotions. "He laughed—laughed! Called me a Cornish peasant who had been fortunate to be debauched by him. There were no jewels, no estate, and no prospect of marriage. He was laughing at me when—"

"Constable, good Constable, she does not know what she is saying," interrupted Pentecost Penhallow despairingly.

"That was when you came in," interrupted Master Drew. "One thing confused me. Why was it left until morning to raise an alarm? I supposed it was in the hope that Keehan would die before dawn.

When he did not, good conscience caused you to send for a physician but hoping that he would depart without naming his assailant. That was why you asked me if he had done so. That was your main concern."

"I have admitted responsibility, Master Constable," Penhallow said. "I will admit it in whatever form of tale would best please you."

"You are not a good teller of tales, Master Penhallow. You should bear in mind the line from this new play in which Keehan was to act which says, as I recall it to mind, 'men of few words are the best men.' Too many words allow one to find an avenue through them. Instead of saying nothing, your pretense allowed me to discover your untruths."

"I admit responsibility, good Constable. She is only seventeen and a life ahead of her, please . . . I did this—"

"Enough words, man! Unless you wish to incriminate yourself and your family," snapped the constable, "I have had done with this investigation." He put his hand in his pocket and drew out a purse. "I found this in Master Keehan's room. The physician took his fee out of it. There is enough to give Master Keehan a funeral. Perhaps there might be a few pence over, though there is not enough to clear his debt. But I think that debt has now been expunged in a final way."

Pentecost Penhallow and his daughter were staring at him in bewilderment.

Master Drew hesitated. Words were often snares for folk, but he felt an explanation was needed. "Law and justice sometimes disagree. You have probably never heard of Aristotle but he once wrote, 'Whereas the law is passionless, passion must ever sway the heart of man.' Rigorous adherence to the letter of the law is often rigorous injustice."

"But what of—?"

"What happened here is that a penniless player met his death by the hand of a person or persons unknown. They might have climbed the wall and entered by the open window to rob him. It often happens in this cruel city. Hundreds die by violence, and hundreds more by disease among its teeming populace. The courts give protection to the rich, to the well connected, to gentlemen. But it seems that Master Keehan was not one of these; otherwise, I might have had recourse to pursue this investigation with more rigor."

He turned for the door, paused, and turned back for a moment.

"Master Penhallow, I know not what conditions now prevail in your country of Cornwall. Do you take advice, and if it be possible, return your family to its protective embrace and leave this warren of iniquity and pestilence that we have created by the banks of this foul-smelling stretch of river. I doubt if health and prosperity will ever be your fortune here."

The young girl, eyes shining with tears, moved forward and grasped his arm. *"Dursona dhys!"* she cried, leaning forward and kissing the constable on the cheek. *"Durdala-dywy!* . . . Bless you, Master Constable. Thank you."

Smiling to himself, Master Drew paused outside the Red Boar Inn before wandering the short distance to the banks of the Thames. The smells were overpowering. Gutted fish and offal. The stench of sewerage. Those odious smells, to which he thought that a near lifetime of living in London had inured him, suddenly seemed an affront to his nostrils. Yet thousands of people were arriving in London year after year, and the city was extending rapidly in all directions. A harsh, unkind city that attracted the weak and the wicked, the hopeful and the cynics, the trusting and the swindler, the credulous and the cheat. Never was there such an assemblage of evil. The Puritan divines did not have to look far if they wished to frighten people with an image of what hell was akin to.

He sighed deeply as he glanced up and down the riverbanks.

A boy came along the embankment path bearing a placard and ringing a handbell. Master Drew peered at the placard.

It was an announcement that the King's Players would be performing Master Will Shakespeare's *The Life of King Henry V* at the Globe Theatre that evening.

Master Whelton Keehan would not be playing the role of King Hal.

Master Hardy Drew suddenly found some lines from another of Will Shakespeare's plays coming into his mind. Where did they come from? *The Tragedy of Macbeth!* The last performance Whelton Keehan had given.

> *Tomorrow, and tomorrow, and tomorrow,*
> *Creeps in this petty pace from day to day*
> *To the last syllable of recorded time;*
> *And all our yesterdays have lighted fools*
> *The way to dusty death. Out, out brief candle!*
> *Life's but a walking shadow, a poor player*
> *That struts and frets his hour upon the stage*
> *And then is heard no more.*

The Revenge of
— the Gunner's Daughter —

The last French shot had fallen a full quarter-mile aft of the *Deerhound* as she slipped into the sheltering fog that was rolling down through the Oresund from the Kattegat and across the Kjoge Bight, south of Copenhagen. That had been twenty minutes ago, and since then there had followed an uneasy quiet, free of the noise of battle; the sea's quiet of creaking wooden spars, the fretful snap of canvas and the whispering waves against the sides of the twenty-two-gun sloop as she became immersed in the thick white mist that now concealed her from her vengeful pursuer.

Captain Richard Roscarrock, captain of His Majesty's sloop *Deerhound*, stood head to one side, in a listening attitude on the quarterdeck, hands clasped tightly behind him, lips compressed. Finally he raised his head; his shoulders seemed to relax.

"Hands to shorten sail, Mr. Hart." He turned to the midshipman next to him, a lad scarcely out of his teenage. "Quietly does it," he snapped hastily as the youngster raised his hand to his mouth to shout the order. "Quietly all! We don't want Johnny Frenchman to hear us. We'll take in the tops'ls and mains'l. Pass the word! And have the hands take a care for the damage on the mainmast; the main topgallant mast seems to be badly splintered. And for heaven's sake, get a couple of hands to secure the mainstay; it'll cause damage if it swings loose for much longer."

Midshipman Hart brought his hand to his forehead so that his original motion ended in a cursory salute. He went forward to gather the hands.

Gervaise, the first lieutenant, moved closer to his captain. His voice was quiet. "I don't think the Frenchman has followed us, sir," he observed. "He's probably beating back into the Baltic now that he has discovered we are in these waters."

Roscarrock agreed mentally but gave a noncommittal grunt by way of response. He had been long enough in command to realize that it was not politic to discuss his thoughts with his juniors.

Unstead, the second officer, joined them. "Did you see the cut of her, sir? I'll bet ten guineas on that being the *Épervier* of Rambert's squadron."

"Will we try to rejoin Admiral Gambier, sir?" pressed Gervaise.

Roscarrock sniffed to indicate his irritation. "In good time, Mr. Gervaise. And I am well aware of what ship it was, Mr. Unstead. We'll haul to and will use the cover of this fog to assess our situation. The French gunners were good, and we have sustained some damage. Look at our mainmast."

The sloop had encountered the French seventy-four-gun man-o'-war by accident, sailing around the headland of Stevns Klint and running abruptly under her guns before Roscarrock could wear the ship, turning the helm to windward. The Frenchman had opened fire almost immediately on the smaller vessel. The French guns had inflicted a lot of damage on the English sloop before her swifter sailing ability, good seamanship, and the descending fog across the bight had allowed a means of escape.

Roscarrock knew that he must have sustained several casualties. He could see for himself that the main topgallant mast had been splintered, the rigging and spars still hanging dangerously. The last shots the French had fired had been high and chain shot, which had ripped into the rigging. Captain Roscarrock also knew there had been at least one, probably two shots landed on the gun deck. However, his first concern was whether the *Deerhound* had been holed below the waterline, and his second concern was whether the damage to his masts was irreparable and would prevent him returning quickly to the main British fleet of Sir James Gambier to warn him of the presence of the French.

Lieutenant Gervaise had already read his mind and passed word for the master's mate, bosun, purser, cooper, chief gunnery officer, and doctor: all the heads of the various departments that ran a ship-of-war.

The group of men came after in ones and twos and gathered before the captain on the quarterdeck. They were tired but wore that look of relief at finding themselves still alive. Faces were blackened by powder burns; clothes were torn and stained with blood.

"Has the word been passed for the gunnery officer?" Captain Roscarrock asked, looking round and not seeing the third lieutenant who fulfilled this role.

An elderly sailor, with petty officer insignia, touched his forehead briefly. "Beg pardon, sir. Gunnery officer's dead. I'll make his report."

The first lieutenant blinked a moment. The second officer, Unstead, whistled tactlessly. Roscarrock broke in harshly as if he had not noticed their reactions.

"And where's the bosun?"

"Dead, sir," replied the master's mate dryly.

"Then his mate should be here."

"Dead as well, sir. I'll attend to the report," the man replied.

"Very well. Damage?"

"No shots below the waterline. Main topgallant mast splintered and upper rigging tangled and dangerous. There is no way we can replace topmast shrouds nor the futtock shrouds. She should be able to take the mains'l and we can run without tops'ls, though it will slow us down."

"What about the mizzentop mast?"

"We were lucky there. A chain shot went through the sheet, but it can be patched. That was the shot that impacted against the mainmast."

Roscarrock nodded swiftly. "Do your best. We'll attempt to re-join the fleet as soon as this fog bank clears. Then we'll effect proper repairs. If our main fleet have already captured Copenhagen, we should have no problem." Roscarrock turned back to a grizzled petty officer. "What's the situation with the guns?"

The elderly man raised a finger to his forelock. "Four guns and their crews out of action, Cap'n. Three guns totally destroyed."

Not as bad as Roscarrock expected—still eighteen guns remaining in action. "Purser? What's our status?"

"Most of the stores are safe, sir. Only two water casks were smashed by shot, but we can replace them. The biggest loss is one of the rum casks."

"The men will have to lose their rum ration until we can replenish the cask. Cooper, how about replacing the water casks?"

"I'll have new casks made by tomorrow if we have easy sailing."

Roscarrock was coming to the report that he disliked most of all. "Mr. Smithers, what's the total casualties?"

The sloop was lucky in that it carried a surgeon. Sloops of His Britannic Majesty's navy did not usually have the luxury of carrying a surgeon and had to rely on the cook-cum-barber to double in that capacity.

"Thirteen dead, twenty-four wounded, five seriously," intoned the florid-faced surgeon with an enthusiasm that seemed to indicate he relished his work.

Roscarrock's mouth thinned. "How seriously injured?"

"Three will be dead before nightfall, sir."

Roscarrock's jaw tightened for a moment. Then he asked, "What ranks among the dead?"

"Two midshipmen and . . . and Lieutenant Jardine; four petty officers, and the rest"—the surgeon shrugged—"the rest were other ranks. Of the wounded, all are seamen, sir."

Roscarrock glanced quickly at the surgeon. "Jardine was killed, you say?"

It was the petty officer gunner who answered. "Beg pardon, sir. Lieutenant Jardine was on the gun deck, laying the guns, when he—"

Roscarrock interrupted with a frown. Lieutenant Jardine was the chief gunnery officer. There was no need for an explanation as to where his station had been during the action. "We'll get the details later. And the midshipmen who were killed?"

"Little Jack Kenny and Tom Merritt," the surgeon replied.

"Very well," Roscarrock said after a moment's silence. "Very well, I want this ship cleared and ready for action again within the hour."

There was a chorus of "aye aye's," and the petty officers dispersed to their jobs. The surgeon went with them to take charge of the wounded.

Lieutenant Gervaise was shaking his head. "Jardine, eh? There'll be a lot of ladies at Chatham who will shed a tear, no doubt." He did not sound grief-stricken.

Lieutenant Unstead was positively smug. "And there'll be a lot of husbands who will sleep more comfortably at night," he added sarcastically.

Jardine had been third officer on the sloop. He had been a youthful, handsome, and vain man with a reputation for the ladies, especially for other men's wives. Roscarrock did not rebuke Unstead, because he was aware that, before they had left the port of Chatham, Unstead had actually challenged Jardine to a duel: something to do with his wife, Phoebe. The duel had been prevented by the provost marshal on shore, and both officers were severely reprimanded.

Roscarrock did not bother to comment. He knew that most of the officers and men would not be sorry to hear of Jardine's sudden demise. His handsome looks disguised a cruel temperament. He had been too fond of inflicting discipline with a rope's end. Roscarrock had tried to keep Jardine in check, but the man was possessed of a brutal nature that enjoyed imposing pain on those who could not retaliate. It was not good for discipline for a ship's company to see their officers in conflict, and so Roscarrock was unable to show his disapproval of Jardine before the men. He had to support the punishments that his junior gave out and reprimand him only in private. No, there would be no false grieving in the *Deerhound* over Jardine.

"Mr. Hart!"

The young midshipman came running forward, touching his hat to his captain.

"Lieutenant Jardine is dead. As senior midshipman, you are now acting third lieutenant. I want you to go round and make a list of all casualties. The surgeon will have his hands full tending the wounded."

"Aye aye, sir."

"Report back to me within the hour."

Roscarrock swung round, dismissing the youthful officer with a curt salute, and turned to his first officer.

"Make sure that the men know the urgency of our situation, Mr. Gervaise. I shall be below in my cabin for a while."

In a sloop, a captain's quarters were small, dark, and stuffy. A small curtain separated his sleeping quarters, a single bunk, a cupboard, and space for a chest, from his day cabin, in which there was space for a desk and a couple of chairs. Roscarrock went to the desk and pulled out a half-filled bottle of brandy. He uncorked it and poured out a glass. For a moment he held it up to the light that permeated through the cabin, seeing the amber liquid reflecting in the dull gray light. Then his features broke into a smile and he raised the glass, as if in silent toast, before swallowing in one mouthful.

He replaced the bottle, sat down, and drew out the ship's log. Then he took out pen and ink.

Kjoge Bight, 2 September 1807, he wrote at the top of his entry, and then sat back to consider how, in brief form, he should address the events of the brief but fierce engagement.

He had just finished the details and realized that Midshipman

Hart had not returned with the list of names to enter in the log. But at that moment there was an urgent tap on the door.

Frowning, he uttered the word: "Come!"

Midshipman Hart stood flush-faced in the doorway. He seemed in a state of great excitement.

Roscarrock frowned irritably. "You're late! Do you have the casualty list?"

Midshipman Hart placed a piece of paper on the captain's desk but continued to stand in a state of some agitation.

Roscarrock suppressed a sigh. "What is it?"

"Beg to report, sir," he began, "concerning the death of Lieutenant Jardine—"

"What about the death of Jardine?" Roscarrock demanded sharply, causing the young man to pause awkwardly again as if trying to find the right phrases.

"There are some . . . some curiosities about the manner of his death, sir. I—I don't know quite how to put it."

Roscarrock sat back with a frown, placing his hands before him, fingertips together. "Curiosities?" He savored the word softly. "Perhaps you would explain what you mean by that word?"

"It would be better if you would come to the gun deck, sir. Begging your pardon, it would be easier to show you rather than to tell you."

The young man was clearly embarrassed. He added quickly, "I've asked the surgeon to join us there."

Roscarrock sat quietly for a moment or two. Then, with a sigh, he reached for his hat and stood up. "This is highly unusual, Mr. Hart, but I will come, as you seem to set such store by my attendance."

"Thank you, sir, thank you." Midshipman Hart seemed greatly relieved.

As Roscarrock followed the young man up onto the deck and allowed him to lead the way toward the gun deck, his expression was bleak. "I cannot see what is curious about a death in battle that needs a captain in attendance when a report is made of the fact, Mr. Hart. I presume you have a good reason for dragging me to look at a corpse?"

Midshipman Hart jerked his head nervously. "I think you will understand when I show you, sir."

They descended on to the gun deck. The *Deerhound* mounted eleven cannon on either side. The first thing that struck one in that confined space, which had a clearing of only five feet between decks so that often the men crouched to perform their fighting duties, was the stench. The acrid gunpowder and smoke predominated, but it mingled with the smell of burnt wood, recent fires that had been doused where French shot had ignited combustible materials. There, too, was that odor of charred flesh, that indescribable nauseous combination of the reek of the wounded and the stench of urine.

Captain Roscarrock drew out a square of lavender-soaked linen, which he always carried, and held it to his nose, glancing around him distastefully.

The deck was a shambles where the French shot had hit. Wood was splintered. Ropes and tackle lay in chaotic profusion. There was blood everywhere, and canvas covered several bodies that had not yet been cleared away.

Roscarrock saw at once that the French shot had blown away part of the first four gunports on the starboard side, which had been the side of the ship he had presented to the enemy in his attempt to turn. Three guns were mangled heaps of metal, almost unrecognizable. A fourth, as the gunner had reported, was damaged but not so badly as the first three.

Yet it was not to that scene of chaos that the young midshipman led him but to a gun that was listed in the gunnery chart as number six portside, the central gun position of the eleven-gunport broadside. There was no damage here, but an isolated body was lying just behind the gun, which was being lashed into its position by two sailors.

The florid-faced surgeon, Smithers, was standing by the body, over which a canvas tarpaulin had been placed.

Midshipman Hart came to a halt by it and turned to his captain. "Lieutenant Jardine, sir," he said, pointing almost dramatically at the body.

Roscarrock's eyes narrowed. "I think I presumed as much," he said without humor. "Now, Mr. Hart, what exactly demands my presence here?"

Hart strained forward like an eager dog trying to please its owner. "Well, sir, this position here, behind number six gun, was where the gunnery lieutenant was positioned to direct our broadsides."

Roscarrock tried not to sound irritated. "I am aware, Mr. Hart, of the battle stations of my officers," he replied.

The boy actually winced, and Roscarrock felt almost sorry for his sharpness. However, a ship-of-war in His Majesty's navy was not the place to deal in polite manners.

"Get on with it, Mr. Hart."

Midshipman Hart swallowed nervously. "Well, sir, Lieutenant Jardine was not killed by French shot nor collateral damage from its fall."

The midshipman turned to the doctor. He was smiling as if amused by something.

"Lieutenant Jardine sustained his fatal injuries having been struck by that gun when in recoil." He indicated the cannon being lashed back to its bulkhead moorings.

Roscarrock stared at him for a moment. "I see," he said slowly. "Are you telling me that when number six gun was fired, it recoiled into Jardine and killed him? That Jardine was standing too near the gun when it was fired?"

Smithers actually chuckled. "Precisely so, Captain. Precisely so."

Roscarrock knew there was no love lost between the surgeon and the late third lieutenant. He decided to ignore the man's humor.

"If he was so close behind the gun when it recoiled, then it would seem that this was an accident but that the fault lay with him.

We will give his family the benefit of hearing he died in action and not by an accident that could have been avoided."

Midshipman Hart cleared his throat. "It was not exactly an accident, sir," he ventured.

Roscarrock turned quickly to him with a frown. "What's that you say?" he snapped.

Midshipman Hart blanched at his captain's disapproving tone but stood his ground. "I do not think this was an accident, sir."

There was a moment's silence.

"Then, pray, sir, how else do you explain it?" Roscarrock allowed a little sarcasm to enter into his voice. "Jardine is standing behind the gun; when it is fired, the gun recoils and slams into him, causing injuries from which he dies. Do I have the right of it, Surgeon Smithers?" he demanded of the doctor without turning to him.

"You do, sir; you do, indeed," echoed the smiling surgeon.

"Then we are agreed so far. Now, Mr. Hart, if, as you claim, this was no accident, are you saying that Lieutenant Jardine deliberately stood in a position where he, as gunnery officer, knew the gun would recoil on him?"

"No, sir, I do not."

"Then what are you saying," Roscarrock demanded harshly, "for I am at a loss to understand your argument?"

"I am saying that murder may have been committed, sir."

There was an awkward silence.

The young midshipman stood defiantly under the close scrutiny of his captain.

When Roscarrock spoke, his voice was quiet. "Murder, Mr. Hart? Murder? That is a most serious accusation."

Midshipman Hart raised his jaw defensively. "I have considered the implications of my accusation, sir."

"Then, perhaps, you would be good enough to take me through the facts which would lead me to follow your line of thinking."

Hart was eager now to demonstrate his arguments. "I have accepted that Lieutenant Jardine was an experienced gunnery officer.

His station in any battle was to stand amidships behind guns number six on both port and starboard, a position where he could command the broadsides on both sides of the ship. His usual position was center ship, where no gun could recoil back if properly secured."

Roscarrock said nothing. All this was common knowledge that was shared by even the young powder monkeys aboard. The boys who carried powder and shot to the cannon learned immediately they came aboard to avoid accidents such as getting caught in gun recoil.

Hart paused, and when his captain made no further comment, he went on quickly. "Each cannon is secured to its position by stay ropes which allow for recoil but control the extent of the recoil. Therefore, a gun can only jump back a yard or so at most."

Roscarrock was still silent.

"In the case of number-six gun—" Hart turned to where members of the crew had now finished lashing the gun back into its position. "—the gun recoiled back across the deck and struck Lieutenant Jardine without being halted by the stay ropes."

Roscarrock's eyes narrowed slightly. "Are you telling me that the gun was not secured?"

"That is correct, sir. It was not secured. I believe that this was a deliberate act and no accident."

"Deliberate? It could have been caused by a frayed stay rope which had not been picked up during an inspection."

Midshipman Hart shook his head vehemently. "Two main ropes secure the gun. Both ropes would have had to be frayed and have snapped asunder at precisely the same moment. A frayed rope breaking on one side would not cause a straight recoil. The gun would have swung at an angle on its side as the stay rope on the other side would have pulled it to a halt there."

"What are you saying, then?"

Midshipman Hart turned to the gun and picked up a couple of rope's ends. "These are the ropes that attached the gun to the bulkhead to limit its recoil." He held them out for Roscarrock's inspection. "If you will observe, sir, you will see that both ropes were cut almost through by a sharp implement, a knife, to the point where the force of pressure from the first recoil would have snapped the remaining strands."

Roscarrock examined the rope ends in silence before handing them back to the young midshipman. "Very well, Mr. Hart. Suppose we accept that someone did this in order to kill Lieutenant Jardine; we must then assume that whoever did it knew that in a battle Jardine would be standing behind that gun. His battle station was well known. But how would they been so sure as to the moment the gun was to be fired? They would have had to sever the ropes only when they were certain of an engagement, for tackle is inspected every three days on this ship."

Midshipman Hart inclined his head thoughtfully. "You are quite right, sir."

"Exactly so. You will agree that to achieve this purpose, the severing of the ropes had to be done just before we engaged the French. In those seconds during the very call to battle stations. There would surely have been witnesses to the deed."

"Lieutenant Jardine was not popular with the men, sir." It was Surgeon Smithers who made the deadpan comment.

There was no argument in that.

Roscarrock turned as if irritated to find Smithers still there, grinning broadly. "Very well, Doctor. I am sure that you have other duties to fulfill. I would ask you not to comment to any other person about this matter until we have cleared it up."

Thus dismissed, the surgeon left to attend to those injured who needed his skills.

Roscarrock turned back to the young man. "Accepting the stay ropes on the cannon were tampered with in the way you suggest and for the purpose of causing the death of Lieutenant Jardine, and leaving aside the opportunity of that action, the surgeon is right—Lieutenant Jardine was not a popular officer on this ship. Any member of the crew could have done this. Even one of your fellow midship-men."

Hart raised his eyebrows in protest.

"Yes," went on Roscarrock, before he could speak. "I know all about the punishments that Lieutenant Jardine handed out."

One of the spiteful punishments that Jardine liked to order was having the master-of-arms inflict floggings on midshipmen who fell foul of his temper. They were made to "kiss the gunner's daughter": that was, they were stretched over the barrel of a cannon and beaten with a birch stick. "The gunner's daughter" was naval slang for a cannon.

Roscarrock modulated his tone to speak in a friendly, reason-able fashion. "Look, Hart, most of the ship's company will not shed a tear when Jardine"—he gestured to the body under the tar-paulin—"is tipped over the side. One-fifth of the ship's company are pressed men. Jardine was commander of the press-gang at Chatham. There's vengeance in their minds. And, as for the rest . . ." Roscarrock shrugged. "Better to forget the reason why; his family will rest more comfortably knowing that he died doing his duty."

Midshipman Hart stood his ground. A look of stubbornness seemed to fill the features of the young midshipman. "Sir, my father is a parson, and I was raised to believe in truth and justice. I cannot agree to such a subterfuge. If a man has been murdered, then his killer must be found."

Roscarrock sighed wearily. "If you must, pursue this matter, Mr. Hart. I see no purpose in it when there are a dozen other dead and dying to be accounted for in this engagement and probably more of us will die before we reach our home port again."

"I would like to pursue my inquiry, sir," the young man insisted stubbornly.

"Who is the gun captain of number six, portside?" Roscarrock demanded ominously after a short pause. "Pass the word for him. Perhaps we can settle the matter now."

The gun captain was a muscular seaman in his late thirties. He stood nervously before them.

"How do you explain this, Evans?" demanded Roscarrock, a hand encompassing the gun and the body.

Evans shrugged slightly. "Ain't got no explanation, sir," he muttered. "The stay ropes jest snapped, and the cannon went straight back into the lieutenant. Broke the rammer's foot as it jolted over it."

The rammer was the man who stood by ready to ram wad and shot into the barrel.

"Did anyone notice that the stay ropes were frayed before you put your match to the gun?"

Evans shook his head vehemently. "The Frenchie was upon us and firing, sir. We just loaded with shot and waited for the order to fire."

"Please, sir . . . ," Midshipman Hart intervened, indicating that he wished to ask a question.

Roscarrock nodded his assent.

"Where were you when we beat to quarters, Evans?"

The gun captain shifted his weight from one foot to another. "We were already on our way up from the lower deck. We'd heard the first cry that a Frenchie had been sighted, and so we came running for the gun deck, knowing a fight was in the offing. While we were running up, we heard the drum start beating to quarters."

"And when did Lieutenant Jardine arrive?"

"Why, he was already at his station and cursing us for our slowness, though 'twas unfair, as we were one of the first guns ready and run out, begging your pardon, sir. However, I do swear he was on the gun deck before we sighted the Frenchie."

"You are sure about that? There was no time for anyone else to be on the gun deck at your gun between the sighting of the Frenchman and the arrival of Lieutenant Jardine?"

"The master's mate was with him, sir."

"Pass the word for the master's mate," called Roscarrock to a passing seaman. Then he turned back to the gun captain. "What happened then?"

"There came the command from yourself, sir." Evans glanced nervously at Roscarrock. "Lieutenant Jardine relayed your order to fire when our guns began to bear. The Frenchie got in a first shot that smashed number-two gun and killed the crew 'fore they had time to fire. Then we fired and . . . well, you know what happened."

Roscarrock dismissed the man with a wave of his hand just as the master's mate arrived. "Were you on the gun deck before we beat to quarters?"

The grizzled veteran frowned at his captain. "That I was. I accompanied Lieutenant Jardine, who wanted to inspect the readiness of the gun deck. We were here a full ten minutes before we beat to quarters. Then I went directly to my station, leaving the lieutenant here."

"That is all," dismissed Roscarrock, turning to the midshipman. "Well, Mr. Hart, your theory seems to be flawed. If Lieutenant Jardine was already on the gun deck when we sighted the Frenchman, how could anyone have cut the stay ropes with the intent to kill him before the gun crews came into action?"

Midshipman Hart was evidently trying to fathom this out. His face brightened. "Unless the stay ropes were cut beforehand."

Roscarrock chuckled cynically. "Are you telling me that whoever cut them was foresighted? A fortune-teller? That he cut the ropes with the premonition that we would shortly be in action and Jardine would be standing in that position? Why, we might have gone this entire voyage without firing a shot in anger—"

"That's it! cried the young man excitedly. "Not in anger, not firing a shot in anger . . ."

Roscarrock regarded him with perplexity. "What are you talking about?"

"Don't you recall last night, sir? You called all officers to your cabin and said that there would be a gunnery drill some time this morning to check our efficiency. That explains why Lieutenant Jardine was already on the gun deck before we sighted the Frenchman. He was ensuring his guns were in readiness."

"I don't follow."

"All the officers knew that gunnery drill would take place. And every officer was told to ensure no crew member knew this so that it was to be a good measure of their efficiency. Even Surgeon Smithers was at the officers' call when you announced the drill."

"Are you now saying that one of my officers is responsible for Jardine's death? That knowing the gunnery drill was ordered and also knowing where Jardine's station was, they cut through the stay ropes and waited for the drill?"

"I am saying that one of the officers on this ship is responsible for his murder, sir. Only the officers knew of the impending gunnery drill and had time to tamper with the ropes."

Roscarrock pursed his lips. "I think that your argument is rather far-fetched. But"—he raised a hand to interrupt the midshipman's protest—"I'll not gainsay your wish to make further inquiries. Remember that you are making serious charges, Mr. Hart. I will not record our conversations in the log until you come to me with evidence. Now, I am afraid that I have other pressing matters to attend to."

Returning to the quarterdeck, Roscarrock found his first lieutenant, Gervaise, issuing orders to the ship's carpenter.

He stiffened slightly as the captain approached, and dismissed the craftsman. "There's still some rigging tackle in a dangerous condition on the mainmast by the crow's nest. We won't be able to clear it until we get in port waters. The Frenchie was using some chain shot to try to dismast us. It's still lodged up there. We'll have to use the mizzentop lookout position."

"Very well. What about the foremast?"

"The master's mate is overseeing the jury rig now. It'll mean a new sail there. We can be under way within half an hour."

Roscarrock glanced around at the enshrouding fog. "Unless it's my imagination, this fog is thinning. Let's hope the Frenchie hasn't stuck around to find out what has happened to us. We won't have the speed to outrun him without full sails."

Gervaise did not seem unduly worried. "Rambert's a cautious cove, sir. Remember how his squadron failed to support Admiral de Villeneuve off Cape Finisterre a few years back? It was Rambert then who ran for a fog bank to escape our squadron rather than engage us. I think he'll keep his ship back and not venture after us."

"Let's hope you are right, Mr. Gervaise."

Gervaise hesitated awkwardly. "Sir, what's this Surgeon Smithers was chortling about Lieutenant Jardine's death?"

Roscarrock swung round in annoyance. Damn the loose-mouthed doctor to hell! "What was Smithers saying?" he demanded.

"Oh, he seemed amused by the fact Jardine killed himself by accident and won't get the glory of dying in battle. Is it true?"

"Lieutenant Jardine was killed by a gun recoiling into him, that's all," Roscarrock said shortly.

Gervaise abruptly began to chuckle. "Bless me! It's really true? Not killed in action? No fame and glory in death for Jardine?"

Roscarrock's eyes narrowed. "I am fully aware that you didn't like Jardine, Mr. Gervaise."

Gervaise stopped chuckling, and his mouth suddenly hardened. "Didn't like him? That is an understatement. I hated him, and if I had been a better man with sword or pistol, like young Unstead, I would have called out the bastard long ago. Ask Smithers, as well. He once tried to foist his attentions on Smithers's daughter Prudence." The words were spoken softly, but there was vehemence in them.

Roscarrock turned away in embarrassment. He pretended to examine the drifting fog again. "Hands on deck for the committal of the dead to the sea in half an hour. I want to be under way immediately afterwards if this clears." He made to turn down the companionway but then paused and added, "Make sure we can muster a fighting trim if Johnny Frenchman suddenly appears again."

Lieutenant Gervaise raised a hand to his hat.

In his cabin, Roscarrock sat for a while absently drumming his fingers on his desktop while listening to the faint sounds of shouted orders and answering cry of the hands as they performed their various tasks to return the ship to readiness.

Little time seemed to pass before there was a sharp tap on the door.

It was Midshipman Hart. His face wore a satisfied expression. He seemed bursting with news.

"Come in, Mr. Hart," Roscarrock invited. "From your expression, I presume that you have solved your mystery?"

"I believe that I now know the means whereby it can be solved."

Roscarrock raised his eyebrows for a moment and then sat back, relaxing as far as his small wooden chair would allow. "So what is your conclusion?"

"Exactly as I said, sir. Lieutenant Jardine's death was accomplished with malice aforethought. Knowing the gun drill was going to be held this morning, one of the officers of this ship cut the stay ropes some time during the night so that number-six gun would recoil back and strike the lieutenant. However, before the gun drill was due to take place, a real engagement ensued when we sighted the Frenchman. The result was just the same. The gun killed the lieutenant."

"That much you have claimed before. You were going to report to me when you could sustain your hypothesis. Can you do so?"

Hart smiled broadly. "As you gave me permission to pursue the task, sir, I took the liberty of searching Lieutenant Jardine's dunnage."

"You searched his personal possessions?"

"I did so, sir. I believe that given what I have found, I can demonstrate the reality of my theory and present a prima facie case against an officer."

Roscarrock leaned forward quickly. "How so?"

"It is well known that Lieutenant Jardine had innumerable affairs, that he was a ladies' man, a seducer of women."

Roscarrock spread his hands, palm downward on his desk. "Go on," he instructed.

"There were several letters in his locker all written to him by the same female hand and signature together with a small portrait. A portrait of a young lady. A rather attractive young lady."

"Well?"

"The letters were signed each time 'your own adoring P.' In one letter, dated on the very evening we left Chatham, this lady, P, writes to Jardine that she fears for his life while on board the *Deerhound*. She suspects that her husband has discovered the affair and means to find an excuse to kill him. She begs him to find an excuse to absent himself from the ship at the earliest opportunity. There is some emotional material about them eloping to some foreign place together."

Roscarrock drew his finger along the side of his nose thoughtfully. "The letters signed with the initial *P*, you say? I don't think that will get you far. By coincidence, I know the names of the wives of three officers begins with *P*. Midshipman Hope is married to a young lady named Penelope. Lieutenant Gervaise's wife is named Peggy, and Lieutenant Unstead's wife is Phoebe. . . ." Roscarrock suddenly paused as if a thought had struck him.

Midshipman Hart was nodding excitedly. "Lieutenant Unstead already challenged Lieutenant Jardine to a duel in Chatham. It was stopped by the Provost Marshal. The cause of the duel was that Lieutenant Jardine had insulted Lieutenant Unstead's wife. Lieutenant Unstead's wife is named, as you say, Phoebe."

Roscarrock inclined his head as though unwilling to admit the possibility. "It is still a theory. How can you prove it?"

"By the miniature portrait, sir."

"So far as I recall, no one on board, except Jardine, ever met Mrs. Unstead, so we have no knowledge of her features."

"Then all we have to do is wait until we return to Chatham and then compare the portrait with the features of those of the officers' ladies whose names begin with *P*. I will wager, however, that the features match those of Mrs. Unstead. Then we will have our assassin."

Captain Roscarrock regarded the eager young midshipman with a serious expression. "Mr. Hart, I think you have done well. However, we cannot let a word of this slip out, because if it was thought that you had this evidence, your own life would not be worth that of a weevil in a ship's biscuit. Do you have these letters and the portrait?"

Midshipman Hart reached into his uniform jacket and drew out a sheaf of papers and a small silver-framed oval object.

"I was going to give them to you, sir, so that you could lock them away until we return to Chatham."

He handed them across.

Roscarrock gave them a cursory glance. "One thing, Mr. Hart." He smiled softly. "Although you suspect Lieutenant Unstead, would it not be more appropriate to suspect all officers, for you might be doing him an injustice?"

"Indeed, sir. I am trying to keep an open mind in case I am wrong."

"Why, then, am I not among your suspects? I could well play the part of a jealous husband."

Midshipman Hart smiled and shook his head. "I did entertain the notion, sir, but then I dismissed it."

"Dismissed it? On what grounds, pray?" demanded Roscarrock in amusement.

"I found out from your steward, sir, that your wife's name begins with the letter *M* and not *P*."

Roscarrock's smile broadened. "You believe in attending to minutiae, Mr. Hart. You are right. My wife's name is Mary. You will go far in the service. Very well. I shall keep these letters and the miniature portrait under lock and key until we are safely home in Chatham. Do not mention a word of such a find. Until we reach our home port, it might be wise to let it be known that your inquiries have been resolved and there is nothing suspicious about Jardine's death."

"Aye, sir."

Roscarrock turned and placed the letters in his locker with the miniature portrait.

There came the sound of a ship's bell.

"Nearly time for the burial service," sighed Roscarrock. "Ask Mr. Gervaise to pass the word."

Captain Roscarrock had been wrong. The fog was patchy and did not thin immediately. It lay around the *Deerhound* for two hours more after the committal of the bodies to the sea. Roscarrock impatiently paced the quarterdeck for a while, awaiting its clearance, but it hung with persistence. Now and then, Roscarrock heard officers exchanging a whisper and a chuckle. Crewmen passed to their duties, smirking. The reason was obvious. The news that Lieutenant Jardine had been killed in an accident was spreading round the ship. No glory for Lieutenant Jardine, just a casualty of bad fortune. It seemed that Midshipman Hart had spread the word that there was no more to the curious manner of the gunnery lieutenant's death than ill fate.

Eventually, Roscarrock returned to his cabin and set himself to wait for the fog to clear. It was another hour before Midshipman Hart knocked on the door and touched his hat. "Mr. Gervaise's compliments, sir. The fog is clearing rapidly now. There is a nor'-northwesterly wind beginning to blow."

Roscarrock stood up. "Excellent. Take a run up aloft and scan the horizon. I don't think the Frenchman has remained nearby, but we don't want any surprises. I will come on deck immediately."

Hart touched his hat again and turned out of the cabin.

Roscarrock reached for the brandy bottle and poured a generous glass from its amber contents.

Time seemed to pass interminably.

There was a sudden commotion on deck.

He raised his glass and swallowed quickly.

There was a cry: "Pass the word for the captain!"

Almost immediately one of the youngest midshipmen knocked at his door, a lad no more than fourteen years old.

"Mr. Gervaise's compliments, sir," came his childish piping treble. "Would you come on deck immediately, sir?"

Roscarrock grabbed his hat and followed the boy on to the quarterdeck.

He glanced around as he came out of the companionway. "What is it, Gervaise? Is it the Frenchman?"

Gervaise's face was pale. "Young Hart, sir. He came on deck, sprang into the stays, and went scrambling up the mainmast to the crow's nest. He was up there before I could warn him! Didn't I mention earlier that the chain shot had frayed the rigging and splintered the spars there? All above the mains'l was unstable. Young Hart just slipped, lost his footing, and came crashing down to the main deck."

He indicated toward where a group of sailors were gathered around something that looked like a bundle of clothes.

Surgeon Smithers rose from his knees by it and glanced upward toward the captain. He stood his head in a studied fashion. "Neck clean broke, Cap'n," he called.

Roscarrock turned back to Gervaise. "Was there no way the boy could have been warned before he went up the main rigging?" he demanded.

Gervaise shook his head. "What was the boy climbing up there for anyway?"

"I told him to go aloft," replied Roscarrock. "I wanted a sweep around with the fog clearing to see if the Frenchman was anywhere in sight. I didn't realize that he would go for the mainmast. I thought everyone had been warned that it was unstable. I presumed that he would use the mizzenmast crow's nest, which would give a good clearance of the horizon, but . . ."

"Poor little sod," muttered Lieutenant Unstead roughly. He had been standing behind Lieutenant Gervaise. "One more body to go over the side, I suppose. I'll get the sail-maker to stitch up another canvas and shot."

An hour later the sloop was tacking across the wind, moving painfully slowly north-northwest across the hight toward the waiting British fleet.

Captain Richard Roscarrock sat at his desk and unlocked the cupboard, drawing forth the small miniature. He gazed down at the young, soft face, with the golden ringlets and pert red lips that smiled out from it. He stared in disapproval for a moment and then returned it, taking out the sheaf of letters that had been so emotionally addressed to Lieutenant Jardine and signed "your own adoring P."

They were outpourings of a desperate and naive love. Hart had been right. The last letter had alerted Jardine to the young woman's suspicion that her husband had found out about their affair and was a threat to Jardine's life. It was clear that the husband, whose name was not indicated in the letter, was a fellow officer on board the *Deerhound*.

Roscarrock gave a low sigh, folded them up, and returned them to the locker.

He drew some clean sheets of paper toward him and reached for the pen and ink.

He addressed his letter to *Mrs. Mary Roscarrock, care of the Rat and Raven Inn, Chatham*. Then he paused a few moments for thought before beginning: *My dearest wife, Polly* . . . He paused and smiled grimly to himself. It was a good thing young Hart's education had been lacking in that he had not realized Polly was used as a diminutive of Mary.

THE PASSING SHADOW

"And talk of Time slipping by you, as if it was an animal of rustic sports with its tail soaped."
—"The Passing Shadow" in *Our Mutual Friend*

The two men sat opposite each other, either side of a dark oak table in the dark, tiny snug of the Thameside tavern. There were no windows in the curious three-cornered little room. A gas burner, jutting from the wall above the solitary table, gave a curious flickering light, reflecting reddish on the red oak paneling. The elder man was in his early fifties, small of stature, immaculately dressed and coiffured, his curly hair receding from a broad forehead. A small "goatee" beard and mustache gave him the appearance of an intellectual, perhaps a professor. The other man was younger, in his thirties, fair of skin, with wide blue eyes and auburn hair. His handsome features had an indefinable Irish quality about them, although when he spoke, his soft, well-modulated tones were clearly those of someone educated in England.

There had been a momentary silence between them while a young girl had brought a tray into the snug on which reposed a decanter of port and two glasses. She had placed it on the table between them and left with a bobbed curtsy, for she was well aware of the identity of the older guest that now sat gazing moodily at the cut-glass decanter as the gaslight caused it to flicker and flash with a thousand points of light.

"I think that you are worried, esteemed father-in-law." The younger man broke the silence with a smile.

The elder man turned with a disapproving frown and commenced to pour the port into the glasses. "You know that I hate being addressed as father-in-law," he reproved.

The young man shrugged. "Since I married your daughter, Kate, I have been at odds as to how to address you. Since I am called Charles and you are called Charles, it would sound like some echo in the conversation if we hailed each other with that mode of address."

The elderly man's eyes lightened with humor. "In that case, let us agree. I shall call you Charley, and you may address me as Charles; otherwise, we shall have to resort to the formal Mr. Collins and Mr. Dickens."

He pushed the port across the table, and his son-in-law dutifully raised the glass. "Your health, Charles," his son-in-law toasted solemnly.

"Yours, too, Charley. I hope your new novel sells well."

"*Straithcairn?*" The young man laughed whimsically. "Alas, I will never succeed as a novelist like my brother Wilkie. He has made more out of his *Woman in White* than I have made out of both my novels. My art lies in illustration, as you know. I am more of an artist than writer, as was my father."

"Although I believe that your grandfather wrote?"

"Indeed, he did, sir. But had to leave his native Ireland to come to this country in order to earn a living as a picture restorer. Being no man of business, he failed to provide for his family."

"In that, we share a common background, Charley. That is what endears me to you. Moreover, I respect your critical opinion."

"Which brings us neatly to my point. You are clearly worried. I suspect it is about this novel that you have been working on of late. I was wondering why you have brought me to this unfamiliar Limehouse region, away from our usual London haunts, where we might bump into friends and colleagues."

Dickens sighed. "Unfamiliar? My godfather, old Christopher

Huffman, sold oars, masts, and ships' gear just round the corner from here in Church Row It was in old Huffman's house there that my father once placed me on the table and told me to sing to the assembled company—to show me off. No, Charley, this place is not so remote for me. Over twenty years ago, I used some of this very area as background"—he waved his hand to encompass the surroundings—"as description in my book *Dombey and Son*."

Charles Collins was silent for a moment.

"But you are worried," he pressed.

Dickens compressed his lips for a moment and then nodded slowly. "You are discerning, Charley. Yes. I am worried."

"About the new book?"

Again, his father-in-law nodded.

"Care to tell me what the book is about?"

"I have a character who has been left a fortune provided that he marries a girl. I've called the girl Bella. Bella Wilfer. My character, I've called him John, has been out of England for fourteen years. Now, while the fortune is attractive, John has decided to return to London under an assumed name to assess the situation. If John doesn't marry Bella, then a man called Boffin stands to inherit the fortune. John gets a job as Boffin's secretary. John becomes the mutual friend of Boffin and the Wilfers. In fact, I have titled my draft *Our Mutual Friend*. The upshot is that John and Bella fall in love, and John declares his real identity and inherits the money."

Charles Collins pulled a face. "It sounds like a romantic comedy of deceit with a happy ending."

Dickens scowled and shook his head. "No, that's just it. It seems to lack spontaneity. It's become a sordid tale of deceit and money. It's full of pessimism. I seem to hear the words of that confounded woman Mrs. Lewes—George Eliot—whatever her name really is, who said that I scarcely ever pass from the humorous and external to the emotional and tragic, without becoming as transient in my unreality as . . . Oh, damnation!" He cut himself short. "She's right. It reads like a dry treatise on morals, not a story."

"Well, I have noticed that you have been growing increasingly pessimistic with life in general," observed his son-in-law seriously.

"The story is too dry and dusty," went on Dickens, ignoring the observation. "I need to insert some drama, some excitement, some mystery—"

The door of the snug suddenly burst open, and a middle-age woman stood nervously on the threshold. She was a round-faced lady who was, in fact, the proprietess of the tavern.

"Lud!" she exclaimed in agitation. "Mr. Dickens, sir, I am all of a tremble."

The two men rose immediately for, indeed, the lady was suiting the words to the action and stood trembling in consternation before them.

Dickens came forward and took the landlady by the arm. "Calm yourself, Miss Mary." His voice held a reassuring quality. "Come, still your nerves with a glass of port and tell us what ails you."

"Port, sir? Gawd, no, sir." 'Tis gin that I would be having if drink be needed at all. But it can wait, Mr. Dickens, sir. " 'Tis advice I do be needing. Advice and assistance."

Dickens regarded her patiently. "Pray, what then puts you so out of spirits? We will do our best to help."

"A body, sir. A body. Washed up against our very walls."

The tavern walls were built on the river's edge, and those dark, choppy waters of the Thames could often be heard slapping at the bricks of the precariously balanced building.

Charley Collins grimaced. "Nothing unusual in that, Miss Mary," he pointed out, adopting his father-in-law's manner of addressing the landlady. In fact, every drinking man along the waterfront knew the landlady of the Grapes simply as Miss Mary. "Dwelling along the waterfront here, you have surely grown used to bodies being washed up?"

It was true that the Thames threw up the dead and dying every day. Suicides were commonplace; there were gentlemen facing ruin in various forms who took a leap from a bridge as a way out and the poor unable to cope with the heavy oppression of penury. Among the latter sort were a high percentage of unfortunate young women, unable to endure the profession that was their only alternative to starvation. Often there were unwanted children. And there were bodies of those who had met their ends by the hands of others for gain, jealousy, and all manner of motives. The flotsam and jetsam of all human misery and degradation floated along the dark, sulky river. Indeed, there were also unsavory stories of watermen, "river finders," who plied their trade on the river, taking drunks from the riverside taverns to drown them in the Thames, though not before emptying their pockets of anything valuable, or to sell their corpses for medical dissection. Death and the river were not mutually exclusive. In fact, many along the riverbanks were called dredgers, dredging coal or valuables lost overboard from the ships that pushed their way along the river to the London docks.

"I would send for a constable at once, Miss Mary," advised Dickens, about to be reseated.

Whereupon the lady let out a curious wailing sound that returned him to a standing position with some alacrity. "I would be doing that, but it be young Fred who be fishing out the body, and the peelers is just as like to say 'e robbed the corpse. Now, if you were there to see fair play . . . they'd respect a man like you, Mr. Dickens."

"If I recall a'right, Fred is your nephew?"

"Me own poor departed sister's son, gawdelpus."

Dickens smiled skeptically. "What makes you think the police would believe that this corpse had been robbed?"

The landlady blinked and then realized what he meant. She looked defensive. "'E only looked to see if there were anything to identify 'im, Mr. Dickens. The corpse, that is. Fred, I mean," she ended in confusion.

Dickens raised a cynical eyebrow. "I presume that there was no means of identification . . . nor any valuables on him?"

"Bert ain't no dredger, Mr. Dickens. 'E's a lighterman. Makes a good living, an' all." There was a note of indignation in her voice.

Dredgers found almost all the bodies of persons who had been drowned and would seek to obtain rewards for the recovery of the bodies or make money through the fees obtained by bearing witness at inquests. But no recovered body and no corpse handed to the coroner would ever have anything of value on it. Dredgers would see to that.

"I am curious, Miss Mary," interrupted Charley Collins, "why do you think that a policeman, seeing this body, might want to accuse anyone of robbing it? Plenty of corpses are washed up without anything on them and often without means of identification."

His father-in-law looked approvingly at him. "A good point. Come, Miss Mary, the question is deserving of an answer."

"The man is well dressed, Mr. Dickens, and Freddie . . . well, 'e thinks . . . that is, Fred thinks that 'e was done in, begging your pardon."

"Done in? Murdered?" asked Collins.

"Back of 'is skull bashed, in, sez Fred."

"And why would the constabulary think Fred might be involved?

Miss Mary sniffed awkwardly. "Well, 'e did three months in chokey last year. Po'lis 'ave long memories."

Collins frowned. "Chokey?"

"Prison," explained Dickens. "I believe the derivation is from the Hindustani *chauki*. Well, Miss Mary, Mr. Collins and I will come and take a look at the corpse. Don't worry. Fred will have nothing to fear if he is honest with us."

They followed her from the snug. The tavern building had a dropsical appearance and had long settled down into a state of hale infirmity. In its whole construction it had not a straight floor and hardly a straight line; but it had outlasted, and clearly would yet outlast, many a better-trimmed building, many a sprucer public house. Externally it was a narrow lopsided wooden jumble of corpulent windows heaped one upon the other as one might heap as many toppling oranges, with a crazy wooden veranda impending over the water, indeed the whole house, inclusive of the complaining flagstaff on the roof, impended over the water, but seemed to have got into the condition of a fainthearted diver who has paused so long on the brink that he will never go in at all.

The snug, which they had originally settled to savor their port wine, was a curious little haven in the tavern: a room like a three-cornered hat into which no direct ray of sun, moon, or star ever penetrated but which was regarded as a sanctuary replete with comfort. The name *Cozy* was painted on its door, and it was always by that name that the snug was referred to.

Miss Mary, the proprietess, pushed her stately way through the taproom and into the dark lane outside. It was a long cobbled lane whose buildings towered on either side, almost restricting the thoroughfare. It was appropriately called Narrow Street, running parallel with the River Thames and separate from it only by such buildings as the Grapes, from which they had emerged. She took a lantern by the door and conducted them round the corner of the building, down a small slipway, which led to the bank of the river.

A young man was there, also with a lantern, waiting for them. At his feet lay a dark shape. "Thank Gawd!" he stuttered as they emerged from the darkness. "Thought I were gonna be stuck 'ere."

Dickens and Collins halted above the shape at his feet. Dickens took the lantern from the young man and, bending down, held it over the shape.

The body was that of a man of about thirty. He was well dressed in a suit of dark broadcloth and a white shirt that had obviously been clean at one stage but was now discolored by the dark Thames water and mud with bits of flotsam and jetsam that adhered to it.

"Handsome," muttered Collins, examining the man's features.

"And a man who took a pride in his appearance," added Dickens.

"How so?"

Dickens raised one of the man's wrists and held the lantern near the well-manicured fingernails.

"The arms are not yet stiffening with rigor mortis, so he is not long dead."

He searched for a wound.

"Back of the skull, guv'nor? Head bashed in," suggested the young man.

"Fred, isn't it?" asked Dickens.

"That's me, guv'nor."

"How did you find this body?"

"Came down 'ere to empty the . . . the waste," he quickly corrected what he was about to say with a frowning glance at Miss Mary. "Saw him half in and half out of the water. Dragged him up and then called Miss Mary."

"And you searched him? Anything to identify him?"

"Not a blessed thing. Straight out."

Dickens could not hide his smile. "Nothing on him at all?"

"Said so, didn't I?"

"Very well, Fred. You cut along to the police at Wapping Steps. That's the nearest station. Bring the majesty of the law hither as quickly as you can." He turned to Miss Mary. "You best get back to your customers. There is nothing that you can do here."

Left alone, Dickens began a thorough search of the man's pockets.

Collins smiled skeptically. "You don't expect to find anything, do you?"

"I never expect anything. In that way I am never disappointed. But it is always best to make sure."

"The dredgers will have got to him before now."

"Not so. This man is young. His body appears in good health and better dressed than most people in these parts. What dredger do you know who would leave the possibility of a reward for finding the body even if they have taken everything from the pockets? A rich person would obviously need an inquest, and there would be the fee from the coroner if they took it along. No, the man was killed, and the killer went through the pockets before tipping the body in the river. Ah—"

Dickens suddenly pulled from an inside waistcoat pocket what appeared to be a piece of narrow ribbon. It formed a small circle, tied in a bow.

"A woman's ribbon?" asked Collins with a frown.

Dickens held it under the lamp. "A piece of red ribbon. Mean anything to you?"

Collins shook his head. "A lady's hair ribbon?" he guessed.

"Come, man . . ." Dickens was indignant. "Think of law. This is the sort of ribbon a legal brief is tied up with. You'll see this ribbon is still tied in a bow as if it has been slipped off a rolled document, a brief, without being untied, and thrust into our man's waistcoat. Now look at the suit he wears; it appears to be black broadcloth. The man is without doubt a lawyer of some type."

Collins gazed at his father-in-law in astonishment. "Next you will be telling me his name," he observed dryly.

"Easy enough—Wraybrook."

"Oh, come!" sneered Collins. "I can see the logic which leads you to guess that the man is a lawyer . . . that has to be proved, by the way . . . but where do you get the name Wraybrook from?"

Dickens held the lamp up so that Collins could see that he had loosened the corpse's starched high white collar.

"Laundresses are invaluable these days. One of them has had the goodness to write the name on the underside of the collar with some indelible marker."

He refastened the collar and completed his search before standing up.

"Poor devil. A young lawyer, his skull smashed in and thrown into the Thames. I wonder why."

"Robbery? That's the usual form."

Dickens stood frowning down for a moment.

There was a noise from the lane as a figure came hurrying around the corner of the tavern and down the slipway toward them. It was the figure of a heavy man. As he came into the light of their raised lantern, they could see he was dressed in the uniform of the Metropolitan Police. He carried a torch, which he shone on them both.

"I'm told there was a body discovered here?" he said gruffly.

Dickens smiled. "And you are? . . ."

"Sergeant, sir. Sergeant Cuff of Thames Division." The sergeant suddenly peered closely at him. "Beg pardon, sir, aren't you—?"

"I am."

"Did you—?"

"No. The landlady of the Grapes called us to have a look. A young man, Fred, found it. He works in the taproom of the inn."

"Ah, just so." The sergeant nodded. "He came to the station to tell us, so I cut along here smartish while he made a statement." The torch moved down to the corpse at their feet. "No need to bother you further, then—you and Mr.—?"

"My son-in-law, Charles Collins."

"Right then, sir. I'll take charge from now on."

"Then we shall leave you to it, Sergeant—?"

"Sergeant Cuff, sir. Thank you, sir."

"They reentered the Grapes and returned to the Cozy, and as Dickens handed back Miss Mary's lantern, he informed her that a police sergeant had arrived to take charge of things.

To their surprise, a moment later Fred came in. He smiled with some relief. "Gave 'em the statement and they told me to go," he announced in satisfaction.

Dickens nodded with a frown. Then he turned to Miss Mary and asked: "I don't suppose you have a *Kelly's Post Office Directory* to hand?"

"Matter of fact, Mr. Dickens, I do have such a volume," she said, and turning behind her bar, extracted the volume from beneath the counter.

Dickens took it into the snug, sat down, and began to turn the pages.

"Looking for Wraybrook the solicitor, I suppose?" observed Collins, finishing the decanted port and peering at his empty glass with regret.

"Except he is not listed. Let's see, this is last year's and would have been compiled the year before. That makes it two years out of date. Perhaps our man, Wraybrook, only established himself within the last year or two."

"Perfectly logical."

Dickens put down the directory, pages open on the table, and sighed.

Miss Mary entered the snug at that moment.

"I just came to see if you needed a new decanter, gentlemen." Her eyes fell on the directory. "Did you find what you were looking for, Mr. Dickens?"

Dickens shook his head. "Regretfully, I did not."

Miss Mary glanced slyly at the open pages. "Lawyers, eh? Well, if you are in need of lawyers, there are plenty to choose from there. Personally, I always prefer to steer clear of them. My late husband said—"

"We were looking for a lawyer who does not seem to be listed there," interrupted Dickens, who had no desire to hear the wisdom of Miss Mary's late husband.

Collins nodded sympathetically. "Perhaps you can call in at the offices of Kelly's. They might have a listing for Wraybrook in their next year's edition."

Miss Mary started and stared at him. "Wraybrook, you say, sir? You don't mean Mr. Eugene Wraybrook?"

Dickens frowned suspiciously at her. "Do you know a lawyer named Wraybrook?"

"He's a young gent, sir. A solicitor right enough. But he's only been in the country six months. They say he's from India. Not that he's Indian, sir. Oh, no, English, same as you and me. Pleasant enough young man. He has rooms at the top end of Narrow Street here, and one of them is his office. Not that he gets much work, I'm told. Decent enough and polite and pays his bills prompt-like."

"Would you recognize Mr. Wraybrook?"

"I would, six."

"And young Fred?"

"Fred, sir? I don't think so. Fred works in the evenings, and Mr. Wraybrook only comes here for lunch now and again."

"Did you take a good look at the body on the slipway?" asked Dickens curiously.

Miss Mary shook her head. "Not I, sir. Can't stand the sight of corpses and . . . Why do you ask, sir?" She frowned, and then her eyes widened suddenly. "You don't mean that . . . that . . .?"

Dickens rose quickly. "Do you know where this Wraybrook has his rooms? What number in Narrow Street?"

"I only know it's the top end, sir. But—"

"Would you give us about fifteen minutes, Miss Mary, and then go out and tell the policeman who is loitering outside with the corpse where we have gone?"

Dickens hurried from the tavern with Collins hard on his heels.

At the darkened top of Narrow Street they came to a cluster of tall tenement buildings crowding over the cramped lane and shutting out all natural light. A few gas lamps gave an eerie glow, and beneath these were some street urchins playing five stones. For a three-penny piece, one of them indicated the tenement in which he knew the solicitor resided. The rooms were on the second floor. There was a single gas burner on every landing, and so it was easy to find a dark door on which was affixed a small handwritten card bearing the name *E. Wraybrook, Bachelor of Law.*

Dickens tried the door, but it was locked.

Collins watched with some surprise as Dickens reached up and felt along the ridge at the top of the door and grunted in dissatisfaction when his search revealed nothing. He stood looking thoughtfully.

"What is it?"

"Sometimes people leave a key in such a place," Dickens said absently. "I expect Sergeant Cuff to be here soon, and I do not want to force the door. Ah , "

He suddenly dropped to one knee and pushed experimentally at a small piece of planking near the door, part of the skirting board. It seemed loose, and a small section gave way, revealing the cavity beyond. Dickens felt inside with his gloved hand and came up smiling. There was a key in his hand.

"Strange how people's habits follow a set course."

A moment later they entered the rooms beyond. There was a strange odor, which caused Collins to sniff and wrinkle his features in bewilderment.

"Opium? The smell of dope?"

"No, Charley," replied his father-in-law. "It's the smell of incense, popular in the East. I think it is sandalwood. Find the gas burner, and let us have some light."

The first room was plainly furnished and was, apparently, an office for prospective clients of the solicitor. On the desk there was a rolled sheaf of papers. Legal documents. Dickens absently took from his pocket the red ribbon, rolled the paper, and slipped the ribbon over it. He shot a glance of satisfied amusement at Collins. He then removed the ribbon, put it back in his pocket, and examined the documents. It was not helpful.

"A litigation over the ownership of a property," he explained. "And a cover note from an agent offering a fee of a guinea for resolving the matter."

He returned the document to the desk and glanced around.

"By the look of this place, it is hardly used and indicates that our Mr. Wraybrook had few clients."

A door led into the living quarters. There was an oil lamp on a side table. It was a sturdy brass-based lamp, slightly ornate, and a very incongruous ornamented glass surround from which dangled a series of globular crystal pieces held on tiny brass chains.

"Light that lamp, Charley," instructed Dickens. "I can't see a gas burner in this room."

Collins removed the glass and turned up the wick on the burner, lighting it before resetting the glass. The crystals jangled a little as he picked it up.

Beyond the door was a bed sitting room. Collins preceded Dickens into the room. Again the furnishings were sparse. It seemed that the late Mr. Wraybrook did not lead a luxurious life. There was little that was hidden from their gaze. A tin traveling trunk at the bottom of the bed showing that its owner was a man recently traveled. The wardrobe, when opened, displayed only one change of clothes and some shirts. The dressing table drawers were empty apart from some socks and undergarments.

"Gene! I thought that . . . Oh!"

A voice had spoken from the doorway behind them. They swung round. There was a young woman standing there. She was not well dressed and was not out of place among the residents of Narrow Street.

She stared at them, slightly frightened. "What are you doing here?" she demanded, silently strident. "Where's Gene . . . Where's Mr. Wraybrook?"

Dickens assumed a stern and commanding attitude. "We will ask the questions, young lady. Who are you?"

The girl seemed to recognize the voice of authority. "Polis ain't cher?"

"Name?" demanded Dickens officiously.

"Beth Hexton. I lives 'ere."

The East End accent did not seem to fit with the delicate features of the girl. Collins could see that whatever her education, she was very attractive, a kind of ethereal beauty that his artist's eye could see in the kind of paintings that Millais and Rossetti and Hunt indulged in. She would not be out of place as a model for an artist of the High Renaissance.

"Here? In these rooms?" he queried.

"Naw!" The word was a verbal scowl. "In this 'ouse. Me dad's Gaffer Hexton," she added, as if that might mean something.

"Ah, Gaffer Hexton." Dickens smiled, "And he might be—?"

"Owns two wagerbuts on the river. Thought all you peelers 'ad 'eard o' me dad."

A wagerbut was a slight sculling craft often used for races along the Thames.

"A dredger?" Dickens said softly.

"Ain't we all got a livin' t' make?" replied the girl defensively.

"How well do you know Mr. Wraybrook?" he demanded.

Her cheeks suddenly flushed. "'E's a friend, a real gen'leman."

"A friend, eh?"

"Yeah. What's 'e done? Where yer taken 'im?"

There was a movement in the other room, and they swung round. They had a glimpse of a stocky, dark-haired man making a hurried exit through the door.

Dickens frowned. "Who was that?" he asked.

"'Im? That's Bert 'egeton." The girl spoke scornfully.

"And he is?"

"'E's the local schoolteacher. Fancies 'imself. Thinks I fancy 'im. *I don't think!*" she added with sardonic humor. "'E's out of 'umor since Gene . . . since Mr. Wraybrook asked me to step out wiv 'im."

Dickens glanced at Collins with raised eyebrows. Although Dickens was certainly no social prude, it seemed a little incongruous that a solicitor would "step out" with a dredger's daughter. But then, she was an attractive girl, and if a local schoolteacher was seeking her favors, why not a solicitor?

A movement at the door, and a dry, rasping cough interrupted them again.

It was the thickset policeman, Sergeant Cuff. "Well, Mr. Dickens . . . for someone who did not know the corpse, you seemed to have reached here pretty quickly."

There was a little scream from the girl. She had gone pale, the back of her hand to her mouth, staring at the detective.

Dickens made an irritated clicking noise with his tongue. "Miss Hexton was a friend of Wraybrook," he admonished.

"'E's dead?" cried the girl in a curious wail.

"Murdered, miss," the policeman confirmed without sympathy.

The girl let out another wail and went running out of the room. They heard her ascending the stairs outside.

"Congratulations on your diplomatic touch, Sergeant," Dickens reproved sarcastically.

Sergeant Cuff sniffed. "The girl's a dredger's daughter. Gaffer Hexton. He would rob a corpse without thinking any more about it. In fact, he was going to be one of my next port of calls. He and his daughter probably set Wraybrook up to be done in, if they didn't do it themselves. Wraybrook was a godsend to these river thieves. Whoever did him in has made themselves a fortune."

Dickens frowned. "You seem very positive that it was a robbery." Then he started. "You've just implied that you knew Wraybrook and knew that he had something of value on him. Look around you, Sergeant Cuff. Would a rich man be living in these frugal rooms?"

Sergeant Cuff had a superior smile. "We're not stupid in the force, Mr. Dickens. Of course I knew Wraybrook. Been watching him for some months. I recognized the body at once but had to wait for a constable to arrive before I came on here. I suppose that you haven't touched anything?"

"Nothing to touch," retorted Dickens in irritation.

"I don't suppose there would be. How did you come to know Wraybrook?"

"I didn't. His name was on his shirt collar. A laundry mark. I deduced he was a solicitor by the cut of his cloth and went to look him up in *Kelly's*. Miss Mary at the Grapes saved me the trouble as she knew of a Eugene Wraybrook and indicated where he lived. It was as simple as that."

"Very clever. Had you confided in me that you had seen the name, I would have saved you the trouble of coming along. Wraybrook arrived in London six months ago from India. We had word from the constabulary in Bombay that Wraybrook was suspected of a theft from one of the Hindu temples. The theft was of a large diamond that had been one of the eyes in the statute of some hea-thenish idol. But while he was suspected, there was no firm evidence to arrest the man. He was allowed to travel to England, and we were asked to keep a watch on him. It was expected that he would try to sell the diamond and make capital on it. He was a clever cove, Mr. Dickens. I suppose, being a solicitor and all, he was careful. Settled in these rooms and plied for business. Not much business, I assure you. Seems he was eking out some living from his savings. We're a patient crowd, Mr. Dickens, we watched and waited. But that's all. . . . Until tonight. I guess someone else had found out about the diamond. He must have kept it on his person the whole time, be-cause we searched these rooms several times, unbeknown to him." Sergeant Cuff sighed deeply. "I suspect the girl and Gaffer Hexton, and that's where my steps take me next."

He touched his hat to Dickens and Collins and turned from the room.

Dickens stood rubbing his jaw thoughtfully.

Collins sighed and picked up the lamp. Its crystal hangings tin-kled a little as he did so.

"That's that. I think we should return to our decanter of port."

Dickens was staring at the lamp. There was an odd expression on his face.

"Let's take that lamp into the office where we can have a look at it under the gaslight."

Collins frowned but did not argue.

Dickens stood, appearing to examine the dangling crystals for a while, and then he grunted in satisfaction. He instructed Collins to put the lamp on the table, turn it out, and then he bent forward and wrenched one of the crystals from its slight chain with brute force, wrenching the links of the chain open. He held up the crystal to the gas burner. Then he walked to the window and drew it sharply across the surface. The score mark had almost split the glass pane.

"And that, dear Charley, unless I am a complete moron, is the missing diamond. By heavens, it's quite a big one. No wonder anyone would get light-fingered in proximity to it. I suspect that on the proceeds of a sale to an unscrupulous fence, even allowing for such exorbitant commission that such a person would take, one could live well for the rest of one's life."

His son-in-law frowned. "What made you spot it?"

"Look at the crystals—clear, pure white glass. When this bauble was hanging by them, it emitted a strange yellow luminescence, a curious quality of light. If it was crystal, then it could not be the same crystal, and it is entirely a different shape. Round and yellow. When I peered closely at it just now, I saw that its fitting on the chain was unlike the others. My dear Charley, if you are going to hide something, the best place to hide it is where everyone can see it. Make it a commonplace object. I assure you that nine times out of ten it will not be spotted."

Collins grinned. "I'll tell Wilkie that. My brother likes to know these things."

"Well, let's follow the redoubtable Sergeant Cuff. I think that this will take the main plank out of his theory that Wraybrook was murdered for the sake of the diamond."

As they left the late Eugene Wraybrook's rooms, a thickset man was hurrying down the stairs. He moved so quickly that he collided with Dickens, grunting as he staggered with the impact. Then, without an apology, the man thrust him aside and continued on.

"Mr. Bert Hegeton," muttered Dickens, straightening his coat. "He seems in a great hurry. Oops. I think he's dropped something."

Indeed, a small thin leather covering of no more than two and a half inches by three and a half inches lay on the top stair where it had fallen from the man's pocket.

"What is it?" asked Collins.

Dickens bent and retrieved it. "A card case, that's all. Visiting cards. Not the sort of thing one would expect a schoolteacher in this area to have." He was about to put it on the wooden three-cornered stand in the corner of the landing when he paused and drew out the small pieces of white cardboard inside. He grimaced and showed one to Collins.

They were cheaply printed and bore the same legend as on the handwritten pasteboard on Wraybrook's door. Dickens smiled grimly.

They ascended the stairs. They could hear Sergeant Cuff's gruff tones and Beth Hexton's sobbing replies.

Sergeant Cuff looked annoyed when they entered the room unannounced.

"You'll excuse me, Sergeant." Dickens smiled, turning directly to the girl. "Does Mr. Hegeton live in this tenement?"

The girl stared at him from a tearstained face.

"Mr. Dickens . . . ," began the sergeant indignantly, but Dickens cut him short with a gesture. "I need an answer," he said firmly.

"On the next floor above this," the girl said, trying to regain some of her composure.

"A jealous type?"

"Jealous?"

"Come, Miss Hexton. You said that he was attracted to you and you rejected him. Isn't that so? In turn, you were attracted to Mr. Wraybrook?"

The girl nodded. "Gene was a gen'leman."

"So you have told us. But Bert Hegeton was not?"

"He was a beast. Yes, he and Gene had an argument this morning over me." Her eyes suddenly widened. "Bert said he would do for Gene. 'E said that. Told Gene that he wouldn't stand for him pinching 'is girl. I was never Bert's girl. Straight out, I wasn't."

Sergeant Cuff was shaking his head. "Come, Mr. Dickens, this won't do at all. We know that whoever killed Wraybrook robbed him and the cause was—"

He stopped because Dickens was holding out his hand toward him. On his palm lay the diamond.

"It was where we could all see it, in the crystals of the lamp," explained Collins.

Dickens then held out the visiting card case. "Hegeton just brushed past me on the stairs and dropped this. I think he killed Wraybrook in a jealous passion, removed certain items from the corpse to make it look like the work of dredgers, and left him in the river. He came back here, and then he found Sergeant Cuff and us in the house and panicked. Instead of hiding the things that he had taken from the body in his room, he decided to go to dispose of them in the river. Fortunately, for you, Cuff, he dropped Wraybrook's visitor's cards on the way out."

He paused while Sergeant Cuff digested his words.

"Jealousy, over the girl?"

"Exactly so."

Sergeant Cuff was thoughtful.

There came the sound of footsteps ascending.

"Then we won't have long to see if your theory is a reality," Sergeant Cuff said grimly. "I have had a couple of constables outside with strict orders not to let anyone leave the house until I gave permission. If Hegeton has Wraybrook's personal possessions on him, then he would have been unable to discard them, and he should still have them on him now."

They turned as a police constable came through the door, ushering the white-faced Hegeton before him.

"What's all this?" he cried angrily. "You can't—"

"I can and I do," Sergeant Cuff said calmly. "Empty your pockets."

Hegeton needed a little persuasion, but after a short while a number of items lay on the table before him, including a silver hunter watch.

Cuff picked it up and glanced at it. "Bert Hegeton? That's your name?"

The thickset man nodded resentfully.

"Then you would not be bearing the initials *EW*, would you. The inscription on the watch is 'EW from his friends, Advocates Club. Bombay.' You are right, Mr. Dickens. This is our man."

Beth Hexton gave a little scream and lunged toward the school-teacher but was held back by Sergeant Cuff.

"You killed him, you swine. You killed him!" she cried.

Bert Hegeton turned a pleading face to her. "I did it to protect you, Beth. He wouldn't marry you. Not him with his high-and-mighty airs. He only wanted one thing. He would have discarded you after that. I love you, Beth. I—"

The girl again leaped forward, beating at him with her fists.

The constable and Sergeant Cuff separated them.

Half an hour later Dickens and Collins were back in the Cozy of the Grapes, sipping their port. Dickens had been frowning in concentration ever since they had returned. Suddenly his features dissolved into a rare smile of satisfaction.

"Damn it, Charley! I can feed parts of this little drama into my book and use it to make the tale come alive."

Collins was cautious. "You'll need to change the names, surely?"

"Nothing simpler. Bert Hegeton now . . ." Dickens paused in thought. "Why, I do believe that is easy enough. *Hegeton* in Old English means a place without a hedge. Do you know there is such a place name in the county of Middlesex, which has now been corrupted into the name Headstone? So let us have Bert . . . no Bradley, sounds more distinguished, Bradley Headstone." He smiled in satisfaction.

"Eugene Wraybrook?" queried his son-in-law.

"Even easier. Just change the ending of Wraybrook into another word meaning exactly the same thing—*brook* becomes *burn*. Wrayburn. The name still means the place of the remote stream."

Collins grinned. His father-in-law enjoyed etymology and playing with words. "So what about poor Beth Hexton?"

"Beth is Elizabeth, so we make her Lizzie. Hexton can become Hexam. And there we have my new characters. I can get on now, build up some enthusiasm about rewriting my book. I can even bring in Beth's father, the dredger. Gaffer Hexam. Ah, to hell with those critics who would say my work is becoming full of dry moral rectitude. Away with such shadows."

He struck a pose. Collins knew that his father-in-law liked to perform.

> Hence, horrible shadow.
> Unreal mockery, hence. Why, so being gone.
> I am a man again.

Collins nodded slowly. "Well, there was no detective needed in *Macbeth,* but this has, indeed, been a neat piece of detection."

"These shadows passing before us, Charley, are the substance of the writer's craft," mused Dickens. "You can let time slip by you with its shadows, who have the agility of a fox, now you see them, now you don't. The writer must capture them before they disappear. Mind you, I think I can dispense with the character of Sergeant Cuff."

Charles Collins grimaced. "I felt sorry for poor Sergeant Cuff, off on the wrong track about the diamond and the reason for the murder." He suddenly grinned. "I'll have to tell this story to my brother, Wilkie. He's been saying that he wants to write a novel in which a policeman is called upon to solve a theft of some enormous diamond and subsequent murders. This might give him some ideas."

Dickens chuckled with a shake of his head. "A policeman solving crimes of theft and murder in a novel? I'll have to have a word with your brother. No one will believe a policeman as a detective hero."

"I seem to recall that when Sir James Graham set up his detective department twenty years ago, it was you who used your campaigning journalism to break down public hostility to having a dozen Metropolitan Police sergeants working among them in plain clothes solving crimes."

Dickens pursed his lips in irritation. "That's different," he snapped. "You are talking about a police detective in a novel. The reading public will never buy such a book."

THE AFFRAY AT
— THE KILDARE STREET CLUB —

My narratives of the adventures of Mr. Sherlock Holmes, the well-known consulting detective, have always attempted a modicum of discreetness. There is so much of both a personal and professional nature that Holmes confided in me which I have not passed on to posterity—much, I confess, at Holmes's personal request. Indeed, among Holmes's personal papers, I had noticed several aide-mémoirs that would have expanded my sketches of his cases several times over. It is not often appreciated that while I indulged in my literary diversions, Holmes himself was possessed of a writing talent as demonstrated by over a score of works ranging from his *Practical Handbook of Bee Culture* to *The Book of Life: the science of observation and deduction.* But Holmes, to my knowledge, had made it a rule never to write about any of his specific cases.

It was therefore with some surprise that, one day during the spring of 1894, after the adventure I narrated as "The Empty House," I received from Holmes a small sheaf of handwritten papers with the exhortation that I read them in order that I might understand more fully Holmes's involvement with the man responsible for the death of the son of Lord Maynooth. Holmes, of course, did not want these details to be revealed to the public. I did acquire permission from him at a later date to the effect that they could be published after his death. In the meantime, I have appended this brief foreword to be placed with the papers and handed both to my bankers and executors with the instruction that they may be released only one hundred years from this date.

It may, then, also be revealed a matter that I have always been sensitive about, in view of the prejudices of our age. Sherlock Holmes was one of the Holmes family of Galway, Ireland, and, like his brother, Mycroft, was a graduate of Trinity College, Dublin, where his closest companion had been the poet Oscar Fingal O'Flahertie Wills Wilde, who even now, as I write, languishes in Reading Gaol. This is the principal reason why I have been reticent about acknowledging Holmes's background, for it would serve no useful purpose if one fell foul of the bigotry and intolerance that arises out of such a revelation. Many good men and true, but with such backgrounds, have found themselves being shunned by their professions or found their businesses have been destroyed overnight.

This revelation will probably come as no surprise to those discerning readers who have followed Holmes's adventures. There have been clues enough of Holmes's origins. Holmes's greatest adversary, James Moriarty, was of a similar background. Most people will know that the Moriarty family are from Kerry, the very name being an Anglicization of the Irish name Ó Muircheartaigh, meaning, interestingly enough, "expert navigator." Moriarty once held a chair of mathematics in Queen's University in Belfast. It was in Ireland that the enmity between Holmes and Moriarty first started. But that is a story which does not concern us.

If there were not clues enough, there was also Holmes's fascination with the Celtic languages, of which he was something of an expert. In my narrative "The Devil's Foot," I mentioned Holmes's study on *Chaldean Roots in the Ancient Cornish Language*. I did not mention that this work won high praise from such experts as the British Museum's Henry Jenner, the greatest living expert on the Cornish language. Holmes was able to demonstrate the close connection between the Cornish verb and the Irish verb systems.

The Holmes family were well known in Galway. Indeed, it was

Holmes's uncle, Robert Holmes, the famous Galway barrister and Queen's Counsel, whom the Irish have to thank for the organization of the Irish National School system for the poorer classes, for he was a member of the Duke of Leinster's seven-man education commission in the 1830s and 1840s, responsible for many innovative ideas.

These few brief words will demonstrate, therefore, the significance of this aide-mémoire, which Holmes passed to me in the spring of 1894.

My initial encounter with my second most dangerous adversary happened when I was lunching with my brother, Mycroft, in the Kildare Street Club, in Dublin, during September of 1873. I was barely twenty years old at the time, and thoughts of a possible career as a consulting detective had not yet formulated in my mind. In fact, my mind was fully occupied by the fact that I would momentarily be embarking for England, where I had won a demyship at one of the Oxford Colleges with the grand sum of 95 pounds per annum.

I had won the scholarship having spent my time at Trinity College, Dublin, in the study of chemistry and botany. My knowledge of chemistry owed much to a great Trinity scholar, Maxwell Simpson, whose lectures at the Park Street Medical School advanced my knowledge of organic chemistry considerably. Simpson was the first man to synthesize succinic acid, a dibasic acid obtained by the dry distillation of amber. It was thanks to this great countryman of mine that I had produced a dissertation thought laudable enough to win me the scholarship to Oxford.

Indeed, I was not the only Trinity man to be awarded a demyship to Oxford that year. My friend, Wilde, a brilliant Classicist, a field for which I had no aptitude at all, was also to pursue his education there. Wilde continually berated me for my fascination with sensational literature and one day promised that he would write a horror story about a portrait that would chill even me.

My brother, Mycroft, who, like most of the Holmes family of

Galway, was also a product of Trinity, had invited me to lunch at the Kildare Street Club. Mycroft, being seven years older than I, had already established his career in the Civil Service and was working in the fiscal department of the Chief Secretary for Ireland in Dublin Castle. He could, therefore, afford the 10 pounds per annum, which gave him access to the opulence of the red brick Gothic-style headquarters of the Kildare Street Club.

The club was the center of masculine Ascendancy life in Ireland. Perhaps I should explain that these were the Anglo-Irish elite, descendants of those families that England had dispatched to Ireland to rule the unruly natives. The club was exclusive to members of the most important families in Ireland. No "Home Rulers," Catholics nor Dissenters were allowed in membership. The rule against Catholics was, however, "bent" in the case of the O'Conor Don, a direct descendant of the last High King of Ireland, and a few religious recalcitrants, such as the earls of Westmeath, Granard, and Kenmare, whose loyalty to England had been proved to be impeccable. No army officer below the rank of major, nor below a naval lieutenant-commander was allowed within its portals. And the only people allowed free use of its facilities were visiting members of the Royal Family, their equerries and the viceroy himself.

My brother, Mycroft, basked and prospered in this colonial splendor, but I confess, it was not to my taste. I had been accepted within this elite sanctuary as guest of Mycroft only, who was known as a confidant of the Chief Secretary and therefore regarded as having the ear of the viceroy himself. I had been persuaded to go only because Mycroft wished to celebrate my demyship and see me off to Oxford in fraternal fashion. I did not want to disappoint him.

The dining room of the club was truly luxuriant. The club had the reputation of providing the best table in Dublin.

A solemn-faced waiter, more like an undertaker, led us through the splendidly furnished dining room to a table in a bay window overlooking St. Stephen's Green, for the club stood on the corner of Kildare Street and the green itself

"An aperitif, gentlemen?" intoned the waiter in a sepulchral voice.

Mycroft took the opportunity to inform me that the cellar was of excellent quality, particularly the stock of champagne. I replied that I believed that I would commence with a glass of sherry and chose a Palo Cortaldo while Mycroft, extravagantly, insisted on a half bottle of Diamant Bleu.

He also insisted on a dozen oysters, which I observed cost an entire shilling a dozen, and were apparently sent daily from the club's own oyster bed near Galway. I settled for pâté de foie gras and we both agreed to indulge in a steak with a bottle of Bordeaux, a rich red St. Estèphe from the Château MacCarthy.

In truth, Mycroft was more of a gourmand than a gourmet. He was physically lazy and already there was a corpulent aspect to his large frame. But he also had the Holmes's brow, the alert, steel-gray, deepset eyes, and firmness of lips. He had an astute mind and was a formidable chess player.

After we had made our choice, we settled down, and I was able to observe our fellow diners.

Among those who caught my immediate eye was a dark-haired man who, doubtless, had been handsome in his youth. He was now in his mid-thirties, and his features were fleshy and gave him an air of dissoluteness and degeneracy. He carried himself with the air of a military man, even as he slouched at his table imbibing his wine, a little too freely, I fear. His discerning brow was offset by the sensual jaw. I was aware of cruel blue eyes; drooping, cynical lids; and an aggressive manner even while seated in repose. He was immaculately dressed in a smart dark coat and cravat with a diamond pin that announced expensive tastes.

His companion appeared less governed by the grape than he, preferring coffee to round off his luncheon. This second man was tall and thin, his forehead domed out in a white curve, and his two eyes deeply sunken in his head. I would have placed him about the same age as his associate. He was clean-shaven, pale, and ascetic looking. A greater contrast between two men, I could not imagine.

The scholarly man was talking earnestly, and his military companion nodded from time to time, as if displeased at being disturbed in his contemplation of his wineglass. The other man, I saw, had rounded shoulders, and his face protruded forward. I observed that his head oscillated from side to side in a curious reptilian fashion.

"Mycroft," I asked after a while, "who is that curious pair?"

Mycroft glanced in the direction I had indicated. "Oh, I would have thought you knew one of them—you being interested in science and such like."

I hid my impatience from my brother. "I do not know; otherwise, I would not have put forward the question."

"The elder is Professor Moriarty."

At once I was interested. "Moriarty of Queen's University, in Belfast?" I demanded.

"The same Professor Moriarty," confirmed Mycroft smugly.

I had at least heard of Moriarty, for he had the chair of mathematics at Queen's and written *The Dynamics of an Asteroid,* which ascended to such rarefied heights of pure mathematics that no man in the scientific press was capable of criticizing it.

"And the man who loves his alcohol so much?" I pressed. "Who is he?"

Mycroft was disapproving of my observation. "Dash it, Sherlock, where else may a man make free with his vices but in the shelter of his club?"

"There is one vice that he cannot well hide," I replied slyly. "That is his colossal male vanity. That black hair of his is no natural color. The man dyes his hair. But, Mycroft, you have not answered my question. His name?"

"Colonel Sebastian Moran."

"I've never heard of him."

"He is one of the Morans of Connacht."

"A Catholic family?" For Ó Mórain, to give the name its correct Irish form, which meant "great," were a well-known Jacobite clan in Connacht.

"Hardly so," rebuked Mycroft. "His branch converted to the Anglican faith after the Williamite conquest. Sebastian Moran's father was Sir Augustus Moran CB, once British Minister to Persia. Young Moran went through Eton and Oxford. The family estate was near Derrynacleigh but I believe, after the colonel inherited, he lost it in a card game. He was a rather impecunious young man. Still, he was able to buy a commission in the Indian Army and served in the First Bengalore Pioneers. He has spent most of his career in India. I understand that he has quite a reputation as a big-game hunter. The Bengal tiger mounted in the hall, as we came in, was one of his kills. The story is that he crawled down a drain after it when he had wounded it. That takes an iron nerve."

I frowned. "Nerve, vanity, and a fondness for drink and cards is sometimes an unenviable combination. They make a curious pair."

"I don't follow you?"

"I mean, a professor of mathematics and a dissolute army officer lunching together. What can they have in common?"

I allowed my attention to occupy the problem but a moment more. Even at this young age I had come to the conclusion that until one has facts, it is worthless wasting time trying to hazard guesses.

My eye turned to the others in the dining room. Some I knew by sight, and one or two I had previously been introduced to in Mycroft's company. Among these diners was Lord Rosse, who had erected the largest reflecting telescope in the world at his home in Birr Castle. There was also the hard-drinking Viscount Massereene and Ferrard and the equally indulgent Lord Clonmell. There was great hilarity from another table where four young men were seated, voices raised in good-natured argument. I had little difficulty recognizing the Beresford brothers of Curraghmore, the elder of them being the Marquess of Waterford.

My eye eventually came to rest on a corner table where an elderly man with silver hair and round chubby red features was seated. He was well dressed, and the waiters constantly hovered at his elbow to attend to his bidding like moths to a fly. He was obviously someone of importance.

I asked Mycroft to identify him.

"The Duke of Cloncury and Straffan," he said, naming one of the premier peers of Ireland.

I turned back to examine His Grace, whose ancestors had once controlled Ireland, with some curiosity. It was said that a word from Cloncury's grandfather could sway the vote in any debate in the old Irish Parliament; that was before the Union with England. As I was unashamedly scrutinizing him, His Grace was helped from his chair. He was, I judged, about seventy-something years of age, a short, stocky man but one who was fastidious in his toilet, for his mustache was well cut and his hair neatly brushed so that not a silver strand of it was out of place.

He retrieved a small polished leather case, the size of a dispatch-box, not more than twelve inches by six by four. It bore a crest in silver on it, and I presumed it to be Cloncury's own crest.

His Grace, clutching his case, made toward the door. At the same time, I saw Professor Moriarty push back his chair. Some sharp words were being exchanged between the professor and his lunching companion, Colonel Moran. The professor swung round and marched swiftly to the door, almost colliding with the elderly duke at their portals. At the last moment, when collision seemed inevitable, the professor halted and allowed His Grace to move through the doors before him.

"Some argument has taken place between the professor and his companion," I observed aloud. "I wonder what the meaning of it is?"

Mycroft looked at me in disgust. "Really, Sherlock, you always seem to be prying into other people's affairs. I would have thought you had enough on your plate preparing for your studies at Oxford."

Even at this time, I had become a close observer of people's behavior, and it is without any sense of shame that I record my surveillance into the lives of my fellow luncheon-room occupants.

I returned my attention to the colonel, who was sitting looking disgruntled at his wineglass. A waiter hovered near and made some suggestion, but Moran swung with an angry retort, indicating the empty wine bottle on the table, and the waiter backed away. The colonel stood up, went through the motions of brushing the sleeves of his coat, and strode out of the dining room. I noticed that he would be returning, for he had left his glass of wine unfinished. Sure enough, the waiter returned to the table with a half-bottle of wine uncorked and placed it ready. The colonel, presumably having gone to make some ablutions, returned after some fifteen minutes and reseated himself. He seemed in a better mood, for he was smiling to himself.

I was distracted to find that my brother was continuing to lecture me. "I know you, Sherlock. You are an extremely lazy and undisciplined fellow. If a subject doesn't interest you, you just ignore it. It is a wonder that you have achieved this demyship, for I did not expect you to gain a degree at all."

I turned to my elder brother with a chuckle. "Because we are brothers, Mycroft, we do not have to share the same concerns. Your problem is your love of good food and wine. You are an indulger, Mycroft, and physical inertia will cause the body to rebel one of these days." I spoke with some conceit, for during my time at Trinity I had taken several cups for swordsmanship, for boxing, and was acknowledged a tolerable singlestick player.

"But you must consider what you will do with your career, Sherlock. Our family have always been in government service, law, or academic spheres. I fear you will fail your qualifications because of being so easily distracted by minutia."

"But minutia is important in life . . . ," I began.

At that moment we were interrupted by a disturbance at the door of the dining room.

The pale-faced waiter hurried into the room and made his way to where the elderly Duke of Cloncury and Straffan had been sitting. I watched in bemusement as the man first scrutinized the table carefully, then the top of the seats around the table, and then—I have never witnessed such a thing before—the waiter actually went on his knees and examined under the table before, finally, his cadaverous features slightly reddened by his exertions, he hurried back to the door, where the head waiter had now entered and stood with a troubled face.

There was a lot of shaking of heads and shrugs that passed between the two. The head waiter left the room.

As the waiter who had conducted the search was passing our table, I hailed the fellow, much to Mycroft's astonished disapproval.

"Has His Grace mislaid something?" I queried.

The waiter, the same individual who had conducted us to our table when we entered, turned mournful eyes upon me. There was a glint of suspicion in them. "Indeed, he has, sir. How did you know?"

"I observed that you were searching on and around the table where he had recently been seated. From that, one deduces that he had lost something that he thought he had with him at that table."

The man's gaze fell in disappointment at the logic of my reply.

"What has he lost?" I pressed.

"His toilet case, sir."

Mycroft gave an ill-concealed guffaw. "A toilet case? What is a man doing bringing a toilet case into a dining room?"

The waiter turned to Mycroft. "His Grace is a very fastidious

and eccentric person, Mr. Holmes." The man evidently knew Mycroft by sight "He carries the case with him always."

"A valuable item?" I hazarded.

"Not really, sir. At least, not financially so."

"Ah, you mean it has great sentimental value for the Duke?" I
suggested.

"It was a gift which King William gave to one of His Grace's ancestors as a personal memento when the man saved his life during
the battle at the Boyne. And now, gentlemen, if you have not seen
the item . . ."

He went on his way.

Mycroft was passing his napkin over his mouth, "Now how
about a port or brandy in the hall?"

The lofty hall of the club, with its big-game trophies and blazing fire and staircase of elaborately carved stonework, was where
members gathered for their after-luncheon drinks and cigars.

We rose and made our way out of the dining room. Our path led
us by the table of Colonel Moran, and as we passed by I noticed that
the colonel's dark suit was ill chosen, for it showed up his dandruff. I
grant you it is such small observations that sometimes irritate my
fellows. But if one is prone to dandruff, at least one should have the
good sense to wear a light color in which the telltale white powder
and silver hairs would be less noticeable.

As we made our way into the hall, we saw the elderly Duke of
Cloncury and Straffan standing with the head waiter and a gentleman who Mycroft informed me was the chairman of the directors
of the club.

His Grace was clearly distressed. "It is priceless! A value beyond
measure!" He was almost wailing.

"I cannot understand it, Your Grace. Are you sure that you had
it with you in the dining room?"

"Young man," snapped the elderly duke, "do you accuse me of
senility?"

The "young man," who was about fifty years of age, blanched and took a step backward before the old man's baleful gaze. "Not at all, Your Grace, not at all. Just tell me the facts again."

"After finishing my luncheon, I went into the washroom. I washed my hands and then brushed my hair. It is my custom to do so after luncheon. I took my silver hairbrush from my leather case, which I always carry with me. I remember clearly that I returned it to the case. I left the case on the washstand and went into the toilet. I came out, washed my hand, and then realized that the case was no longer there."

The head waiter was looking glum. "I have already suggested to His Grace that the case might have been left in the dining room and sent one of the waiters to check. It was not there."

The old man bristled. "Knew it would be a damned waste of time. Said so. I know where it went missing. I'd start interrogating your employees, sir. At once!"

The club chairman looked unhappy. "Your Grace, please allow us time to search the premises before we start anything so drastic. Perhaps it has simply been mislaid? . . ."

"Mislaid!" The word was an explosion. "Dammit! Mislaid! Do you take me for a fool, sir? I demand that an interrogation of your employees begin at once. I suggest that you now send for the DMP!"

The mention of the Dublin Metropolitan Police had made the chairman slightly pale. "Your Grace, the reflection on our reputa-tion—"

"Damn your reputation, sir! What about my hairbrush!" quiv-ered the old man.

It was then I felt I should intervene. "Excuse me, Your Grace," I began.

Rheumy blue eyes turned on me and assessed my youthful years. And who the devil are you, sir?"

"My name is Holmes. I might be able to help you."

"You, you young jackanapes? What do you mean?"

I heard my brother tut-tutting anxiously in the background at my effrontery.

"With your permission, I think I might be in a position to recover the lost item."

Cloncury's eyes narrowed dangerously. "Do you have it, you impudent whippersnapper?" he demanded. "By God, if you are responsible . . . "

Mycroft came to my help. "Excuse me, Your Grace, this is my younger brother, Sherlock Holmes."

Cloncury glanced up and recognized Mycroft, knowing him to have the ear of the viceroy. He looked slightly mollified. "Why didn't he introduce himself properly then, hey? Very well, young Holmes, what do you mean by it?"

"With your permission, sir," I went on, unperturbed, "I would like to put a few questions to the chairman of the club."

The chairman began to flush in annoyance.

"Go ahead, then, Mr. Holmes," instructed Cloncury. "I am sure that the chairman will be in favor of anything that stops the incursion of the police into this establishment."

It seemed that the chairman, albeit reluctantly, was in favor.

"Well, sir, if I remember correctly, the washroom is next to the cloakroom, is it not?"

"Yes."

"Is the washroom attended?"

"It is not."

"And the cloakroom? Is it attended at all times?"

"Of course it is."

"Your Grace, will you be so good as to show me where it was that you left your toilet box?"

We turned in a body, headed by the duke, and passed into the washroom. He pointed to one of the ornate marble washbasins at the far end of the room. It was one of a dozen such washbasins lining the entire left-hand-side wall of the chamber, which was fronted by a series of mirrors for the use of the members. The right-hand-side wall was fitted with toilet cubicles in dark mahogany and brass fittings, except for a small area behind the main door. The marble-tiled wall here was unimpeded by anything except for a small opening. It was about two feet square, framed in mahogany and with a hatch door.

I pointed to it. "I presume that this hatch connects the washroom with the cloakroom?"

"Naturally," barked the chairman. "Now what is all this about?"

I turned and led them out of the washroom and into the cloakroom, where a uniformed attendant leaped from his chair, dropping a half-smoked cigarette into an ashtray and looking penitently from one to another of us.

"Can I help you gentlemen?" he stuttered.

"Yes, you can," I assured him. "You can bring me the garment that you are holding for Colonel Sebastian Moran. I think you will find that it is a heavy riding cloak or one of those new-style long, loose coats which, I believe, is called an Ulster."

The attendant returned my gaze in bewildered fashion.

The chairman pushed forward. "Good God, sir, what do you mean by it? Colonel Moran is a respected member of this club. Why are you presuming to ask for his coat?"

The Duke of Cloncury was looking at me with a frown of disapproval. "You'd better have a good explanation, young Holmes," he muttered.

"I believe that you want the return of your toilet case?" I asked blandly.

"Gad, you know I do."

I turned to the attendant. "Have you been on duty for the last half an hour?"

"That I have, sir."

"A short while ago, Colonel Moran knocked on the hatch from the washroom side and asked if you could pass him his coat for a moment. Is that correct?"

The man's jaw dropped in astonishment. "It is, sir. He said he wanted to comb his hair and had left the toilet items in his coat. And the coat was, indeed, one of those new-style Ulsters, sir."

"I believe the colonel then came around from the washroom, into the cloakroom, in order to hand you back the coat?"

"That is exactly what he did, sir."

I turned and smiled at the astonished company, perhaps a little too superior in my attitude.

"How the hell did you know that?" growled the chairman.

"Now, my man," I said, ignoring him but speaking again to the attendant. "Would you fetch Colonel Moran's Ulster?"

The attendant turned, picked down the garment, and handed it to me in silence.

I took it and weighed it carefully with one hand before reaching into the inside lining. There were several large pockets there as was the fashion with such garments. The leather box was tucked neatly into one of them.

"How did you know?" gasped Cloncury, seizing his precious box eagerly.

"Know? I merely deduce from facts, sir. If you will open the box and check the brush? I think you may find that in the brush are some strands of dark black hair. The color of Colonel Moran's hair, which is easy to spot, as it is dyed."

It took the duke but a moment to confirm that I was right.

"I think the colonel is someone given to seizing opportunity. A chance taker," I told them. "He followed His Grace into the washroom when His Grace had already entered the toilet. He saw the leather case there. He knew it had great sentimental value for His Grace. Perhaps he thought he might be able to blackmail Cloncury for its return, probably through an intermediary, of course. He seized the opportunity, asking for his Ulster to be passed through the hatch in order to conceal the box in order to get it out of the club. He chanced that members would not be searched. . . ."

"It would be unthinkable that a member of this club would be searched," muttered the chairman. "We are all gentlemen here!"

I chose not to comment. "He could not carry the box out of the washroom into the cloakroom without observation. When I saw the hatch, I knew that he had only to ask for his coat to be passed through, place the box in his pocket unobserved, and the theft was complete."

"How did you know it was an Ulster or a riding cloak?" demanded His Grace.

"He would have to be possessed of a heavy coat such as an Ulster or riding cloak with large enough interior pockets to conceal the box in."

"Why not pass the coat back through the hatch once he had hidden the box in the coat?" demanded Mycroft. "Why do you think that he came out of the washroom door, into the hall, and then into the cloakroom to return the cloak to the attendant?"

"Moran was cautious. Passing it back through the hatch might cause the attendant to feel the box and become suspicious, especially after Cloncury raised the alarm. So he carried it round and handed it to the attendant holding it upright by the collar. The extra weight would not be noticed. Is that correct?"

The attendant nodded confirmation.

"What made you think there would be hairs on the brush and that they would be his?" queried His Grace, staring dubiously at the black dyed hairs that were entangled on his silver-backed brush.

"Because Moran is a vain man and could not resist cocking a snoot at you, Your Grace, by brushing his own hair while you were within feet of him. It fits in with Moran's character, a demonstration of his nerve, for any moment you might have opened the door and discovered him. Chance is his adrenaline."

"Holmes, this is amazing!" gasped Cloncury.

"It was another Trinity man who alerted me to the importance of careful observation," I informed him. "Jonathan Swift. He wrote that a stander-by may sometimes see more of the game than he who plays it." I could not resist turning to Mycroft and adding, sotto voce, "And Trinity almost refused to give Swift a degree because they thought he was too lazy and undisciplined!"

The chairman of the club signaled the uniformed club doorman and his assistant. They looked ex-military men.

"You will find Colonel Moran in the dining room," he instructed. "Ask him to join us immediately. If he will not comply, you have my permission to escort him here with as much force as you have cause to use."

The two men went off briskly about their task.

A moment later, the colonel, whose appearance suggested that he had polished off the rest of the wine, was firmly propelled into our presence.

His red-rimmed eyes fell on his Ulster and on Cloncury holding his precious leather case. The man's face went white in spite of the alcoholic infused cheeks.

"By Gad, sir, you should be horsewhipped!" growled the Duke of Cloncury and Straffan menacingly.

"This is a fabrication!" bluffed Moran feebly. "Someone put the box in my inside coat pocket."

I could not forbear a grin of triumph. "How did you know that it was the box which had been stolen? And how did you know it was found in your *inside* coat pocket, Colonel?"

Moran knew the game was up.

"Moran," the chairman said heavily, "I shall try to persuade His Grace not to bring charges against you for the sake of the reputation of this club. If he agrees, it will be on the condition that you leave Ireland within the next twelve hours and never return. I will circulate your name in society so that no house will open its doors to you again. I will have you blackballed in every club in the land."

The Duke of Cloncury and Straffan gave the matter a moment's thought and then agreed to the conditions. "I'd horsewhip the beggar, if it were me. Anyway. I think we all owe young Mr. Sherlock Holmes our thanks in resolving this matter."

Moran glowered at me. "So you tipped them off, you young interfering—" He made a sudden aggressive lunge at me.

Mycroft inserted his large frame between me and Moran. His fist impacted on the colonel's nose, and Moran went sprawling back, only to be neatly caught by the doorman and his assistant.

"Kindly escort Colonel Moran off the premises, gentlemen," ordered the chairman, "and you do not have to be gentle."

Moran twisted in their grasp to look back at me with little option but to control his foul temper.

"I have your measure, Sherlock Holmes," he glowered, seething with an inner rage as they began to propel him toward the door. "You have not heard the last of me."

It was as Mycroft was sharing a cab in the direction of my rooms in Lower Baggott Street that he frowned and posed the question: "But I cannot see how you could have identified Moran as the culprit in the first place."

"It was elementary, Mycroft." I smiled. "When we left the luncheon room and passed behind Moran's chair, I saw that the colonel had dandruff on his shoulders. Now he had jet-black hair. But with the dandruff lay a number of silver strands. It meant nothing to me at the time, for I was not aware of the facts. When I discovered that the missing case contained a hairbrush and comb, everything fell into place. The duke not only had silver hair, but, I noticed, he also had dandruff to boot. By brushing his hair in such a foolhardy gesture, Moran had transferred the dandruff and silver hair to his own shoulders. It was easy to witness that Moran was a vain man. He would not have allowed dandruff and hair, if it had been his, to lie on his shoulders when he entered a public dining room. Indeed, I saw him rise from his table and go out, brushing himself as he did so. The sign of a fastidious man. He had, therefore, unknowingly picked it up during his short absence. Everything else was a matter of simple deduction."

As Moran had been thrown out of the Kildare Street Club, he had called out to me that I had not heard the last of him. Indeed, I had not. But I could not have conceived of how our paths would meet at that time, nor of the sinister role Moran's friend, Professor Moriarty, would play in my life. While Moriarty became my most implacable foe, Colonel Sebastian Moran was certainly the second most dangerous man that I ever had to deal with.

THE SPECTER OF
━ TULLYFANE ABBEY ━

Somewhere in the vaults of the bank of Cox and Co., at Charing Cross, there is a travel-worn and battered tin dispatch box with my name, John H. Watson MD, Late Indian Army, painted on the lid. It is filled with papers, nearly all of which are records of cases to illustrate the curious problems which Mr. Sherlock Holmes had at various times to examine.

—"The Problem of Thor Bridge"

This is one of those papers.

I must confess that there are few occasions on which I have seen my estimable friend, Sherlock Holmes, the famous consulting detective, in a state of some agitation. He is usually so detached that the word *calm* seems unfit to describe his general demeanor. Yet I had called upon him one evening to learn his opinion of a manuscript draft account I had made of one of his cases which I had titled "The Problem of Thor Bridge."

To my surprise, I found him seated in an attitude of tension in his armchair, his pipe unlit, his long pale fingers clutching my handwritten pages, and his brows drawn together in disapproval. "Confound it, Watson," he greeted me sharply as I came through the door. "Must you show me up to public ridicule in this fashion?"

I was, admittedly, somewhat taken aback at his uncharacteristic greeting. "I rather thought you came well out of the story," I replied defensively. "After all, you helped a remarkable woman, as you yourself observed, while, as for Mr. Gibson, I believe that he did learn an object lesson—"

He cut me short. "Tush! I do not mean the case of Grace Dunbar, which, since you refer to it, was not as glamorous as your imaginative pen elaborates on. No, Watson, no! It is here"—he waved the papers at me—"here in your cumbersome preamble. You speak of some of my unsolved cases as if they were failures. I only mentioned them to you in passing, and now you tell me, and the readers of the *Strand Magazine,* that you have noted them down and deposited the record in that odious little tin dispatch box placed in Cox's Bank."

"I did not think that you would have reason to object, Holmes," I replied with some vexation.

He waved a hand as if dismissing my feelings. "I object to the manner in which you reveal these cases! I read here, and I quote . . ." He peered shortsightedly at my manuscript. "'Some, and not the least interesting, were complete failures, and as such will hardly bear narrating, since no final explanation is forthcoming. A problem without a solution may interest the student, but can hardly fail to annoy the casual reader. Among these unfinished tales is that of Mr. James Phillimore, who, stepping back into his own house to get his umbrella, was never more seen in this world.' There!" He glanced up angrily.

"But, Holmes, dear fellow, that is precisely the matter as you told it to me. Where am I in error?"

"The error is making the statement itself. It is incomplete. It is not set into context. The case of James Phillimore, whose title was Colonel, incidentally, occurred when I was a young man. I had just completed my second term at Oxford. It was the first time I crossed foils, so to speak, with the man who was to cause me such grief later in my career . . . Professor Moriarty."

I started at this intelligence, for Holmes was always unduly reticent about his clashes with James Moriarty, that sinister figure whom Holmes seemed to hold in both contempt as a criminal and regard as an intellect.

"I did not know that, Holmes."

"Neither would you have learned further of the matter, but I find that you have squirreled away a reference to this singular event in which Moriarty achieved the better of me."

"You were bested by Moriarty?" I was now really intrigued.

"Don't sound so surprised, Watson," he admonished. "Even villains can be victorious once in a while." Then Holmes paused and added quietly, "Especially when such a villain as Moriarty enlisted the power of darkness in his nefarious design."

I began to laugh, knowing that Holmes abhorred the supernatural. I remember his outburst when we received the letter from Morrison, Morrison, and Dodd which led us into "The Adventure of the Sussex Vampire." Yet my laughter died on my lips as I caught sight of the ghastly look that crossed Holmes's features. He stared into the dancing flames of the fire as if remembering the occasion.

"I am not in jest, Watson. In this instance, Moriarty employed the forces of darkness to accomplish his evil end. Of that there can be no shadow of doubt. It is the only time that I have failed, utterly and miserably failed, to prevent a terrible tragedy whose memory will curse me to the grave."

Holmes sighed deeply and then appeared to have observed for the first time that his pipe was unlit and reached for the matches.

"Pour two glasses from that decanter of fine Hennessy on the table and sit yourself down. Having come thus far in my confession, I might as well finish the story in case that imagination of yours decides to embellish the little you do know."

"I say, Holmes—," I began to protest, but he went on, ignoring my words.

"I pray you, promise never to reveal this story until my clay has mingled with the earth from which I am sprung."

If there is a preamble to this story, it is one that I was already knowledgeable of and which I have already given some account of in the memoir I entitled "The Affray at the Kildare Street Club." Holmes was one of the Galway Holmes. Like his brother, Mycroft, he had attended Trinity College, Dublin, where he had, in the same year as his friend Oscar Wilde, won a demyship to continue his studies at Oxford. I believe the name Sherlock came from his maternal side, his mother being of another well-established Anglo-Irish family. Holmes was always reticent about this background, although the clues to his Irish origins were obvious to most discerning people. One of his frequent disguises was to assume the name of Altamont as he pretended to be an Irish-American. Altamont was his family seat near Ballysherlock.

Armed with this background knowledge, I settled back with a glass of Holmes's cognac and listened as he recounted a most singular and terrifying tale. I append it exactly as he narrated it to me.

"Having completed my first term at Oxford, I returned to Dublin to stay with my brother Mycroft at his house in Merrion Square. Yet I found myself somewhat at a loose end. There was some panic in the fiscal office of the chief secretary where Mycroft worked. This caused him to be unable to spare the time we had set aside for a fishing expedition. I was therefore persuaded to accompany Abraham Stoker, who had been at Trinity the same year as Mycroft, to the Royal to see some theatrical entertainment. Abraham, or Bram as he preferred to be called, was also a close friend of Sir William and Lady Wilde, who lived just across the square, and with whose younger son, Oscar, I was then at Oxford with.

"Bram was an ambitious man who not only worked with Mycroft at Dublin Castle but wrote theatrical criticism in his spare time and by night edited the *Dublin Halfpenny Press*, a journal which he had only just launched. He was trying to persuade me to write on famous Dublin murders for it, but as he offered no remuneration at all, I gracefully declined.

"We were in the foyer of the Royal when Bram, an amiable, booming giant with red hair, hailed someone over the heads of the throng. A thin, white-faced young man emerged to be clasped warmly by the hand. It was a youth of my own age and well known to me; Jack Phillimore was his name. He had been a fellow student at Trinity College. My heart leaped in expectation, and I searched the throng for a familiar female face which was, I will confess it, most dear to me. But Phillimore was alone. His sister Agnes, was not with him at the theater.

"In the presence of Bram, we fell to exchanging pleasantries about our alma mater. I noticed that Phillimore's heart was not in exchanging such bonhomie nor, to be honest, was mine. I was impatient for the opportunity to inquire after Phillimore's sister. Ah, let the truth be known, Watson, but only after I am not in this world.

"Love, my dear Watson. Love! I believe that you have observed that all emotions, and that one in particular, are abhorrent to my mind. This is true, and since I have become mature enough to understand, I have come to regard it as opposite to that true cold reason which I place above all things. I have never married lest I bias my judgment. Yet it was not always my intention, and this very fact is what led to my downfall, causing the tragedy which I am about to relate. Alas, Watson, if . . . but with an *if* we might place Paris in a bottle.

"As a youth I was deeply in love with Agnes Phillimore who was but a year older than I. When Jack Phillimore and I were in our first year at Trinity, I used to spend time at their town house by Stephen's Green. I confess, it was not the company of Phillimore that I sought then but that of Agnes.

"In my maturity I could come to admire *the* woman, as you insist I call Irene Adler, but admiration is not akin to the deep, destructive emotional power that we call love.

"It was when Bram spotted someone across the foyer that he needed to speak to that Phillimore seized the opportunity to ask abruptly what I was doing for recreation. Hearing that I was at a loose end, he suggested that I accompany him to his father's estate in Kerry for a few days. Colonel James Phillimore owned a large house and estate in that remote county. Phillimore said he was going down because it was his father's fiftieth birthday. I thought at the time that he placed a singular emphasis on that fact.

"It was then that I managed to casually ask if his sister Agnes was in Dublin or in Kerry. Phillimore, of course, like most brothers, was ignorant that his sister held any attraction for the male sex, least of all one of his friends. He was nonchalant. 'To be sure she is at Tullyfane, Holmes. Preparing for her marriage next month.'

"His glance was distracted by a man jostling through the foyer, and so he missed the effect that this intelligence had on me.

"'Married?' I gasped. 'To whom?'

"'Some professor, no less. A cove by the name of Moriarty.'

"'Moriarty?' I asked, for the name meant little to me in that context. I knew it only as a common County Kerry name. It was an Anglicizing of the Irish name Ó Muircheartaigh, meaning 'expert navigator.'

"'He is our neighbor, he is quite besotted with my sister, and it seems that it is arranged that they will marry next month. A rum cove, is the professor. Good education and holds a chair of mathematics at Queen's University in Belfast.'

"'Professor James Moriarty,' I muttered savagely. Phillimore's news of Agnes's intentions had shattered all my illusions.

"'Do you know him?' Phillimore asked, observing my displeasure. 'He's all right, isn't he? I mean . . . he's not a bounder, eh?'

"'I have seen him once only and that from a distance in the Kildare Street Club,' I confessed. I had nothing against Moriarty at that time. 'My brother Mycroft pointed him out to me. I did not meet him. Yet I have heard of his reputation. His *Dynamics of an Asteroid* ascended to such rarefied heights of pure mathematics that no man in the scientific press was capable of criticizing it.'

"Phillimore chuckled.

" 'That is beyond me. Thank God I am merely a student of theology. But it sounds as though you are an admirer.'

" 'I admire intellect, Phillimore,' I replied simply. Moriarty, as I recalled, must have been all of ten years older than Agnes. What is ten years at our age? But to me, a callow youth, I felt the age difference that existed between Agnes and James Moriarty was obscene. I explain this simply because my attitude has a bearing on my future disposition.

" 'So come down with me to Tullyfane Abbey,' pressed Phillimore, oblivious to the emotional turmoil that he had created in me.

"I was about to coldly decline the invitation when Phillimore, observing my negative expression, was suddenly very serious. He leaned closed to me and said softly: 'You see, Holmes, old fellow, we are having increasing problems with the family ghost, and as I recall, you have a canny way of solving bizarre problems.'

"I knew enough of his character to realize that jesting was beyond his capacity.

" 'The family ghost?'

" 'A damned infernal specter that is driving my father quite out of his wits. Not to mention Agnes . . . '

" 'Your father and sister are afraid of a specter?'

" 'Agnes is scared at the deterioration in my father's demeanor. Seriously, Holmes, I really don't know what to do. My sister's letters speak of such a bizarre set of circumstances that I am inclined to think that she is hallucinating or that my father has been driven mad already.'

"My inclination was to avoid opening old wounds now by meeting Agnes again. I could spend the rest of my vacation in Marsh's Library, where they have an excellent collection of medieval cryptogram manuscripts. I hesitated—hesitated and was lost. I had to admit that I was intrigued to hear more of the matter in spite of my emotional distress, for any mystery sends the adrenaline coursing in my body.

"The very next morning I accompanied Jack Phillimore to Kingsbridge Railway Station and boarded the train to Killarney. En route he explained some of the problems.

"Tullyfane Abbey was supposed to be cursed. It was situated on the extremity of the Iveragh Peninsula in a wild and deserted spot. Tullyfane Abbey was, of course, never an abbey. It was a dignified Georgian country house. The Anglo-Irish gentry in the eighteenth century had a taste for the grandiose and called their houses *abbeys* or *castles* even when they were unassuming dwellings inhabited only by families of modest fortune.

"Phillimore told me that the firstborn of every generation of the lords of Tullyfane were to meet with terrible deaths on the attainment of their fiftieth birthdays even down to the seventh generation. It seems that first lord of Tullyfane had hanged a young boy for sheep stealing. The boy turned out to be innocent, and his mother, a widow who had doted on the lad as insurance for comfort in her old age, had duly uttered the curse. Whereupon, each lord of Tullyfane, for the last six generations, had met an untimely end.

"Phillimore assured me that the first lord of Tullyfane had not even been a direct ancestor of his, but that his great-grandfather had purchased Tullyfane Abbey when the owner, concerned at the imminent prospect of departing this life on his fiftieth birthday, decided to sell and depart for healthier climes in England. This sleight of hand of ownership had not prevented Jack's great-grandfather, General Phillimore, from falling off his horse and breaking his neck on his fiftieth birthday. Jack's grandfather, a redoubtable judge, was shot on his fiftieth birthday. The local inspector of the Royal Irish Constabulary had assumed that his untimely demise could be ascribed more to his profession than to the paranormal. Judges and policemen often experienced sudden terminations to their careers in a country where they were considered part of the colonial occupation by ordinary folk.

"'I presume your father, Colonel James Phillimore, is now approaching his fiftieth birthday and hence his alarm?' I asked Phillimore as the train rolled through the Tipperary countryside toward the Kerry border.

"Phillimore nodded slowly.

"'My sister has, in her letters, written that she has heard the specter crying at night. She reports that my father has even witnessed the apparition, the form of a young boy, crying on the turret of the abbey.'

"I raised my eyebrows unintentionally.

"'Seen as well as heard?' I demanded. 'And by two witnesses? Well, I can assure you that there is nothing in this world that exists unless it is due to some scientifically explainable reason.'

"'Nothing in this world,' muttered Phillimore. 'But what of the next?'

"'If your family believes in this curse, why remain at Tullyfane?' I demanded. 'Would it not be better to quit the house and estate if you are so sure that the curse is potent?'

"'My father is stubborn, Holmes. He will not quit the place, for he has sunk every penny he has into it apart from our town house in Dublin. If it were me, I would sell it to Moriarty and leave the accursed spot.'

"'Sell it to Moriarty? Why him, particularly?'

"'He offered to buy Father out in order to help resolve the situation.'

"'Rather magnanimous of him,' I observed. 'Presumably he has no fear of the curse?'

"'He reckons that the curse would only be directed at Anglo-Irish families like us, while he, being a pure Milesian, a Gael of the Gaels, so to speak, would be immune to the curse.'

"Colonel Phillimore had sent a calèche to Killarney Station to bring Phillimore and me to Tullyfane Abbey. The old colonel was clearly not in the best of spirits when he greeted us in the library. I noticed his hand shook a little as he raised it to greet me.

"'Friend of Jack's, eh? Yes, I remember you. One of the Galway Holmeses. Mycroft Holmes is your brother? Works for Lord Hartington, eh? Chief Secretary, eh?'

"He had an irritating manner of putting *eh* after each telegraphic phrase as a punctuation.

"It was then that Agnes Phillimore came in to welcome us. God, Watson, I was young and ardent in those days. Even now, as I look back with a more critical eye and colder blood, I acknowledge that she was rare and wonderful in her beauty. She held out her hand to me with a smile, but I saw at once that it lacked the warmth and friendship that I thought it had once held for me alone. Her speech was reserved, and she greeted me as a distant friend. Perhaps she had grown into a woman while I held to her image with boyish passion? It was impossible for me to acknowledge this at that time, but the passion was all on my side. Ah, immature youth, what else is there to say?

"We dined in somber mode that evening. Somber for me because I was wrestling with life's cruel realities; somber for the Phillimores because of the curse that hung over the house. We were just finishing the dessert when Agnes suddenly froze, her fork halfway to her mouth. Then Colonel Phillimore dropped his spoon with a crash on his plate and gave a piteous moan.

"In the silence that followed I heard it plainly. It was the sound of a sobbing child. It seemed to echo all around the room. Even Jack Phillimore looked distracted.

"I pushed back my chair and stood up, trying to pinpoint the direction from which the sounds came.

"'What lies directly beneath this dining room?' I demanded of the colonel. He was white in the face, too far gone with shock to answer me.

"I turned to Jack Phillimore. He replied with some nervousness.

"'The cellars, Holmes.'

"'Come, then,' I cried, grabbing a candelabra from the table and striding swiftly to the door.

"As I reached the door, Agnes stamped her foot twice on the floor as if agitated.

"'Really, Mr. Holmes,' she cried, 'you cannot do battle with an ethereal being!'

"I paused in the doorway to smile briefly at her.

"'I doubt that I shall find an ethereal being, Miss Phillimore.'

"Jack Phillimore led the way to the cellar, and we searched it thoroughly, finding nothing.

"'What did you expect to find?' demanded Phillimore, seeing my disappointment as we returned to the dining room.

"'A small boy, corporeal in form and not a spirit,' I replied firmly.

"'Would that it were so,' Agnes greeted our return without disguising her look of satisfaction that I could produce no physical entity in explanation. 'Do you not think that I have caused this house to be searched time and time again? My father is on the verge of madness. I do believe that he has come to the end of his composure. I fear for what he might do to himself.'

"'And the day after tomorrow is his fiftieth birthday,' added Phillimore soberly.

"We were standing in the entrance to the dining room when Malone, the aging butler, answered a summons to the front door by the jangle of the bell.

"'It's a Professor Moriarty,' he intoned.

"Moriarty was tall and thin, with a forehead domed in a white curve and deeply set eyes. His face protruded forward and had a curious habit of slowly oscillating from side to side in what, in the harsh judgment of my youth, I felt to be a curiously reptilian fashion. I suppose, looking back, he was handsome in a way and somewhat distinguished. He had been young for his professorship, and there was no doubting the sharpness of his mind and intellect.

"Agnes greeted him with warmth while Phillimore was indifferent. As for myself, I felt I had to suppress my ill humor. He had come to join us for coffee and brandy and made sympathetic overtures to the colonel over his apparent state of ill health.

" 'My offer still stands, dear sir,' he said. 'Best be rid of the abbey and the curse in one fell swoop. Not, of course, that you would lose it entirely, for when Agnes and I are married, you will always be a welcome guest here. . . .'

"Colonel Phillimore actually growled. A soft rumbling sound in the back of his throat, like an animal at bay and goaded into response.

" 'I intend to see this through. I refuse to be chased out of my home by a specter when Akbar Khan and his screaming Afghans could not budge me from the fort at Peiwar Pass. No, sir. Here I intend to stay and see my fiftieth birthday through.'

" 'I think you should at least consider James's offer, Father,' Agnes rebuked him. 'This whole business is affecting your nerves. Better get rid of the place and move to Dublin.'

" 'Nonsense!' snapped her father. 'I shall see it through. I will hear no more.'

"We went to bed early that night, and I confess, I spent some time analyzing my feelings for Agnes before dropping into a dozing slumber.

"The crying woke me. I hauled on a dressing gown and hastened to the window through which a full white moon sent its soft light. The cry was like a banshee's wail. It seemed to be coming from above me. I hastened from the room and in the corridor outside I came across Jack Phillimore, similarly attired in a dressing gown. His face looked ghastly.

" 'Tell me that I am not dreaming, Holmes,' he cried.

" 'Not unless we share a dream,' I replied tersely. " 'Do you have a revolver?'

"He looked startled.

" 'What do you hope to achieve with a revolver?' he demanded.

" 'I think it might be efficacious in dealing with ghosts, ghouls, and apparitions.' I smiled thinly.

"Phillimore shook his head.

"'The guns are locked below in the gun room. My father has the key.'

"'Ah well,' I replied in resignation, 'we can probably proceed without them. This crying is emanating from above. What's up there?'

"'The turret room. That's where Father said he saw the apparition before.'

"'Lead me to the turret room, then.'

"Spurred on by the urgency of my tone, Phillimore turned to lead the way. We flew up the stairs of a circular tower and emerged onto a flat roof. At the far end of the building rose a similar, though larger, tower or, more accurately, a round turret. Encircling it, ten feet above the roof level there ran a small balcony.

"'My God!' cried Phillimore, halting so abruptly that I cannoned in to him.

"It took me a moment to recover before I saw what had caused his distress. On this balcony there stood the figure of a small boy. He was clearly lit in the bright moonlight and yet, yet I will tell you no lie, Watson, his entire body and clothes glowed with a strange luminescence. The boy it was who was letting out the eerie, wailing sounds.

"'Do you see it, Holmes?' cried Phillimore.

"'I see the young rascal, whoever he is!' I yelled, running toward the tower over the flat roof.

"Then the apparition was gone. How or where, I did not observe.

"I reached the base of the tower and looked for a way to scramble up to the balcony. There was only one way of egress from the roof. A small door in the tower which seemed clearly barred on the inside.

"'Come, Phillimore, the child is escaping!' I cried in frustration.

"'Escaping, eh?' It was the colonel who emerged out of the darkness behind us. His face was ashen. He was clad only in his pajamas.

AN ENSUING EVIL

'Specters don't need to escape, eh! No, sir! Now that you have seen it, too, I can say I am not mad. At least, not mad, eh?'

"'How do I get into the turret?' I demanded, ignoring the colonel's ranting.

"'Boarded up for years, Holmes,' Phillimore explained, moving to support his frail father for fear the old man might topple over. 'There's no way anyone could have entered or left it.'

"'Someone did,' I affirmed. 'That was no specter. I think this has been arranged. I think you should call in the police.'

"The colonel refused to speak further of the matter and retired to bed. I spent most of the night checking the approaches to the turret room and was forced to admit that all means of entrance and exit seemed perfectly secured. But I was sure that when I started to run across the roof toward the tower, the boy had bobbed away with such a startled expression that no self-respecting ghost in the middle of haunting would have assumed.

"The next morning, over breakfast, I was forceful in my exhortations to the colonel that he should put the matter forthwith in the hands of the local police. I told him that I had no doubts that some bizarre game was afoot. The colonel had recovered some of his equilibrium and listened attentively to my arguments.

"Surprisingly, the opposition came from Agnes. She was still in favor of her father departing the house and putting an end to the curse.

"We were just finishing breakfast when Malone announced the arrival of Professor Moriarty.

"Agnes went to join him in the library while we three finished our meal, by the end of which, Colonel Phillimore had made up his mind to follow my advice. It was decided that we accompany Colonel Phillimore directly after breakfast to discuss the matter with the local Inspector of the Royal Irish Constabulary. Agnes and Moriarty joined us, and having heard the story from Agnes, Moriarty actually said that it was the best course of action, although Agnes still had her doubts. In fact, Moriarty offered to accompany us. Agnes excused herself a little ungraciously, I thought, because she had arranged to make an inventory of the wines in the cellar.

"So the Colonel, Phillimore, Moriarty, and I agreed to walk the two miles into the town. It must be observed that a few miles' walk was nothing for those who lived in the country in those days. Now, in London, everyone is forever hailing hansom carriages even if they merely desire to journey to the end of the street.

"We left the house and began to stroll down the path. We had barely gone twenty yards when the colonel, casting an eye at the sky, excused himself and said he needed his umbrella and would be but a moment. He turned, hurried back to his front door, and entered. That was when he disappeared from this world forever.

"The three of us waited patiently for a few moments. Moriarty then said that if we continued to stroll at an easy pace, the colonel would catch us up. Yet when we reached the gates of the estate, I began to grow concerned that there was still no sign of the colonel. I caused our party to wait at the gates. Ten minutes passed, and then I felt I should return to find out what had delayed the Colonel.

"The umbrella was still in the hall stand. There was no sign of the colonel. I rang the bell for old Malone and he swore that as far as he was aware the colonel had left with us and had not returned. There was no budging him on that point. Grumbling more than a little, he set off to the colonel's room; I went to the study. Soon the entire house was being searched as Jack Phillimore and Moriarty arrived back to discover the cause of the delay.

"It was then that Agnes emerged from the cellars, looking a little disheveled, an inventory in her hand. When she heard that her father had simply vanished, she grew distraught and Malone had to fetch the brandy.

"In the wine cellar, she told me, she had heard and seen nothing. Moriarty volunteered to search the cellar just to make the examination of the house complete. I told Phillimore to look after his sister and accompanied Moriarty. While I disliked the man, there was no doubt that Moriarty could hardly have engineered the colonel's disappearance as he had left the house with us and remained with us outside the house. Naturally, our search of the cellars proved futile. They were large, and one could probably have hidden a whole army in them if one so desired. But the entrance from the hall led to the area used for wine storage, and no one could have descended into the cellar without passing this area and thus being seen by Agnes. No answer to Colonel James Phillimore's disappearance presented itself to me.

"I spent a week at Tullyfane attempting to form some conclusion. The local RIC eventually gave up the search. I had to return to Oxford, and it became obvious to me that neither Agnes nor Moriarty required my company further. After that, I had but one letter from Jack Phillimore, and this several months later and postmarked at Marseille.

"Apparently, at the end of two weeks, a suicide note was found in the colonel's desk stating that he could not stand the strange hauntings in Tullyfane Abbey. Rather than await the terrible death on his fiftieth birthday, he proposed to put an end to it himself. There was attached a new will, giving the estate to Agnes in acknowledgment of her forthcoming marriage and the house in Stephen's Green to Jack. Phillimore wrote that although the will was bizarre, and there was no proof of his father's death, he nevertheless had refused to contest it. I heard later that this was against the advice of Phillimore's solicitor. But it seemed that Jack Phillimore wanted no part of the curse or the estate. He wished his sister joy of it and then took himself to Africa as a missionary where, two years later, I heard that he had been killed in some native uprising in British East Africa. It was not even on his fiftieth birthday. So much for curses.

"And Agnes Phillimore? She married James Moriarty and the property passed to him. She was dead within six months. She drowned in a boating accident when Moriarty was taking her to Beginish, just off the Kerry coast, to show her the columnar basaltic formations similar to those of the Giant's Causeway. Moriarty was the only survivor of the tragedy.

"He sold Tullyfane Abbey and its estate to an American and moved to London to become a gentleman of leisure, although his money was soon squandered due to his dissipated lifestyle. He resorted to more overt illegal activities to replenish his wealth. I have not called him the 'Napoleon of crime' without cause.

"As for Tullyfane, the American tried to run the estate, but fell foul of the Land Wars of a few years ago when the Land Leaguers forced radical changes in the way the great estates in Ireland were run. That was when a new word was added to the language— boycott—when the Land Leaguers ostracized Charles Boycott, the estate agent of Lord Erne at Lough Mask. The American pulled out of Tullyfane Abbey, which fell into ruin and became derelict.

"Without being able to find out what happened when James Phillimore stepped back beyond his front door to retrieve his umbrella, I was unable to bring the blame to where, I believed with every fiber in my body, it lay; namely, to James Moriarty. I believe that it was Moriarty who planned the whole dastardly scheme of obtaining the estate which he presumed would set him up for life. He was not in love with poor Agnes. He saw her as the quick means of becoming rich and, not content to wait for her marriage portion, I believe he forged the suicide note and will and then found an ingenious way to dispatch the colonel, having failed to drive him insane by playing on the curse. Once he had secured the estate, poor Agnes became dispensable.

"How he worked the curse, I was not sure until a singular event was reported to me some years later.

"It was in London, only a few years ago, that I happened to encounter Bram Stoker's younger brother, George. Like most of the Stoker brothers, with the exception of Bram, George had gone into medicine and was a Licentiate of the Royal College of Surgeons in Dublin. George had just married a lady from County Kerry, actually the sister of the McGillycuddy of the Reeks, one of the old Gaelic nobility.

"It was George who supplied me with an important piece of the jigsaw. He was actually informed of the occurrence by none other than his brother-in-law, Dennis McGillycuddy, who had been a witness to the event.

"About a year after the occurrences at Tullyfane Abbey, the body of a young boy was found in an old mine working in the Reeks. I should explain that the Reeks are the mountains on the Iveragh Peninsula which are the highest peaks in Ireland and, of course, Tullyfane stands in their shadows. The boy's body had not badly decomposed, because it had lain in the ice-cold temperatures of the small lochs one gets in the area. It so happened that a well-known Dublin medical man, Dr. John MacDonnell, the first person to perform an operation under anesthetic in Ireland, was staying in Killarney. He agreed to perform the autopsy because the local coroner had noticed a peculiar aspect to the body; he observed that in the dark the corpse of the boy was glowing.

"MacDonnell found that the entire body of the boy had been coated in a waxy yellow substance; indeed, it was the cause of death, for it had so clogged the pores of his skin that the unfortunate child had simply been asphyxiated. Upon analysis, it was discerned that the substance was a form of natural phosphorus, found in the caves in the area. I immediately realized the significance of this.

"The child, so I presumed, was one of the hapless and miserable wretches doomed to wander the byways of Ireland, perhaps orphaned during the failure of the potato crops in 1871, which had spread starvation and typhus among the peasants. Moriarty had forced or persuaded him to act the part of the wailing child whom we had observed. This child was our specter, appearing now and then at Moriarty's command to scream and cry in certain places. The phosphorus would have emitted the ethereal glow.

"Having served his purpose, Moriarty, knowing well the properties of the waxy substance with which he had coated the child's body, left the child to suffocate and dumped the body in the mountains."

I waited for some time after Holmes had finished the story, and then I ventured to ask the question to which he had, so far, provided no answer. As I did so, I made the following preamble.

"Accepting that Moriarty had accomplished a fiendish scheme to enrich himself and that it was only in retrospect you realized how he managed to use the child to impersonate a specter—"

Holmes breathed out sharply as he interrupted. "It is a failure of my deductive capabilities that I have no wish to advertise, Watson."

"Yet there is one thing—just how did Moriarty manage to spirit away the body of James Phillimore after he stepped back inside the door of the house to retrieve his umbrella? By your own statement, Moriarty, Jack Phillimore, and yourself were all together, waiting for the colonel, outside his house. The family retainer, old Malone, swore the colonel did not reenter the house. How was it done? Was Malone in the pay of Moriarty?"

"It was a thought that crossed my mind. The RIC likewise questioned old Malone very closely and came to the conclusion that he was part of no plot. In fact, Malone could not say one way or another if the colonel had returned, as he was in the kitchen with two housemaids as witnesses at the time."

"And Agnes? . . ."

"Agnes was in the cellar. She saw nothing. When all is said and done, there is no logical answer. James Phillimore vanished the moment he stepped back over the threshold. I have thought about every conceivable explanation for the last twenty years and have come to no suitable explanation except one. . . ."

"Which is?"

"The powers of darkness were exalted that day, and Moriarty had made a pact with the devil, selling his soul for his ambition."

I stared at Holmes for a moment. I had never seen him admit to any explanation of events that was not in keeping with scientific logic. Was he correct that the answer lay with the supernatural, or was he merely covering up for the fact of his own lack of knowledge or, even more horrific to my susceptibilities, did the truth lie in some part of my old friend's mind which he refused to admit even to himself?

Pinned to John H. Watson's manuscript was a small yellowing cutting from the *Kerry Evening News;* alas the date had not been noted.

"During the recent building of an RIC Barracks on the ruins of Tullyfane Abbey, a well-preserved male skeleton was discovered. Sub-Inspector Dalton told our reporter that it could not be estimated how long the skeleton had lain there. The precise location was in a bricked-up area of the former cellars of the abbey.

"Doctor Simms-Taafe said that he adduced, from the condition of the skeleton, that it had belonged to a man in midlife who had met his demise within the last twenty or thirty years. The back of the skull had been smashed in due to a severe blow, which might account for the death.

"Sub-Inspector Dalton opined that the death might well be linked with the disappearance of Colonel Phillimore, then the owner of Tullyfane Abbey, some thirty years ago. As the next owner, Professor James Moriarty was reported to have met his death in Switzerland, the last owner having been an American who returned to his homeland, and the Phillimores being no longer domiciled in the country, the RIC are placing the matter in their file of unsolved suspicious deaths."

A few lines were scrawled on the cutting in Dr. Watson's hand, which ran, "I think it was obvious that Colonel Phillimore was murdered as soon as he reentered the house. I have come to believe that the truth did lie in a dark recess of my old friend's mind which he refused to admit was the grotesque and terrible truth of the affair.

Patricide, even at the instigation of a lover with whom one is besotted, is the most hideous crime of all. Could it be that Holmes had come to regard the young woman herself as representing the powers of darkness?" The last sentence was heavily underscored.

─── THE SIREN OF SENNEN COVE ───

Of the many adventures and curious hazards that I have shared with my good friend Sherlock Holmes, the well-known consulting detective, there is one that still brings an icy chill to my bones and a tingle to the hairs on the nape of my neck. I can still recall the apprehension—nay, the unutterable fear—that gripped me when I saw the pale specter of that naked, dancing woman who had lured so many seamen to their watery deaths—and she no more than ten yards away from where Holmes and I huddled in an open dinghy on the tempestuous seas off the rocky granite coast of Cornwall.

Lest Holmes rebuke me for starting my account at the end rather than at the beginning, let me remind those of my readers who have followed my record of his adventures that, in the spring of 1897, Dr. Moore Agar of Harley Street had prescribed to my friend a complete rest, should he wish to avoid a breakdown in his health. We had taken a small cottage near Poldhu Bay, near Mullion, on the Lizard Peninsula almost, but not quite, on the farthest extremity of Cornwall.

It was here that the ancient Cornish language had arrested Holmes's attention and he received a consignment of books on philology and set himself to writing a monograph on what he perceived as Chaldean roots in that branch of the Celtic languages.

Our idyll was rudely interrupted when, taking tea at the local vicarage with its incumbent, Mr. Roundhay, we became involved with the strange case of Mortimer Tregennis, which I have recounted as "The Adventure of the Devil's Foot." It was a stimulating exercise in deduction but, as Holmes remarked at the end of it, he was pleased to get back to the study of the Cornish language.

Only three days elapsed before we had a visitor who would send us helter-skelter into a case that made the investigation of the death of Mortimer Tregennis seem a mere diversion in mental entertainment by comparison with the terrifying peril it presented.

It was just before noon. I was taking the sun in a garden chair outside our cottage, sipping a preprandial sherry. Although it was April, it was a warm day and not at all breezy. Holmes was enclosed in the room we had set aside as his study, poring over a newly acquired volume that had arrived by that morning's mail. It was *Some Observations on the Rev. R. Williams' Preface to his Lexicon Cornu-Britannicum,* written by no less a luminary than Prince Louis Lucien Bonaparte. That is why I recall it so well; the idea of one of the Bonaparte family becoming a philologist and an authority on the Cornish language was a matter which intrigued me.

Holmes had scooped up the book and disappeared into his study after breakfast, promising faithfully to appear for luncheon because our daily help, Mrs. Chirgwin, was preparing it, and she did not take kindly to her meals being missed.

I was, therefore, sitting, reading the *Falmouth Packet* when I heard the sound of a carriage rattling along the track that led to our cottage. I reluctantly placed my sherry and newspaper aside and stood up, waiting to receive the unexpected visitor with some curiosity. We were so isolated that visitors were an unusual phenomenon.

It took a moment for the carriage to appear from behind a clump of trees and come to a halt before the garden gate. It was a sturdily built carriage, one more often seen in the country than in town. But it was clearly the vehicle of some well-to-do personage.

A tall, dark-faced coachman leaped down and opened the door. From the interior, a short, well-built man alighted and glanced about him. He had a shock of white hair, a red face and was well dressed, bearing the hallmarks of a country squire. In fact, he seemed almost a caricature of one.

He saw me and hailed even as he opened the gate and came toward me. "Mr Sherlock Holmes?"

"I am his colleague, Dr. Watson," I replied. "Can I be of assistance, sir?"

The man frowned impatiently. "It is Mr. Holmes that I must see."

"I am afraid that he is busy at the moment. May I take your name, sir, and I will see—?"

"It's all right, Watson," came Holmes's voice from behind me. He was leaning out of his study window, which he had opened. "I heard the carriage arriving. What can I do for you?"

The white-haired man examined him for a moment with intense blue eyes; a keen examination that seemed to miss nothing.

"A moment of your time is what I require, sir. Perhaps some advice at the end of it. My name is Sir Jelbart Trevossow. It is a name not unknown in these parts."

Holmes stared at the man in amusement. "That's as may be, sir, yet, unfortunately, it is a name unknown to me," he replied amiably. "Nevertheless, I have a moment before luncheon. Watson, old fellow, bring Sir Jelbart into our little parlor, and I will be there directly."

I smiled a little at the mortification on the country squire's face. He was apparently unused to people not recognizing him nor having his wishes obeyed instantly. I gestured to the door with a slight bow.

His mouth tightened, but he moved inside to the room we had set aside as our common parlor. I followed him and closed the cottage door behind me.

"Now, sir," I said, "may I offer you some refreshment? Something to keep out the chill? A whiskey or a sherry, perhaps?"

"I do not agree with strong spirits, Doctor," Sir Jelbart snapped. "I am of the Wesleyan religion, sir. My views are firm on strong drink and tobacco. . . ." He sniffed suspiciously, for Holmes's noxious weed could be discerned all over our small cottage.

"Then be seated, sir," I invited. "Perhaps Mrs. Chirgwin might be prevailed upon to make you some tea?"

"I will have nothing, thank 'ee," he replied firmly, sitting down. His attitude was somewhat pugnacious.

Holmes entered at that moment, and I was thankful for it, raising my eyes to the ceiling to indicate to him that our guest was of an awkward nature.

Holmes stretched himself at his ease in an armchair opposite our visitor and, undaunted by the look that would have sent others straight to the fires of hell, he took a pipe from his pocket and lit up.

"I do not agree with tobacco, sir," snapped our guest.

Holmes's good-natured expression did not change. "Each to their own enjoyment, sir," he replied indifferently. "Myself, I think best over a pipe or two of shag tobacco. The coarser, the better."

Sir Jelbart eyed Holmes for a moment, and when he saw that he was dealing with someone of an equal steel will, he suddenly relented. Holmes would doubtless have pointed out that by giving way so easily on the matter, Sir Jelbart's business must have been of considerable importance to him.

"Now, sir"—Holmes smiled—"perhaps we can discuss the reason for this visit, for I presume you have not come merely to pass the time of day with me on our respective likes and prejudices?"

Sir Jelbart Trevossow cleared his throat more in an expression of annoyance than to help him in his speech. "I am not one to waste time, Mr. Holmes. I have business interests, sir. I was a stockholder in the company which owned the barque *Sophy Anderson*. Ten years ago you investigated her loss, which could have bankrupted those who had financed her voyage. I was one of them."

Holmes leaned back for a moment, his eyes closed as he recalled the case. "Exactly ten years ago," he agreed. He turned to me. "It is not a case that you have as yet recorded, Watson, old fellow."

"I did mention it in passing when I was relating the case of 'The Five Orange Pips,'" I replied in defense. "I felt that it was too pedestrian a case to excite the temperament of readers of *The Strand Magazine*, Holmes. As I recall—"

Sir Jelbart cleared his throat again in annoyance.

Holmes smiled politely.

"Pray, proceed," he said, waving a hand.

"I came to you, Mr. Holmes, knowing that you have some dealings with the mysteries of the sea."

"A number of my cases have been concerned with the disappearance or foundering of ships. The cutter *Alicia*, for example, and the *Friesland*, on which Watson and I nearly lost our lives—"

"Mr. Holmes," interrupted Sir Jelbart, "do you know how many ships—and I mean ships of some tonnage, not merely little coasters—have been lost on this coast alone during the last fifteen years?"

Holmes speculated. "A half-dozen, a dozen, perhaps?"

"One hundred and eight," our guest informed us solemnly. "This, sir, is a wrecker's coast, always has been. The people scavenge from the sea."

Holmes pursed his lips. "If memory serves me well, three years ago the new Merchant Shipping Act, especially part nine on the law of salvage and wrecks, should now prevent any lucrative business being made out of wrecking."

"Not at all, sir. My brother, Captain Silas Trevossow, is the local Excise Officer. He will tell you that wrecking is still as virile a business as ever it was."

"Most interesting, Sir Jelbart, but I cannot yet see what has brought you to my door."

"I come to you for assistance, Mr. Holmes. As soon as I learned that you were staying in the Duchy, I knew that you were the one man who could help."

"I am still waiting for your explanation."

"I live in Chy Trevescan, a house near Sennen Cove, at the far end of the Cornish peninsula. It is by Land's End. The area is a gray granite place, and its village was once called the first and last on this island. It stands on an open, rocky tableland, and to the west the land ends in granite cliffs facing the sea.

"Sennen Cove is about one and a quarter miles from the village, and this is reached by a narrow road which drops down very steeply between the hills to the sea and then extends along the sea's edge into a long sandy beach that curves along the margin of Whitesand Bay, a mile or so of sandy beach. The people in the area usually live by pilchard fishing or lifting lobsters. Whitesand Bay appears a hospitable shoreline, but the Brisons Rocks are a mile offshore, and in the distance is Cape Cornwall, where the seas can smash a great ship to matchwood if it is unlucky enough to founder there. There is another group of rocks to the south, the Tribbens, of which the largest is Cowloe."

Sir Jelbart paused.

Holmes made no move, asked no question.

Our visitor decided to continue. "During the last two weeks, three vessels have foundered on the Tribbens."

"Pray what is so singular about these three sinkings out of the hundred or so others you enumerate that causes you so much concern?" demanded Holmes.

Jelbart looked at him in surprise. "I have not as yet said that there was anything singular about them. How did you—?"

"Elementary," Holmes replied wearily. "You would not come here, bear to sit in the proximity of my pipe, and refer to these three specific vessels out of the hundreds of sinkings if they were but simple additional statistics. Something must have caused you some great concern. Pray elucidate."

Sir Jelbart leaned forward. "There were several survivors from the wrecks. They all recount a singular manifestation that was the cause of their ships foundering on the rocks."

"Which is?"

"They claim the ships were lured ashore by a siren."

"A siren?" Holmes smiled quickly. "I presume that you do not mean a signal device like a horn?"

"No sir, I do not!" spluttered our guest indignantly. "I mean a spirit, a seductress, an enchantress."

I could not control my amusement, but Holmes calmly began to refill his pipe. "I think that you had better clarify your statement, Sir Jelbart."

"These ships were heading for the Port of St. Ives. Coasters, they were. Many local captains cut across the mouth of Whitesand Bay instead of standing out to sea. They steer a course between the Carn Bras Longships, rocky islands to the west, and the inshore rocks in order to make up sea time. The wrecks have happened at night. Usually there are no problems for local skippers on this course, for there are lights at strategic points, and the captains of these vessels know the waters well. All three captains of the wrecked coasters had run this course many times."

"How did this enchantress manifest herself?" I ventured.

"Each survivor says that she was a specter that appeared to the crew dancing on the rocks."

So serious was the man that I could not suppress a chuckle. "But Holmes . . . ," I began when I saw him silencing me with a disdainful glance.

"In what form did this specter manifest itself?" he repeated my question. "Some specifics, please."

"A woman. Gad sir, a naked woman, dancing on one of the rocks. But the figure was large and shimmered white. Indeed, many of the survivors said that they could see right through her."

"Did anyone hear anything?"

"Not at the time of the sinking, but in the nights following, some locals report that they have heard a heavy breathing from the direction of the rocks. So loud was it that it was heard ashore when the wind was in the right direction. A sound of hissing breath like some giant was hiding behind the rocks. The locals are in fear of the Tribbens, even though it was a favorite spot to lift lobsters."

"No music? No panpipes?" I smiled sarcastically.

Before the man could answer, Holmes had cut in. "Nothing else was seen around these rocks? Has anyone ventured to examine them?"

"No, sir. The survivors were scared out of their wits, sailors being so superstitious. The fear at the sight of the specter caused the crews to panic, the captains to lose control. It takes only a moment's distraction to put a vessel on those rocks. Some seventy-five men have perished, sir, and the news is abroad about the siren of Sennen Cove luring the men to their deaths."

"And you have come to me. Why?"

"Because, in spite of the merriment of your colleague"—he glanced dourly at me—"I do not believe in ghosts, sir. I am a Methodist. A plain man raised in a plain religion. A man who believes in rationality. I think there is some mischief afoot, but I cannot find an explanation."

Holmes laid down his pipe for a moment, leaning back in his chair and placing his hands fingertips together, and gave Sir Jelbart a careful scrutiny. "I am sure that you have some explanation, Sir Jelbart. Some theory to propose to me?"

"I have made a study of shipwrecks along this coast, Mr. Holmes. That is why I know the statistics. I believe that wreckers are at work."

"From what you say, this Sennen Cove is not so far removed from civilization that a gang of wreckers could work with impunity," I intervened. "Unless it is a conspiracy of the entire local populace."

"On the contrary, Doctor," Sir Jelbart said, "the coastline is not the easiest place to police."

"But three vessels, sir . . . if what you say is correct . . . that would cause a more careful watch to be kept?"

"No, indeed. That's the confounded point of the matter. The stories of the specter have scared off local people. Imagine, sir, tales of this siren, this seductress dancing naked on a rock whose sides are so sheer that no one could land on it, let alone find a shelf on which to balance. And the size of her . . . they say the figure is at least twelve feet tall. No one in those parts will venture even to the shore after dark, not even Mr. Neal, our minister. He now goes around warning people to stay clear of the area unless they wish to see the enchantress and suffer the fate of Lot's wife when she turned back to look upon Sodom and Gomorrah,"

"Does he now?" mused Holmes. "You say that your brother is in the Excise? Have you made your views known to him?"

"I have."

"And what does he say?"

"He does not share them."

"Why?"

"Because the ships founder and sink. Little wreckage, if any, is swept ashore. He argues that if wreckers are the cause, what happens to their spoils? They go straight to the bottom. There seems nothing to profit from. He believes, therefore, that we can rule wrecking out."

"It is a sound, logical deduction," agreed Holmes.

"Nevertheless, the alternative is preposterous. I must believe that the matter has a rational explanation. I refuse to believe that it is a siren luring passing ships onto the rocks. A specter? A ghost? This is why I have come to you, Mr. Holmes. You, I am sure, cannot believe in the supernatural."

"On the contrary," Holmes replied seriously. "What is the supernatural but nature which has not yet been explained? Tell me, Sir Jelbart, in what condition was the weather when these ships foundered?"

"The weather?"

"Yes, was it a tempestuous night, was there a sea fog, were high seas running?"

Sir Jelbart shook his head. "On the contrary. The wrecks occurred on fine nights. Good visibility and calm seas. That is why the captains of these doomed vessels took the passage so close to the Tribbens Rocks. In bad weather, a good seaman would have stood out to sea and given his ship plenty of sea room."

"Has your brother, Captain Trevossow, made an investigation of the area?"

"He intends to do so this very night. That is why I have been encouraged to come to you, for I fear for his life. The *Torrington Lass* is sailing from Penzance overnight around the coast to St. Ives. She should pass the Tribbens at midnight. My brother intends to be aboard to inspect the rocks as they sail by."

"Isn't that dangerous in view of what has transpired to the previous ships?" I asked.

"It will be a clear night tonight with calm weather," he replied. "In normal circumstances, there should be no danger. However . . ." He ended with an eloquent shrug.

"Surely, your brother is a practical man," Holmes said, "and would be prepared for any unusual occurrence?"

"He is not the skipper and crew," pointed out Sir Jelbart.

"You have piqued my curiosity, Sir Jelbart," Holmes said thoughtfully.

Just then Mrs. Chirgwin put her head around the parlor door and announced that the midday meal was ready and she would not be blamed if it was to get cold, gentleman caller or no.

Holmes arose, smiling. "Pray, stay to lunch with us, Sir Jelbart, and, afterward we will accompany you back to this Sennen Cove. We will stay overnight if you can accommodate us. By the way, do you have access to a rowing boat and a competent seaman who would be prepared to row us out to these haunted rocks?"

Sir Jelbart rose and held out his hand. "I do, indeed, sir. I am glad the instinct that brought me hither has been proved a good one."

The journey from Poldhu Bay around the great stretch of Mount's Bay, through the town of Penzance, along the inhospitable inland road, passing such strange un-English-sounding places as Buryas, Trenuggo, Crows-an-Wra, Treave, and Carn Towan, before reaching the village of Sennen, was longer than I had expected. We finally arrived at Sir Jelbart's house of Chy Trevescan in the early evening. It was this journey, through the desolate landscape, with standing stones and ancient crosses that illustrated, for me at least, that Cornwall was, indeed, "the land beyond England." A strange, ancient place, lost in time.

The sun was low in the sky, almost directly in our eyes, as we came along the road above Whitesand Bay heading south to Sennen. I saw a spectacular stretch of sandy beach about a mile long and curving. Sir Jelbart was full of local folklore. It was here, apparently, that the Saxon King Athelstan landed during his attempt to conquer the Celts of Cornwall. It was here that the Pretender Perkin Warbeck came ashore from Ireland in his vain attempt to seize the English Crown. The sea was calm now, but our guide told us that it usually came rolling shoreward in long breakers.

"There is a small craft out there by that point," observed Holmes. "It seems to have a curious engine fitted on its stern."

Sir Jelbart glanced toward it. It was anchored at the north end of the bay, the opposite end of the large bay to the location of Sennen Cove.

"That's Aire's Point." He screwed up his eyes to focus on the point. "Ah, that is young Harry Penwarne's boat."

"What's he doing?"

"No idea. He's a bit of an inventor. Amateur, of course. He once explained it all to me. The Penwarne place is just by Aire's Point at Tregriffian. Sad history."

"Why so?" asked Holmes.

"The Penwarnes are one of the old families in these parts, but young Harry's father was a gambler. He lost most of the family fortune. Shot himself while young Harry was studying at the Sorbonne in Paris about ten years ago. Harry returned here and has tried to keep Tregriffian House going. Inventive young man. Full of all these modern technological ideas, but he worries too much. Frequently seen him with bloodshot eyes. Burning the midnight oil, what?"

Chy Trevescan was certainly a large house in anyone's estimation. But it was an ugly house. Squat and brooding, thickset, just like the granite countryside. As we drove up to the main door, we noticed that a small pony and trap stood outside. It was a single horse, two-wheeled affair. Standing on the step was a solemn-faced man whose black broadcloth proclaimed him as a minister.

"Sir Jelbart," the man greeted him even before he descended, "I do not approve of this enterprise. I have heard that your brother is sailing on the *Torrington Lass* tonight, and I do not approve."

"Our local minister, Mr. Neal," explained Sir Jelbart under his breath. Then aloud: "I fail to see what business it is of yours, sir. You have abrogated your responsibility to your flock by not demonstrating that what is happening on the Tribbens Rocks is not the Devil's work. Now my brother and I must take matters into our own hands."

Mr. Neal's face was distorted in anger. "As your minister, I forbid it. You have no right to interfere with matters of the otherworld. It is God's wish that these vessels be stricken down, for their crews must be debauched. They are being punished for their sins; otherwise God would intervene and save them from their doom! I tell you, it is God who drives those ships on the Tribbens Rocks! Their vines are vines of Sodom, grown on the terraces of Gomorrah; their grapes are poisonous, the clusters bitter to the taste. . . ."

"Deuteronomy!" snapped Holmes suddenly, the sharpness of his voice causing the minister to stop, blinking. "But hardly appropriate. God would surely not waste his time organizing shipwrecks, Mr. Neal, in order to punish those souls who have met their fate on those rocks."

"I warn you, sir," cried the minister, "do not attempt to interfere or you, too, will be doomed—the way of the wicked is doomed. . . ."

"But the Lord watches over the way of the righteous," replied Holmes solemnly, quoting from the same psalm.

The minister turned toward his governess's cart. "You have been warned!" he cried as he climbed into his pony and trap and disappeared down the driveway.

Sir Jelbart bade us come inside for refreshment while he sent for the local fisherman whom he trusted. Holmes suggested that only he and myself, together with the boatman, need set out on the expedition to examine the rocks. The boatman's name was

Noall Tresawna, a simple, thickset man. Holmes explained what he wanted, and the man made no demur. When Holmes asked him if he had heard about the supernatural phenomenon, Tresawna nodded.

"Are you not a little apprehensive, my friend?" asked Holmes. "We must rely on your nerve and experience in a little boat out there among the rocks."

"I do be a God-fearing man, master," Tresawna replied. "I say my prayers and keep the commandments, and I place my fate in God's hands. For it is written in the Good Book:

Happy is the man
who does not take the wicked for his guide
nor walk the road that sinners tread
nor take his seat among the scornful . . .

Holmes broke in:

. . . the law of the Lord is his delight
the law his meditation night and day.

Tresawna looked impressed. "Aye, master, that do be so, and thus I be not afear'd of specters."

Toward midnight, Tresawna met us at the kitchen door of the house and led us by the light of a storm lantern across fields to a cliff top, which was a point overlooking the Tribbens. The point was called Pedn-men-du, which Holmes afterward told me meant "the head of black stone." A dangerous stairlike path descended to where he had moored his boat. The night was a dark blue velvet. Bright white stars winked in the sky, and the moon was only in its first quarter and thus shedding little illumination.

Once inside the boat, Tresawna extinguished the lantern, for he knew the seas around the coast better in what little natural light there was than by artificial means.

Holmes bent close to me as we sat in the stern. "Have you brought your revolver as I requested, Watson?"

"I have. But do you expect me to shoot at a twelve-foot-high naked dancer?" I inquired sarcastically.

"Not quite, old fellow. I expect a more tangible, flesh-and-blood target to present itself."

The little boat rocked its way through the calm, dark seas along the tower cliffs of Pedn-men-du, out to a point where we could see the line of white surf breaking along the stretch of Whitesand Bay.

"There be the Tribbens now, sir," called our boatman, pointing toward the black shadows that were looming up ahead of us. We could hear the whispering seas sighing and crashing gently against them.

"They don't look so menacing," I ventured.

"Not to us in this small boat, sir," Noall Tresawna agreed. "But a large vessel with a lower keel could be ripped open by the hidden jagged rocks that be just a few feet below us."

"Is that what happened to the vessels that have been sunk here?" asked Holmes.

"That's about it, sir. A good skipper can take his vessel up between Tal-y-men and Kettle's Bottom to the west or between Kettle's Bottom and the Peal on the east. After that, it is a straight run between Shark's Fin and the Tribbens and out across the bay. But I hear tell from those who have survived that the curiosity to see the dancing lady caused them to steer too close to the rocks on their starboard and before they knew it, the ship's keels were sheared away, like a knife going through butter."

"Is it a deep bottom here?"

"Not too deep as happens, but deep enough."

"What do you think is the cause of these vessels foundering? Do you think it is wreckers?"

"Not for me to say, sir. I wouldn't say so. If it were wreckers, why choose a place where the ships aren't driven ashore so that you could pick up the cargoes? That's what they did in the old days. But here, the ships go down and lay on the bottom. There's no currents to bring anything ashore."

The rocks were now closer. The one closest to the cliffs was almost an island in its size, and this, Tresawna told us, was called Cowloe. Beyond these rocks were two other large pinnacles jutting from the sea.

Holmes glanced at his pocket watch. "Nearly midnight. The *Torrington Lass* should be approaching here soon, if Sir Jelbart's timing of her sailing is correct."

Tresawna rested on his oars. Everything was silent except for the incessant whispering of the sea.

Then suddenly a curious white light seemed to illuminate the waters between the rocks.

A cold fear seized me such as I had never known.

I have been in some pretty tight spots, I can tell you. Not even when I received my wound at the battle of Maiwand, facing the hordes of Afghan tribesmen, thinking that I was about to breathe my last, did I feel such fear.

I gripped Holmes's arm in a vise.

"God, Holmes! Look there! Tell me that it is an illusion! Tell me that you don't see it?"

On the farthest rock, a cold white light bathed.

And in that white ethereal light stood the figure of a giant woman, nearly twelve feet high. It was a strange flickering; one which had a transparent quality, for I could see the rock through the image. The figure was that of an attractive woman. Quite beautiful. She was naked. She moved in voluptuous contortions, dancing in such provocative poses that I have never seen before; seductive, alluring, moving as an enchantress to ensnare weak souls.

The hairs on the nape of my neck rose. I could not draw my attention away from the figure. I felt like a rabbit before a snake.

"Fascinating!" muttered Holmes at my side.

From a distance there came a sound of a ship's horn.

"Come, Watson, old fellow, get a grip of yourself." Holmes nudged me. "That's the *Torrington Lass* approaching."

I stared at him in bewilderment. "But, Holmes, don't you see her . . . God help us, it is a phantom! . . ."

Holmes had turned sharply to Tresawna. "Have you brought the rockets ready, as I asked?"

"I have, Mr. Holmes." The man had kept his gaze averted from the rocks while muttering some prayer.

"Then we must send them up at once. There is no time to get nearer the rocks before the *Torrington Lass* will be down upon them."

Tresawna had three rockets of the sort carried by ships as distress signals. He placed one in the bow and struck a match. Within moments it took off into the night sky.

About half a mile away, we could see the lights of the steam packet heading in our direction.

Tresawna set off the remaining two rockets and eventually we saw the ship turn westward and move on its northerly course.

"Now," cried Holmes triumphantly, "make for the rocks."

Even as we turned and Tresawna began to row with all his might toward the rocks, there came a crack much like a rifle shot. The ethereal white light suddenly vanished, and all was dark and quiet.

"'Vast rowing," snapped Holmes.

We sat in silence. There was no sound except the whispering sea again.

Holmes gave a deep sigh. "I don't think there will be anything more we can do until daylight. We won't see anything more tonight. Best take us back to Chy Trevescan and meet us there again tomorrow as soon as it is light."

Holmes was in one of his infuriating moods, not answering any questions, not even when our host, Sir Jelbart, demanded to know what adventure had befallen us.

The next morning we had just finished breakfast when a tall

naval officer arrived and was greeted familiarly by Sir Jelbart. He introduced the man as his brother Captain Silas Trevossow. The Captain had ridden over from St. Ives that morning. Holmes admitted responsibility for sending up the rockets to prevent the *Torrington Lass* being lured onto the rocks.

"Thank God you did. The skipper and his crew were petrified. They froze like ice as a fear gripped the ship. Only when we saw your danger signals was the skipper brought back to his senses, and he seized the wheel to alter course."

"You are in time to come with us, Captain," Holmes invited. "I think you might find this interesting, and I assure you, by this evening you will have apprehended the person behind these sinkings. A most evil genius."

An hour later found Holmes, Captain Trevossow, Noall Tresawna and myself out by the rocks again, though they seemed less menacing in daylight.

"That is the rock on which we saw the dancing woman," Holmes pointed. "Make for that."

We came close to the rock on which the giant woman had been dancing.

"Look!" I cried. "Look at the angle of the face of this rock. No physical entity could stand on it, much less dance. It is almost a forty-five-degree sheer angle."

"Close to sixty degrees, Watson," replied Holmes unmoved. "As smooth a rock face as ever you would see, and look at the covering on it."

I frowned, examining it.

"Covering? That is only guano."

"Exactly, my medical friend. The long-accumulated dung of sea fowl, a yellow white substance as if the rock, that flat, almost vertical surface, has been whitewashed."

"I don't see how that concerns us."

Holmes merely shook his head sadly and glanced around. "Now, Tresawna, head for that other rock there."

He indicated a large pinnacle raising itself above the water some fifteen yards away. This was easy to land on as the waves were not at all rough, and Holmes insisted on climbing onto it while we held the boat steady. He took with him a small canvas bag, which he had brought from Sir Jelbart's house. He spent some time examining a particular area, all the while glancing back to the first guano-covered rock as if taking measurements or alignments.

Eventually he turned to a third rock at an angle to both of these. He seemed to measure the distance to it. It was about another fifteen yards away, rising higher than the others and larger. Holmes scrambled back into the boat.

"What did you find, Mr. Holmes?" asked Captain Trevossow, for Holmes had put several items into the canvas bag. He handed it to the captain, who glanced into it.

"Be careful," Holmes admonished. "They are sharp."

"Why, they are only fragments of glass."

"Only?" Holmes raised an eyebrow. "In fact, they are more than glass. They are fragments of a shattered concave mirror."

He answered no more questions but instructed Tresawna to row toward the third rock that he had indicated.

This pinnacle had a natural sea pool at the foot of it, making an excellent landing place, and we could all climb out and follow a little circular path that went around the islandlike rock to a small cave. It was no higher than four feet at its entrance.

Holmes gave a cry of elation as he beheld it. He immediately bent down and entered. There was only room for himself in the cave, but we heard, almost at once, a further cry of exaltation. He reemerged pushing a large square glass container with some metal pieces in it, zinc and some other substance. This seemed to have been discarded at the back of the cave. Holmes brought it forward. There was a chemical smell to it which I hazarded was ammonium chloride.

"What do you make of that?" he announced.

Captain Trevossow and I exchanged a bewildered glance and shrugged.

Holmes sighed impatiently. "This is a Leclanche cell, and a pretty strong one," he said irritably when he saw we were lost.

"An electric battery?" Captain Trevossow frowned. "What's that doing on this godforsaken rock?"

Holmes gave him one of his enigmatic looks. "I am sure that we will be able to find the answer very soon."

He suddenly took his magnifying glass from his pocket and examined a flat-topped rock that was in the center of the entrance. He went down on his hands and knees and seemed to take a sighting from the rock, gazing straight out across the sea to the smaller pinnacle on which he had found the mirror fragments.

"You'll notice the grooves here and the scraping of metal on this rock," he inquired of us.

We both nodded, still confused.

Holmes stood up with a smile of satisfaction. "Excellent. I think that we will now pay a visit on Mr. Harry Penwarne at Tregriffian House."

It took some time to row back to the shore and collect Sir Jelbart from Chy Trevescan. Leaving Noall Tresawna to attend to his boat, Sir Jelbart and his brother, Holmes and myself, climbed into the carriage and made the journey through Sennen along the road above Whitesand Bay to Tregriffian House.

Harry Penwarne was no more than thirty-five. A young man whose boyish looks seemed to have a hardness to them. He smiled only with a movement of his facial muscles, but he bade us welcome to his house. I thought his eyes held a suspicious look in them. Then I realized that they were quite bloodshot. His manservant was a muscular man also with dour looks, who appeared less like a servant and more like a soldier or sailor. He spoke little, but I detected a French accent when he did.

"What can I do for you, Sir Jelbart?" he inquired. "What brings you and your friends to my house?"

Holmes intervened immediately. "You'll forgive me," he said, "but when I saw your diving experiments the other day, I just had to come and meet you."

Penwarne's eyes narrowed. He glanced at Sir Jelbart, who was looking in astonishment at Holmes.

"I didn't know it was generally known that I was making such experiments."

Holmes smiled. "My dear sir, I have been reading Kleingert of Breslau's experimentations with diving equipment, and it seemed obvious you were using a machine to send compressed air to the diver."

Harry Penwarne frowned. "Are you involved in deep-sea diving, Mr. Holmes?"

"I have a little knowledge," confessed Holmes. "Though I confess to being a mere amateur. I know that there are some new French inventions which have extended the time divers can remain underwater."

"You mean the new compressor modification by Laplace of the Sorbonne?" inquired Penwarne.

"Exactly so. I understand that you, also, were a student at the Sorbonne?"

"I graduated from there ten years ago."

"Pray what were you studying?"

"Marine engineering, of course."

"I think, at that time, Dr. Marey was experimenting at the Sorbonne with his new invention, wasn't he?"

"Dr. Marey? I do not know the gentleman." Penwarne shook his head. "I am not a medical man, Mr. Holmes."

Holmes looked at him sharply. "I did not say that he was a doctor of medicine."

Penwarne's mouth tightened.

"However, you are right. He was a physician, but his experiments were concerned with another discipline. Ten years ago, he invented the first motion pictures using a single camera."

"Is that supposed to be of interest to me?" asked Penwarne defensively. "My study is marine engineering, sir."

"You are possessed of a bright mind, Mr. Penwarne. You saw the potential of Marey's camera and started your own development of it. But two years ago, Auguste and Louis Lumiere patented their cinematograph in Paris. They produced a combined camera and projector operating at sixteen frames a second. You were devastated. You were working on a similar system, but they were first with the patent. Therefore, I believe that you have turned your invention to a more dreadful use."

"I have no idea what you mean," protested Penwarne. His face was white now. His nervousness was self-evident. For the first time, I began to see the direction in which Holmes was leading.

"Your father was impecunious. You needed desperately to re-store the family fortune; otherwise, you were faced with selling Tre-griffian House to pay his debts. So a new plan came to your mind, one that would make you a mass murderer but rich. Using your pro-jector, and a piece of film, you lured three ships to their doom. You went into the wrecking business as many folks in these parts used to do over a hundred years ago."

"How do you claim that I managed to lure them?"

"With a film of some dancer that you probably made in Paris. Because of the angles involved to ensure the ships saw the image, you had to reflect your image via a third means. A concave mirror would bounce the image, which your projector shone onto it, across to the large rock covered with guano. That almost whitewash sub-stance made a suitable screen on which to project it."

"Rubbish," snorted the now trembling Harry Penwarne. "The ships went down off the rocks. If I were able to do such a thing, how could I have collected the salvage from those wrecks?"

"You went diving there at night, with your assistant. People heard the whining and gasping of your compressed air apparatus, but being anchored behind the rocks, they did not see your boat. I presume that you went down looking only for the ship's safe and tak-ing cash and jewels. Perhaps you planned to lift some of the less eas-ily negotiable materials at a later day. . . ."

Harry Penwarne half rose from his chair, but his pale face and dark staring eyes were not on Holmes. They were staring past him.

"Jean-Claude!" he cried in French. "We can bluff it out. Don't give the game away! . . ."

I turned at once and saw Penwarne's manservant leveling a revolver at Holmes.

I confess that I was considered something of a crack shot when I was serving in the Northumberland Fusiliers, but until that instant I had never shot so well. I did so from my lap, for thus far only could I draw my revolver and let off a shot that impacted on the hand of Jean-Claude. He cried out in pain. The gun fell from his hand. Captain Trevossow leaped forward and scooped it up to cover the manservant.

I was now covering Harry Penwarne, but the shock of the discovery of his nefarious crimes sent the young man into a state of incapability. He collapsed back in his chair.

"I cannot believe it!" cried the astounded Sir Jelbart. "What made you suspect young Harry?"

"When I realized that he was using a compressed air machine on his boat, as I said. Also, when you told me about noticing his bloodshot eyes. It's a condition caused by breaking blood vessels in the eye, a hazard of deep-sea diving that has not been overcome yet."

Sir Jelbart shook his head. "Astounding," he muttered.

"You were absolutely right in your theory, Sir Jelbart. The only problem I had was to discover how it was done. A search of the house will probably supply the evidence," Holmes said airily. "You will find cameras, projectors, the electrical batteries he ferried out to the cave to work the projector, and above all, the film of the young woman dancing."

"What was the meaning of the broken glass, Mr. Holmes?" asked Captain Trevossow. "Why was it broken?"

"Previously, no one had noticed the mirror that Penwarne had erected to reflect the image where it was needed, so that it could be seen from the ships. He was able to row to the rock and retrieve it at his leisure. Last night, however, he realized someone was near the rocks investigating. Our rockets gave us away. To destroy the evidence of the concave mirror, he used a rifle or pistol to shatter it to save time in rowing across from where he had the camera. He switched off his projector, dismantled it, and hurried home in his boat with his accomplice, Jean-Claude. In his rush, he forgot to take the used Leclanche battery."

As Holmes predicted, in a cellar of the old house, an entire laboratory was discovered with Penwarne's experiments and models of cameras and projectors and various pieces of film he had shot.

Holmes spent a long time examining them with intense interest.

"In many ways, our friend Penwarne's development of the camera, projector, and the film he used seems more advanced than Lumiere's. The coated celluloid is inspirational. In other circumstances, Penwarne might have been a genius and pioneer of this new cinematography and made his fortune. Instead, like all twisted genius, he resorted to crime. Doubtless, he and his accomplice will make that early morning walk to meet the end of a hemp rope at Bodmin Moor. When all is said and done, he was stupid."

I frowned. "Why stupid, Holmes?"

"Because the most successful criminal is one who does not draw attention to himself or his crime. A naked siren dancing on a rock—why, that is enough to bring all manner of interested persons rushing to this isolated part of Cornwall. The supernatural always entices people like moths are enticed to a candle. Sooner or later, he would have been discovered."

"But you discovered him the sooner, Holmes," I pointed out.

"It required no great mental effort on my part, dear fellow. I fear that people will think the less of my powers of deduction if they perceive this as a case of which I am proud. Therefore, I entreat you not to publish any account of it until after I have shuffled off this mortal coil."

He gave a deep sigh.

"Now, I hope, we can return to our cottage and suffer no more interruptions. After all, I am down here to rest from such activities. Once again, my dear Watson, I think we may dismiss the matter from our mind, and go back with a clear conscience to the study of those Chaldean roots that are surely to be traced in the Cornish branch of the great Celtic speech."

THE KIDNAPPING
— OF MYCROFT HOLMES —

I was watching the face of my estimable friend, Sherlock Holmes, who sat opposite me at the breakfast table. He was examining the telegraph that Mrs. Hudson had brought up with the tea tray, his features mirroring his perplexity. The tea was left untouched.

"Some bad news, Holmes?" I ventured, no longer able to contain my curiosity.

He glanced up and blinked. Then he held out the flimsy sheet of paper toward me. "A most singular communication from my brother, Mycroft."

I took the telegraph and read: *Should anything happen to me, do not trust the man who is Gentle. If I disappear, look for me near the Lump of Goats in the land of the Race of Ciar.—Mycroft.*

I started to chuckle. "Is he fond of a tipple, this brother of yours?" I said. "It sounds as though he were the worse for a glass or two when he wrote it."

But Holmes's face was serious, and he seemed concerned. "You do not know Mycroft. It is some cipher that I must solve. He must be in trouble if he cannot telegraph me in plain language."

Holmes retired to his armchair, and soon I became aware of the wreath of smoke rising slowly from his pipe. It reminded me that I was short on tobacco and so, finishing my breakfast, I went out to the local tobacconist. I also bought a newspaper. When I returned, barely fifteen minutes later, I found Holmes in a high state of agitation.

"Watson," he cried as I entered, "thank God you have returned. I need you to accompany me on a short trip."

"Whatever is the matter, dear fellow?" I demanded, never having seen him moved to such emotion before.

"You'll need an overnight case," he went on, not heeding my question, "and pack your service revolver. I fear that there may be difficult times ahead."

"Where are we off to?" I inquired.

"Dublin," he said shortly.

"To Ireland?" I was astonished. "Whatever for?"

He turned to me with a haunted look in his eyes. "I received another telegraph but ten minutes ago. It is my brother, Mycroft. He has been kidnapped."

It seems that I should pause in my narrative to make some explanation of those matters that Holmes was always reticent about my sharing with the English public in the accounts I made of his adventures. Of course, to the discerning eye, many clues as to the nature of Holmes's background have been plainly visible in my chronicles, although it was at his insistence that I never clearly spelled them out. I refer to the fact that Sherlock Holmes is Irish or, to be more precise, Anglo-Irish. Holmes had, however, a fear of prejudice, and this was not without cause. Therefore, I have promised him (and stipulated to my executors) that my accounts of those cases directly concerned with his background, such as the one I am about to relate, will not be released until one hundred years after his death.

Sherlock Holmes was of the Holmes family of Galway, which settled in Ireland in the seventeenth century. His uncle, Robert Holmes, was the famous Galway barrister whom the Irish have to thank for the organization of their National Schools. The Sherlock family on his mother's side, after which he was named, arrived in Meath at the time of Henry II's invasion of Ireland. He achieved distinction at Trinity College, Dublin, before winning a scholarship to Oxford—emulating his equally brilliant friend from Dublin, Oscar Wilde. His Irish background led to his interest in the Celtic languages and his subsequent authorship of such monographs as *Chaldean Roots in the Ancient Cornish Language*.

It was shortly after we met that I realized the acuteness of his ear in linguistic manners.

"Watson," he had said reflectively. "A name very common in northeast Ulster. I detect a County Down diction. You are probably descended from the old Scottish family of Mac Bhaididh, for that is usually Anglicized as Watson or MacWhatty or MacQuatt."

"Astounding, Holmes!" I gasped. "How did you know? I began my education in England at the age of seven!"

"Elementary, my dear Watson." He smiled mischievously. "You still retain the rising inflection at the ends of sentences. The musical rhythm of an accent is harder to displace than pronunciation."

It may also be remembered that Holmes's two greatest antagonists—Professor Moriarty and Colonel Moran—shared his Irish background. Indeed, like seems to have attracted like. Had I a gold sovereign for every time someone with an Irish name and background crossed our path, I would be a rich man. Take our landlady, Mrs. Hudson. Many visitors who lacked a fine ear mistook her as Scottish, and Holmes (who was possessed of a perverse sense of humor) was not loath to play up this charade. She was, in actuality, an Irish lady who had been married to one of the numerous Hudsons of Kilbaha in County Kerry.

I make this brief digression merely so that the background to this extraordinary story may be more fully appreciated.

Holmes had been summoned to Dublin that day—a little over a year since we'd first met—by a laconic telegraph that read: *Mycroft kidnapped. Meet me at Merrion Square. Superintendent Mallon, DMP.* He explained that his brother, Mycroft, had his rooms in Merrion Square. DMP stood for the Dublin Metropolitan Police.

Having caught the nightboat train at Paddington, we arrived at Kingstown, the port near Dublin, in the early hours of Saturday morning May 6, 1882. I make mention of the date for the sake of the more historically minded reader, as this was an historic time for Ireland and its relations with Britain. During the journey—a wild, dark trip across the storm-blown Irish sea spent mainly in the first

class lounge nursing whiskeys to keep down the mal de mer—
Holmes told me something of his brother, Mycroft. Mycroft was
seven years older than Holmes, a graduate of Trinity College,
Dublin, who had decided to make his career in Dublin Castle, the
seat of the imperial administration in Ireland. He worked in the fiscal department of the Under Secretary, a permanent official who
was head of the Civil Service. According to Holmes, his brother was
possessed of a brilliant mind but was indolent and not given to
sports or physical exercise and so was heavy in build.

"Why would anyone want to kidnap him?" I queried. "Is kidnapping usual in Ireland?"

Holmes replied with a shake of his head. "Not at all. But it does
not escape my notice that there is some political unrest in the country at this time. Have you been following Irish political events in the
newspapers?"

I confessed that I had not and was surprised that Holmes had
been, as he had always confessed his knowledge of political matters
to be feeble. After this exchange, Holmes became moody and refused to speculate further.

The journey from Kingstown into Westland Row, via the Dublin
and South Eastern Railway, was made in morose silence. Holmes
now and then would take out the two telegraphs he had received
and examine them with a deep furrow of concentration on his broad
brow.

Alighting from the train at Westland Row Railway Station,
Holmes ignored the cabbies and conducted me, with unerring step,
to a magnificent square of Georgian houses a short walk from the
station. He went directly to one of the terraced buildings and
paused before the door. I saw that it was ajar. Holmes pushed at it
tentatively. It swung open, revealing a shadowy, cavernous hallway.

"Mycroft's rooms are on the second floor," he explained as I followed him inside and up the stairs.

He halted before a door with a glimmering gaslight beside it,
which illuminated a small brass frame affixed to one of the wooden

panels. A card inserted in the frame read MYCROFT HOLMES, ARTIUM BACCALAUREUS. Holmes tapped on the door. It swung open immediately, and a large, florid-faced uniformed constable stood scowling at us.

"Is Mallon here?" asked Holmes before the constable could speak. "I am Sherlock Holmes."

"Superintendent Mallon is . . . ," began the constable ponderously, but another man, seeming to be in his early forties, quickly appeared at his shoulder.

"I am John Mallon," he said. There was no disguising his Ulster accent. "I have heard of you from my colleague Lestrade of Scotland Yard. You are the younger brother of Mr. Mycroft Holmes? I suppose by your presence here that you must have heard the news? Well, there is nothing that I can tell you at this stage. You should not have made the journey—"

Holmes cut him short by handing him one of the telegraphs. I perceived that it was the one summoning Holmes to Dublin, which had seemed to be sent by Mallon.

The detective glanced at it, and a frown gathered on his brow. "I did not send this," he said.

"So I have gathered. The questions are—who did and why?"

Mallon glanced at the paper again. "This was sent from the GPO in Sackville Street. Anyone could have sent it."

"Curious that you are here to meet me in accordance with the summons."

"Coincidental. No one knew I was coming here until midnight last night. That was when the local police notified me that your brother was missing."

At this stage, Mallon stood aside and gestured for Holmes to enter his brother's rooms. I followed and was met with a look of disapproving query.

"This is my friend and colleague Doctor Watson," explained Holmes, at which Mallon reluctantly acknowledged my existence before calling out, "MacVitty!"

At the summons, a tall cadaverous-looking man came from an inner room. He was dressed so that no one would doubt that he was exactly what he appeared to be—a gentleman's gentleman. Mallon inquired whether MacVitty had sent the telegraph to London. The man shook his head. Then he turned his keen eyes on Holmes and greeted him as one known of old. "It's good to see you again, Master Sherlock, but I'd rather it were under better conditions."

"I gather that you summoned the police, MacVitty," Holmes replied kindly. "Let's hear the details."

"Not much to tell. Master Mycroft was expected home on Thursday night. He was going to dine in and not at his club. He gave me specific orders to have a sea trout and a chilled bottle of Pouilly-Fumé ready. When he did not turn up, I thought he had changed his mind. But then Mr. O'Keeffe came down. He said that he had been invited to brandy and cigars. Mr. O'Keeffe works with Master Mycroft at the Castle, sir."

"You said 'came down,'" Holmes said quickly.

"Mr. O'Keeffe has rooms on the top floor of this building. He waited awhile before returning to his own apartment. When Master Mycroft did not show up for breakfast, I sent for the police."

"And that was Friday morning?" queried Holmes sharply.

"The local police did not think it necessary to act until late last night," said Mallon defensively. "There are many reasons why an unattached gentleman might not return home at night. . . ."

"It is strange that you turn up now, Mallon," mused Holmes, "at the precise time the telegraph asked me to meet you here."

Mallon's eyes narrowed. "I am not sure what you mean."

"Information is a two-way street. I know that you are no ordinary policeman, Mallon. You are the director of the detective branch of G Division, which is devoted to political matters such as investigating the Irish Republican Brotherhood, the Land League, and other such extremist movements. I know that you were the very man who arrested Charles Parnell of the Irish Party at Morrison's Hotel last

October. This doubtless implies that your superiors believe a political motive is behind my brother's disappearance."

Mallon smiled sourly. He seemed to be irritated by the reference to his superiors. "It is the job of G Division to make itself acquainted with everything that happens to highly placed political personages—especially in this day and age."

"Yet you have formed no opinion of what has occurred?"

"Not as yet, Mr. Holmes."

Holmes sighed and then, with a quick beckoning gesture to me, he headed for the door. "We shall doubtless be in touch again, Mallon," he said. "We will take rooms in the Kildare Street Club."

Outside the door, he addressed me in a low tone. "Come, Watson. We will speak with Mr. O'Keeffe. He should not have departed for work as yet," he added, with a glance at his fob watch.

We started up the stairs only to be met by a young man coming down them. He was well dressed and carried himself in a lackadaisical manner.

"Mr. O'Keeffe?" queried Holmes, acting on impulse.

The young man halted, then frowned as he examined us. "That's me," he said. "Who might you be?"

"I am Sherlock Holmes, the brother of Mycroft. This is my friend Doctor Watson."

O'Keeffe's expression was one of friendly concern. "Has old Mycroft turned up?"

Holmes shook his head. "I understand that you were to have had brandy and cigars in his room on the evening that he went missing?"

"I thought there was something odd going on that evening," the young man confessed, apparently crestfallen at our negative news.

Holmes's eyes narrowed slightly. "Odd? In what way?"

"We left the Castle together and walked down towards Nassau Street. We'd made arrangements to meet later, so I left him on the corner of Nassau and Dawson, as I had an appointment. I had gone but a few yards when something made me glance back. I saw Mycroft speaking to a couple of singular covers. Not out of place, you understand, but clearly rough diamonds. Thickset fellows. One seemed to be jabbing him in the ribs with his finger. I turned back, but as I did so, a carriage pulled up, a fair-sized one. It was covered in a calèche, I think it is called. You know the sort. There was an emblem on the door, as I recall—a scallop shell depicted in white. It appeared to me that Mycroft was pushed into the carriage by the two men, who then followed him in. It was rolling away down Nassau Street before I got anywhere near it."

Holmes stood thoughtfully rubbing his chin. "Perhaps just as well," he muttered.

The young man was puzzled. "Why, what do you mean?"

"I believe that Mycroft was propelled into the carriage at the point of a revolver, and had you interfered, you would have been shot."

"Do you really think so?" O'Keeffe seemed astounded.

"I would be prepared to wager on it," Holmes assured him. "This was the last you saw of Mycroft, I presume?"

"Indeed, it was. I did not feel alarmed enough to mention this to anyone then. Later I turned up at his rooms as we had arranged, hoping he would give me an explanation of his carriage ride. But MacVitty told me that Mycroft had not returned, even though he had ordered his supper to be ready. I waited awhile, but he did not turn up." He looked directly at Holmes. "I suppose it would not be difficult to trace a carriage with such an emblem?"

"Did you send a telegraph to me?" Holmes said, ignoring his question.

"Never thought of it, old boy—couldn't even if I had. Mycroft said he had a younger brother in London somewhere, but I had no way of knowing your address." He suddenly glanced at his pocket watch. "Sorry, have to dash. Lots to do today. The new Lord Lieutenant and Chief Secretary are arriving to take over the administration. Must be at the Castle and spruced up. Have to act as the

Viceroy's ADC at the Viceregal Lodge tonight. Don't worry, old boy. G Division will sort things out. I saw Mallon of the DMP arrive a short while ago. You're in safe hands."

With a flourish of his hat, the young man passed on his way.

I saw that Holmes's face was glum. "Perhaps we'd better have a wash and brush up," I ventured. "It wasn't an easy overnight journey on the train and boat. We will do no good if we are in a state of fatigue."

Holmes agreed. We were about to leave the house when Superintendent Mallon came out of Mycroft's rooms. He seemed surprised to find us still in the house. "I'll walk with you to Kildare Street, gentlemen," he offered as he opened the door.

I was sure Holmes was going to refuse and was surprised when he accepted. "That is good of you, Superintendent."

"The old city is in a fine state with the arrival of the new Lord Lieutenant," said Mallon obliviously as we left the house. "They say that Gladstone has taken leave of his senses and done a deal with the Republicans. He's let the leaders out of jail. Given them their cherished land reforms. The next thing we'll see is a parliament back here in Dublin. Give these Fenians an inch, and they'll take a mile. They say that's the purpose for which Lord Cavendish has just replaced Lord Cowper as Viceroy."

I did not follow Irish politics, although I knew something about the recent land war against the big landowners—a reaction to the worsening conditions experienced by Irish tenant farmers. There had been the famous case of Captain Boycott, Lord Erne's estate manager, who had been ostracized by his workers and the local community. The campaign had been led by members of the Land League and Irish Party, who also wanted self-government for Ireland.

"There'll be trouble, mark my words, if Cavendish does start to give the Fenians more concessions," went on Mallon. "And you don't have to stretch the imagination to see the connections between them. I hear Cavendish is even related to Parnell's wife. Parnell, Davitt, Sexton, and Dillon—the Fenian leaders—are already on their way to London to discuss matters with Gladstone, while Cavendish and his new Chief Secretary Burke arrive here."

I subsequently learned that Mallon used the term *Fenian* to describe anyone who supported any form of devolved government and not merely Irish Republicans. His voice droned a bit. I was sure that poor Holmes, distracted as he was about his brother's disappearance and the mysterious faked telegraph he had received, was totally uninterested in the superintendent's political musings.

When Mallon left us, I asked why Holmes had been so enthusiastic for him to accompany us to Kildare Street.

"Didn't you see the calèche drawn up across the street, Watson?" he asked in surprise. "A black carriage with a white scallop shell emblem on its doors?"

The Kildare Street Club was housed in an opulent red brick Gothic-style building at the end of the street that bore its name. The club, as Holmes informed me, was exclusive to the most important families in Ireland. No Catholics were allowed in membership, nor anyone who was known to support Irish efforts to secure "home rule." In fact, no army officer below the rank of major, nor naval officer below a lieutenant-commander, was even allowed within its portals. It turned out that Mycroft Holmes was an honored member. Sherlock Holmes was welcomed in his brother's name.

We spent the morning at the great General Post Office in Sackville Street, opposite an edifice called Nelson's Pillar, which seemed a pale imitation of the monument in London's Trafalgar Square. I kept a wary eye on all carriages, but there was no sign of the black one with a white scallop shell emblem. We also made inquiries about the emblem and were told that it was the emblem of no less a person than Lord Maynooth, a leading spokesman of the Liberal Government. I pointed out that such a man could not possibly be involved in kidnapping and that O'Keeffe must have mistaken the emblem.

Holmes, however, felt that we should pay a call on the noble

THE KIDNAPPING OF MYCROFT HOLMES

lord later in the day. Our inquiries about the mysterious telegraph proved fruitless, and eventually we returned to the Kildare Street Club for a late luncheon, greatly despondent at our lack of success.

After lunch, a drowsiness overtook me. It was Thursday night since I had slept, and here we were on Saturday afternoon. Holmes noticed my eyelids drooping and advised me to take an hour's nap.

"Nonsense, old fellow," I protested. "If you are off to see our titled friend, then I shall come with you."

He shook his head. "I am going to rest for an hour or so, as well, Watson. We'll go to see Lord Maynooth this evening."

I went to my room but not before I had made Holmes swear that he would make no move without me. I then collapsed onto my bed. It seemed that only moments had passed before I was being shaken awake. Holmes was bending over me.

"Come on, Watson," he hissed. "The game's afoot!"

I blinked and struggled up. "So soon? What? . . ."

"It's early evening, old fellow. You've been asleep for nearly four hours," he admonished.

I leaped from the bed with a curse. "Why didn't you awaken me earlier?"

Holmes shrugged. "No cause. It was only a short while ago that our mystery friend made contact again. Here . . ."

He shoved a plain piece of paper into my hand. It was addressed simply to Mr. S. Holmes. It read: *Sorry I missed you at Merrion Square this morning. Be at the corner of Dawson Street and the north side of St. Stephen's Green at 7 P.M. You may bring your friend with you.*

I looked at Holmes, aghast. "But it is a quarter to," I cried, catching sight of the clock on the mantelshelf.

"Have no concern. The place is but a minute from here. Come on. And don't forget that revolver of yours."

We arrived punctually at 7 P.M. at the allotted place. Almost at once a black covered carriage, drawn by two black nags, pulled away from the curb on the opposite side of the road by the fenced park

221

and turned a semicircle across the thoroughfare to come to a rest where we stood. Holmes grabbed my sleeve and indicated the door. There was a white scallop shell emblem on it. There were very few people about, most having already dispersed for their evening meals. I placed my hand on the butt of my pistol inside my coat pocket.

The door of the carriage opened, and a soft Irish voice called, "Would you be so good as to step inside the carriage, Mr. Holmes? Doctor Watson, as well."

"Who are you?" demanded Holmes. "Are you holding my brother for ransom?"

"Your questions will be answered if you step inside," went on the voice in good humor. "And advise your friend not to do anything rash with the revolver he is handling in his pocket. He is covered at this moment and would be ill-advised to attempt any indiscretion, as it would certainly prove fatal."

Holmes glanced at me in resignation. "Best do as he says, Watson."

He climbed into the carriage, and I followed. We sat with our backs to the driver. Two shadowy figures were seated before us. The vehicle started with a jerk, throwing both of us forward. Before I had time to recover, one of the men had leaned forward and expertly searched me, removing my revolver. A moment later, Holmes also suffered a similar scrutiny.

"Both clean, Cap'n," muttered a voice.

Then the modulated, wry tones of the first speaker came out of the darkness. "There now, that is more civilized. We don't want any nasty accidents, do we? Remember, my companion has you both covered."

"Who are you?" I demanded, feeling much put out at being disarmed by these ruffians. "I presume you are not the noble lord who is the owner of the crest on this carriage?"

"Shall we say that I have a loan of it, Doctor," chuckled the man.

"I suppose you are the person who masqueraded as Superintendent Mallon?" asked Holmes.

"A good bit of sport, I thought. Mallon is no friend to us, but I thought you might respond to a telegraph from the DMP."

"I presume that you are Fenians?" Holmes observed.

"*Na Fianna,* the mythical warriors who protected the High Kings of Ireland," the man affirmed playfully. "It is a name to be proud of. Though we generally call ourselves the Irish Republican Brotherhood."

I felt a coldness in my being as I realized we were in the hands of the notorious Irish revolutionary movement.

"Can I ask why you are holding my brother?"

"You are leaping to conclusions, Mr. Holmes, which does your reputation no credit. We are going on a short journey, and when we arrive all will be explained."

With that a silence fell among us while the carriage rocked and clattered over the cobbles of the streets. The blinds were drawn, and I was painfully aware of the man with the revolver covering us, so there was no way I could observe where we were going.

The journey ended abruptly as the carriage came to a halt and the door was flung open by another shadowy figure who ordered us out. He also held a pistol. We were in a small enclosed yard. The man who had been addressed as Cap'n led the way into a house. It looked bare and uninhabited. He lit a lantern and led us along a gloomy corridor to a door at the far end. He tapped on it in a curious, measured manner. A voice answered, and he ushered us through into the room beyond. Inside were three men seated behind a table. There were two chairs placed before it, in which we were motioned to be seated.

"Let me apologize for the unorthodox manner in which you have been brought here, Mr. Holmes. You, too, Doctor Watson." The speaker, an elderly silver-haired man with a clear English accent, was seated in the center of the trio.

I was about to reply angrily when Holmes sat down. "I am surprised to see you here, my lord," he said to the speaker respectfully, "even though it was your carriage which brought us." Clearly this was none other than Lord Maynooth.

"I don't doubt it," replied the man. "But it is, perhaps, better that no names are mentioned, as Her Majesty's Government will deny this meeting has taken place. My colleagues"—he gestured to the men on either side of him—"represent the interests of the Irish Parliamentary Party and of the Irish Republican Brotherhood."

I think Holmes was just as astounded as I was at this further revelation.

Lord Maynooth continued. "May I inquire what your politics are, Mr. Holmes?"

"Perhaps you would be more specific?" Holmes was diffident.

I had to confess that I had been surprised during the time that I had known Holmes by his apparent singular lack of current political knowledge. I had once mentioned the death, during the previous year, of that great Scotsman, Thomas Carlyle, and he had naively asked me who he was. I subsequently discovered that Holmes often pretended a lack of knowledge as a means of avoiding political discussion. He did have some profound views, as I later learned.

"I refer to the current state in Ireland," Lord Maynooth replied.

"I support the Prime Minister's actions in the Land Act reforms," replied Holmes easily. "I believe the Coercion Acts of last year were a mistake and a tragedy. The arrest of elected politicians such as Parnell and Davitt was an unwise course in the extreme. I am old enough to remember the 1867 uprising in this country. Such heavy-handed methods will only ensure another one, therefore I would also support the reinstatement of a domestic parliament in Ireland."

"You are a Home Ruler, then, Mr. Holmes?" The question came from a well-dressed man with a dark beard on the left of the three men.

"I believe that is precisely what I have indicated," Holmes replied shortly.

"Well, Mr. Holmes, we are in dire straits," Lord Maynooth continued, "and it was necessary to confirm your sympathies. Yes, dire straits. The kidnapping of your brother is, you'll forgive me, but a sideshow in this grave matter."

Holmes looked grim. I saw his lips compress momentarily into a thin line. "We each have our priorities," he acknowledged curtly.

It seemed that it had been agreed that Lord Maynooth was to do most of the talking. "Our main task is to prevent anarchy from brewing in Ireland and spreading to the Imperial Government itself in London. Your reputation is known, Mr. Holmes, and when your brother was kidnapped, we could think of no one better than you to solve this difficulty. Your brother was working for us."

"Us?" Holmes's voice was sharp. "Again I must ask you to be specific. You have indicated what interests you represent—Government, Irish Party, and Republicans—but for what purpose have such disparate interests come together?"

"Simply for the sake of peace in these islands. We are all pledged to support the Kilmainham Treaty agreed upon between Prime Minister Gladstone and Mr. Parnell, the leader of the Irish Party. But there are some who wish no dilution of the Union who would see it destroyed—certain landowning families with vested interests, as well as those on the extreme edge of the Republican movement who have no patience for moderate political advance. Both sides object to the Kilmainham agreement and the release of the Irish prisoners. Among the fiercest critics are Viceroy Lord Cowper and Chief Secretary Forster. That is why Gladstone made them resign yesterday and replaced them."

"Where does Mycroft come into this?" interposed Holmes.

"Mycroft Holmes had alerted us to a plot, emanating from certain highly placed people, the purpose of which is to plunge this country into a catastrophic situation. He communicated that he knew the organizer of the plot. He was on his way to meet with our agent at Trinity College when he was kidnapped."

Holmes was leaning forward with a frown. "Who kidnapped him?"

"Have you heard of the Invincibles?"

Holmes reflected for a moment. "They were formed last year—a breakaway group from the IRB. They are extremists who believe in violence as a way to secure their aims."

"They are but a handful and have been publicly denounced by both the IRB and the Irish Party," said the sandy-haired man on the right, a little defensively I thought.

"We believe that there is a Unionist faction manipulating the Invincibles," went on Lord Maynooth. "Oh, unbeknownst to them, of course. They mean to create unrest, destroy the Kilmainham agreement, overturn the reforms, and discredit Parnell—preventing any hope of achieving Home Rule for Ireland. Doing so would also discredit Mr. Gladstone's Liberal Government, and its collapse would be inevitable. The effects on the whole empire might be chaotic."

"And the IRB are supportive of Parnell and Gladstone's joint policies?"

The sandy-haired man stirred a little and shrugged. "We are a pragmatic body, Mr. Holmes. Our uprising was crushed fifteen years ago. The Invincibles are as much of a threat to us as they are to anyone else. The way forward in practical terms, at this time, is to ensure that land reforms are achieved, as a first step toward eventual Home Rule—the day when the Irish nation will be able to decide its own future without London. We believe that some sinister plot is being concocted to discredit us, one which would set Ireland back a hundred years and bring back the Penal Laws. We know the plot must be put into action soon."

"Why soon?"

"Because today the new Viceroy, Lord Frederick Cavendish, and his Chief Secretary, Burke, arrived in Dublin to take over from the more conservative hands of Lord Cowper and Forster," explained Lord Maynooth.

The dark-bearded man summed up. "We ask you, Mr. Holmes, to help us find your brother and identify the leader of this plot, so that we may save the country from chaos."

Holmes answered without hesitation. "You may rely on my full assistance and that of my colleague, Doctor Watson here. But, gentlemen, I need clues. I need—"

There was a disturbance from outside the door. The mysterious "cap'n" made an apologetic gesture and withdrew. We could hear raised voices outside.

When the door opened again and the man returned, his face was deadly pale. "Too late!" he announced quietly.

"Too late?" cried Holmes, starting forward. "You mean Mycroft—"

The man stared at him for a moment and then shook his head. "Far worse, I fear. Gentlemen—" He turned to the three men sitting tensely behind the table. "—this evening, as they were walking outside the Viceregal Lodge on the grounds of Phoenix Park, Lord Cavendish and Chief Secretary Burke were stabbed to death. They have been assassinated. The Irish National Invincibles have admitted responsibility."

There was a silence that seemed to last a long time.

Lord Maynooth rose, his face cold and grim. "Reaction in England will be inevitable. Even though the Irish Party and the IRB have disassociated themselves from the Invincibles, they will be painted with the same brush. Arrests will follow, new Coercion Acts will be enforced, and the cause for land reform and Home Rule will be set back for generations."

The dark-bearded man on the left stood up also. "There is nothing to be done," he said simply.

Holmes rose in outrage. "And what of Mycroft?" he demanded.

"The plot is revealed. He is as good as dead," said Maynooth quietly.

"I refuse to accept that," Holmes said stubbornly.

"The country will be in a panic now," the dark-haired man said. "You brother is, sadly, expendable."

Only the man on the right, the IRB representative who had remained seated, looked compassionately at Holmes. "You have my support," he said quietly. "I suggest that we all reseat ourselves and see if we can save something out of this debacle."

The other two appeared reluctant but finally reseated themselves. Holmes had taken out one of the two telegraphs he had received in London and was examining it hastily. "Mycroft provided me with the clues, but I need a key. The answer is probably staring me in the face."

They looked at him in bewilderment. Holmes thrust the telegraph forward. They peered curiously at it. The quiet man, to the right, shook his head in bewilderment. "There isn't anything there, Mr. Holmes. It's all gibberish. It does not make sense in anyone's language."

Holmes stared at the man as if he had been struck. "Language!" he suddenly cried, causing us all to think that he had taken leave of his senses. "Language! Do you have an English-Irish Dictionary?"

We fretted impatiently for a quarter of an hour before a messenger sent for the purpose returned with a volume.

"Most dictionaries are Irish-English, but I found this old one from 1732, published in Paris . . . ," he started to explain. Holmes snatched it out of his hand, sat down by the lantern, and began busily turning pages. When he finally looked up, his face was flushed with triumph.

"Gentlemen, you must arrest O'Keeffe of Dublin Castle. He is your link with the Invincibles."

The cap'n let out a derisory whistle. "O'Keeffe? I know him. He's an Orangeman and would have no truck with the Invincibles."

"Nevertheless, he is the man whose name Mycroft was going to reveal. He had even invited O'Keeffe to come to his rooms on the night of his disappearance . . . I believe that was in order for your agents to arrest him."

Lord Maynooth examined Holmes with narrowed eyes. "You will have to tell us how you did this conjuring trick, sir," he demanded.

"Plenty of time afterward," Holmes snapped. "In the meantime, we must also find out if there is any building of note near

Maulnagower in County Kerry. Perhaps a country house owned by someone in the world of politics. It is my belief that Mycroft is being held there."

A sudden stillness had descended over the room. The eyes of our companions had turned to the dark-bearded man who had been seated to the left and seemed to represent the Irish Party.

"But isn't that where your country house is . . . ," began Lord Maynooth. Before he could finish, the dark-bearded man had uttered a curse and tried to leap for the door. He was expertly grappled by the cap'n and held in an arm lock.

"Holmes, this is amazing!" I cried. "How can you possibly have deduced that? Where did you get your information from?"

Holmes shot me a pitying glance. "We have been in possession of the main clues the whole time. All we lacked was the key to interpreting them. It was only when our Republican friend referred to 'language' that I realized that chat key was."

"Then let us in on the secret before we proceed, Mr. Holmes, for we are curious," pressed the silver-haired man. "Our colleague's action has proclaimed his guilt but how—?"

"My brother knew that he was in some danger. He had to warn me. He knew that he was facing a combination of two elements—the extreme Unionist faction and the extreme Republican faction. Between the two, little moves in Ireland that is not known about. Any telegraph sent from the GPO would be reported on by their agents, spies, and informers. Mycroft had to send the information to me in London in case the worst happened. So he encrypted a message to me, hoping that I would understand." He gestured to the telegraph.

"How could you interpret this through the Irish language?" demanded the silver-haired man.

"They key was the Irish language itself. Mycroft knew that I have made a study of the ancient Celtic languages and had worked, now and then, on preparing a monograph on the Chaldean roots that I perceived therein."

"How does that help?"

"Simply enough. I realized that Mycroft was identifying someone. The very man whom he was going to warn you against. What does he say?"

"He warns you not to trust a gentleman but does not say who," I said, peering at the telegraph.

"No!" Holmes almost exploded in irritation. "Observe more carefully! He says do not trust a man who is Gentle. Look, he uses a capital *G* in the word *Gentle.*

"A mistranscription by the clerk at the telegraph office?" I hazarded.

"It is deliberate. That was when I suddenly realized that an Irish word for *gentle* is *caomh.*" He pronounced the word *ceeve.* "That is the root of the name *O Caoimh,* which we commonly Anglicize as O'Keeffe." They were looking at him with wonder on their faces.

"Certain things O'Keeffe claimed now endorse this view. He said he was a witness to Mycroft's kidnapping and described Lord Maynooth's carriage. I suppose he knew your carriage?"

"Of course," agreed Maynooth. "But why describe it as the kidnapper's vehicle?"

"A clever fellow is O'Keeffe. He wanted to confuse me, put me on a wrong scent. All he needed was twelve hours to bring his plot to fruition. He also mentioned that he was acting as ADC to the Viceroy tonight. What would possess the Viceroy and his Chief Secretary to be walking outside the Viceregal Lodge in the darkness of the evening alone? Where was O'Keeffe? Did he suggest that exercise and lure them into that fatal ambush?"

"Very well, Mr. Holmes. We will bring O'Keeffe in. But how did you learn of the house in Kerry?"

"Once I understood the code Mycroft was using, the rest was obvious. The land of the race of Ciar was simple. The race of Ciar were called the Ciarraighe—Anglicized as Kerry—who gave their name to their territory. So now we must look for the place called 'lump of goats.' The word *lump* is *meall* in Irish, but mall in a place name is usually interpreted as a knoll. The knoll of goats—*Meall na nGabher.* Mycroft and I spent a vacation, when we were children, near a place Anglicized as Maulnagower in Kerry. He presumed that I would recognize it."

It did not take us long to discover that the Irish Party representative had been playing a double game and had plotted Parnell's re-arrest so that he would emerge as leader of a new extreme party. A short while later we were embarking at Kingsbridge Station, in the west of the city, on a train to Kerry with a score or so of armed men from the Royal Irish Constabulary. The train clattered through the darkness to a place called Killarney, where we switched to a slower local train heading toward a town called Cahirciveen. In the dawn light, the house at Maulnagower was surrounded. There were only four armed men guarding it.

Called upon to surrender, they put up a fight. One was killed, another wounded, before we burst in. In an upstairs room, bound hand and foot on a bed, was the person of Mycroft Holmes. He was badly bruised, and there was a cut over one eye. When he was sitting up on the bed and rubbing his wrists to restore circulation, he finally smiled dourly at his younger brother. "It took you a while to fathom my cryptogram," he admonished. "I expected you to be here yesterday."

Holmes regarded him with sibling disapproval. "I expected you to be dead. Why did they keep you alive?"

"Oh, they certainly had planned a Kerry bog for me. But firstly they wanted to know exactly what I knew and who I had passed it on to before they rid themselves of my company. O'Keeffe was due to come down later today or tomorrow and then . . ." He shrugged. "Where is O'Keeffe, by the way?"

"Hopefully, he has been arrested by the good Superintendent Mallon," Holmes assured him.

"Capital! A strange fanatic, is O'Keeffe. The worst kind. But I believe that there were more important people manipulating him— powerful politicians and military men who do not want to see any devolution of power to the Irish people."

"So O'Keeffe was only a minor cog in the wheels of this conspiracy?"

"An important cog," corrected Mycroft. "He was acting as an intermediary between the powerful factions involved and those who were set to do the dirty work."

Holmes sighed. "I suppose that we'd best return to Dublin and see what O'Keeffe has to confess."

O'Keeffe had nothing to say. Superintendent Mallon had led the raid on O'Keeffe's rooms in Merrion Square and had not been too subtle about it. He had charged up the stairs with a dozen men of the Dublin Metropolitan Police. As they had begun to break in the door there had been the crack of a revolver. When they had finally broken in, O'Keeffe was no longer in this world. He had shot himself in the head.

Mallon, considered the hero of the day, was not admonished for this. Between May 14 and June 9 of the following year, five of the Invincibles were duly executed for the Phoenix Park murders; eight others were sentenced to long terms of imprisonment. The informer who had turned state's evidence to secure the convictions was eventually shot dead on the SS *Melrose Castle* off Cape Town some months later. The Invincibles, as an organization, disappeared as quickly as it had materialized.

However, Holmes regarded the case as one of his worst failures, for he had not solved it in time to prevent the Phoenix Park murders and public outrage over the killings forced the Government to disregard the Kilmainham agreement. Parnell and other Irish leaders, having been released from prison only four days before the murders, were subjected to harassment and arrest, Gladstone was compelled to abandon his movement toward Home Rule, block further land reforms, and introduce more coercion acts in Ireland as troop reinforcements were poured into the country. Ireland, which had stood on the brink of a peaceful settlement, was plunged once again into chaos. Whoever had pulled O'Keeffe's strings to induce him to manipulate the extremist Invincibles took those secrets to the grave. No one ever determined who it had been.

Mycroft Holmes, for his own personal safety, left service in Dublin Castle and, with the personal patronage of Gladstone, removed to London as an interdepartment Government adviser. Tragedy stalked Lord Maynooth, who was sent to be governor of one of the Australian colonies. His second son was shot dead in his locked bedroom at his Park Lane residence, a crime Holmes was able to lay at the door of Colonel Moran. Holmes, for public consumption, proposed that the motive had been a disagreement over cards. Privately, he thought it had been a more sinister political assassination designed to keep Maynooth in line.

The upheaval in his native land brought about by the murders had a profound effect on Sherlock Holmes. It was shortly after the closing of the case that his long periods of lethargy and indolence began, along with his use of narcotics when he had no puzzle to concentrate his gifted mind upon—to ease what he described as the "unutterable boredom" of his life.

I know that the case of his brother's kidnapping had changed his character into more cynical extremes by a realization of just how far those close to the center of power would go to protect their self-interest. In the year before he finally retired to the Sussex coasts, Sherlock Holmes caused a furor by refusing an offered knighthood from Edward VII. Why did he refuse that accolade? Holmes told me that he had done so because he believed that Ireland had been shabbily treated by the Imperial Establishment. Nevertheless, he had made me agree that I would not allow any of the cases involving his Irish background to be released to the public until long after his death.

— A STUDY IN ORANGE —

Somewhere in the vaults of the bank of Cox and Co., at Charing Cross, there is a travel-worn and battered tin dispatch box, with my name, John H. Watson, MD, late Indian Army, painted on the lid. It is filled with papers, nearly all of which are records of cases to illustrate the curious problems which Mr. Sherlock Holmes had at various times to examine.

— "The Problem of Thor Bridge"

This is one of those papers.

It was my estimable friend, the consulting detective Mr. Sherlock Holmes, who drew the printing error to my attention.

"Really, my dear Watson!" he exclaimed, one morning over breakfast, as he thrust the copy of *Collier's Magazine* toward me. "How can you let something like this slip by? I have often found myself remarking on the considerable liberties that you have taken in your accounts of my cases, but this date is an error in the extreme. Detail, my dear Watson. You must pay attention to detail!"

I took the copy of the magazine from his hands and glanced at the page on which his slim forefinger had been tapping in irritation. *Collier's* had just published my account of the case of "Black Peter," in which Holmes had been able to clear young John Neligan of the accusation of murder of Captain "Black Peter" Carey. He had caused the arrest of the real culprit, Patrick Cairns. The case had occurred some eight years before, in 1895 to be precise. Indeed, it had only been with some caution that I had decided to write it at all. Although the events happened in Sussex, all three men were Irish sailors, and Holmes was always reticent when it came to allowing the public to read anything that associated him with Ireland.

This was, I must hasten to say, not due to any bigotry on the part of Holmes. It was simply a stricture of my old friend that no reference be made that might associate him with his Anglo-Irish background. He was one of the Holmes family of Galway. Like his brother, Mycroft, he had started his studies at Trinity College, Dublin, before winning his demyship to Oxford following the example of his fellow Trinity student Oscar Wilde. On arrival in England, Holmes had encountered some xenophobic anti-Irish and anticolonial hostilities. Such prejudices so disturbed him that he became assiduous in his attempts to avoid any public connection with the country of his birth. This eccentricity had been heightened in later years by public prejudicial reaction to the downfall and imprisonment of the egregious Wilde, whom he had known well.

While Holmes allowed me to recount some of his early cases in Ireland, such as "The Affray at the Kildare Street Club," "The Specter of Tullyfane Abbey," and "The Kidnapping of Mycroft Holmes," purportedly by Fenians, I had faithfully promised my friend that these accounts would be placed in my bank with strict instructions that they not be released until fifty years after my death or the death of my friend, whichever was the later event.

I was, therefore, fearful of some error that I had associated him in some manner with the nationality of the three men involved in the case of "Black Peter," that I took the magazine from him and peered cautiously at the page.

"I was very careful not to mention any Irish connection in the story," I said defensively.

"It is where you pay tribute to my mental and physical faculties for the year '95 that the error occurs," Holmes replied in annoyance.

"I don't understand," I said, examining the page.

He took back the magazine from me and read with careful diction: "In this memorable year '95, a curious and congruous succession of cases had engaged his attention, ranging from his famous investigation of the sudden death of Cardinal Tosca—an inquiry which was carried out by him at the express desire of His Holiness the Pope. . . ."

He paused and looked questioningly at me.

"But the case was famous," I protested. "It was also publicly acknowledged that the pope asked specifically for your help. I kept some of the articles that appeared in the public press. . . ."

"Then I suggest you go to your archive of tittle-tattle, Watson," he interrupted sharply. "Look up the article."

I moved to the shelves where I maintained a few scrapbooks in which I occasionally pasted such articles of interest connected with the life and career of my friend. It took me a little while to find the six column inches that had been devoted to the case by the *Morning Post*.

"There you are," I said triumphantly. "The case of Cardinal Tosca was recorded."

His stare was icy. "And have you noticed the date of the article?"

"Of course. It is here, for the month of November 1891. . . ."

"*Eighteen ninety-one?*" he repeated with studied deliberation.

I suddenly realized the point that he was making.

I had set the date down as 1895. I had been four years out in my record.

"It is a long time ago," I tried to justify myself. "It is easy to forget."

"Not for me," Holmes replied grimly. "The case featured an old adversary of mine whose role I did not discover until after that man's own death while in police custody in early 1894. That was why I knew that the date that you had ascribed to the case was wrong."

I was frowning, trying to make the connection. "An old adversary? Who could that be?"

Holmes rose abruptly and went to his little Chubb Safe, bent to it, and twiddled with the locking mechanism before extracting a wad of paper.

"This," he said, turning to me and tapping the paper with the stem of his pipe, "was what I found in my adversary's apartment when I went to search it after his death. It is a draft of a letter. Whether he sent it or not, I am not sure. Perhaps it does not matter. I believe that it was fortuitous that I found it before the police, who would doubtless have made it public or, worse, it might have fallen into other hands so that the truth might never have been known to me. It is a record of my shortcomings, Watson. I will allow you to see it but no other eyes will do so during my lifetime. You may place it in that bank box of yours with your other scribbling. Perhaps after some suitable time has passed following my death, it can be opened to public scrutiny. That I shall leave to posterity."

I took the document from him and observed the spidery handwriting that filled its pages.

I regarded Holmes in bewilderment. "What is it?"

"It is the true story of how Cardinal Tosca came by his death. You have had the goodness to claim the case as one of my successes. This will show you how I was totally outwitted. The man responsible wrote it."

My jaw dropped foolishly. "But I was with you at the time. You solved the case to the satisfaction of Scotland Yard. Who—?"

"Colonel Sebastian Moran, the man who I once told you was the second most dangerous man in London. He was my adversary, and I did not know it. Read it, Watson. Read it and learn how fallible I can be."

The Conduit Street Club, London W1
May 21, 1891

My dear "Wolf Shield":
So he is dead! The news is emblazoned on the newspaper billboards at every street corner. His friend, Watson, has apparently given an interview

to reporters in Meiringen, Switzerland, giving the bare details. Holmes and Moriarty have plunged to their deaths together over the Reichenbach Falls. Sherlock Holmes is dead, and in that news I can find no grief for Moriarty, who has dispatched him to the devil! Moriarty, at his age, was no street brawler and should have sent his hirelings to do the physical work. So Moriarty's untimely end was his own fault. But that he took that sanctimonious and egocentric meddler to his death is a joy to me.

Holmes was always an irritant to me. I remember our first clash in the Kildare Street Club in Dublin, back in '73. He was but a young student then, just gone up to Oxford. He and his brother, Mycroft, who, at the time, was an official at Dublin Castle, were lunching in the club. It chanced that Moriarty and I were also lunching there. It was some paltry misunderstanding over a ridiculous toilet case with that old idiot, the Duke of Cloncurry and Straffan, that Holmes's meddling caused me to be thrown out of the Club and banned from membership.

It was not the last time that little pipsqueak irritated me and thwarted my plans. But there is one case where he was not successful in his dealings with me. Now my own ego must lay claim to having got the better of that Dublin jackeen. I proved the better man but, alas, he went to his death without knowing it. I would have given anything that he had plunged to his death knowing that Sebastian Moran of Derrynacleigh had outwitted him while he claimed to be the greatest detective in Europe! But, my dear "Wolf Shield," let me tell you the full story, although I appreciate that you know the greater part of it. You are the only one that I can tell it to for, of course, you were ultimately responsible for the outcome.

In November of 1890 His Eminence Cardinal Giacomo Tosca, nuncio of Pope Leo XIII, was found dead in bed in the home of a certain member of the British Cabinet in Gayfere Street not far from the Palace of Westminster. The facts, as you doubtless recall, created a furor. You will remember that Lord Salisbury headed a Conservative government that was not well disposed to papal connections at the time. The main reason was the government's stand against Irish Home Rule summed up in their slogan—"Home Rule is Rome Rule." That very month Parnell had been reelected leader of the Irish Party in spite of attempts to discredit him.

The Irish Party controlled four-fifths of all Irish parliamentary seats in Westminster. They were considered a formidable opposition.

A doctor named Thomson, called in to examine the body of the papal nuncio, caused further speculation by refusing to sign a death certificate, as he told the police that the circumstances of the death were indistinct and suspicious. The doctor was supported in this attitude by the local coroner.

The alarums that followed this announcement were extraordinary. The popular press demanded to know whether this meant the papal nuncio was murdered. More important, both Tory and Liberal newspapers were demanding a statement from government on whether the nuncio had been an intermediary in some political deal being negotiated with Ireland's Catholics.

What was Cardinal Tosca doing in the house of the Conservative government Minister Sir Gibson Glassford? More speculation was thrown on the fire of rumor and scandal when it was revealed that Glassford was a cousin, albeit distant, of the Earl of Zetland, the Viceroy in Dublin. Moreover, Glassford was known to represent the moderate wing of the Tories and not unsympathetic to the cause of Irish Home Rule.

Was there some Tory plot to give the Irish self-government in spite of all their assurances of support for the Unionists? All the Tory leaders, Lord Salisbury, Arthur Balfour, Lord Hartington, and Joseph Chamberlain among them, had sworn themselves to the Union and made many visits to Ireland declaring that Union would never be severed. Yet here was a cardinal found dead in the house of a Tory minister known to have connections with Ireland. It came as a tremendous shock to the political world.

Catholic bishops in England denied any knowledge of Cardinal Tosca being in the country. The Vatican responded by telegraph also denying that they knew that Cardinal Tosca was in England. Such denials merely fueled more speculation of clandestine negotiations.

As for Sir Gibson Glassford himself—what had he to say to all this? Well this was the truly amusing and bizarre part of the story.

Glassford denied all knowledge of the presence of Cardinal Tosca in his house. Not only the press but also the police found this hard to believe.

In fact, the Liberal press greeted the minister's statement with derision, and editorials claimed that the government was covering up some dark secret. There were calls for Glassford to resign immediately. Lord Salisbury began to distance himself from his junior minister.

Glassford stated that he and his household had retired to bed at their usual hour in the evening. The household consisted of Glassford himself, his wife, two young children, a nanny, a butler called Hogan, a cook, and two housemaids. They all swore that there had been no guests staying in the house that night and certainly not His Eminence.

In the morning, one of the housemaids, descending from her room in the attic, noticed the door of the guest's room ajar and the glow of a lamp still burning. An attention to her duties prompted her to enter to extinguish the light, and then she saw Cardinal Tosca. His clothes were neatly folded at the foot of the bed, his boots placed carefully under the dressing table chair. He lay in the bed clad in his nightshirt. His face was pale and his eyes wide open.

The maid was about to apologize and leave the room, thinking this was a guest whose late arrival was unknown to her, when she perceived the unnatural stillness of the body and the glazed stare of the eyes. She turned from the room and raised the butler, Hogan, who, ascertaining the man was dead, informed his master, after which the police were called.

It was not long before the clothing and a pocketbook led to the identification of His Eminence.

The household was questioned strenuously, but no one admitted ever seeing Cardinal Tosca on the previous night or on any other night; no one had admitted him into the house. Glassford was adamant that he and his wife had never met the cardinal, or even heard of him, let alone extended an invitation to him to be entertained as a guest in their house.

Inquiries into the Catholic community in London discovered that Cardinal Tosca had arrived in the city incognito two days before and was staying with Father Michael, one of the priests at St. Patrick's Church in Soho Square. This was the first public Catholic Church to be opened in England since the Reformation. It had been consecrated in 1792. But Father Michael maintained that he did not know the purpose of Cardinal

Tosca's visit. The Cardinal had simply told him that he had arrived from Paris by the boat train at Victoria and intended to spend two days in important meetings. He exhorted Father Michael not to mention his presence to anyone, not even to his own bishop.

Now, and this was the point that troubled the police the most, according to Father Michael, the cardinal had retired to his room in the presbytery, that is the priest's house, in Sutton Street, Soho, at ten o'clock in the evening. Father Michael had looked in on His Eminence because the cardinal had left his missal in the library and the priest thought he might like to have it before retiring. So he saw the cardinal in bed in his night attire and he was looking well and fit. At seven o'clock the next morning, Cardinal Tosca was found dead by the housemaid a mile and a half away in Sir Gibson Glassford's house in Gayfere Street, Westminster.

The press redoubled their calls for Glassford to resign, and the Liberal press started to call on Lord Salisbury's entire government to offer their resignation. Riots had burst out in Belfast instigated by Unionists, and various factions of the Orange Order, the sectarian Unionist movement, were on the march, and the thundering of their intimidating lambeg drums was resounding through the streets of the Catholic ghettoes.

The police confessed that they had no clue at all. They did, however, treat the butler, poor Hogan, to a very vigorous scrutiny and interrogation, and it was discovered that he had some tenuous links to the Irish Party, having some cousin in membership of the party. Glassford, a man of principle, felt he should stand by his butler and so added to the fuel of speculation.

The police admitted that they were unsure of how the cardinal came by his death, let alone why, and were unable to charge anyone with having a hand in it.

Because of the suspicion of an Irish connection, which was mere prejudice on the part of the authorities due to the Catholic connection, the case was handed over to the Special Irish Branch, which is now more popularly referred to as the Special Branch of Scotland Yard. The Police Commissioner James Monro had formed this ten years before to fight the Irish Republican terrorism. The head of the Special Branch was Chief Inspector John G. Littlechild. And it was through the private reports of Detective

Inspector Gallagher that I was able to observe, in some comfort, the events that now unfolded.

It was some seven days after the revelation of Cardinal Tosca's death that Chief Inspector Littlechild received a visit from Mycroft Holmes. This was a singular event, as Mycroft Holmes, being a senior government official in Whitehall, was not given to making calls on his juniors. With Mycroft Holmes came his insufferable younger brother, Sherlock. My friend Gallagher, who had the information as to what had transpired directly from Littlechild himself, told me about this meeting. Littlechild had been handed an embossed envelope bearing a crest. No word was said. He opened it and found a letter entirely in Latin, a language of which he had no knowledge. It showed the arrogance of the Holmes Brothers that they did not offer a translation until the Chief Inspector made the request for one.

It was a letter from none other than Gioacchino Pecci, who for thirteen years had sat on the papal throne in Rome as Leo XIII. The letter requested that the police allow Sherlock Holmes to investigate the circumstances of the death of the papal nuncio and provide whatever support was required. Mycroft Holmes added that the prime minister had himself sanctioned the request, presenting a note from Lord Salisbury to that effect.

I was told that Littlechild had an intense dislike of Sherlock Holmes. Holmes had not endeared himself to Littlechild, because he had often insulted some of Scotland Yard's best men—Inspector Lestrade, for example. Inspector Tobias Gregson and Inspector Stanley Hopkins had also been held up to public ridicule by Holmes's caustic tongue. But what could Littlechild do in such circumstances but accept Holmes's involvement with as good a grace as he could muster?

Holmes and his insufferable and bumbling companion, Watson, were to have carte blanche to question Sir Gibson Glassford's household and make any other inquiries he liked. Littlechild had thankfully made one condition, which was to come in handy for me. Detective Inspector Gallagher was to accompany Holmes at all times so that the matter would remain an official Scotland Yard inquiry. Thus it was that I was kept in touch with everything that the so-called Great Detective was doing while he was entirely unaware of my part in the game.

This is the part of the story that my friend Gallagher narrated to me.

The first thing that Holmes informed Gallagher of was that he had telegraphed Cardinal Tosca's secretary in Paris. The secretary confirmed that Cardinal Tosca had caught the boat train to London, promising to return within forty-eight hours. The journey had been prompted by the arrival of a stranger at Cardinal Tosca's residence in Paris late one night. The secretary had the impression that the visitor was an American by the way he spoke English with an accent. When asked his business, the man presented a small pasteboard that had a name and a symbol on it. The secretary could not remember the name but was sure that the device was harp-shaped. The man spent a few minutes with the cardinal, and the next morning the cardinal caught the boat train. Moreover, the cardinal insisted on traveling alone, which was highly unusual.

Inspector Gallagher pointed out that had Holmes consulted him, he would have been informed that this information was already in police hands, having consulted the cardinal's secretary. Holmes was too conceited to be abashed by the fact. He believed that nothing was achieved unless he personally achieved it.

Gallagher accompanied Holmes and Watson in a hansom cab to their first port of call: the local mortuary where the body of the cardinal was being preserved, much to the outcry of the Catholic Church, who felt it scandalous that His Eminence was thus prevented a lying in state and burial according to their practices.

Holmes insisted that he and Watson should examine the body, and this was done, after much argument, in the company of the original examining doctor, Thomson, and the coroner, with Gallagher looking on without enthusiasm. In fact, Gallagher found Holmes's involvement quite objectionable. He seemed to claim authority over the medical experts and leaned over the corpse, using a large magnifying glass as he examined it.

He suddenly let out a hiss of breath and turned to his companions. "Do you not remark on the slight bruising on this neck vein," he remarked, pointing dramatically, like one who has discovered something unique.

"I did so remark on it, Mr. Holmes," Dr. Thomson replied patiently. The coroner was clearly displeased.

"If you will read my report, that matter was made clear . . . ," he began, but Holmes actually waved him into silence.

"But what of the puncture wound which is discernible under my glass. What of that, sir?" he demanded of the doctor.

"I found it irrelevant," replied Thomson. "A bite of some sort, that is all."

Holmes turned to his crony, the sycophantic Watson. "Watson, please observe this mark and bear in mind that I have brought it to the attention of these . . . gentlemen."

Gallagher thought that he was being quite insulting, and so did Dr. Thomson and the coroner, who waited with unconcealed impatience for Holmes to complete his study.

Finally, Holmes turned to Gallagher and demanded to see the clothes that had been found with His Eminence's body.

"Is there any question that these clothes found by the body belong to the cardinal?" he asked as the parcel was handed to him.

"None whatsoever," he was assured. "Father Michael himself examined and identified them."

The cardinal's pocketbook, rosary, and pocket missal were all contained in the package.

"I presume that none of this material has been removed or tampered with?" queried Holmes.

Gallagher flushed with mortification. "Scotland Yard, Mr. Holmes, is not in the habit of removing or altering evidence, as you well know."

Holmes seemed oblivious of his insults, and he searched through the pocket book, which contained some banknotes in both French and English currencies and little else apart from two pasteboard visiting cards. They bore the name "T. W. Tone" on them and a little harp device surmounted by a crown. Holmes showed them to Watson and said quietly, "Note these well, Watson, old friend." It was as if Gallagher was not supposed to hear, but he did so and duly reported the fact to me.

Holmes then frowned and peered closely at the bundle of clothes.

"Wasn't the cardinal supposed to be wearing a nightshirt? Pray, where is that?"

"It was wrapped separately from the other clothing," Gallagher assured him, producing it. "As this was what the body was clad in, it was considered that it should be kept separate in case it provided any clues."

The insufferable Holmes took out the nightshirt and started to examine it. A curious expression crossed his features as he sniffed at it. Turning, he picked up the other clothing and sniffed at that. He spent so long smelling each item alternatively that Gallagher thought him mad.

"Where have these been stored during these last several days?"

"They have been placed in sacking and stored in a cupboard here in case they were needed as evidence."

"In a damp cupboard?"

"Of course not. They have been kept in a dry place."

Half an hour later saw them at Father Michael's presbytery, where His Eminence had last been seen alive. He treated the poor priest in the same brusque manner as he had the doctor and coroner. His opening remarks were, apparently, exceedingly offensive.

"Did the cardinal take narcotics, according to your knowledge?" he demanded.

Father Michael looked astounded, so shocked that he could say nothing for a moment and then, having regained control of his sensibilities, after Holmes's brutal affront, shook his head.

"He was not in the habit of using a needle to inject himself with any noxious substance?" Holmes went on, oblivious of the outrage he had caused.

"He was not—"

"—to your knowledge?" Holmes smiled insultingly. "Did the cardinal receive any letters or messages while he was here?"

Father Michael admitted no knowledge on the matter, but, at Holmes's insistence, he summoned the housekeeper. She recalled that a man had presented himself at the door of the presbytery demanding to see His Eminence. Furthermore, the housekeeper said the man was well muffled, with hat pulled down and coat collar pulled up, thus presenting no possibility of identification. She did remember that he had spoken with an Irish accent. He had presented a card with a name on it. The housekeeper could not remember the name but recalled that the card had a small device embossed on it, which she thought was a harp.

Gallagher could not forbear to point out that Scotland Yard had asked these questions prior to Holmes's involvement.

"Except the question of narcotics," replied Holmes, a patronizing expression on his face.

Holmes then demanded to see the bedroom where Father Michael had bade good night to His Eminence. He carefully examined it.

"I perceive this room is on the third floor of the house. That is irritating in the extreme."

Father Michael, Gallagher, and even Watson exchanged a puzzled glance with one another as Holmes went darting around the bedroom. In particular, he went through Cardinal Tosca's remaining clothing, sniffing at it like some dog trying to find a scent.

Holmes then spent a good half an hour examining the presbytery from the outside, much to the irritation of Gallagher and the bemusement of Watson.

From Soho they took a hansom cab to Sir Gibson Glassford's house in Gayfere Street. Glassford was apparently close to tears when he greeted them in his study.

"My dear Holmes," he said, holding the Great Detective's hand as if he were afraid to let go of it. "Holmes, you must help me. No one will believe me; even my wife now thinks that I am not telling her all I know. Truly, Holmes, I never saw this prelate until Hogan showed me the dead body in the room. What does it mean, Holmes? What does it mean? I would resign my office, if that would do any good, but I fear it would not. How can this strange mystery be resolved?"

Holmes extracted his hand with studied care and removed himself to the far side of the room. "Patience, Minister. Patience. I can proceed only when I have facts. It is a mistake to confound strangeness with mystery. True, the circumstances of this matter are strange, but they only retain *their mystery until the facts are explained. Watson, you know my methods. The grand thing is to be able to reason backward."*

Watson nodded, as if he understood, but he looked unhappy. Inspector Gallagher was pretty certain that the bumbling doctor had not a clue of what the arrogant man was saying. Glassford looked equally bewildered and had the courage to say so.

"Facts, my dear sir!" snapped Holmes. "I have no facts yet. It is a capital mistake to theorize before one has facts. Insensibly, one begins to twist facts to suit theories, instead of theories to suit facts."

He made Glassford, his wife, and all the servants go through the evidence they had already given to the police and then demanded to see the bedchamber in which His Eminence had been found.

"I observe this bedroom is on the fourth floor of your house. How tiresome!"

Once again, he wandered around the bedroom, paying particular attention to the carpeting, exclaiming once or twice as he did so.

"Seven days. I suppose it would have been an impossibility to think anything would have remained undisturbed."

The note of accusation caused Detective Inspector Gallagher to flush in annoyance. "We did our best to secure the evidence, Mr. Holmes," he began.

"And your best was to destroy whatever evidence there was," snapped Holmes conceitedly.

He then led the way outside the house and stood peering around as if searching for something. But he seemed to give up with a shake of his head. He was turning away when his eyes alighted on two men on the opposite side of the road who were peering down an open manhole. From the steps of the house, an elderly woman, clutching a Pekingese dog in her arms, was observing their toil, or rather lack of it, with disapproval.

An expression of interest crossed Holmes's features, and he went over to them. "Good afternoon, gentlemen," he greeted the workmen. "I observe by your expression that something appears amiss here."

The workmen gaped at him, unused to being addressed as gentlemen.

"Naw, guv'nor," replied one, shaking his head. "We do reckon ain't

A STUDY IN ORANGE

naw'fing wrong 'ere." He glanced at the elderly lady and said in an ag-
grieved voice. "But seems we've gotta check, ain't we?"

The elderly lady was peering shortsightedly at Holmes. "Young man!"
She accosted him in an imperial tone. "I don't suppose you are an employee of the local sewerage works?"

Holmes swung round, leaving the two workmen still gazing morbidly
down the hole in the road, and he smiled thinly. "Is there some way I can
be of assistance, madam?"

"I have not seen eye to eye with your workmen there. They assure me
that I have been imagining excavations near my house by the sewerage company. I do not imagine things. However, since these excavations
have ceased, or rather the sounds of them, which have been so oppressive
to my obtaining a decent night's repose, I presume that we will no longer
be bothered by these nightly disturbances?"

"Nightly disturbances?" Holmes asked with quickening interest.

When she confirmed that she had complained a fortnight prior to the
sewerage company of nightly disturbances caused by vibration and muffled banging under the street, causing her house to shake, one of the workmen summoned courage to come forward.

He raised a finger to his cap. "Beggin' yer pardon, lady, but wiv all
due respect an' that, ain't bin none of our lads a digging dahn 'ere. No
work bin done in this 'ere area fer months naw."

Holmes stood regarding the old woman and the workmen for a moment, and then with a cry of "Of course!" he bounded back to Glassford's
house, and his knocking brought Hogan, the butler, to the door again.

"Show me your cellar," he ordered the startled man.

Sir Gibson emerged from his study, disturbed by the noise of
Holmes's reentry into the house, and looked astounded. "Why, what is it,
Mr. Holmes?"

"The cellar, man," snapped Holmes dictatorially, totally disregarding
the fact that Glassford was a member of the government.

In a body, they trooped down into the cellar. In fact, several cellars
ran under the big house, and Hogan, who had now brought a lamp, was
ordered to precede them through the wine racks, a coal storage area, a

boiler room, and areas filled with bric-a-brac and assorted discarded fur-niture along one wall.

"Have any underground excavations disturbed you of late? These would have been during the night," Holmes asked as he examined the cel-lar walls. Glassford looked perplexed.

"Not at all," he replied, and then turned to his butler. "Your room is above here at the back of the house, isn't it, Hogan? Have you been disturbed?"

The butler shook his head.

"Does the Underground railway run in this vicinity?" Holmes pressed.

"We are not disturbed by the Underground here," replied Sir Gibson. "The Circle Line, which was completed six years ago, is quite a distance to the north of here."

"That wall would be to the north," Holmes muttered, and turning to Hogan ordered the man to bring the lamp close while he began examining the wall. He was there fully fifteen minutes before he gave up in irritation. Inspector Gallagher was smiling to himself and could not help making the thrust: "Your theory not turning out as you would hope, Mr. Holmes?"

Holmes scowled at him. "We will return to Father Michael's," he al-most snarled.

At the presbytery, he demanded to see the priest, and being shown into the study asked without preamble: "Do you have a cellar?"

Father Michael nodded.

"Pray precede me to it," demanded Holmes arrogantly.

The priest did so, with Holmes behind him and Watson and Gallagher trailing in the rear. It was an ordinary cellar, mostly used for the storage of coal and with wine racks along one side. Holmes moved hither and thither through it like a ferret until he came to a rusting iron door.

"Where does this lead?" he demanded.

Father Michael shrugged. "It leads into the new crypt. As you know, we are rebuilding the church and creating a crypt. The door used to lead into another cell, but it has not been opened ever since I have been here."

"Which is how long?" asked Holmes, examining it carefully.

"Ten years."

"I see," muttered the Great Detective. Then he smiled broadly. "I see." He said it again almost as if to impress everyone that he had spotted some solution to the mystery.

"And does an Underground railway run near here?"

Father Michael shook his head. "Our architect ascertained that before we began to rebuild the church. We needed to ensure strong foundations."

Gallagher felt he could have done a dance at the crestfallen expression on Holmes's face. It lasted only a moment, and then Holmes had swung round on him.

"I want to see the Metropolitan Commissioner of Sewers and maps of the system under London."

Gallagher felt he was dealing with a maniac now. It seemed that Holmes had devised some theory that he was determined to prove at all cost.

Mr. Bert Small, manager of the sewerage system, agreed to see Holmes and provide plans of the area at the company's Canon Row offices, just opposite the Palace of Westminster on the corner of Parliament Street.

"I cannot see the connection I wish to make," Holmes said in resignation, pushing the plans away from him in disgust. "There seems no way that one could negotiate the sewers from Soho Square to Gayfere Street, at least not directly in a short space of time. And the Underground railway does not run anywhere near Father Michael's nor Glassford's houses."

It was then that Bert Small came to the rescue of Holmes, demonstrating that it was not intellect alone that helped him solve his cases but good fortune and coincidence.

"Maybe you are looking at the wrong underground system, Mr. Holmes," he suggested. "There are many other underground systems under London apart from sewers and the new railway system."

Holmes regarded him with raised eyebrows. "There is another system of tunnels that runs under Westminster?"

Mr. Small rose and took down some keys, smiling with superiority. "I will show you."

It took but a few minutes for Mr. Bert Small—the man of the moment, as Gallagher cynically described him—to lead them from his office *around the corner to Westminster Bridge. Here Mr. Small led them down a flight of steps to the Embankment to the base of the statue of Queen Boadicea, in her chariot with her two daughters. There was a small iron door here, which he unlocked, then suggested that they follow him.*

A flight of iron steps led them into a tunnel. Mr. Small seemed to swell with pride, and he pointed out that it was situated just above the lower-level interceptory sewer that ran below the level of the Thames. They could see that it was built of brickwork but arched rather than circular and was about six feet high. It was designed, said Mr. Small, to carry cast-iron pipes with water and gas.

He took a lantern and shone it along the dark, forbidding way.

Gallagher was conscious of the river seeping through the brickwork, dripping down the walls on either side and, above all, he was aware of the smell, the putrid stench of the river and the echoing tunnel before them. Holmes began to sniff with a sigh of satisfaction.

Mr. Small pointed down the tunnel. "These tunnels run from here along the river as far as the Bank of England, Mr. Holmes. These are Sir Joseph Bazalgette's tunnels, which he completed fifteen years ago," he said proudly. "You have probably seen, gentlemen, that Sir Joseph died a few months ago. The tunnel system under London was his finest achievement and—"

Holmes was not interested in the eulogy of the civil engineer who had built the tunnels. "And are there other connections?"

"Altogether there are eleven and a half miles of these sorts of tunnels. They fan out through the city," replied Mr. Small, blinking at being cut short.

"Do they connect with Soho Square and Gayfere Street?" Holmes demanded.

"There are none of these tunnels that would connect directly. You would have to go from Soho Square down to Shaftesbury Avenue to find an entrance and then you would have to exit here and walk to Gayfere Street."

"Then that's no good to me," snapped Holmes irritably. "Let's return to the surface."

Detective Inspector Gallagher smiled to see the Great Detective so put out that whatever theory he had could not be sustained.

As they emerged onto the Embankment, Mr. Small, perhaps seeking to mollify Holmes's bad humor, was prompted to make another suggestion.

"There is yet another tunnel system, Mr. Holmes," he finally ventured. "That might pass in the general direction that you have indicated, but I am not sure. I do have a plan of it back at the office. But it has been closed down for over a decade now."

Holmes asserted that he would like to see the plans.

Gallagher believed that Holmes was off on another wild goose chase and, being just across the road from his office at Scotland Yard, he left Holmes and Watson with Mr. Small. He returned to report the progress to his chief, Littlechild. It was two hours later that Gallagher received a curt note from Holmes asking him to meet him at Glassford's house within half an hour and bring a posse of armed police officers, who were to station themselves in the front and back of the building.

Gallagher reluctantly carried out Holmes's orders after consulting with Chief Inspector Littlechild, who checked with the commissioner.

Holmes met Gallagher at the door of Glassford's house and immediately took him down into the cellar. The first thing that Gallagher noticed was an aperture to the south side of the cellar that had previously been covered by piles of old furniture. Beyond this hole was a tunnel of some ten feet in length, dug through the London clay. But within ten feet it met a well-constructed brick-lined tunnel. It was of arched brickwork some four and a half feet in height and four feet wide and a small-gauge railway line ran through it. Gallagher was puzzled, for this was certainly not a tunnel connected with the rail system. Holmes ordered a policeman to be stationed as a guard at this point and then invited Gallagher to join him in Sir Gibson Glassford's study.

Holmes had gathered everyone in Glassford's study. There was the minister himself, his wife, and all the servants, nanny, cook, housemaids, and the butler, Hogan. The Great Detective was looking pleased as punch with himself, and Gallagher reported that the spectacle was repulsive in the extreme.

"The case was simple," exclaimed Holmes in his usual pedantic style. "I drew your attention to the bruising and puncture mark over the vein in *the cardinal's neck. To most people who have dealt with the administration of narcotics, the puncture mark was the sign of a hypodermic syringe. Usually, this is the method by which a medication or drugs is introduced under the skin of the patient by means —"*

"I think we know the method, Holmes," muttered Gallagher. "Dr. Thomson did not agree with you. Indeed, he conducted tests which showed no sign of any foreign substance, let alone narcotics or poison, being introduced into the body of the cardinal which would cause death."

"There was no need to introduce such foreign matter," Holmes went on, looking like a cat that has devoured cream. "The hypodermic contained no substance whatsoever."

"But how —?" began Sir Gibson.

"It contained nothing but air," went on Holmes. "It caused an air embolism — a bubble of air — to be introduced into the bloodstream. That was fatal. Cardinal Tosca was murdered."

Gallagher sighed deeply.

"We already suspected that . . . ," he protested.

"I have now demonstrated your suspicion to be a fact," replied Holmes scornfully. "Now that we know the method, the next question is how was the body transported here?"

"You have been at pains to prove your theory that there is a passage through the underground sewers from Soho Square to here," muttered Gallagher.

Holmes smiled condescendingly. "As you have now observed, it is no theory. It was obvious that the body had to be removed from Soho Square to Gayfere Street. Hardly through the streets in full view, I think, eh, Watson?" Holmes chuckled at his own humor. "It was clear to me that the body had been removed through a dank, smelly sewer. A tunnel where the clothes the body was being transported in, in this case, his nightshirt, had come into contact with the excretions running from the walls. The odors were still apparent after some days in police storage. There was no odor on the cardinal's other clothing. Those transporting the body had carried them wrapped separately in a bag or some other casing, which protected them. The only question was — through what manner of tunneling was this achieved?"

He paused, presumably to bask in their admiration of his logic. He met only bemusement.

"The body was transported not through the sewers, as it happened, Gallagher. In 1861 the Pneumatic Dispatch Company built an underground rail system. The plan was to transport only mail. However, two years later the Post Office opened its own system and this, coupled with the fact that the pneumatic system had begun to develop mechanical faults and air leakage, caused the plans to extend it to be shelved. Ten years ago, that entire system was abandoned and was also forgotten."

Holmes paused, waiting like a conjuror about to pull a rabbit from a hat.

"Except by Mr. Small," pointed out Gallagher, not wishing Holmes to claim the approbation.

"And by the group of people intent on mischief. The body of the cardinal was carried, with his clothing, from his bedroom in the presbytery down to the cellar. In spite of assurances that the door had not been opened in ten years, I observed scuff marks showing that it had been opened recently. The body was removed into the new crypt where workmen had, in their excavations, made contact with the old pneumatic tunnel. The tunnel came directly toward Westminster. In preparation for this ghastly event, which had been well planned, a tunnel had been excavated in advance into the cellar of Sir Gibson's house. I was alerted by the complaints that had been made to the local sewerage company by the old lady opposite who had been disturbed by it. I subsequently found out that, being elderly, she had removed her bedroom to a lower floor, near ground level. That was how she had been disturbed in the night. I found it curious that her concerns were not shared by anyone in this house."

"But I have already told you that only the butler lives on the lower floor," pointed out Sir Gibson, "and Hogan has not complained of any such noises. Have you, Hogan?"

The man shook his head morosely.

"Well," went on Holmes obliviously, "our conspirators, for that is what they are, had enticed their victim from France on the pretense that he was wanted to mediate in some negotiations between this government *and members of the Irish Republican Brotherhood. The idea appealed to Cardinal Tosca's vanity, and he came here obeying the conspirators' exhortation not to tell anyone else. He was killed and the body brought through this underground system."*

"But for what purpose?" demanded Glassford. "Why was he killed and placed in my house?"

"The purpose was to achieve exactly what this has nearly achieved. An attempt to discredit you as a member of government, and to stir up antagonism against any movement by the Irish Party to press forward again with its political campaign in parliament."

"I don't understand."

"What group of people would best benefit by discrediting both a government pledged to the Unionist cause and to those who seek only Home Rule within the United Kingdom? Both those objectives would receive an irrevocable blow by the involvement of a Tory Minister in the murder of a cardinal and the suspicion of some conspiracy between them. Where would sympathy go to?"

"I presume the more extreme Irish Nationalists—the Republicans."

"Watson, your revolver!" cried Holmes suddenly.

It was too late. Hogan had pulled his own revolver. "Everyone stay where they are!" he shouted.

"Don't be a fool, Hogan," snapped Gallagher, moving forward, but Hogan waved his weapon threateningly.

"I am not a fool," the butler cried. "I can see where this is leading, and I shall not suffer alone."

"You'll not escape," cried Holmes. "The police have already surrounded this place."

Hogan simply ignored them.

He stepped swiftly back, removing the key from the lock of the study door. Then he slammed the door shut, turned the key, and they heard him exiting the house.

When Gallagher threw his weight against the door, Holmes ordered him to desist.

"He'll not get far."

In fact, Hogan hardly reached the corner of the street before members of the Special Branch called him to stop and surrender. When he opened fire, he was shot and died immediately. Which was, from my viewpoint, my dear "Wolf Shield," just as well.

Holmes had reseated himself with that supercilious look of the type he assumed when he thought he had tied up all the loose ends.

"Hogan was a member of the Irish Republican Brotherhood, the Fenians. He had ingratiated himself into your employ, Sir Gibson, and was told to wait for orders. The diabolical plot was to use the murder of His Eminence to bring about the fall of your government."

"And we know the name of the man who lured the cardinal here," Watson intervened importantly, speaking almost for the first time in the entire investigation. "We should be able to track him down and arrest him."

Holmes looked at his acolyte with pity. "Do we know his name, Watson?"

"Why, indeed! He overlooked the fact that he left his card behind. T. W. Tone. Remember?"

"T. W. Tone—Theobald Wolfe Tone is the name of the man who led the Irish uprising of 1798," Sir Gibson intervened in a hollow voice. Watson's face was red with chagrin. Sir Gibson glanced at Holmes. "Can we find out who the others were in this plot, Mr. Holmes?"

"That will be up to the Special Branch," Holmes replied, almost in a dismissive fashion. "I fear, however, that they will not have much success. I suspect those who were involved in this matter are already out of the country by now."

"Why did Hogan remain?"

"I presume that he thought himself safe or that he remained to report firsthand on the effects of the plot."

Glassford crossed to Holmes with an outstretched hand.

"My dear sir," he said, "my dear, dear sir. I . . . the country . . . owe you a great debt."

Holmes's deprecating manner was quite nauseating. Gallagher told me that he found his false modesty was truly revolting.

It is true that when the government released the facts of the plot, as Holmes had given it to them, the case of the death of Cardinal Tosca became a cause célèbre. Holmes was even offered a small pension by the government, and he refused, perhaps more on account of its smallness than any modesty on his part. He even declined a papal knighthood from the grateful Bishop of Rome.

Sickening, my dear "Wolf Shield." It was all quite sickening.

But, as you well know, the truth was that Holmes did not come near to resolving this matter. Oh, I grant you that he was able to work out the method by which I killed Cardinal Tosca. I admit that I had thought it rather an ingenious method. I had stumbled on it while attending a lecture in my youth at Trinity College. It was given by Dr. Robert MacDonnell, who had begun the first blood transfusions in 1865. MacDonnell had given up the use of the syringe because of the dangers of embolism or the air bubble which causes fatality when introduced into the bloodstream. My method in the dispatch of the cardinal was simple, first a whiff of chloroform to prevent struggle and then the injection.

My men were waiting, and we transferred the body in the method Holmes described. Yes, I'll give him credit as to method and means. He forced Hogan to disclose himself. Hogan was one of my best agents. He met his death bravely. But Holmes achieved little else. . . . We know the reason, my dear "Wolf Shield," don't we?

Well, now that Holmes has gone to his death over the Reichenbach Falls, I would imagine that you might think that there is little chance of the truth emerging? I have thought a great deal about that. Indeed, this is why I am writing this full account in the form of this letter to you. The original I shall deposit in a safe place. You see, I need some insurance to prevent any misfortune befalling me. As well you know, it would be scandalous should the real truth be known of who was behind the death of Cardinal Tosca and why it was done.

With that bumptious irritant Sherlock Holmes out of the way, I hope to lead a healthy and long life. Believe me —

Sebastian Moran (Colonel)

Having read this extraordinary document I questioned Holmes about whether he had any doubts as to its authenticity.

"Oh, there is no doubt that it is in Moran's hand and in his style of writing. You observe that I still have two of his books on my shelves? *Heavy Game of the Western Himalayas* and *Three Months in the Jungle.*"

I remembered that Holmes had purchased these volumes soon after the affair of "The Empty House."

"Moran was many things, but he was no coward. He might even have been a patriot in a peculiar and perverted way. His family came from Conamara and had become Anglicans after the Williamite Conquest of Ireland. His father was, in fact, Sir Augustus Moran, Commander of the Bath, once British Minister to Persia. Young Moran went through Eton, Trinity College, Dublin, and Oxford. The family estate was at Derrynacleigh. All this you knew about him at the time of our encounter in the affair of 'The Empty House.' I did not mean to imply that he was without faults when I said Moran was no coward and a type of patriot. He had a criminal mind. He was a rather impecunious young man, given to gambling, womanizing, petty crime, and the good life.

"He bought himself a commission in the India Army and served in the First Bengalore Pioneers. He fought in several campaigns and was mentioned in dispatches. He spent most of his army career in India, and I understand that he had quite a reputation as a big-game hunter. I recall that there was a Bengal tiger mounted in the hall of the Kildare Street Club, before he was expelled from it, which he killed. The story was that he crawled down a drain after it when he had wounded it. That takes iron nerve."

I shook my head in bewilderment. "You call him a patriot? Do you mean he was working for the Irish Republicans?"

Holmes smiled. "He was a patriot. I said that Moran had criminal tendencies but was no coward. Unfortunately the talents of such people are often used by the State to further its own ends. You have observed that Moran admits that Inspector Gallagher kept him informed of our every move in the case. Unfortunately Gallagher was killed in the course of duty not long after these events, so we are not able to get confirmation from him. I think we may believe Moran, though. So why was Moran kept informed? Colonel Moran was working for the Secret Service."

I was aghast. "You don't mean to say that he worked for our own Secret Service? Good Lord, Holmes, this is amazing. Do you mean that our own Secret Service ordered the cardinal to be killed? That's preposterous. Immoral. Our government would not stand for it."

"If, indeed, the government knew anything about it. Unfortunately, when you have a Secret Service, then it becomes answerable to no one. I believe that even behind the Secret Service there was another organization with which Moran became involved."

"I don't follow, Holmes."

"I believe that Moran and those who ordered him to do this thing were members of some extreme Orange faction."

"Orange faction? I don't understand." I threw up my hands in mystification.

"The Orange Order was formed in 1796 to maintain the position of the Anglican Ascendancy in Ireland and prevent the union of the Dublin colonial parliament with the parliament of Great Britain. However, the Union took place in 1801, and the Orange Order then lost support. Its patrons, including royal dukes and titled landowners, quickly accepted the new status quo, being either paid off with new titles or financial bribes. The remaining aristocratic support was withdrawn when the Order was involved in a conspiracy to prevent Victoria inheriting the throne and attempting to place its Imperial Grand Master, His Royal Highness, the Duke of Cumberland, on the throne instead. The failure of the coup, Catholic Emancipation 1829, the removal of many of the restrictions placed on members of that religion, as well as the Reform Acts, extending more civil rights to people, all but caused the Orange Order to disappear.

"Those struggling to keep the sectarian movement alive realized it needed to be a more broad-based movement, and it opened its membership to all Dissenting Protestants, so that soon its ranks were flooded by Ulster Presbyterians who had previously been excluded from it. Threatened by the idea that in a self-governing Ireland the majority would be Catholic, these Dissenters became more bigoted and extreme.

"The attempt to destroy the Irish Party seeking Home Rule, which is now supported by the Liberals, was addressed by diehard Unionists in the Tory Party like Lord Randolph Churchill, who advised the party to 'play the Orange Card.' The support of Churchill and the Tories made the Orange Order respectable again, and Ascendancy aristocrats and leading Tories, who had previously disassociated themselves from the Order, now felt able to rejoin it. The Earl of Enniskillen was installed as Grand Master of the Order two years before these events and, with the aid of the Tories, continued to dedicate the Order to the Union and Protestant supremacy."

"But why would they plan this elaborate charade?" I asked.

"Remember what had happened in that November of 1890? The rift in the Irish Party was healing, and Parnell had been reelected its leader. Once more they were going to present a united front in Parliament, and Lord Salisbury was faced with going to the country soon. Something needed to be done to discredit the moderates within Salisbury's Cabinet to bring them back 'on side' with the Unionists against any plans to give Ireland Home Rule to help them remain in power."

"But to kill a cardinal—"

"—having enticed him from Paris to this country thinking he was going to meet with members of the Irish Nationalists," interposed Holmes.

"—to deliberately kill a cardinal to cause such alarms and . . . why, Holmes, it is diabolical."

"Unfortunately, my dear Watson, this becomes the nature of governments who maintain secret organizations that are not accountable to anyone. I was tried and found wanting, Watson. This case was my biggest single failure."

"Oh come, Holmes, you could not have known. . . ."

Holmes gave me a pitying look.

"You must take Moran's gibes and insults from whence they came. You could do no more," I assured him.

He looked at me with steely eyes. "Oh yes, I could. I told you about how important it is to pay attention to detail. From the start I committed the most inexcusable inattention to detail. Had I been more vigilant, I could have laid this crime at the right door. It is there in Moran's text, a fact made known to me right from the start and which I ignored."

I pondered over the text but could find no enlightenment.

"The visitor's cards, Watson. The mistake over the visitor's cards presented by the mysterious caller to the cardinal."

"Mistake? Oh, you mean the name being T. W. Tone, the name of someone long dead? I didn't realize that it was a false name."

"The name was merely to confirm the notion that we were supposed to be dealing with Irish Republicans. No, it was not that. It was the harp device, which was also meant to lead us into thinking that it was presented by an Irish nationalist, being the Irish national symbol. The fact was that the harp was surmounted by a crown—that is the symbol of our colonial administration in Ireland. No nationalist could bear the sight of a crown above the harp. I should have realized it."

Holmes sat shaking his head for a while, and then he continued:

"Place the case of Cardinal Tosca in your trunk, Watson. I don't want to hear about it ever again."

Even then I hesitated.

"Granted that Moran worked for some superior—have you, in retrospect, come to any conclusion as to who Moran's superior was? Who was the man who gave him the order and to whom he was writing his letter?"

Holmes was very serious as he glanced back at me. "Yes, I know who he was. He died in the same year that Moran was arrested for the murder of Lord Maynooth's son. You recall that Moran died in police custody after his arrest? It was supposed to be a suicide. I realized that should have been questioned. But then I heard of the death of . . ." He paused and sighed. "Moran's superior was a brilliant politician but a ruthless one. He, more than most, reawakened the Orange hatreds against the Catholic Irish in order to maintain the Union."

"He was a member of the government?" I cried, aghast.

"He had been until just prior to this event, but he was still influential."

"And this code name 'Wolf Shield'? You were able to tell who it was by that?"

"That part was simple. The name, sounding so Anglo-Saxon, I simply translated 'Wolf Shield' back into Anglo-Saxon, and the man's name became immediately recognizable. But let him now rest where his prejudices cannot lacerate his judgment any more."

In deference to my old friend's wishes, I have kept these papers safely, appending this brief note of how they fell into my hands. It was Holmes, with his biting sense of humor, who suggested I file it as "A Study in Orange," being his way of gentle rebuke for what he deemed as my melodramatic title of the first case of his with which I was involved. With this note, I have placed Moran's manuscript into my traveling box, which is now deposited in my bank at Charing Cross. I have agreed with Holmes's instructions that my executors should not open it until at least fifty years have passed from the dates of our demise.

The one thing that I have not placed here is the name of Moran's superior, but that anyone with knowledge of Anglo-Saxon personal names could reveal.

The Eye of Shiva

The harsh monsoon winds were rattling fiercely at the closed shutters of the British Residency building. The Residency itself stood on an exposed hillock, a little way above the crumbling banks of the now turbulent Viswamitri River as it frothed and plunged its way through the city of Baroda to empty into the broad Gulf of Khambhat. The building had been secured from the moaning wind and rain by the servants; the lamps were lit, and the male guests still lounged in the dining room, unperturbed by the rising noise of the storm outside.

The ladies had withdrawn, shepherded away by Lady Chetwynd Miller, the wife of the Resident, while the decanter of port began to pass sun-wise around the eight remaining men. The pungent odor of cigar smoke began to permeate the room.

"Well," demanded Royston, a professional big-game hunter who was staying a few days in Baroda before pushing east to the Satpura mountains to hunt the large cats that stalked the ravines and darkened crevices there. "Well," he repeated, "I think the time has come to stop teasing us, Your Excellency. We all know that you brought us here to see it. So where is it?"

There was a murmur of enthusiastic assent from the others gathered before the remnants of the evening meal.

Lord Chetwynd Miller raised a hand and smiled broadly. He was a sprightly sixty-year-old; a man who had spent his life in the service of the British Government of India and who now occupied the post of Resident in the Gujarat state of Baroda. He had been

Resident in Baroda ever since the overthrow of the previous despotic Gaekwar or ruler. Baroda was still ruled by native princes who acknowledged the suzerain authority of the British Government in India but who had independence in all internal matters affecting their principality.

Five years previously a new Gaekwar, Savaji Rao III, had come to power. If the truth were known, he had deposed his predecessor with British advice and aid, for the previous Gaekwar had not been approved of by the civil servants of Delhi. Indeed, he had the temerity to go so far as to murder the former Resident, Colonel Phayre. But the British Raj had not wanted it to appear as though they were interfering directly in the affairs of Baroda. The state was to remain independent of the British Government of India. Indeed, the secret of the success of the British Raj in India was not in its direct rule of that vast subcontinent, with its teeming masses, but in its persuasion of some six hundred ruling princes to accept the British imperial suzerainty. Thus much of the government of India was in the hands of native hereditary princes who ruled half the land mass and one quarter of the population under the "approving" eye of the British Raj.

Baroda, since Savaji Rao III had taken power, was a peaceful city of beautiful buildings, of palaces, ornate gates, parks and avenues, standing as a great administrative center at the edge of cotton-rich plains and a thriving textile-producing industry. A port with access to the major sea lanes and a railway center with its steel railroads connecting it to all parts of the subcontinent.

After the establishment of the new regime in Baroda, the British Raj felt they needed a man who was able to keep firm control on British interests there. Lord Chetwynd Miller was chosen, for he had been many years in service in India. Indeed, it was going to be his last appointment in India. He had already decided that the time had come for retirement. He was preparing for the return to his estates near Shrewsbury close to the Welsh border before the year was out.

"Come on, Chetwynd," urged Major Bill Foran, of the Eighth Bombay Infantry, whose task it was to protect the interests of the British Residency and the community of British traders who lived in Baroda. He was an old friend of the Resident. "Enough of this game of cat and mouse. You are dying to show it to us just as much as we are dying to see it."

Lord Chetwynd Miller grinned. It was a boyish grin. He spread his hands in a deprecating gesture. It was true that he had been leading his guests on. He had invited them to see the Eye of Shiva and kept them waiting long enough.

He gazed around at them. Apart from Bill Foran, it could not be said that he really knew the other guests. It was one of those typical Residency dinner parties, whereby it was his duty to dine with any British dignitaries passing through Baroda. Lieutenant Tompkins, his ADC, had compiled this evening's guest list.

Royston he knew by reputation. There was Father Cassian, a swarthy, secretive-looking Catholic priest who seemed totally unlike a missionary. He had learned that Cassian was a man of many interests—not the least of which was an interest in Hindu religion and mythology. There was Sir Rupert Harvey. A bluff, arrogant man, handsome in a sort of dissolute way. He had just arrived in Baroda and seemed to dabble in various forms of business. Then there was the tall languid Scotsman, James Gregg. Silent, taciturn and a curious way of staring at one as if gazing right through them. He was, according to the list, a mining engineer. For a mere mining engineer, Tompkins had observed earlier, Gregg could afford to stay at the best hotel in Baroda and did not seem to lack money.

The last guest sat at the bottom of the table, slightly apart from the others. It was Lord Chetwynd Miller's solitary Indian guest, Inspector Ram Jayram, who, in spite of being a Bengali by birth, was employed by the Government of Baroda as its chief of detectives. Ram Jayram had a dry wit and a fund of fascinating stories, which made him a welcome guest to pass away the tedium of many soirées. That evening, however, he had been invited especially.

Word had come to Jayram's office that an attempt was going to be made to rob the Residency that night, and Lord Chetwynd Miller had accepted Jayram's request that he attend as a dinner guest so that he might keep a close eye on events. It was Jayram who suggested to the Resident that the potential thief might be found among the guests themselves. A suggestion that the Resident utterly discounted.

But the news of the Resident's possession of the fabulous ruby—the Eye of Shiva—was the cause of much talk and speculation in the city. The Resident was not above such vanity that he did not want to display it to his guests on the one evening in which the ruby was his.

Lord Chetwynd Miller cleared his throat. "Gentlemen . . . ," he began hesitantly. "Gentlemen, you are right. I have kept you in suspense long enough. I have, indeed, invited you here, not only because I appreciate your company, but I want you to see the fabled Eye of Shiva before it is taken on board the SS *Caledonia* tomorrow morning for transportation to London."

They sat back, expectantly watching their host.

Lord Chetwynd Miller nodded to Tompkins, who clapped his hands as a signal.

The dining room door opened, and Devi Bhadra, Chetwynd Miller's majordomo, entered, pausing on the threshold to gaze inquiringly at the lieutenant.

"Bring it in now, Devi Bhadra," instructed the ADC.

Devi Bhadra bowed slightly, no more than a slight gesture of the head, and withdrew.

A moment later he returned carrying before him an ornate tray on which was a box of red Indian gold with tiny glass panels in it. Through these panels everyone could see clearly a white velvet cushion on which was balanced a large red stone.

There was a silence while Devi Bhadra solemnly placed it on the table in front of the Resident and then withdrew in silence.

As the door shut behind him, almost on a signal, the company leaned toward the ornate box with gasps of surprise and envy at the perfection of the ruby that nestled tantalizingly on its cushion.

Father Cassian, who was nearest, pursed his lips and gave forth an unpriestly-like whistle. "Amazing, my dear sir. Absolutely!"

James Gregg blinked; otherwise, his stoic face showed no expression. "So this is the famous Eye of Shiva, eh? I'll wager it has a whole history behind it?"

Royston snorted. "Damned right, Gregg. Many a person has died for that little stone there."

"The stone, so it is said, is cursed."

They swung round to look at the quiet Bengali. Jayram was smiling slightly. He had approved the Resident's suggestion that if one of his guests was going to make an attempt on the jewel, it were better that the jewel be placed where everyone could see it so that such theft would be rendered virtually impossible.

"What d'you mean, eh?" snapped Sir Rupert Harvey irritably. It had become obvious during the evening that Harvey was one of those men who disliked mixing with "the natives" except on express matters of business. He was apparently not used to meeting Indians as his social equals and showed it.

It was Major Foran who answered. "The inspector—" Did he emphasize the Bengali's rank just a little? "The inspector is absolutely right. There is a curse that goes with the stone, isn't that right, Chetwynd?"

Lord Chetwynd Miller grinned and spread his hands. "Therein is the romance of the stone, my friends. Well, how can you have a famous stone without a history, or without a curse?"

"I believe I sense a story here," drawled Gregg, reaching for his brandy, sniffing it before sipping gently.

"Will you tell it, sir?" encouraged Royston.

Lord Chetwynd Miller's features bespoke that he would delight in nothing better than to tell them the story of his famous ruby— the Eye of Shiva.

"You all know that the stone is going to London as a private gift from Savaji Rao III to Her Majesty? Yesterday the stone was officially handed into my safekeeping as representative of Her Majesty. I have made the arrangements for it to be placed on the SS *Caledonia* tomorrow to be transported to London."

"We all read the *Times of India*," muttered Sir Rupert, but his sarcasm was ignored.

"Quite so," Lord Chetwynd Miller said dryly. "The stone has a remarkable history. It constituted one of a pair of rubies which were the eyes of a statue of the Hindu god Shiva—"

"A god of reproduction," chimed in Father Cassian, almost to himself. "Both benign and terrible, the male generative force of Vedic religion."

"It is said," went on the Resident, "that the statue stood in the ancient temple of Vira-bhadra in Betul country. It was supposedly of gold, encrusted with jewels, and its eyes were the two rubies. The story goes that during the suppression of the 'Mutiny,' a soldier named Colonel Vickers was sent to Betul to punish those who had taken part. He had a reputation for ruthlessness. I think he was involved with the massacre at Allahabad—"

"What was that?" demanded Gregg. "I know nothing of the history here."

"Six thousand people, regardless of sex or age, were slaughtered at Allahabad by British troops as a reprisal," explained Father Cassian in a quiet tone.

"The extreme ferocity with which the uprising was suppressed was born of fear," explained Major Foran.

"Only way to treat damned rebels!" snapped Royston. "Hang a few, and the people will soon fall into line, eh?"

"In that particular case," observed the Resident, screwing his face up in distaste, "the Sepoys who had taken part in the insurrection were strapped against the muzzles of cannons and blown apart as a lesson to others."

"Military necessity," snapped Major Foran, irritated by the implied criticism.

THE EYE OF SHIVA

The Resident paused a moment and continued. "Well, it is said that Vickers sacked the temple of Vira-bhadra and took the rubies for himself while he ordered the rest of the statue melted down. This so enraged the local populace that they attacked Vickers and managed to reclaim the statue, taking it to a secret hiding place. Vickers was killed, and the rubies vanished. Stories permeated afterward that only one ruby was recovered by the guardians of the temple. A soldier managed to grab the other one from Vickers's dying hand. He, in his turn, was killed, and the stone had a colorful history until it found its way into the hands of the Gaekwar of Baroda."

Inspector Ram Jayram coughed politely. "It should be pointed out," he said slowly, "that the Gaekwar in question was not Savaji Rao III but the despot whom he overthrew a few years ago."

The Resident nodded agreement. "The jewel was found in the Gaekwar's collection, and Savaji Rao thought it would be a courteous gesture to send the jewel to Her Majesty as a token of his friendship."

Gregg sat staring at the red glistening stone with pursed lips. "A history as bloody as it looks," he muttered. "The story is that all people who claim ownership of the stone, who are not legitimate owners, meet with bad ends."

Sir Rupert chuckled cynically as he relit his cigar. "Could be that Savaji Rao has thought of that and wants no part of the stone? Better to pass it on quickly before the curse bites!"

Lieutenant Tompkins flushed slightly, wondering whether Sir Rupert was implying some discourtesy to the Queen-Empress. He was youthful, and this was his first appointment in India. It was all new to him and perplexing, especially the cynicism about Empire that he found prevalent among his fellow veteran colonials.

"The only curse, I am told, is that there are some Hindus who wish to return the stone to the statue," Father Cassian observed.

Sir Rupert turned to Inspector Jayram with a grin that was more a sneer. "Is that so? Do you feel that the stone should belong back in the statue? You're a Hindu, aren't you?"

Jayram returned the gaze of the businessman and smiled politely. "I am a Hindu, yes. Father Cassian refers to the wishes of a sect called the Vira-bhadra, whose temple the stone was taken from. They are worshippers of Shiva in his role of the wrathful avenger and herdsman of souls. For them he wears a necklace of skulls and a garland of snakes. He is the malevolent destroyer. I am not part of their sect."

Sir Rupert snorted as if in cynical disbelief. "A Hindu is a Hindu," he sneered.

"Ah, so?" Inspector Jayram did not appear in the least put out by the obvious insult. "I presume that you are a Christian, Sir Rupert?"

"Of course!" snapped the man. "What has that to do with anything?"

"Then, doubtless, you pay allegiance to the Bishop of Rome as Holy Father of the Universal Church?"

"Of course not . . . I am an Anglican," growled Sir Rupert.

Jayram continued to smile blandly. "But a Christian is a Christian. Is this not so, Sir Rupert?"

Sir Rupert reddened as Father Cassian exploded in laughter. "He has you there," he chuckled as his mirth subsided a little.

Jayram turned with an appreciative smile. "I believe that it was one of your fourth-century saints and martyrs of Rome, Pelagius, who said that labels are devices for saving people the trouble of thinking. Pelagius was the great friend of Augustine of Hippo, wasn't he?"

Father Cassian smiled brightly and inclined his head. "You have a wide knowledge, Inspector."

Sir Rupert growled angrily and was about to speak when Lord Chetwynd Miller interrupted. "It is true that the story of the curse emanated from the priests of the sect of Vira-bhadra, who continue to hunt for the stone."

Royston lit a fresh cheroot. He preferred them to the cigars provided by their host.

"Well, it is an extraordinary stone. Would it be possible for me to handle it, Your Excellency?"

The Resident smiled indulgently. "It will be the last chance. When it gets to London, it will doubtless be locked away in the royal collection."

He took a small key from his waistcoat pocket and bent forward, turning the tiny lock that secured the box and raising the lid so that the stone sparkled brightly on its pale bed of velvet.

He reached forward and took out the stone with an exaggerated air of carelessness and handed it to the eager Royston.

Royston held the stone up to the light between his thumb and forefinger and whistled appreciatively. "I've seen a few stones in my time, but this one is really awe inspiring. A perfect cut, too."

"You know something about these things, Royston?" inquired Sir Rupert, interested.

Royston shrugged. "I don't wish to give the impression that I am an expert, but I've traded a few stones in my time. My opinion is probably as good as the next man's."

He passed the ruby to Father Cassian, who was seated next to him. The priest took the stone and held it to the light. His hand trembled slightly, but he assumed a calm voice. "It's nice," he conceded. "But the value, as I see it, is in the entire statue of the god. I place no value on solitary stones, but only in an overall work of art, in man's endeavor to create something of beauty."

Sir Rupert snorted as an indication of his disagreement with this philosophy and reached out a hand.

Father Cassian hesitated, still staring at the red stone.

At that moment there came the sound of an altercation outside. The abruptness of the noise caused everyone to pause. Lieutenant Tompkins sprang to his feet and strode to the door. As he opened it, Lady Chetwynd Miller, a small but determined woman in her mid-fifties, stood framed in the doorway.

"Forgive me interrupting, gentlemen," she said with studied calm. Then looking toward her husband, she said quietly, "My dear,

Devi Bhadra says the servants have caught a thief attempting to leave your study."

Lord Chetwynd Miller gave a startled glance toward Inspector Jayram, then rose and made his way to the door. Tompkins stood aside as the Resident laid a reassuring hand on Lady Chetwynd Miller's arm.

"Now then, dear, nothing to worry about. You go back to your ladies in the drawing room, and we'll see to this."

Lady Chetwynd Miller seemed reluctant but smiled briefly at the company before withdrawing. The Resident said to his ADC: "Ask Devi Bhadra to bring the rascal here into the dining room."

He turned back with a thin smile toward Inspector Jayram. "It seems as if your intelligence was right. We have a prisoner for you to take away, Inspector."

Jayram raised his hands in a curiously helpless gesture. "This is technically British soil, Excellency. But if you wish me to take charge? . . . Let us have a look at this man."

At that moment, Lieutenant Tompkins returned with Devi Bhadra together with a burly Sepoy from Foran's Eighth Bombay Infantry. They frog-marched a man into the dining room. The man was thin, wearing a *dhoti,* a dirty loincloth affected by Hindus, an equally dirty turban, and a loose robe open at the front. He wore a cheap jeweled pendant hung on a leather thong around his neck.

The Resident went back to his seat and gazed up with a hardened scowl. "Bring the man into the light and let us see him."

The man was young, handsome, but his face was disfigured in a sullen expression. His head hung forward. Devi Bhadra prodded the man forward so that the light from the lanterns reflected on his face.

"I have searched him thoroughly, sahib. He has no weapons."

"Do you speak English?" demanded Lord Chetwynd Miller.

The man did not reply.

The British Resident nodded to Devi Bhadra, who repeated the question in Gujarati, a language of the country. There was no response.

"Forgive me," Inspector Jayram interrupted. "I believe the man might respond to Hindi."

Devi Bhadra repeated his question, but there was no reply.

"Looks like your guess was wrong," observed Royston.

Inspector Jayram rose leisurely and came to stand by the man. His eyes narrowed as he looked at the pendant. Then he broke into a staccato to which the captive jerked up his head and nodded sullenly.

Jayram turned to the Resident with an apologetic smile. "The man speaks a minor dialect called Munda. I have some knowledge of it. He is, therefore, from the Betul district."

"Betul?" The Resident's eyes widened as he caught the significance of the name.

Jayram indicated the pendant. "He wears the symbol of the cult of Vira-bhadra."

"Does he? The beggar!" breathed Lord Chetwynd Miller.

"Well," drawled Gregg. "If he were after this little item, he was out of luck. We had it here with us."

He held up the ruby.

The captive saw it and gave a sharp intake of breath, moving as if to lunge forward but was held back by the powerful grip of Devi Bhadra and the Sepoy.

"So that's it?" snapped Major Foran. "The beggar was coming to steal the stone?"

"Or return it to its rightful owners," interposed Father Cassian calmly. "It depends on how you look at it."

"How did you catch him, Devi Bhadra?" asked Foran, ignoring the priest.

"One of the maids heard a noise in your study, sahib," said the man. "She called me, and I went to see if anything was amiss. The safe was open, and this man was climbing out of the window. I caught hold of him and yelled until a Sepoy outside came to help me."

"Was anything missing from the safe?"

"The man had nothing on him, sahib."

"So it was the stone that he was after?" concluded Gregg in some satisfaction. "Quite an evening's entertainment that you've provided, Your Excellency."

The captive burst into a torrent of words, with Jayram nodding from time to time as he tried to follow.

"The man says that the Eye of Shiva was stolen and should be returned to the temple of Vira-bhadra. He is no thief but the right hand of his god seeking the return of his property."

The Resident sniffed. "That's as may be! To me he is a thief, who will be handed over to the Baroda authorities and punished. As Gregg said, it was lucky we were examining the stone while he was trying to open the safe."

Major Foran had been inspecting the stone, which he had taken from Gregg, and he now turned to the prisoner. "Would you like to examine the prize that you missed?" he jeered.

They were unprepared for what happened next. Both the Sepoy and Devi Bhadra were momentarily distracted by the bright, shining object that Foran held out. Not so their prisoner. In the excitement of the moment, they had slackened their grip to the extent that the muscular young man seized his chance. With a great wrench, he had shaken free of his captors, grabbed the stone from the hand of the astonished major, and bounded across the room as agilely as a mountain lion. Before anyone could recover from their surprise, he had flung himself against the shuttered windows.

The wood splintered open as the man crashed through onto the veranda outside.

The dinner company was momentarily immobile in surprise at the unexpected abruptness of the man's action.

A second passed. On the verandah outside, the Betulese jumped to his feet and began to run into the evening blackness and the driving rain.

It was the ADC, Lieutenant Tompkins, who first recovered from his surprise. He turned and seized the Sepoy's Lee Enfield rifle. Then he raised it to his shoulder. There was a crack of an explosion which brought the company to life.

Foran was through the door onto the veranda in a minute. Lord Chetwynd Miller was only a split second behind, but he slipped and collided with Sir Rupert, who was just getting to his feet. The impact was so hard that Sir Rupert was knocked to the floor. The Resident went down on his knees beside him. Father Cassian was the first to spring from his chair, with an expression of concern, to help them up. The Resident was holding on to Cassian's arm when he slipped again and, with a muttered expression of apology, climbed unsteadily to his feet. By then it was all over.

The young man in the *dhoti* was lying sprawled facedown. There was a red, telltale stain on his white dirty robe that not even the torrent of rain was dispersing. Foran had reached his side and bent down, feeling for a pulse and then, with a sigh, he stood up and shook his head.

He came back into the dining room, his dress uniform soaked by the monsoon skies. As he did so, the dining room door burst open, and Lady Chetwynd Miller stood on the threshold again, the other ladies of her party crowding behind her.

The Resident turned and hurried to the door, using his body to prevent the ladies spilling into the room.

"My dear, take your guests back into the drawing room. Immediately!" he snapped, as his wife began to open her mouth in protest. "Please!" His unusually harsh voice caused her to blink and stare at him in astonishment. He forced a smile and modulated his tone. "Please," he said again. "We won't be long. Don't worry, none of us have come to any harm." He closed the door behind them and turned back, his face ashen.

"Well," drawled Foran, holding his hand palm outward and letting the others see the bright glistening red stone that nestled there, "the young beggar nearly got away with it."

The Resident smiled grimly and turned to his majordomo.

"Devi Bhadra, you and the Sepoy remove the body. I expect

Inspector Jayram will want to take charge now. Is that all right with you, Foran?"

Major Foran, nominally in charge of the security of the Residency, indicated his agreement, and Devi Bhadra motioned the Sepoy to follow him in the execution of their unpleasant task.

Lord Chetwynd Miller turned to his ADC and clapped him on the shoulder. The young man had laid aside the Lee Enfield and was now sitting on his chair, his face white, his hand shaking.

"Good shooting, Tompkins. Never saw better."

Foran was pouring the young officer a stiff brandy. "Get that down you, lad," he ordered gruffly.

The young lieutenant stared up. "Sorry," he muttered. "Never shot anyone before. Sorry." He took a large gulp of his brandy and coughed.

"Did the right thing," confirmed the Resident. "Otherwise the beggar would have got clean away—" He turned to Jayram and then frowned.

Inspector Jayram was gazing in fascination at the stone that Foran had set back in its box. He took it up with a frown passing over his brow. "Excuse me, Excellency," he muttered.

They watched him astounded as he reached for a knife on the table and, placing the stone on the top of the table, he drew the knife across it. It left a tiny white mark.

White-faced, Major Foran was the first to realize the meaning of the mark. "A fake stone! It is not the Eye of Shiva!"

Jayram nodded calmly. He was watching their faces carefully.

Sir Rupert was saying, "Was the stone genuine in the first place? I mean, did Savaji Rao give you the genuine article?"

"We have no reason to doubt it," Major Foran replied, but his tone was aghast.

Royston, who had taken the stone from where Jayram had left it on the table, was peering at it in disbelief. "The stone was genuine when we started to examine it," he said quietly.

The Resident was frowning at him.

"What do you mean?"

"I mean . . ." Royston stared around thoughtfully. "I mean that this is not the stone that I held in my hand a few minutes ago."

"How can you be so sure?" demanded Gregg. "It looks exactly the same to me."

Royston held up the defaced stone to the light. "See here . . . there is a shadow in this stone, a tiny black mark that indicates its flaw. The stone I held a few moments ago did not have such a mark. That I can swear to."

"Then where is the real stone?" demanded Father Cassian. "This stone is a clever imitation. It is worthless."

Major Foran was on his feet, taking the stone and peering at it with a red, almost apoplectic stare. "An imitation, by George!"

The Resident was stunned.

"I bet that Hindu chappie had this fake to leave behind when he robbed the safe. The real one must still be on his body," Lieutenant Tompkins gasped.

"On his body or in the garden," grunted Foran. "By your leave, sir, I'll go and get Devi Bhadra to make a search."

"Yes, do that, Bill," instructed the Resident quietly. He was obviously shocked. Foran disappeared to give the orders.

There was a moment's silence, and then Jayram spoke. "Begging your pardon, Excellency, you will not find the stone on the body of the dead priest."

Lord Chetwynd Miller's eyes widened as they sought the placid dark brown eyes of Jayram. "I don't understand," he said slowly.

Jayram smiled patiently. "The Betul priest did not steal the real ruby, Your Excellency. Only the fake. In fact, the real ruby has not left this room."

"You'd better explain that," Father Cassian suggested. "The ruby has been stolen. According to Lord Miller, the genuine stone was given into his custody. And according to Royston there, he was holding the genuine stone just before we heard Devi Bhadra capture that beggar. Then the Hindu priest was brought here into this room. He grabbed the stone from Foran, and the real stone disappears. Only he could have had both fake and real stone."

Foran had come back through the shattered window of the dining room. Beyond they could see Devi Bhadra conducting a search of the lawn where the man had fallen.

"There is nothing on the dead man," Foran said in annoyance. "Devi Bhadra is examining the lawn now."

"According to Inspector Jayram here," interposed Gregg heavily, "it'll be a waste of time."

Foran raised an eyebrow.

"Jayram thinks the ruby never left this room," explained Father Cassian. "I think he believes the Hindu priest grabbed the fake when he tried to escape."

Jayram nodded smilingly. "That is absolutely so," he confirmed.

The Resident's face was pinched. "How did you know?" he demanded.

"Simple common sense, Excellency," replied the Bengali policeman. "We have the stone here, the genuine stone. Then we hear the noise of the Betulese being captured as he makes an abortive attempt to steal the stone from your study—abortive because the stone is here with us. He is brought to this room, and there he stands with his arms held between Devi Bhadra and the Sepoy. He makes a grab at what he thinks is the ruby and attempts to escape. He believes the stone genuine."

"Sounds reasonable enough," drawled Sir Rupert. "Except that you have no evidence that he was not carrying the fake stone on him to swap."

"But I do. Devi Bhadra searched the culprit thoroughly. He told us; he told us twice that he had done so and found nothing on the man. If the fake stone had been on the person of the priest of Vira-bhadra, then His Excellency's majordomo would have found it before he brought the priest here, into the dining room."

"What are you saying, Jayram? That old man Shiva worked some magic to get his sacred eye back?" grunted Gregg, cynically.

Jayram smiled thinly. "No magic, Mr. Gregg."

"Then what?"

"The logic is simple. We eight are sat at the table. The genuine stone is brought in. We begin to examine it. We are interrupted in our examination by the affair of the priest of Vira-bhadra. Then we find it is a faked stone. The answer is that someone seated at this table is the thief."

There was a sudden uproar.

Sir Rupert was on his feet, bawling. "I am not going to be insulted by a . . . a . . . ."

Jayram's face was bland. "By a simple Bengali police inspector?" he supplied helpfully. "As a matter of fact, I was not being insulting to you, Sir Rupert. My purpose is to recover the stone."

Lord Chetwynd Miller slumped back into his chair. He stared at Ram Jayram. "How do you propose that?"

Jayram spread his hands and smiled. "Since none of our party have left the room, with the exception of Major Foran," he bowed swiftly in the soldier's direction, "and he, I believe, is beyond reproach, the answer must be that the stone will still be on the person of the thief. Is this not logical, Your Excellency?"

Lord Chetwynd Miller thought a moment and then nodded, as though reluctant to concede the point.

"Good. Major Foran, will you have one of your Sepoys placed on the veranda and one at the door? No one is to leave now," Jayram asked.

Foran raised a cynical eyebrow. "Are you sure that I'm not a suspect?"

"We are all suspects," replied Jayram imperturbably. "But some more so than others."

Foran went to the door and called for his men, giving orders to station themselves as Jayram had instructed.

"Right." Jayram smiled. "We will now make a search, I think."

"Then we'll start with you," snapped Sir Rupert. "Of all the impertinent—"

Jayram held up a hand, and the baronet fell silent. "I have no objection to Major Foran searching my person." He smiled. "But, as a matter of fact, Sir Rupert, I was thinking of saving time by starting with you. You see, when there was the disturbance of the Betulese being brought in here, at that time you were the one holding the stone."

Royston whistled softly. "That's right, by Jove! I held the genuine stone. Then I passed it on to Father Cassian and . . ."

The priest looked uncomfortable. "I passed it on to Sir Rupert just as the commotion occurred."

Sir Rupert's face was working in rage. "I'll not stand for this!" he shouted. "A jumped-up punkah-wallah is not going to make me—"

Major Foran moved across to him with an angry look. "Then I'll make you, if you object to obeying the inspector's orders, Sir Rupert," he said quietly.

Sir Rupert stared at them and then with a gesture of resignation began to empty his pockets.

Jayram, still smiling, raised his hand. "A moment, Sir Rupert. There may not be any need for this."

Inspector Foran hesitated and stared in surprise at the Bengali. "I thought . . . ," he began.

"The commotion started. Our attention was distracted. When our attention focused back on the jewel, who was holding it?"

They looked at one another.

Gregg stirred uncomfortably. "I guess I was," he confessed.

Foran nodded agreement. "I took the stone from him, and that's when we discovered it was a fake."

Gregg rose to his feet, and they all examined him with suspicion. "You won't find anything on me," Gregg said with a faint smile. "Go ahead."

Jayram returned his smile broadly.

"I am sure we won't. You, Mr. Gregg, did not take the stone from the hands of Sir Rupert, did you?"

Gregg shook his head and sat down abruptly.

"No. I took it from the box where Sir Rupert had replaced it. He put it back there when the Hindu priest was being questioned."

"Just so. The stone was genuine as it passed round the table until it reached Sir Rupert, who then replaced it in the box. Then Mr. Gregg took the stone from the box and passed it round to the rest of us. It was then a fake one."

Sir Rupert was clenching and unclenching his hands spasmodically. Major Foran moved close to him.

"This is a damned outrage, I tell you," he growled. "I put the stone back where I found it."

"Exactly," Jayram said with emphasis. *"Where you found it."*

They realized that he must have said something clever, or made some point that was obscure to them.

"If I may make a suggestion, Major," Jayram said quietly. "Have your Sepoys take Father Cassian into the study and hold him until I come. We will remain here."

The blood drained from Father Cassian's face as he stared at the little Bengali inspector. His mouth opened and closed like a fish for a few seconds. Everyone was staring at him with astonishment. If nothing else, Cassian's expression betrayed his guilt.

"That's a curious request," observed Foran, recovering quickly. "Are you sure that Father Cassian is the thief?"

"Will you indulge me? At the moment, let us say that Father Cassian is not all that he represents himself to be. Furthermore, at the precise moment of the disturbance, Cassian was holding the stone. Sir Rupert had asked him for it. Our attention was momentarily distracted by Lady Miller at the door. When I looked back, the stone had been replaced in its holder. Sir Rupert, seeing this, took up the stone, examined it, and replaced it. The only time it could have been switched was when Cassian held it, before he replaced it in the casket."

Cassian half rose, and then he slumped down. He smiled in resignation. "If I knew the Bengali for 'it's a fair cop,' I'd say it. How did you get on to me, Jayram?"

Jayram sighed. "I suspected that you were not a Catholic priest. I then made a pointed reference to Pelagius to test you. Any Catholic priest would know that Pelagius is not a saint and martyr of the fourth century. He was a philosopher who argued vehemently with Augustine of Hippo and was excommunicated from the Roman church as a heretic. You did not know this."

Cassian shrugged. "I suppose we can't know everything," he grunted. "As I say, it's a fair . . ." He had reached a hand into his cassock. Then a surprised look came over his features. He rummaged in his pocket and then stared at Jayram. "But . . . ," he began.

Jayram jerked his head to Foran. Foran gave the necessary orders. After the erstwhile "Father" Cassian had been removed, against a background of stunned silence, Foran turned back to Jayram.

"Perhaps you would explain why you have had Cassian removed to be searched. The search could easily have been done here."

"The reason," Jayram said imperturbably, "is that we will not find the stone on him."

There was a chorus of surprise and protest.

"You mean, you know he is innocent?" gasped Foran.

"Oh no. I know he is guilty. When our attention was distracted by the entrance of the captive, Father Cassian swapped the genuine stone and placed the fake on the table for Sir Rupert to pick up later. It was the perfect opportunity to switch the genuine stone for the faked stone. Cassian is doubtless a professional jewel thief who came to Baroda when he heard that Savaji Rao was going to present the Eye of Shiva to the Resident for transportation to England."

"You mean, Cassian was already prepared with an imitation ruby?" demanded Royston.

"Just so. I doubt whether Cassian is his real name. But we will see."

"But if he doesn't have the stone, what can we charge him with, and moreover, who the hell has the genuine stone?" demanded Foran.

"Father Cassian can be charged with many things," Jayram

assured him. "Traveling on a fake passport, defrauding . . . I am sure we will find many items to keep Father Cassian busy."

"But if he doesn't have the genuine Eye of Shiva, who the devil has it?" repeated Lieutenant Tompkins.

Jayram gave a tired smile. "Would you mind placing the genuine ruby on the table, Your Excellency?"

There was a gasp as he swung round to Lord Chetwynd Miller.

Lord Chetwynd Miller's face was sunken and pale. He stared up at Jayram like a cornered animal, eyes wide and unblinking.

Everyone in the room had become immobile, frozen into a curious theatrical tableau.

The Resident tried to speak, and then it seemed his features began to dissolve. He suddenly looked old and frail. To everyone's horror, except for the placid Jayram, he reached into the pocket of his dinner jacket and took out the rich red stone and silently placed it on the table before him.

"How did you know?" he asked woodenly.

Ram Jayram shrugged eloquently. "I think your action was one made on—how do you say—'the spur of the moment'? The opportunity came when our prisoner tried to escape. You instinctively ran after him. You collided with Sir Rupert, and both went down. Cassian went to your aid. He had his role as a priest to keep up. There was— how do you call it?—a melee? The jewel accidentally fell from Cassian's pocket unnoticed by him onto the floor. You saw it. You realized what had happened and staged a second fall across it, secreting it into your pocket. You were quick-witted. You have a reputation for quick reactions, Excellency. It was an excellent maneuver."

Foran was staring at the Resident in disbelief. Tompkins, the ADC, was simply pale with shock.

"But why?" Foran stammered after a moment or two.

Lord Chetwynd Miller stared up at them with haunted eyes. "Why?" The Resident repeated with a sharp bark of laughter.

"I have given my life to the British Government of India. A whole life's work. Back home my estates are heavily mortgaged and

I have not been able to save a penny during all my years of service here. I was honest; too scrupulously honest. I refused to take part in any business deal which I thought unethical; any deal from which my position prohibited me. What's the result of years of honest dedication? A small pension that will barely sustain my wife and myself, let alone pay the mortgage of our estate. That together with a letter from the viceroy commending my work and perhaps a few honors, baubles from Her Majesty that are so much worthless scrap metal. That is my reward for a lifetime of service."

Major Foran glanced at the imperturbable face of Jayram and bit his lip.

"So, you thought you saw a way of subsidizing your pension?" Jayram asked the Resident.

"I could have paid off my debts with it," confirmed the Resident. "It would have given us some security when we retired."

"But it was not yours," Sir Rupert Harvey observed in a shocked voice.

"Whom did it belong to?" demanded the Resident, a tinge of anger in his voice. "Was it Savaji Rao's to give? Was it the Queen-Empress's to receive? Since Colonel Vickers stole it from the statue of Shiva in Betul, it has simply been the property of thieves and only the property of the thief who could hold on to it."

"It was the property of our Queen-Empress," Lieutenant Tompkins said sternly. He was youthful, a simple young soldier who saw all things in black-and-white terms.

"She would have glanced at it and then let it be buried in the royal vaults forever. No one would have known whether it was genuine or fake—they would merely have seen a pretty red stone. To me, it was life; comfort and a just reward for all I had done for her miserable Empire!"

Lord Chetwynd Miller suddenly spread his arms helplessly, and a sob racked his frail body. It was the first time that those gathered around the table realized that the Resident was merely a tired old man.

"I have to tell my wife. Oh God, the shame will kill her."

They looked at his heaving shoulders with embarrassment.

"I don't know what to do," muttered Foran.

"A suggestion," interrupted Ram Jayram.

"What?"

"The stone was missing for a matter of a few minutes. It was not really stolen. What happened was a sudden impulse, an overpowering temptation which few men in the circumstances in which His Excellency found himself could have resisted. He saw the opportunity and took it."

Foran snorted. "You sound like an advocate, Jayram," he said. "What are you saying?"

Jayram smiled softly. "A policeman has to be many things, Major. Let us look at it this way—the stone was placed in the safekeeping of the Resident by Savaji Rao. It is his responsibility until it is placed on the ship bound for England. Perhaps the Resident merely placed it in his pocket as a precaution when the thief was brought in. I suggest that you, Major Foran, now take charge of the genuine stone, on behalf of the Resident, and see that it goes safely aboard the SS *Caledonia* tomorrow. Lord Chetwynd Miller has only a few months before his retirement to England, so he will hardly be left in his position of trust much longer. He is a man who has already destroyed his honor in his own eyes—why make his dishonor public when it will gain nothing?"

Foran nodded agreement. "And Cassian must never be informed of how the stone was removed from him."

"Just so," Jayram agreed.

Sir Rupert Harvey rose with a thin-lipped look of begrudging approval at the Bengali. "An excellent solution. That is a Christian solution. Forgiveness, eh?"

Ram Jayram grinned crookedly at the baronet. "A Hindu solution," he corrected mildly. "We would agree that sometimes justice is a stronger mistress than merely the law."

— Murder in the Air —

C hief Steward Jeff Ryder noticed the worried expression on the face of Stewardess Sally Beech the moment that she entered the premier class galley of the Global Airways 747, Flight GA 162. He was surprised for a moment, as he had never seen the senior stewardess looking so perturbed before.

"What's up, Sal?" he greeted in an attempt to bring back her usual impish smile. "Is there a wolf among our first-class passengers causing you grief?"

She shook her head without a change of her pensive expression. "I think one of the passengers is locked in the toilet," she began.

Jeff Ryder's smile broadened, and he was about to make some ribald remark.

"No," she interrupted as if she had interpreted his intention. "I am serious. I think that something might have happened. He has been in there for some time, and the person with whom he was traveling asked me to check on him. I knocked on the door, but there was no reply."

Ryder suppressed a sigh. A passenger locked in the toilet was uncommon but not unknown. He had once had to extricate a two-hundred-and-fifty-pound Texan from an aircraft toilet once. It was not an experience that he wanted to remember.

"Who is this unfortunate passenger?"

"He's down on the list as Henry Kinloch Gray."

Ryder gave an audible groan. "If a toilet door is stuck on this aircraft, then it just had to be Kinloch Gray who gets stuck with it.

Do you know who he is? He's the chairman of Kinloch Gray and Brodie, the big multinational media company. He has a reputation for eating company directors alive, but as for the likes of you and me, poor minnows in the great sea of life . . ." He rolled his eyes expressively. "Oh Lord! I'd better see to it."

With Sally trailing in his wake, Ryder made his way to the premier-class toilets. There was no one about, and he saw immediately which door was flagged as "engaged." He went to it and called softly: "Mr. Kinloch Gray? Is everything all right, sir?" He waited and then knocked respectfully on the door.

There was still no response.

Ryder glanced at Sally. "Do we know roughly how long he has been in there?"

"His traveling companion said he went to the toilet about half an hour ago."

Ryder raised an eyebrow and turned back to the door. His voice rose an octave. "Sir. Mr. Kinloch Gray, sir, we are presuming that you are in some trouble in there. I am going to break the lock. If you can, please stand back from the door."

He leaned back, raised a foot, and sent it crashing against the door by the lock. The flimsy cubicle lock dragged out its attaching screws and swung inward a fraction.

"Sir? . . ." Ryder pressed against the door. He had difficulty pushing it; something was causing an obstruction. With some force, he managed to open it enough to insert his head into the cubicle and then only for a moment. He withdrew it rapidly; his features had paled. He stared at Sally, not speaking for a moment or two. Finally he formed some words. "I think he has been shot," he whispered.

The toilets had been curtained off, and the captain of the aircraft, Moss Evans, one of Global Airways's senior pilots, had been sent for, having been told briefly what the problem was. The silver-haired, sturdily built pilot had hid his concerns as he made his way from the flight deck through the premier-class section, smiling and nodding affably to passengers. His main emotion was one of irrita-tion, for it had been only a few moments since the aircraft had passed its midpoint, the "point of no return," halfway into its flight. Another four hours to go, and he did not like the prospect of divert-ing to another airport now and delaying the flight for heaven knew how long. He had an important date waiting for him.

Ryder had just finished making an announcement to premier-class passengers with the feeble excuse that there was a mechanical malfunction with the forward premier-class toilets, and directing passengers to the midsection toilets for their safety and comfort. It was typical airline jargon. Now he was waiting with Sally Beech for the captain. Evans knew Ryder well, for Jeff had been flying with him for two years. Ryder's usually good humor was clearly absent. The girl also looked extremely pale and shaken.

Evans glanced sympathetically at her; then he turned to the shattered lock of the cubicle door. "Is that the toilet?"

"It is."

Evans had to throw his weight against the door and managed to get his head inside the tiny cubicle.

The body was sprawled on the toilet seat, fully dressed. The arms dangled at the sides, the legs were splayed out, thus preventing the door from fully opening. The balance of the inert body was precari-ous. From the mouth to the chest was a bloody mess. Bits of torn flesh hung from the cheeks. Blood had splayed on the side walls of the cu-bicle. Evans felt the nausea well up in him but suppressed it.

As Ryder had warned him, it looked as though the man had been shot in the mouth. Automatically, Evans peered down, not knowing what he was looking for until he realized that he should be looking for a gun. He was surprised when he did not see one. He peered around again. The hands dangling at the sides of the body held nothing. The floor of the cubicle to which any gun must have fallen showed no sign of it. Evans frowned and withdrew. Some-thing in the back of his mind told him that something was wrong about what he had seen, but he could not identify it.

"This is a new one for the company's air emergency manual," muttered Ryder, trying to introduce some humor into the situation.

"I see that you have moved passengers back from this section," Evans observed.

"Yes. I've moved all first-class passengers from this section, and we are rigging a curtain. I presume the next task is to get the body out of there?"

"Has his colleague been told? The person he was traveling with?"

"He has been told that there has been an accident. No details."

"Very well. I gather our man was head of some big corporation?"

"Kinloch Gray. He was Henry Kinloch Gray."

Evans pursed his lips together in a silent whistle. "So we are talking about an influence backed by megabucks, eh?"

"They don't come any richer."

"Have you checked the passenger list for a doctor? It looks like our man chose a hell of a time and place to commit suicide. But I think we'll need someone to look at him before we move anything. I'll proceed on company guidelines of a medical emergency routine. We'll notify head office."

Ryder nodded an affirmative. "I've already had Sally check if there are any doctors on board. As luck would have it, we have two in the premier class. They are both seated together. C one and C two."

"Right. Get Sally to bring one of them up here. Oh, and where is Mr. Gray's colleague?"

"Seated B three. His name is Frank Tilley, and I understand he is Gray's personal secretary."

"I'm afraid he'll have to stand by to do a formal identification. We'll have to play this strictly by the company rule book," he added again as if seeking reassurance.

∘ ∘ ∘

Sally Beech approached the two men in seats C one and two. They were both of the same age, mid-forties; one was casually dressed with a mop of fiery red hair, looking very unlike the stereotype idea of a doctor. The other appeared neat and more smartly attired. She halted and bent down.

"Doctor Fane?" It was the first of the two names she had memorized.

The smartly dressed man glanced up with a smile of inquiry.

"I'm Gerry Fane. What can I do for you, miss?"

"Doctor, I am afraid that we have a medical emergency with one of the passengers. The captain extends his compliments and would greatly appreciate it if you could come and take a look."

It sounded like a well-repeated formula. In fact, it was a formula out of the company manual. Sally did not know how else to deliver it but in the deadpan way that she had been trained to do.

The man grimaced wryly. "I am afraid my doctorate is a Ph.D. in criminology, miss. Not much help to you. I think that you will need my companion, Hector Ross. He's a medical doctor."

The girl glanced apologetically to the red-haired man in the next seat and was glad to see that he was already rising so that she did not have to repeat the same formula.

"Don't worry, lass. I'll have a look, but I am not carrying my medical bag. I'm actually a pathologist returning from a conference, you understand? Not a GP."

"We have some emergency equipment on board, Doctor, but I don't think that you will need it."

Ross glanced at her with a puzzled frown, but she had turned and was leading the way along the aisle.

Hector Ross backed out of the toilet cubicle and faced Captain Evans and Jeff Ryder. He glanced at his watch. "I am pronouncing death at thirteen-fifteen hours, Captain."

Evans stirred uneasily. "And the cause?"

Ross bit his lip. "I'd rather have the body brought out where I can make a full inspection." He hesitated again. "Before I do, I would like my colleague, Doctor Fane, to have a look. Doctor Fane is a criminal psychologist, and I have great respect for his opinion."

Evans stared at the doctor, trying to read some deeper meaning behind his words. "How would a criminal psychologist be able to help in this matter unless—?"

"I'd appreciate it all the same, Captain. If he could just take a look?" Ross's tone rose persuasively.

Moments later, Gerry Fane was backing out of the same toilet door and regarding his traveling companion with some seriousness.

"Curious," he observed. The word was slowly and deliberately uttered.

"Well?" demanded Captain Evans impatiently. "What is that supposed to mean?"

Fane shrugged eloquently in the confined space. "It means that it's not well at all, Captain," he said with just a hint of sarcasm. "I think we should extricate the body so that my colleague here can ascertain the cause of death, and then we can determine how this man came by that death."

Evans sniffed, trying to hide his annoyance. "I have my company's chairman waiting on the radio, Doctor. I would like to be able to tell him something more positive. I think you will understand when I tell you that he happens to know Mr. Gray. Same golf club or something."

Fane was ironic. "*Knew,* I'm afraid. Past tense. Well, you can tell your chairman that it rather looks as though his golfing partner was murdered."

Evans was clearly shocked. "That's impossible. It must have been suicide."

Hector Ross cleared his throat and looked uneasily at his friend. "Should you go that far, old laddie?" he muttered. "After all—"

Fane was unperturbed and interrupted him in a calm decisive

tone. "Whatever the precise method of inflicting the fatal wound, I would think that you would agree that it looked pretty instantaneous. The front parts of the head, below the eyes and nose, are almost blown away. Nasty. Looks like a gunshot wound to the mouth."

Evans had recovered the power of speech. Now, as he thought about it, he realized the very point that had been puzzling him. It was his turn to be sarcastic.

"If a gun was fired in there, even one of low caliber with a body to cushion the impact of the bullet, it would have had the force to pierce the side of the aircraft, causing decompression. Do you know what a bullet can do if it pierces an aircraft fuselage at thirty-six thousand feet?"

"I did not say for certain that it was a gun." Fane maintained his gentle smile. "I said that it looked like a gunshot."

"Even if it were a gunshot that killed him, why could it not have been a suicide?" the chief steward interrupted. "He was in a locked toilet, for Chrissake! It was locked on the inside."

Fane eyed him indulgently. "I made a point about the instantaneous nature of the wound. I have never known a corpse to be able to get up and hide a weapon after a successful suicide bid. The man is sprawled in there dead, with a nasty mortal wound that was pretty instantaneous in causing death . . . and no sign of any weapon. Curious, isn't it?"

Evans stared at him in disbelief. "That's ridiculous . . ." There was no conviction in his voice. "You can't be serious? The weapon must be hidden behind the door or somewhere."

Fane did not bother to reply.

"But," Evans plunged on desperately, knowing that Fane had articulated the very thing that had been worrying him: the missing weapon. "Are you saying that Gray was killed and then placed in the toilet?"

Fane shook his head firmly. "More complicated than that, I'm afraid. Judging from the blood splayed out from the wound, staining the walls of the cubicle, he was already in the toilet when he was killed and with the door locked from the inside, according to your chief steward there."

Jeff Ryder stirred uncomfortably. "The door *was* locked from the inside," he confirmed defensively.

"Then how—?" began Evans.

"That is something we must figure out. Captain, I have no wish to usurp any authority, but if I might make a suggestion? . . ."

Evans did not answer. He was still contemplating the impossibility of what Fane had suggested.

"Captain? . . ."

"Yes? Sorry, what did you say?"

"If I might make a suggestion? While Hector does a preliminary examination to see if we can discover the cause of death, will you allow me to question Gray's colleague, and then we might discover the why as well as the how?"

Evans lips compressed thoughtfully. "I don't feel that I have the authority. I'll have to speak to the chairman of the company."

"As soon as possible, Captain. We'll wait here," Fane replied calmly. "While we are waiting, Doctor Ross and I will get the body out of the toilet."

Hardly any time passed before Moss Evans returned. By then Ross and Fane had been able to remove the body of Kinloch Gray from the toilet and lay it in the area between the bulkhead and front row of the premier-class seats.

Evans cleared his throat awkwardly. "Doctor Fane. My chairman has given you full permission to act as you see fit in this matter . . . until the aircraft lands, that is. Then, of course, you must hand over matters to the local police authority." He shrugged and added, as if some explanation were necessary: "It seems that my chairman has heard of your reputation as a . . . a criminologist? He is happy to leave the matter in the hands of Doctor Ross and yourself."

Fane inclined his head gravely. "Will you be diverting the aircraft?" he asked.

"My chairman has ordered us to continue to our point of destination, Doctor. As the man is dead, it is pointless to divert in search of any medical assistance."

"Good. Then we have over three hours to sort this out. Can your steward provide me with a corner where I can speak with Gray's colleague? She tells me that he is his personal secretary. I want a word without causing alarm to other passengers."

"See to it, Jeff," Captain Evans ordered the chief steward. He glanced at Fane. "Don't they say that murder is usually committed by someone known to the victim? Doesn't that make this secretary the prime suspect? Or will every passenger have to be checked out to see if they have some connection with Gray?"

Fane smiled broadly. "I often find that you cannot make general rules in these matters."

Evans shrugged. "If it helps, I could put out an address asking all passengers to return to their seats and put on their seat belts. I could say that we are expecting turbulence. It would save any curious souls from trying to enter this area."

"That would be most helpful, Captain," Hector Ross assured him, looking up from his position by the corpse.

Evans hesitated a moment more. "I am going back to the flight deck. Keep me informed of any developments."

Within a few minutes of Evans's leaving, there came the sound of raised voices. Fane looked up to see the stewardess, Sally Beech, trying her best to prevent a young man from moving forward toward them.

The young man was very determined. "I tell you that I work for him." His voice was raised in protest. "I have a right to be here."

"You are in tourist class, sir. You have no right to be here in premier class."

"If something has happened to Mr. Gray, then I demand . . ."

Fane moved quickly forward. The young man was tall, well spoken, and, Fane observed, his handsome looks were aided by a tan that came from a lamp rather than the sun. He was immaculately dressed. He sported a gold signet ring on his slim tapering fingers. Fane had a habit of noticing hands. He felt much could be told about a person from their hands and how they kept their fingernails. This young man obviously paid a great deal of attention to maintaining well-manicured nails.

"Is this Mr. Gray's secretary?" he asked Sally.

The stewardess shook her head. "No, Doctor. This is a passenger from tourist class. He claims to have worked for Mr. Gray."

"And your name is?" queried Fane swiftly, his sharp eyes on the young man's handsome features.

"Oscar Elgee. I was Mr. Gray's manservant." The young man spoke with a modulated voice that clearly betrayed his prep school background. "Check with Frank Tilley, in premier class. He is Mr. Gray's personal secretary. He will tell you who I am."

Fane smiled encouragingly at Sally Beech. "Would you do that for me, Miss Beech, and also tell Mr. Tilley that I would like to see him here when convenient?" When she hurried away, Fane turned back to the new arrival. "Now, Mr. Elgee, how did you hear that there had been an . . . an accident?"

"I heard one of the stewardesses mentioning it to another back in the tourist class," Elgee said. "If Mr. Gray has been hurt—"

"Mr. Gray is dead."

Oscar Elgee stared at him for a moment. "A heart attack?"

"Not exactly. Since you are here, you might formally identify your late employer. We need an identification for Doctor Ross's record."

He stood aside and allowed the young man to move forward to where the body had been laid out ready for Ross's examination. Ross moved to allow the young man to examine the face. Elgee halted over the body and gazed down for a moment.

"Terra es, terram ibis," he muttered. Then his face broke in anguish "How could this have happened? Why is there blood on his face? What sort of accident happened here?"

"That's exactly what we are attempting to find out," Ross told him. "I take it that you formally identify this man as Henry Kinloch Gray?"

The young man nodded briefly, turning away. Fane halted him beyond the curtained area.

"How long did you work for him, Mr. Elgee?"

"Two years."

"What exactly was your job with him?"

"I was his manservant. Everything. Chauffeur, butler, cook, valet, handyman. His *factotum.*"

"And he took you on his trips abroad?"

"Of course."

"But I see he was a stickler for the social order, eh?" smiled Fane.

The young man flushed. "I don't understand."

"You are traveling tourist class."

"It would not be seemly for a manservant to travel first class."

"Quite so. Yet, judging from your reactions to his death, you felt a deep attachment to your employer?"

The young man's chin raised defiantly, and a color came to his cheeks. "Mr. Gray was an exemplary employer. A tough business-man, true. But he was a fair man. We never had a cross word. He was a good man to work for. A great man."

"I see. And you looked after him? Took care of his domestic needs. If I recall the newspaper stories, Harry Gray was always de-scribed as an eligible bachelor."

Fane saw a subtle change of expression on the young man's face. "If he had been married, then he would hardly have needed my ser-vices, would he? I did everything for him. Even repairing his stereo system or his refrigerator. No, he was not married."

"Just so." Fane smiled, glancing again at Elgee's hands. "Repairing a stereo system requires a delicate touch. Unusual for a handyman to be able to do that sort of thing."

"My hobby is model making. Working models." There was a boastful note in his voice.

"I see. Tell me, as you would be in the best position to know, did your employer have any enemies?"

The young man actually winced. "A businessman like Harry Gray is surrounded by enemies." He looked up and saw Sally Beech ushering a bespectacled man into the compartment. "Some enemies work with him and pretended to be his confidants," he added with a sharp note. He paused and frowned as the thought seemed to occur to him. "Are you saying that his death was . . . was suspicious?"

Fane noticed, with approval, that Sally had motioned her new charge to sit down and did not come forward to interrupt him. He turned to the young man.

"That we will have to find out. Now, Mr. Elgee, perhaps you would return to your seat? We will keep you informed of the situation."

The young man turned and went out, hardly bothering to acknowledge the new arrival, who, in turn, seemed to drop his eyes to avoid contact with the personable young man. There was obviously no love lost between the manservant and secretary.

Leaving Hector Ross to continue his examination with the aid of the aircraft's emergency medical kit, Fane went up to where the newcomer had been seated.

Sally Beech, waiting with her charge, gave him a nervous smile. "This is Mr. Francis Tilley. He was traveling with Mr. Gray."

Frank Tilley was a thin and very unattractive man in his midthirties. His skin was pale, and his jaw showed a permanent blue shadow, which no amount of shaving would erase. He wore thick, horn-rimmed spectacles that seemed totally unsuited to his features.

His hair was thin and receding, and there was a nervous twitch at the corner of his mouth.

Fane motioned the stewardess to stand near the door to prevent any other person entering the premier-class compartment, and he turned to Tilley.

"He's dead, eh?" Tilley's voice was almost a falsetto. He giggled nervously. "Well, I suppose it had to happen sometime, even to the so-called great and the good."

Fane frowned at the tone in the man's voice. "Are you saying that Mr. Gray was ill?" he asked.

Tilley raised a hand and let it fall as if he were about to make a point and changed his mind. Fane automatically registered the shaky hand, the thick trembling fingers, stained with nicotine, and the raggedly cut nails.

"He was prone to asthma, that's all. Purely a stress condition."

"Then, why? . . ."

Tilley looked slightly embarrassed. "I suppose that I was being flippant."

"You do not seem unduly upset by the death of your colleague?"

Tilley sniffed disparagingly. "Colleague? He was my boss. He never let anyone who worked for him forget that he was the boss, that he was the arbiter of their fate in the company. Whether the man was a doorman or his senior vice-president, Harry Kinloch Gray was a 'hands on' chairman, and his word was law. If he took a dislike to you, then you were out immediately, no matter how long you had worked with the company. He was the archetypical Victorian self-made businessman. Autocratic, mean, and spiteful. He should have had no place in the modern business world."

Fane sat back and listened to the bitterness in the man's voice. "Was he the sort of man who had several enemies then?"

Tilley actually smiled at the humor. "He was the sort of man who did not have any friends."

"How long have you worked for him?"

"I've spent ten years in the company. I was his personal secretary for the last five of those years."

"Rather a long time to spend with someone you don't like? You must have been doing something right for him not to take a dislike to you and sack you, if, as you say, that was his usual method of dealing with employees."

Tilley shifted uneasily at Fane's sarcasm. "What has this to do with Mr. Gray's death?" he suddenly countered.

"Just seeking some background."

"What happened?" Tilley went on. "I presume that he had some sort of heart attack?"

"Did he have a heart condition then?"

"Not so far as I know. He was overweight and ate like a pig. With all the stress he carried about with him, it wouldn't surprise me to know that that was the cause."

"Was this journey a particularly stressful one?"

"No more than usual. We were on our way to a meeting of the executives of the American subsidiaries."

"And so far as you noticed, Mr. Gray was behaving in his usual manner?"

Tilley actually giggled. It was an unpleasant noise. "He was his usual belligerent, bullying, and arrogant self. He had half a dozen people to sack and he wanted to do it in a public ritual to give them the maximum embarrassment. It gave him a buzz. And then . . ." Tilley hesitated and a thoughtful look came into his eyes. "He was going through some documents from his case. One of them seemed to fascinate him, and after a moment or two he started to have one of his attacks—"

"Attacks? I thought you said that he had no health problems?"

"What I actually said was that he was prone to asthma. He did have these stress-related asthma attacks."

"So you did. So he began to have an asthma attack? Did he take anything for it?"

"He carried one of those inhalers around with him. He was vain and thought that none of us knew about it. The great chairman did not like to confess to a physical weakness. So when he had his attacks, he would disappear to treat himself with the inhaler. It was so obvious. Ironic that he had a favorite quotation from Ecclesiastes, 'Vanitas vanitatum, omnis vanitas'!"

"So are you saying that he went to the toilet to take his inhaler?"

"That is what I am saying. After a considerable time had passed, I did get concerned."

"Concerned?" Fane smiled thinly. "From what you are telling me, concern about your boss's well-being was not exactly a priority with you."

Tilley lips thinned in a sneer. "Personal feelings do not enter into it. I was not like Elgee, who puts his all into the job. I was being paid to do a job, and I did it with integrity and with professionalism. I did not have to like Harry Gray. It was no concern of mine what Harry Gray did or did not do outside of the job he paid me to do. It did not concern me who his lover was nor who his mortal enemies were."

"Very well. So he went to the toilet and did not come back?"

"As I said, after a while, I called the stewardess and she went to check on him. That was no more nor less the concern of my position as his secretary."

"Wait there a moment, Mr. Tilley."

Fane moved to where Sally Beech was standing, still pale and slightly nervous, and said quietly: "Do you think you could go to Mr. Gray's seat and find his attaché case? I'd like you to bring it here."

She returned in a short while with a small brown leather case.

Fane took it to show to Frank Tilley. "Do you identify this as Gray's case?"

The man nodded reluctantly. "I don't think you should do that," he protested as Fane snapped open the clasps.

"Why not?"

"Confidential company property."

"I think an investigation into a possible homicide will override that objection."

Frank Tilley was surprised. "Homicide? . . . But that means . . . murder. No one said anything about murder."

Fane was too busy shifting through the papers to respond. He pulled out a sheet and showed it to Tilley. "Was this what he was looking at just before he began to have breathing difficulties?"

"I don't know. Perhaps. It was a piece of paper like it—that's all I can say."

The sheet was a tear sheet from a computer printout. It had two short sentences on it:

You will die before this aircraft lands. *Memento, "homo,"*
quia pulvis es et in pulverem revertis.

Fane sat back with a casual smile. He held out the paper to the secretary. "You are a Latin scholar, Mr. Tilley. How would you translate the phrase given here?"

Tilley frowned. "What makes you say that I am a Latin scholar?"

"A few moments ago you trotted out a Latin phrase. I presumed that you knew its meaning."

"My Latin is almost nonexistent. Mr. Gray was fond of Latin tags and phrases, so I tried to keep up by memorizing some of those he used frequently."

"I see. So you don't know what this one means?"

Tilley looked at the printed note. He shook his head. "*Memento* means 'remember,' doesn't it?"

"Have you ever heard the phrase memento mori? That would be a more popular version of what is written here."

Tilley shook his head. "Remember something, I suppose?"

"Why do you think the Latin word for 'man' has quotation marks around it?"

"I don't know what it means. I do not know Latin."

"What this says roughly is, 'Remember, man, that you are dust and to dust you will return.' It was obviously written on a computer, a word processor. Do you recognize the type?"

Tilley shook his head. "It could be any one of hundreds of company standards. I hope you are not implying that I wrote Mr. Gray a death threat?"

"How would this have made its way into his attaché case?" Fane said, ignoring the comment.

"I presume someone put it there."

"Who would have such access to it?"

"I suppose that you are still accusing me? I hated him. But not so that I would cut my own throat. He was a bastard, but he was the goose who laid the golden egg. There was no point in being rid of him."

"Just so," muttered Fane thoughtfully. His eye caught sight of a notepad in the case, and he flicked through its pages while Frank Tilley sat looking on in discomfort. Fane found a list of initials with the head, "immediate dismissal" and that day's date.

"A list of half a dozen people that he was about to sack?" Fane observed.

"I told you that he was going to enjoy a public purge of his executives and mentioned some names to me."

"The list contains only initials and starts with O. T. E." He glanced at Tilley with a raised eyebrow. "Oscar Elgee?"

"Hardly," Tilley replied with a patronizing smile. "It means Otis T. Elliott, the general manager of our U.S. database subsidiary."

"I see. Let's see if we can identify the others."

He ran through the other initials to which Tilley added names. The next four were also executives of Gray's companies. The last initials were written as *Ft.*

"F. T. is underscored three times with the words 'no pay off!' written against it. Who's F. T.?"

"You know that F. T. are my initials," Tilley observed quietly. His features were white and suddenly very grave. "I swear that he never said anything to me about sacking me when we discussed those he had on his list. He never mentioned it."

"Well, was there anyone else in the company that the initials F. T. could apply to?"

Tilley frowned, trying to recall, but finally shook his head and gave a resigned shrug. "No. It could only be me. The bastard! He never told me what he was planning. Some nice little public humiliation, I suppose."

Hector Ross emerged from the curtained section and motioned Fane to join him. "I think I can tell you how it was done," he announced with satisfaction.

Fane grinned at his friend. "So can I. Tell me if I am wrong. Gray went into the toilet to use his inhaler to relieve an attack of asthma. He placed the inhaler in his mouth, depressed it in the normal way, and . . ." He ended with a shrug.

Ross looked shocked. "How did you—?" He glanced over Fane's shoulder to where Frank Tilley was still sitting, twitching nervously. "Did he confess that he set it up?"

Fane shook his head. "No. But was I right?"

"It is a good hypothesis but needs a laboratory to confirm it. I found tiny particles of aluminium in the mouth, and some plastic. Something certainly exploded with force, sending a tiny steel projectile into the back roof of the mouth with such force that it entered the brain and death was instantaneous, as you initially surmised. Whatever had triggered the projectile disintegrated with the force. Hence there were only small fragments embedded in his mouth and cheeks. There were some when I searched carefully, around the cubicle. Diabolical."

"This was arranged by someone who knew that friend Gray had a weakness and banked on it. Gray didn't like to take his inhaler in public and would find a quiet corner. The plan worked out very well and nearly presented an impossible crime, an almost insolvable crime. Initially it appeared that the victim had been shot in the mouth in a locked toilet."

Hector Ross smiled indulgently at his colleague. "You imply that you already have the solution?"

"Oh yes. Remember the song that we used to sing at school?

Life is real! Life is earnest!
And the grave is not its goal;
Dust thou art, to dust returnest,
Was not spoken of the soul.

Hector Ross nodded. "It's many a day since I last sang that, laddie. Something by Longfellow, wasn't it?"

Fane grinned. "It was, indeed. Based on some lines from the Book of Genesis—'terra es, terram ibis'—dust thou art, to dust thou shalt return.' Get Captain Evans here, please." He made the request to the Chief Steward, Jeff Ryder, who had been waiting attendance on Ross. When he had departed, Fane glanced back to his friend. "There is something to be said for Latin scholarship."

"I don't follow, laddie."

"Our murderer was too fond of the Latin in-jokes he shared with his boss."

"You mean his secretary?" He glanced at Frank Tilley.

"Tilley claims that he couldn't even translate memento mori."

"Remember death?"

Fane regarded his friend in disapproval. "It actually means 'remember *to* die' and a memento mori is usually applied to a human skull or some other object that reminds us of our mortality."

Captain Evans arrived and looked from Fane to Ross in expectation. "Well, what news?"

"To save any unpleasant scene on the aircraft, Captain, I suggest you radio ahead and have the police waiting to arrest one of your passengers on a charge of murder. No need to make any move until we land. The man can't go far."

"Which man?" demanded Evans, his face grim.

"He is listed as Oscar Elgee in the tourist class."

"How could he—?"

"Simple. Elgee was not only Gray's manservant but I think you'll find, from the broad hints Mr. Tilley gave me, that he was also his lover. Elgee seems to confirm it by a death note with a Latin phrase in which he emphasized the word *homo,* meaning 'man,' but, we also know it was often used as a slang term in my generation for 'homosexual.' "

"How would you know that Elgee was capable of understanding puns in Latin?" asked Ross.

"The moment he saw Gray's body, young Elgee muttered the very words. *Terra es, terram ibis*—dust you are, to dust you will return."

"A quarrel between lovers?" asked Ross. "Love to hatred turned—and all that, as Billy Shakespeare succinctly put it?"

Fane nodded. "Gray was giving Elgee the push, both as lover and employee, and so Elgee decided to end his lover's career in mid-flight, so to speak. There is a note in his attaché case that Elgee was to be sacked immediately without compensation."

Tilley, who had been sitting quietly, shook his head vehemently.

"No there isn't," he interrupted. "We went through the list. I told you that the initials O. T. E. referred to Otis Elliott. I had faxed that dismissal through before we boarded the plane."

Fane smiled softly. "You have forgotten F. T."

"But that's my—"

"You didn't share your boss's passion for Latin tags, did you? It was the F. T. that confused me. I should have trusted that a person with Gray's reputation would not have written *F* followed by a lower case *t* if he meant two initials F. T. I missed the point. It was not your initials at all, Mr. Tilley. It was *Ft* meant as an abbreviation. Specifically, *fac,* from *facere*: 'to do'; and *totum*: 'all things.' *Factotum.* And who was Gray's *factotum?*"

There was a silence.

"I think we will find that this murder was planned for a week or two at least. Once I began to realize what the mechanism was that killed Gray, all I had to do was look for the person capable of devising that mechanism as well as having motive and opportunity. Hold out your hands, Mr. Tilley."

Reluctantly the secretary did so.

"You can't seriously see those hands constructing a delicate mechanism, can you?" Fane said. "No, Elgee, the model maker and handyman, doctored one of Gray's inhalers so that when it was depressed it would explode with an impact into the mouth, shooting a needle into the brain. Simple but effective. He knew that Gray did not like to be seen using the inhaler in public. The rest was left to chance, and it was a good chance. It almost turned out to be the ultimate impossible crime. It might have worked, had not our victim and his murderer been too fond of their Latin in-jokes."

— THE SPITEFUL SHADOW —

"It is so obvious who killed poor Brother Síoda that it worries me."
Sister Fidelma stared in bewilderment at the woebegone expression of the usually smiling, cherubic Abbot Laisran. "I do not understand you, Laisran," she told her old mentor, pausing in the act of sipping her mulled wine. She was sitting in front of a blazing fire in the hearth of the abbot's chamber in the great Abbey of Durrow.

On the adjacent side of the fireplace, Abbot Laisran slumped in his chair, his wine left abandoned on the carved oak table by his side. He was staring moodily into the leaping flames. "Something worries me about the simplicity of this matter. There are things in life that appear so simple that you get a strange feeling about them. You question whether things can be so simple, and sure enough, you often find that they are so simple because they have been made to appear simple. In this case, everything fits together so flawlessly that I question it."

Fidelma drew a heavy sigh. She had only just arrived at Durrow to bring a psalter, a book of Latin psalms written by her brother, Colgú, King of Cashel, as a gift for the abbot. But she had found her old friend Abbot Laisran in a preoccupied frame of mine. A member of his community had been murdered, and the culprit had been easily identified as another member. Yet it was unusual to see Laisran so worried. Fidelma had known him since she was a little girl, and it was he who had persuaded her to take up the study of law. Further, when she had reached the qualification of *Anruth*, one degree below that of *Ollamh*, the highest rank of learning, it had been Laisran who had advised her to join a religious community on being accepted as a *dálaigh,* an advocate of the Brehon Court. He had felt that this would give her more opportunities in life.

Usually, Abbot Laisran was full of jollity and good humor. Anxiety did not sit well on his features, for he was a short, rotund, red-faced man. He had been born with that rare gift of humor and a sense that the world was there to provide enjoyment to those who inhabited it. Now he appeared like a man on whose shoulders the entire troubles of the world rested.

"Perhaps you had better tell me all about it," Fidelma invited. "I might be able to give some advice."

Laisran raised his head, and there was a new expression of hope in his eyes. "Any help you can give, Fidelma . . . Truly, the facts are, as I say, lucid enough. But there is just something about them—" He paused and then shrugged. "I'd be more than grateful to have your opinion."

Fidelma smiled reassuringly. "Then let us begin to hear some of these lucid facts."

"Two days ago, Brother Síoda was founded stabbed to death in his cell. He had been stabbed several times in the heart."

"Who found him and when?"

"He had not appeared at morning prayers. So my steward, Brother Cruinn, went along to his cell to find out whether he was ill. Brother Síoda lay murdered on his bloodstained bed."

Fidelma waited while the abbot paused, as if to gather his thoughts.

"We have, in the abbey, a young woman called Sister Scáthach. She is very young. She joined us as a child because, so her parents told us, she heard things. Sounds in her head. Whispers. About a month ago, our physician became anxious about her state of health. She had become—" He paused as if trying to think of the right word. "—she believed she was hearing voices instructing her."

Fidelma raised her eyes slightly in surprise.

Abbot Laisran saw the movement and grimaced. "She has always been what one might call eccentric, but the eccentricity has grown so that her behavior became bizarre. A month ago I placed her in a cell and asked one of the apothecary's assistants, Sister Sláine, to watch over her. Soon after Brother Síoda was found, the steward and I went to Sister Scáthach's cell. The door was always locked. It was a precaution that we had recently adopted. Usually the key is hanging on a hook outside the door. But the key was on the inside, and the door was locked. A bloodstained robe was found in her cell and a knife. The knife, too, was bloodstained. It was obvious that Sister Scáthach was guilty of this crime."

Abbot Laisran stood up and went to a chest. He removed a knife whose blade was discolored with dried blood. Then he drew forth a robe. It was clear that it had been stained in blood.

"Poor Brother Síoda," murmured Laisran. "His penetrated heart must have poured blood over the girl's clothing."

Fidelma barely glanced at the robes. "The first question I have to ask is why would you and the steward go straight from the murdered man's cell to that of Sister Scáthach?" she demanded.

Abbot Laisran compressed his lips for a moment. "Because only the day before the murder, Sister Scáthach had prophesied his death and the manner of it. She made the pronouncement only twelve hours before his body was discovered, saying that he would die by having his heart ripped out."

Fidelma folded her hands before her, gazing thoughtfully into the fire. "She was violent then? You say that you had her placed in a locked cell with a Sister to look after her?"

"But she was never violent before the murder," affirmed the abbot.

"Yet she was confined to her cell?"

"A precaution, as I say. During these last four weeks she began to make violent prophecies. Saying voices instructed her to do so."

"Violent prophecies but you say that she was not violent?" Fidelma's tone was skeptical.

"It is difficult to explain," confessed Abbot Laisran. "The words were violent, but she was not. She was a gentle girl, but she claimed that the shadows from the Otherworld gave her instructions; they told her to foretell the doom of the world, its destruction by fire and flood when mountains would be hurled into the sea and the seas rise up and engulf the land."

Fidelma pursed her lips cynically. "Such prophecies have been common since the dawn of time," she observed.

"Such prophesies have alarmed the community here, Fidelma," admonished Abbot Laisran. "It was as much for her sake that I suggested Sister Sláine make sure that Sister Scáthach was secured in her cell each night and kept an eye upon each day."

"Do you mean that you feared members of the community would harm Sister Scáthach rather than she harm members of the community?" queried Fidelma.

The abbot inclined his head. "Some of these predictions were violent in the extreme, aimed at one or two particular members of the community, foretelling their doom, casting them into the everlasting hellfire."

"You say that during the month she has been so confined, the pronouncements grew more violent."

"The more she was constrained, the more extreme the pronouncements became," confessed the abbot.

"And she made just such a pronouncement against Brother Síoda? That is why you and your steward made the immediate link to Sister Scáthach?"

"It was."

"Why did she attack Brother Síoda?" she asked. "How well did she know him?"

"As far as I am aware, she did not know him at all. Yet when she made her prophecy, Brother Síoda told me that she seemed to know secrets about him that he thought no other person knew. He was greatly alarmed and said he would lock himself in that night so that no one could enter."

"So his cell door was locked when your steward went there after he had failed to attend morning prayers?"

Abbot Laisran shook his head. "When Brother Cruinn went to Síoda's cell, he found that the door was shut but not locked. The key was on the floor inside his cell. . . . This is the frightening thing. . . . There were bloodstains on the key."

"And you tell me that you found a bloodstained robe and the murder weapon in Sister Scáthach's cell?"

"We did," agreed the abbot. "Brother Cruinn and I."

"What did Sister Scáthach have to say to the charge?"

"This is just it, Fidelma. She was bewildered. I know when people are lying or pretending. She was just bewildered. But then she accepted the charge meekly."

Fidelma frowned. "I don't understand."

"Sister Scáthach simply replied that she was a conduit for the voices from the Otherworld. The shadows themselves must have punished Brother Síoda as they had told her they would. She said that they must have entered her corporeal form and used it as an instrument to kill him, but she had no knowledge of the fact, no memory of being disturbed that night."

Fidelma shook her head. "She sounds a very sick person."

"Then you don't believe in shadows from the Otherworld?"

"I believe in the Otherworld and our transition from this one to that but . . . I think that those who repose in the Otherworld have more to do than to try to return to this one to murder people. I have investigated several similar matters where shadows of the Otherworld have been blamed for crimes. Never have I found such claims to be true. There is always a human agency at work."

Abbot Laisran shrugged. "So we must accept that the girl is guilty?"

"Let me hear more. Who was this Brother Síoda?"

"A young man. He worked in the abbey fields. A strong man. A farmer, not really one fitted in mind for the religious life." Abbot Laisran paused and smiled. "I'm told that he was a bit of a rascal before he joined us. A seducer of women."

"How long had he been with you?"

"A year, perhaps a little more."

"And he was well behaved during this time? Or did his tendency as a rascal, as you describe it, continue?"

Abbot Laisran shrugged again. "No complaints were brought to me, and yet I had reason to think that he had not fully departed from his old ways. There was nothing specific, but I noticed the way some of the younger religieuse behaved when they were near him. Smiling, nudging each other . . . You know the sort of thing?"

"How was this prophecy of Brother Síoda's death delivered?" she replied, ignoring his rhetorical question.

"It was at the midday mealtime. Sister Scáthach had been quiet for some days and so, instead of eating alone in her cell, Sister Sláine brought her to the refectory. Brother Síoda was sitting nearby and hardly had Sister Scáthach been brought into the hall than she pointed a finger at Brother Síoda and proclaimed her threat so that everyone in the refectory could hear it."

"Do you know what words she used?"

"I had my steward note them down. She cried out: 'Beware, vile fornicator, for the day of reckoning is at hand. You, who have seduced and betrayed, will now face the settlement. Your heart will be torn out. Gormflaith and her baby will be avenged. Prepare yourself. For the shadows of the Otherworld have spoken. They await you.' That was what she said before she was taken back to her cell."

Fidelma nodded thoughtfully. "You said something about her knowing facts about Brother Síoda's life that he thought no one else knew?"

"Indeed. Brother Síoda came to me in a fearful state and said that Scáthach could not have known about Gormflaith and her child."

"Gormflaith and her child? Who were they?"

"Apparently, so Brother Síoda told me, Gormflaith was the first girl he had ever seduced when he was a youth. She was fourteen and became pregnant with his child but died giving birth. The baby, too, died."

"Ah!" Fidelma leaned forward with sudden interest. "And you

say that Brother Síoda and Sister Scáthach did not know one another? How then did she recognize him in the refectory?"

Abbot Laisran paused a moment. "Brother Síoda told me that he had never spoken to her, but of course he had seen her in the refectory and she must have seen him."

"But if no words ever passed between them, who told her about his past life?"

Abbot Laisran's expression was grim. "Brother Síoda told me that there was no way that she could have known. Maybe the voices that she heard were genuine?"

Fidelma looked amused. "I think I would rather check out whether Brother Síoda had told someone else or whether there was someone from his village here who knew about his past life."

"Brother Síoda was from Mag Luirg, one of the Uí Ailello. No one here would know from whence he came or have any connection with the kingdom of Connacht. I can vouch for that."

"My theory is that when you subtract the impossible, you will find your answers in the possible. Clearly, Brother Síoda passed on this information somehow. I do not believe that wraiths whispered this information."

Abbot Laisran was silent.

"Let us hear about Sister Sláine," she continued. "What made you choose her to look after the girl?"

"Because she worked in the apothecary and had some understanding of those who were of bizarre humors."

"How long had she been looking after Sister Scáthach?"

"About a full month."

"And how had the girl's behavior been during that time?"

"For the first week it seemed better. Then it became worse. More violent, more assertive. Then it became quiet again. That was when we allowed Sister Scáthach to go to the refectory."

"The day before the murder?"

"The day before the murder," he confirmed.

"And Sister Sláine slept in the next cell to the girl?"

"She did."

"And did she always lock the door of Sister Scáthach's cell at night?"

"She did."

"And on that night?"

"Especially on that night of her threat to Síoda."

"And the key was always hung on a hook outside the cell so that there was no way Sister Scáthach could have reached it?"

When Abbot Laisran confirmed this, Fidelma sighed deeply. "I think that I'd better have a word with Sister Scáthach and also with Sister Sláine."

Fidelma chose to see Sister Scáthach first. She was surprised by her appearance as she entered the gloomy cell the girl inhabited. The girl was no more than sixteen or seventeen years old, thin with pale skin. She looked as though she had not slept for days; large dark areas of skin showed under her eyes, which were black, wide, and staring. The features were almost cadaverous, as if the skin was tightly drawn over the bones.

She did not look up as Fidelma and Laisran entered. She sat on the edge of her bed, hands clasped between her knees, gazing intently on the floor. She appeared more like a lost waif than like a killer.

"Well, Scáthach," Fidelma began gently, sitting next to the girl, much to the surprise of Laisran, who remained standing at the door, "I hear that you are possessed of exceptional powers."

The girl started at the sound of her voice and then shook her head. "Powers? It is not a power but a curse that attends me."

"You have a gift of prophecy."

"A gift that I would willing return to whoever cursed me with it."

"Tell me about it."

"They say that I killed Brother Síoda. I did not know the man. But if they tell me that it was so, then it must be so."

"You remember nothing of the event?"

"Nothing at all. So far as I am aware, I went to bed, fell asleep, and was only awoken when the steward and the abbot came into my cell to confront me."

"Do you remember prophesying his death in the refectory?"

The girl nodded quickly. "That I do remember. But I simply repeated what the voice told me to say."

"The voice?"

"The voice of the shadow from the Otherworld. It attends me at night and wakes me if I slumber. It tells me what I should say and when. Then the next morning I repeat the message as the shadows instruct me."

"You hear this voice . . . or voices . . . at night?"

The girl nodded.

"It comes to you here in your cell?" pressed Fidelma. "Nowhere else?"

"The whispering is at night when I am in my cell," confirmed the girl.

"And it was this voice that instructed you to prophesy Brother Síoda's death? It told you to speak directly to him? Did it also tell you to mention Gormflaith and her baby?"

The girl nodded in answer to all her questions.

"How long have you heard such voices?"

"I am told that it has been so since I was a little girl."

"What sort of voices?"

"Well, at first the sounds were more like the whispering of the sea. We lived by the sea, and so I was not troubled at first for the sounds of the sea have always been a constant companion. The sounds were not disturbing but gentle, kind sounds. They came to me more in my head, soft and sighing. Then they increased. Sometimes I could not stand it. My parents said they were voices from the Otherworld. A sign from God. They brought me here. The abbey treated me well, but the sounds increased. I was placed here to be looked after by Sister Sláine."

"I hear that these voices have become very strident of late."

"They became more articulate. I am not responsible for what they tell me to say or how they tell me to say it," the girl added as if in defense.

"Of course not," Fidelma agreed. "But it seems there was a change. The voice became stronger. When did this change occur?"

"When I came here to this cell. The voice became distinct. It spoke in words that I could understand."

"You mention voices in the plural and singular. How many voices spoke to you?"

The girl thought carefully. "Well, I can only identify one."

"Male or female?"

"Impossible to tell. It was all one whispering sound."

"How did it become so manifest?"

"It was as if I woke up and they were whispering in a corner of the room." The girl smiled. "The first and second time it happened, I lit a candle and peered round the cell, but there was no one there. Eventually I realized that as strong as the voices were, they must be in my head. I resigned myself to being the messenger on their behalf."

"And the voice instructed you to do what?"

"It told me to stand in the refectory and pronounce their messages of doom."

Abbot Laisran leaned forward in a confiding fashion. "Sometimes these messages were of violence against the whole community, and at other times violence against individuals. But it was the one against Brother Síoda that was the most specific and named events."

Fidelma nodded. She had not taken her eyes from the girl's face. "Why do you believe this voice came from the Otherworld?"

The girl regarded her with a puzzled frown. "Where else would it be from? I am a good Christian and say my prayers at night. But still the voice haunts me."

"Have you heard it since the warning you were to deliver to Brother Síoda?"

The girl shook her head. "Not in the same specific way."

"Then in what way?"

"It has gone back to the same whispering inconsistency, the sound of the sea."

Fidelma glanced around the cell. "Is this place where you usually have your bed?"

The girl looked surprised for a moment. "This is where I normally sleep."

Fidelma was examining the walls of the cell with keen eyes. "Who occupied the cells on either side?"

"On that side is Sister Sláine who looks after this poor girl. To the other side is the chamber occupied by Brother Cruinn, my steward."

"But there is a floor above this one?"

"The chamber immediately above this is occupied by Brother Torchán, our gardener."

Fidelma turned to the lock on the door of the cell.

Abbot Laisran saw her peering at the keyhole. "Her cell was locked, and the key on the inside when Brother Cruinn and I came to this cell after Brother Síoda had been found."

Fidelma nodded absently. "That is the one puzzling aspect," she admitted.

Abbot Laisran looked puzzled. "I would have thought it tied everything together. It is the proof that only Scáthach could have brought the weapon and robe into her cell and therefore she is the culprit."

Fidelma did not answer. "How far is Brother Síoda's cell from here?"

"At the far end of this corridor."

"From the condition of the robe that you showed me, there must have been a trail of blood from Brother Síoda's cell to this one?"

"Perhaps the corridor had been cleaned," he suggested. "One of the duties of our community is to clean the corridors each morning."

"And they cleaned it without reporting traces of the blood to you?" She was clearly unimpressed by the attempted explanation. Fidelma rose and glanced at the girl with a smile. "Don't worry, Sister Scáthach. I think that you are innocent of Brother Síoda's death." She turned from the cell, followed by a deeply bewildered Abbot Laisran. "Let us see Sister Sláine now."

At the next cell, Sister Sláine greeted them with a nervous bob of her head.

Fidelma entered and glanced along the stone wall that separated the cell from that of Sister Scáthach's. Then she turned to Sister Sláine, who was about twenty-one or -two, an attractive-looking girl.

"Brother Síoda was a handsome man, wasn't he?" she asked without preamble.

The girl started in surprise. A blush tinged her cheeks. "I suppose he was."

"He had an eye for the ladies. I presume that you were in love with him, weren't you?"

The girl's chin came up defiantly. "Who told you?"

"It was a guess," Fidelma admitted with a soft smile. "But since you have admitted it, let us proceed. Do you believe in these voices that Sister Scáthach hears?"

"Of course not. She's mad and has now proved her madness."

"Do you not find it strange that this madness has only manifested itself since she was moved into this cell next to you?"

The girl's cheeks suddenly suffused with crimson. "Are you implying that—?"

"Answer my question," snapped Fidelma, cutting her short.

The girl blinked at her cold voice. Then, seeing that Abbot Laisran was not interfering, she said: "Madness can alter, it can grow worse . . . It is a coincidence that she became worse after Abbot Laisran asked me to look after her. Just a coincidence."

"I am told that you work for the apothecary and look after sick people? In your experience, have you ever heard of a condition among people where they have a permanent hissing, or whistling in the ears?"

Sister Sláine nodded slowly. "Of course. Many people have such a condition. Sometimes they hardly notice it while others are plagued by it and almost driven to madness. That is what we thought was wrong with Sister Scáthach when she first came to our notice."

"Only at first?" queried Fidelma.

"Until she starting to claim that she heard words being articulated, words that formed distinct messages which, she also claimed, were from the shadows of the Otherworld."

"Did Brother Síoda ever tell you about his affair with Gormflaith, and his child?"

Fidelma changed the subject so abruptly that the girl blinked. It was clear from her reaction that Fidelma had hit on the truth.

"Better speak the truth now, for it will become harder later," Fidelma advised.

Sister Sláine was silent for a moment, her eyes narrowed as she tried to penetrate behind Fidelma's inquisitive scrutiny.

"If you must know, I was in love with Síoda. We planned to leave here soon to find a farmstead where we could begin a new life together. We had no secrets from one another."

Fidelma smiled softly and nodded. "So he did tell you?"

"Of course. He wanted to tell me all about his past life. He told me of this unfortunate girl and her baby. He was very young and foolish at the time. He was a penitent and sought forgiveness. That's why he came here."

"So when you heard Sister Scáthach denounce him in the refectory, naming Gormflaith and relating her death and that of her child, what exactly did you think?"

"Do you mean, about how she came upon that knowledge?"

"Exactly. Where did you think Sister Scáthach obtained such knowledge if not from her messages from the Otherworld?"

Sister Sláine pursed her lips. "As soon as I had taken Sister Scáthach back to her cell and locked her in, I went to find Brother Síoda. He was scared. I thought at first that he had told her or someone else apart from me. He swore that he had not. He was so scared that he went to see Abbot Laisran—"

"Did you question Sister Scáthach?"

The girl laughed. "Little good that did. She simply said it was the voices. She had most people believing her."

"But you did not?"

"Not even in the madness she is suffering can one make up such specific information. I can only believe that Síoda lied to me. . . ." Her eyes suddenly glazed and she fell silent as if in some deep thought.

"Cloistered in this abbey, and a conhospitae, a mixed house, there must be many opportunities for relationships to develop between the sexes?" Fidelma observed.

"There is no rule against it," returned the girl. "Those advocating celibacy and abstinence have not yet taken over this abbey. We still live a natural life here. But Síoda never mixed with the mad one, never with Scáthach."

"But you have had more than one affair here?" Fidelma asked innocently.

"Brother Síoda was my first and only love," snapped the girl in anger.

Fidelma raised her eyebrows. "No others?"

The girl's expression was pugnacious. "None."

"You had no close friends among the other members of the community?"

"I do not get on with the women, if that is what you mean."

"It isn't. But it is useful to know. How about male friends? . . ."

"I've told you, I don't—"

Abbot Laisran coughed in embarrassment. "I had always thought that you and Brother Torchán were friends."

Sister Sláine blushed. "I get on well with Brother Torchán," she admitted defensively.

Fidelma suddenly rose and glanced along the wall once more, before turning with a smile to the girl. "You've been most helpful," she said abruptly, turning for the door.

Outside in the corridor, Abbot Laisran was regarding her with a puzzled expression. "What now?" he demanded. "I would have thought that you wanted to develop the question of her relationships?"

"We shall go to see Brother Torchán," she said firmly.

Brother Torchán was out in the garden and had to be sent for so Fidelma could interview him in his cell. He was a thickset, muscular young man whose being spoke of a life spent in the open air.

"Well, Brother, what do you think of Sister Scáthach?"

The burly gardener shook his head sadly. "I grieve for her as I grieve for Brother Síoda. I knew Brother Síoda slightly but the girl not at all. I doubt if I have seen her more than half a dozen times and never spoken to her but once. By all accounts, she was clearly demented."

"What do you think about her being driven to murder by voices from the Otherworld?"

"It is clear that she must be placed in the care of a combination of priests and physicians to drive away the evilness that has compelled her."

"So you think that she is guilty of the murder?"

"Can there be any other explanation?" asked the gardener in surprise.

"You know Sister Sláine, of course. I am told she is a special friend of yours."

"Special? I would like to think so. We often talk together. We came from the same village."

"Has she ever discussed Sister Scáthach with you?"

Brother Torchán shifted uneasily. He looked suspiciously at Fidelma. "Once or twice. When the abbot first asked her to look after Sister Scáthach, it was thought that it was simply a case of what the apothecaries call tinnitus. She heard sounds in her ears. But then

Sláine said that the girl had become clearly demented, saying that she was being woken up by the sound of voices giving her messages and urging her to do things."

"Did you know that Sláine was having an affair with Síoda?" Fidelma suddenly said sharply.

Torchán colored and, after a brief hesitation, nodded. "It was deeper than an affair. She told me that they planned to leave the abbey and set up home together. It is not forbidden by rule, you know."

"How did you feel about that?"

Brother Torchán shrugged. "So long as Síoda treated her right, it had little to do with me."

"But you were her friend."

"I was a friend and advised her when she wanted advice. She is the kind of girl who attracts men. Sometimes the wrong men. She attracted Brother Síoda."

"Was Brother Síoda the wrong man?"

"I thought so."

"Did she ever repeat to you anything Brother Síoda told her?"

Torchán lowered his eyes. "You mean about Gormflaith and the child? Sister Sláine is not gifted with the wisdom of silence. She told me various pieces of gossip. Oh . . ." He hesitated. "I have never spoken to Scáthach, if that is what you mean."

"But, if Sláine told you, then she might well have told others?"

"I do not mean to imply that she gossiped to anyone. There was only Brother Cruinn and myself whom she normally confided in."

"Brother Cruinn, the steward, was also her friend?"

"I think that he would have liked to have been something more until Brother Síoda took her fancy."

Fidelma smiled tightly. "That will be all, Torchán."

There was a silence as Abbot Laisran followed Fidelma down the stone steps to the floor below.

Fidelma led the way back to Sister Scáthach's cell, paused, and then pointed to the next door. "And this is Brother Cruinn's cell?"

Abbot Laisran nodded.

Brother Cruinn, the steward of the abbey, was a thin, sallow man in his mid-twenties. He greeted Fidelma with a polite smile of welcome. "A sad business, a sad business," he said. "The matter of Sister Scáthach. I presume that is the reason for your wishing to see me?"

"It is," agreed Fidelma easily.

"Of course, of course. A poor, demented girl. I have suggested to the abbot here that he should send to Ferna to summon the bishop. I believe that there is some exorcism ritual with which he is acquainted. That may help. We have lost a good man in Brother Síoda."

Fidelma sat down unbidden in the single chair that occupied the cell. "You were going to lose Brother Síoda anyway," she said dryly.

Brother Cruinn's face was an example of perfect self-control. "I do not believe I follow you, Sister," he said softly.

"You were also losing Sister Sláine. How did you feel about that?"

Brother Cruinn's eyes narrowed, but he said nothing.

"You loved her. You hated it when she and Brother Síoda became lovers."

Brother Cruinn was looking appalled at Abbot Laisran, as if appealing for help.

Abbot Laisran wisely made no comment. He had witnessed too many of Fidelma's interrogations to know when not to interfere.

"It must have been tearing you apart," went on Fidelma calmly. "But instead, you hid your feelings. You pretended to remain a friend, simply a friend to Sister Sláine. You listened carefully while she gossiped about her lover and especially when she confided what he had told her about his first affair and the baby."

"This is ridiculous!" snapped Brother Cruinn.

"Is it?" replied Fidelma as if pondering the question. "What a godsend it was when poor Sister Scáthach was put into the next cell to you. Sister Scáthach was an unfortunate girl who was suffering, not from imagined whispering voices from the Otherworld, but from an advanced case of the sensation of noises in the ears. It is not an uncommon affliction, but some cases are worse than others. As a little child, when it developed, silly folk—her parents—told her that the whistling and hissing sounds were the voices of lost souls in the Otherworld trying to communicate with her and thus she was blessed.

"Her parents brought her here. She probably noticed the affliction more in these conditions than she had when living by the sea, where the whispering was not so intrusive. Worried by the worsening affects, on the advice of the apothecary, Abbot Laisran placed her in the cell with Sister Sláine, who knew something of the condition, to look after her."

Fidelma paused, eyes suddenly hardening on him.

"That was your opportunity, eh, Brother Cruinn? A chance to be rid of Brother Síoda and with no questions asked. A strangely demented young woman who was compelled by voices from another world to do so would murder him."

"You are mad," muttered Brother Cruinn.

Fidelma smiled. "Madness can only be used as an excuse once. This is all logical. It was your voice that kept awakening poor Sister Scáthach and giving her these messages that made her behave so. At first you told her to proclaim some general messages. That would cause people to accept her madness, as they saw it. Then, having had her generally accepted as mad, you gave her the message to prepare for Síoda's death."

She walked to the head of his bed, her eye having observed what she had been seeking. She reached forward and withdrew from the wall a piece of loose stone. It revealed a small aperture, no more than a few fingers wide and high.

"Abbot Laisran, go into the corridor and unlock Sister Scáthach's door, but do not open it nor enter. Wait outside."

Puzzled, the abbot obeyed her.

Fidelma waited and then bent down to the hole.

"Scáthach! Scáthach! Can you hear me, Scáthach? All is now

well. You will hear the voices no more. Go to the door and open it. Outside you will find Abbot Laisran. Tell him that all is now well. The voices are gone."

She rose up and faced Brother Cruinn, whose dark eyes were narrowed and angry.

A moment later, they heard the door of the next room open and a girl's voice speaking with Abbot Laisran.

The abbot returned moments later. "She came to the door and told me that the voices were gone and all was well."

Fidelma smiled thinly. "Even as I told her to do so. Just as that poor influenced girl did what you told her to, Brother Cruinn. This hole goes through the wall into her cell and acts like a conduit for the voice."

"I did not tell her to stab Brother Síoda in the heart," he said defensively.

"Of course not. She did not stab anyone. You did that."

"Ridiculous! The bloodstained robes and weapon were in her cell—"

"Placed there by you."

"The door was locked and the key was inside. That shows that only she could have committed the murder."

Abbot Laisran sighed. "It's true, Fidelma. I went with Brother Cruinn myself to Sister Scáthach's cell door. I told you, the key was not on the hook outside the door but inside her cell and the door locked. I said before, only she could have taken the knife and robe inside and locked herself in."

"When you saw that the key was not hanging on the hook outside the door, Laisran, then did you try to open the door?" Fidelma asked innocently.

"We did."

"No, did *you* try to open the door?" snapped Fidelma with emphasis.

Abbot Laisran looked blank for a moment. "Brother Cruinn tried the door and pronounced it locked. He then took his master keys, which he held as steward, and unlocked the door. He had to wiggle the key around in the lock. When the door was open, the key was on the floor on the inside. We found it there."

Fidelma grinned. "Where Brother Cruinn had placed it. Have Cruinn secured, and I will tell you how he did it later."

After Brother Cruinn was taken away by attendants summoned by the Abbot Laisran, Fidelma returned to the abbot's chamber to finish her interrupted mulled wine and to stretch herself before the fire.

"I'm not sure how you resolved this matter," Abbot Laisran finally said as he stacked another log on the fire.

"It was the matter of the key that made me realize that Brother Cruinn had done this. Exactly how and, more important, why, I did not know at first. I realized as soon as Sister Scáthach told me how she was awoken by the whispering voice at night that it must have come from one of three sources. The voice must have come from one of the three neighboring cells. When she showed me where she slept, I realized from where the voice had come. Brother Cruinn was the whispering in the night. No one else could physically have done it. He also had easy access to Brother Síoda's locked cell because only he held the master keys. The problem was what had he to gain from Brother Síoda's death? Well, now we know the answer—it was an act of jealousy, hoping to eliminate Brother Síoda so that he could pursue his desire for Sister Sláine. That he was able to convince you that the cell door was locked and that he was actually opening it was child's play. An illusion in which you thought that Sister Scáthach had locked herself in her cell. Brother Cruinn had placed the key on the floor when he planted the incriminating evidence of the bloodstained weapon and robe.

"In fact, the door was not locked at all. Brother Cruinn had taken the robe to protect his clothing from the blood when he killed Síoda. He therefore allowed no blood to fall when he came along the corridor with robe and knife to where Sister Scáthach lay in her exhausted sleep. Remember that she was exhausted by the continuous times he had woken her with his whispering voice. He left the incriminating evidence, left the key on the floor, and closed the door. In the morning, he could go through the pantomime of opening the door, claiming it had been locked from the inside Wickedness coupled with cleverness, but our friend Brother Cruinn was a little too clever."

"But to fathom this mystery, you first had to come to the conclusion that Sister Scáthach was innocent," pointed out the abbot.

"Poor Scáthach! It is her parents who should be on trial for filling her susceptible mind with this myth about Otherworld voices when she is suffering from a physical disability. The fact was Scáthach could not have known about Gormflaith. She was told. If one discounts voices from the Otherworld, then it was by a human agency. The question was who was that agency and what was the motive for this evil charade."

Abbot Laisran gazed at her in amazement. "I never cease to be astonished at your astute mind, Fidelma. Without you, poor Sister Scáthach might have stood condemned."

Fidelma smiled and shook her head at her old mentor. "On the contrary, Abbot Laisran, without you and your suspicion that things were a little too cut and dried, we should never even have questioned the guilt or innocence of the poor girl at all."